ROOM
SERVICE

Beverly Brandt

St. Martin's Paperbacks

This book is dedicated to all the people who offer proof that writing is *not* a solitary endeavor:

To Kim Cardascia, an editor of wonderful insight and patience;
To Deidre Knight, an agent who answers my e-mails, even on weekends;
To Alesia Holliday, a new friend who solved an enormous problem;
To Pam Binder, for asking, "How can we help?", and really meaning it;
To Laron Glover, a critique partner who never complains when I say, "I need it back in a week";
To Wendy Linstad, for waking up thinking about my plot problem, instead of her own;
To Emily Kruger, Elizabeth Lee, Alexa Lee, Olger Palma, and Diane Hall-Harris, for not looking at the 1,200 envelopes that needed to be stuffed in one evening and running the other way;
To Kelley Price, for being such a great sister;

And to Wes Brandt, for being right there with me as I dream . . .

ACKNOWLEDGMENTS

THIS book, more than any other I've written, has been a gift. Not because it came to me without having to work for it, but because during the process of publication it made me realize how fortunate I am to be surrounded by so many wonderful people.

I'd like to thank the Expedia Finance team for being so understanding and supportive of my "other" career. Emily, Elizabeth, Olger, Nick, Travis, Amy, Howard, Julie, Joe, Jane, Deborah, Stephanie, Mindy, Ana, Marj— I appreciate how great you've all been!

Thanks to Detective J. J. Rushing of the Scottsdale Police Department for locking my friend Libby up in "The Chair" and walking us through the process of being arrested.

My thanks to Libby Muelhaupt for allowing herself to be detained for my benefit, for providing me with details on Scottsdale's flora and fauna, and for giving me a place to escape to when I really, really needed it.

To Ann Gosch, my friend and copyeditor-on-call, thank you for okaying my use of the word "gotten" and for always being interested in what's going on in my life.

Thanks also to Dr. Norm Gosch for brainstorming the various ways I could make one hundred cattlemen vomit. Doctors are wonderful people to know!

And finally, thanks to an online resource that I hope never goes away. I spent many a happy hour at www.askjeeves.com, looking up everything from the team colors of the Arizona Diamondbacks to possible diseases in dogs. I learned a lot—and I never even had to leave my house!

PROLOGUE

June 22

"DAMN you, Jillian. Please let me in." Katya Morgan pressed the intercom button insistently, her voice hoarse from an hour of pleading with her stepmother and anyone else who would listen.

Jillian Morgan sat in the kitchen of the mansion she had inherited last week and watched her stepdaughter on the television monitor that sat on the built-in desk in the corner. Katya had been staked out in front of the tightly closed wrought-iron gates for over an hour, and the desperation in her voice was becoming more evident with each passing moment.

"You have to let me stay here tonight. I'm sorry for breaking in yesterday. I know I shouldn't have, and I promise I won't try to take anything if you'll just let me in," Katya begged, sounding like a heartbroken child.

"Which is exactly what she is underneath that phony exterior," Jillian muttered to the silent room, her voice echoing off the cold marble countertops. She hated to think of her stepdaughter as a poor little rich girl, since it was difficult to feel too sorry for someone who had never known a day without food or clothes that fit or the best shoes that money could buy. Still, Jillian couldn't help but feel some sympathy for the little girl her stepdaughter had been.

At ten years old, Katya had, in essence, lost both parents in the space of one week.

Not literally, of course. Her mother had been the one to physically die when her car took a curve too fast and rolled over, crushing its only occupant. And the trouble with Katya was that she was a living reminder to Charles Morgan that the woman he had loved with such devoted adoration had died, leaving him alone with her ten-year-old ghost. So he sent his only child away to one fancy boarding school after another—not to some dingy orphanage as in a late-nineteenth-century novel, fortunately, but the poor kid still must have felt as if she were being punished for her mother's death.

Jillian pressed two fingers against the ache pounding in her temples.

When she had asked Katya's father why he had sent his daughter away, Charles had staunchly defended his decision as being in Katya's best interest. But Jillian had noticed the way he could barely stand to look at his exotic-looking raven-haired daughter, the daughter who, at thirty-one, looked exactly like the woman who had died driving the sleek silver convertible her husband had given her for her thirtieth birthday.

The buzzer from beside the locked gates sounded again, and Jillian absently massaged her forehead as she answered her stepdaughter's summons. "Katya, you can't stay here. Stop pressing the bell."

There was a long pause before the intercom rang again.

"Please, Jillian, I don't have anywhere else to go," Katya pleaded, sounding as lost and forlorn as Jillian imagined her stepdaughter felt.

Drawing in a shaky breath, Jillian wiped the tears from her eyes.

She never should have agreed to the terms of Charles's will.

Her stepdaughter did not have the skills required to survive without money. She didn't even know how to fill out a job application. And, even if she had, she had no prior work experience to her credit. Drinking, gambling, lounging around the pool, and partying were not exactly the sort of skills employers sought in their employees. She should have tried harder to convince Katya's father that there must be a better way to make his daughter grow up without having to resort to such desperate measures.

Jillian felt a small bubble of anger toward the man who had died, leaving her to deal with what he hadn't been able to face in his own lifetime. After all, she was only two years older than her stepdaughter. How in the world was she supposed to know how to deal with the now-penniless woman camped out on her doorstep?

The only thing she knew was that no matter how much she might want to help her stepdaughter, she couldn't.

Slowly, she lifted the telephone receiver and pressed the buttons on the keypad.

No, it wasn't an emergency. Yes, she would hold.

The intercom buzzed again, and Jillian flipped the switch to turn the sound off. After an hour of trying to reason with her stepdaughter, of trying to help her see that her only hope was to get a job and get on with the business of living, Jillian was forced to give up. She had done all she could do.

The police operator came back on the phone and Jillian squeezed her eyes tightly shut as she reported a trespasser on her property. When the operator asked the address, Jillian hesitated. Opening her eyes again, she watched the now-silent picture of Katya attempting to budge the immovable gates with her bare hands.

"Your address, please?" the operator repeated.

Jillian let out a deep breath, then gave the address of the only permanent home Katya Morgan had ever known.

CHAPTER ONE

One Week Earlier

I'M an orphan.

Katya Morgan felt the telephone receiver start to slip out of her hand and clenched it tighter. Her fingernails dug into her palm, but she didn't relax her grip as she sat staring out at the sparkling waters of the Caribbean.

Her stepmother's calm voice on the other end of the line sounded soothing, belying her words as she said, "I know this is a shock to you, Katya. Your father did his best to hide the seriousness of his cancer, even from me. I didn't know how sick he was until it was too late."

Katya reached for the pack of Nat Sherman Black & Golds lying on the poolside table next to her. Tapping one slim cigarette out of the pack, she brought the sweet-smelling tobacco to her lips and searched blindly for her lighter, then leaned back in her chaise lounge on the patio of the villa she'd rented for the summer on the island of Saint Martin. Holding the flame to her cigarette, she pulled in a breath of expensive nicotine.

Daddy couldn't be . . . gone. She knew he'd been unwell, but he was going to get better. He'd said so himself.

Pushing her favorite gold-rimmed, purple-tinted Armani sunglasses farther up the bridge of her nose, Katya blinked back tears. "How did he . . ." She paused, swallowing a deep breath of island air, and started again. "Was it bad at the end?"

"No. The morphine helped a lot with the pain. He simply slipped peacefully away in his sleep," Jillian answered in that same soothing tone, the one Katya always thought of as her stepmother's kindergarten-teacher voice.

Katya closed her eyes, trying not to imagine her tough, judgmental, larger-than-life father lying small and withered in his massive mahogany bed. The Caribbean sun beat down on her mercilessly, her island paradise now turned into an unrelenting inferno.

Opening her eyes again, Katya tapped the dead ash off the end of her cigarette with a shapely red fingernail and gazed out at the stunningly glorious day. White sailboats studded water so blue, it nearly screamed to be painted. Lush green islands were dotted about, their brightly colored flowers invisible until you ventured closer, then exploding in bright pinks, golden yellows, and luminescent corals. It was all too perfect, and she couldn't bear to continue looking at it, but couldn't close her eyes again, either, and risk seeing that haunting vision of her father.

As usual, she seemed unable to make the right choice.

Eyes open, eyes closed. What did it matter? Her father was dead, and, at thirty-one, she was an orphan. Without her father, she had no one.

Katya drew in a ragged breath and sat up straighter in her chair. Who was she kidding? Even with her father, she'd had no one.

"I know you and your father didn't always see eye to eye, but he really did love you," Jillian said, as if reading her stepdaughter's thoughts. "It was just so difficult for him. You look so much like your mother, and he loved her so. He took her death very hard."

Katya remained silent as her stepmother continued

on in her same even tone, "The funeral is scheduled for Saturday morning, and the will is to be read later that day."

"I'll be there," Katya mumbled before dropping the receiver onto the table beside her. Her hand shook as she reached out and picked up the fruity cocktail the butler had brought earlier. The ice had melted, causing cool beads of sweat to drip onto her lightly tanned stomach as she lifted the glass to her lips and drained the entire drink in one long swallow.

A wave of grief tinged with anger around the edges washed over her. Why hadn't Daddy told her that he was so ill? Why had their last conversation been identical to every other one for the past fifteen years? If he'd told her he was so sick, she could have . . .

Katya drew in a deep breath and put the now-empty glass back on the patio table.

She could have what? Altered the way she looked so he wouldn't feel as if he were looking back in time every time he saw her? Changed her wild and wicked ways? Become the serious-minded, studious daughter he wanted her to be?

Katya gritted her teeth and pushed a lock of silky dark hair behind her ear. No. She wouldn't have done any of those things, even if she had known how sick her father was.

"I shouldn't have had to change to make him love me," she muttered under her breath, taking a final drag on her cigarette before crushing it out viciously in the Baccarat crystal ashtray.

"Katya, honey, you want to ring for a Bloody Mary?"

Startled, Katya looked up to see the perfectly muscled, perfectly tanned, perfectly nude body of her latest flavor-of-the-season as he pulled himself out of the swimming pool. She had completely forgotten about Antoine, whose real friends, she suspected, called him Tony.

When they had woken up at just past noon, they'd talked about their plans to lounge for a while in the pool, maybe go to lunch at Le Tastevin on the French side of the island or perhaps L'Escargot on the Dutch, then head down to their private beach. Tonight there would be gambling in Philipsburg; they'd hit a party or two and maybe go dancing.

That had been before her stepmother had called to tell her that her father had died.

Katya considered her companion through her lashes. The problem with Antoine was that he was clingy, always dropping endearments into the conversation or making some excuse to touch her. And the last thing she wanted right now was someone trying to console her. What she really wanted was to be alone.

"Actually, Antoine, I've just developed some, ah, female troubles. I think it would be best if we canceled our plans for the day."

In her experience, even remotely hinting at problems with the female reproductive system had the immediate effect of clearing the area within a five-mile radius of heterosexual men. Antoine didn't even stop to pout, as he normally would if she changed their plans at the last minute. Instead, he gave her the predictable "Oh, God, please don't start talking to me about your period" look before scurrying off to the cabana to pull on his linen shorts and silk shirt before making a mad dash out to his rented convertible.

Katya threw her legs over the side of the chaise lounge. The smooth stones of the patio felt warm beneath her bare feet as she headed for the pool overlooking the Baie de l'Embouchure to the north and the island of Saint Bart's to the east. She dropped her sunglasses onto the stone patio before diving into the refreshing water.

Pushing her straight black hair out of her eyes as she surfaced, she paddled over to the edge of the pool that had been constructed to look as if it were an extension of the ocean beyond. She tried focusing her attention on a brilliant white sailboat with its red-and-white-striped spinnaker fluttering in the wind but was unable to stop the tears from welling up in her eyes. She swiped at them with her hand, drying their salty wetness before they could roll down her face.

Crying was not to be tolerated. Her father had taught her that lesson himself. She could still remember the sting of his words, the week after her mother had died. His voice, raised in anger, as he yanked the sterling silver picture frame out of her hands. "Crying won't bring your mother back, so you might as well stop that bawling right now. Do you hear me?" he'd yelled.

And of course she could hear him, he was standing right there in front of her, but she couldn't say anything, couldn't seem to do anything but sit in her mother's favorite chair and stare at her mother's laughing face in the picture and cry. Her father continued his tirade, telling her that crying wasn't going to bring her mother back. But, still, she couldn't stop the tears from coming.

The next day her father had the servants box up all of her mother's belongings and take them away. Then he told her he was sending her away, too. And even at ten, she was smart enough to know she was being punished for not being able to keep her grief to herself.

Closing her eyes against the pressure behind them, Katya laid her head down on the arms she'd crossed over the edge of the pool and made lazy circles in the water with her legs. She had only cried once since that day over twenty years ago, and she wasn't going to do so now.

After all, Daddy had been right. Crying hadn't brought her mother back, and it wasn't going to bring him back, either.

CHAPTER TWO

ALEX Sheridan stood at Charles Morgan's graveside and fought the urge to loosen his tie. For someone who had lived in Arizona virtually his entire life, he should have been accustomed to the late spring heat. Still, ninety-eight degrees was hot, especially with a heavily starched shirt and silk tie that seemed to trap the sun's rays against his chest. If it were up to him, ties would be banned as cruel and unusual punishment against mankind.

A flutter of bright purple and turquoise turned his attention from the heat. The slight June breeze had caught the scarf of the woman standing across from him and set it fluttering in the wind.

The daughter of the deceased. Alex knew her—by reputation, at least. She had been a guest at the Royal Palmetto, the hotel he ran as general manager, several times during the past few years. Rumor had it that she and her father were constantly clashing over her party-girl lifestyle, so Miss Morgan chose to frequent the local hotels whenever she was under obligation to return to Scottsdale for a familial visit. From all accounts, she was a typical spoiled heiress, but an attractive one, Alex noticed, as the breeze continued to tease her. The edges of her straight black hair lifted and fell against the colorful scarf she'd tied over a short sleeveless black dress. The hem of her dress ended north of the mid-thigh mark, and unlike the other women attending her father's funeral, Katya Morgan had left her legs bare.

All nine yards of them.

As the reverend droned on about hope and peace in the afterlife, the breeze picked up a strand of Katya Morgan's hair and pushed it over her shoulder. Alex watched as she tossed her head, turning her face into the wind with her eyes closed. Then she opened them, looking straight at Alex.

He was struck first by the unusual color of her eyes—neither gray nor green but something in between. Then he noticed that they lacked the tears he expected to see in them. Having grown up in a household with six women, Alex was used to feminine tears. But Katya Morgan's eyes were as dry as the Arizona desert.

Oddly, Alex felt more sorry for her then than if she'd been working on her fourth hankie.

She kept her gaze locked on his, her eyes full of sadness and . . . something else he couldn't define. Something like loneliness, only much deeper. Whatever it was, it made Alex shiver despite the heat.

Then he blinked, and the connection was broken. He looked back at her, but she was staring intently at the glossy black coffin and, when she looked back up, her eyes were devoid of any emotion.

It was as if he had simply imagined the moment. As if it had never happened.

"Nothing?" Katya spat the word out of her mouth as if it were a scoop of bargain-priced caviar being fed to her from a metal spoon. "What do you mean, nothing?"

She stalked toward the man who had been her father's friend longer than she had been alive. Even in her low-heeled sandals, she towered over her father's attorney. Unlike most men, Nathan Rosenberg failed to be intimidated by her. Instead, he pushed his small round glasses farther up the bridge of his nose and met her angry glare with his own dispassionate gaze.

"Your father's will is very clear on this point. You are to take nothing from the estate that you didn't purchase yourself. And since you've never held any sort of paying job, I believe that leaves you with nothing except the gifts your father gave you."

Katya took a step backward and sat down in the oversize chocolate-brown leather chair that had been her father's favorite. The fabric had absorbed the scent of the spicy cologne he'd worn for years. It wrapped its comforting arms around her and she resisted the urge to curl up into a ball and pretend that none of this was happening. But ignoring the situation wouldn't get her what she wanted, and neither would becoming angry at Nathan.

Surely there was some mistake, some twist that he was just about to tell her when she'd interrupted. Her father would never do something like this to her.

Katya took a deep breath. "Go on."

Leaning forward, she crossed her legs as she picked her pocketbook up off the floor. Fumbling with the clasp, she drew out her pack of cigarettes. Her hands shook as she flicked the lighter, and she hastily inhaled a lungful of nicotine to calm her unsteady nerves.

Nathan shrugged, looking out over the small group gathered in her father's den. Besides Katya and the handful of servants who had been in Charles Morgan's employ at the time of his death, her stepmother was the only other occupant. "I've already explained the arrangements Charles made for the staff. The remainder of the estate has been bequeathed to the Morgan Family Trust. The trust agreement is not a part of the public record, and I am not at liberty to discuss the details of the trust with anyone other than Jillian Morgan. That's all. I've made copies of the will for each of you in case you'd

like your own attorneys to review it, and the original
will be entered into probate today."

"No!" Katya wailed. "Daddy couldn't have left me
without a cent to my name. He wouldn't do that to me."

Nathan Rosenberg slid a sideways glance at her
stepmother before answering. "I'm sorry, Katya. As a
family friend, I have to tell you that your father was
very disappointed in your behavior these last few years.
He told me many times that he tried to talk to you about
it, but you wouldn't listen. I think he saw this as the
only way to make you realize you can't continue down
your self-destructive path. At least, not with his help."

"But I'll change. I promise. I'll do whatever Daddy
wanted." Katya hated hearing the desperation in her own
voice and tried to swallow it down past the lump in her
throat. She put a hand on Nathan's arm and pleaded,
"I'll do anything, sign anything you want. Please, just
tell me what Daddy wants me to do to get my inheritance."

She saw the pity in Nathan's eyes as he pulled her
hand off his arm. "I'm sorry, Katya. It's too late. There's
nothing I can do. Good-bye." He nodded politely before
gathering up the papers he'd spread out on her father's
desk and putting them into his briefcase.

As the door closed behind him, Katya slid back into
her father's chair. The leather was cold on her bare legs,
so she tugged down the hem of her dress. Taking a deep
pull on her cigarette, she looked blindly around the study
as she tried to gather her thoughts. She'd always remembered this room as being dark, a masculine haven where
her father came to brood about one business venture or
another. The floors were still a dark hardwood, but the
midnight blue paint on the walls had been replaced with
an orange-colored earth tone that lightened the room
considerably. The heavy velvet curtains had been ex-

changed for gauzy white sheers that let in the outside light and made it seem as if Camelback Mountain behind them were a part of the room. If she hadn't known the changes had been wrought by her stepmother, Katya might have admitted to liking the new look. But as it was, she hated that the other woman had come into her father's life and felt that she was free to change whatever she liked—including Daddy's feelings about his only child.

Before today, Katya had felt nothing but a vague sympathy for her stepmother, but this afternoon had changed that. Jillian had changed Daddy's study, and Katya was willing to bet her favorite Prada sandals that this new will had been her stepmother's idea as well. Anger welled up in her chest, rising like bile up her throat.

Tapping the ash from her cigarette into an ashtray, she turned to look at the blonde who had chosen a seat as far away from her stepdaughter as possible.

"So, Jillian, you think you've won, don't you?"

Katya was too far away to read the expression in her stepmother's pale blue eyes. "This isn't a war, Katya. This is reality," Jillian responded dispassionately.

"That's what you think. I'll have you know that I'm going to hire a lawyer to contest this will. I know you put Daddy up to it."

"Think what you must, but I'll warn you, your father made sure his will was airtight. He knew you'd try to fight it. You have very little money now, and you have to be careful how you spend it. You're going to need to find somewhere to live, buy groceries, and clothes—"

"You can stop with the sympathetic act, Jillian. I'm going to spend every last dollar I have fighting you. You won't get away with this." Katya tried to still her shaking hands as she rose from the chair. She'd rather die than let her stepmother see how upset she was. Gathering her purse, she clutched her car keys in one hand.

"You can't take the car."

Katya turned at Jillian's softly uttered words. "Pardon me?"

Her stepmother had stood up and Katya was surprised to notice for the first time that Jillian had lost quite a bit of weight since she'd seen her last. Her dark blue pantsuit hung on her normally curvaceous frame.

Katya viciously crushed the thought that these last few months must have been hard on her stepmother. So the bitch had sacrificed a few pounds for her father's fortune. It was more than a fair trade.

"The car is in your father's name. He went through your things and picked out everything that had been given to you as a gift. I've packed those things up for you. The rest must stay here."

A red flash exploded behind Katya's eyes. This was too much. Her stepmother wasn't content to make sure Katya had been disinherited; she was trying to take her car and clothes, too.

Katya wasn't going to stand for it.

"Like hell it will. I'll take whatever I want. You just try and stop me." Her voice rose with fury as she stormed out of her father's den.

She burst out into the foyer and headed for the wide marble stairs leading up to the second floor where her old bedroom was located.

Her father's head of security stood on the bottom step. "I'm sorry, Miss Morgan. I can't let you go upstairs," he said, laying a firm hand on her shoulder as she tried to pass.

"Would everyone stop telling me they're sorry?" she hissed, trying to shake him off. She wanted to go upstairs, to the bedroom that had been hers since the day she'd been born, climb under the covers, and not come out until this nightmare was over. Why wouldn't they let her do that? "Let me pass," she demanded.

"I'm afraid I can't do that. I have my orders."

"Orders from who?" Katya turned her head to look at her stepmother, who had followed her out into the entryway. "From her?"

"Yes. From Mrs. Morgan."

"You just wait. Once this is resolved, I'll have your job. I'll fire all of you for siding with her."

Katya jerked her arm out of the security man's grasp. She stepped to the heavy front door and would have flung it open if it hadn't weighed quite so much. Instead, it opened slowly on well-oiled hinges, ruining the effect.

Stepping out into the porte cochere, she searched for her red convertible. Daddy had let her drive the car whenever she was in town, and she'd be damned if she'd let Jillian take it from her.

Only it wasn't there. In its place sat a yellow taxi, engine running.

"I truly am sorry, Katya," her stepmother said calmly from behind her. "Believe it or not, I'm doing this for your own good."

Raising her arm, Katya threw her car keys into the pink and white bougainvillea climbing up the trellis at the front of the house. "You'll pay for this, Jillian," she said, not bothering to turn around as she strode over to the waiting cab and let herself in.

"Take me to the Royal Palmetto," she told the cab-driver, settling back into the smelly interior of the taxi.

The tiny rips in the vinyl seat scratched her bare legs as the cab passed through the wrought-iron gates of her childhood home and drove away from Camelback Mountain.

CHAPTER THREE

"HELLO, Alex. This is Jillian Morgan. I'm sorry to disturb you."

Alex Sheridan leaned back in the leather chair in his office at the Royal Palmetto hotel and cradled the telephone between his shoulder and his ear while riffling through the papers on his desk. "You're not disturbing me, Jillian. I'm sorry I didn't get a chance to speak to you after the funeral this morning. There was some flooding at the hotel and I had to get back to deal with it. How are you holding up?"

Her voice had sounded strained, but Alex doubted she'd admit anything to him. He'd known Jillian Morgan for over two years now and had yet to see a crack in the facade she showed to the world.

"I'm fine; thank you for asking." Her polite reply was just what he'd expected.

"You'll let me know if you need anything?"

"Yes." She hesitated. "Actually, Alex, that's why I called. I need to ask a favor."

Alex blinked in surprise. Over the years, he'd worked closely with Jillian to arrange conferences and business meetings at the hotel for her husband, had even been to the Morgans' house for a few cocktail parties and dinners. But he'd never considered his relationship with either Charles Morgan or his wife as anything but business. What in the world could she want from him now?

Well, there was only one way to find out. "Certainly. What can I do for you?" he asked.

Again Jillian hesitated, and Alex straightened in his chair. Something this difficult to ask could only bode badly for him.

"You're going to think I'm crazy." Alex heard her small laugh before she continued, "My stepdaughter is on her way back to the Royal Palmetto, and I need you to . . . well, you see, the thing is . . ." She took a deep breath, then blurted, "She needs a job. Her father disinherited her. She can't pay her bill, and I can't cover it or . . . well, never mind why. I just can't. She's going to need a job to survive, although she may not realize it yet. I thought you might be able to find something for her there at the hotel."

Alex stifled a groan. Give Katya Morgan a job at the hotel? Great, that was just what he needed—to babysit some rich girl whose daddy was no longer around to pamper her. Alex himself had been raised to believe that hard work was its own reward. He'd graduated in the top 5 percent of his high school class and had worked two jobs to put himself through college and graduate with a minimum of debt. He had little sympathy for people like Katya, who simply showed up and expected society to provide for them.

Looking heavenward, he opened his mouth to refuse, then stopped when Jillian's soft voice interrupted, "Please, Alex. I would appreciate it if you could do this for me."

He frowned, thinking of all the business Jillian had brought his way over the past few years. Besides, what were the chances Miss Morgan would accept his offer? A million to one, he'd wager. She'd probably laugh in his face, then run off to marry the richest man she could find. And that would be fine with him. He'd be able to save his business relationship with Jillian just by offering her stepdaughter a position, a position Katya was certain to reject.

"Of course. I'd be happy to help," he answered smoothly as he tilted back in his swivel chair. There were always plenty of openings at the hotel for people willing to work hard. So, what would he offer her?

He blinked and a smile spread across his face. Housekeeping. Yes, that was it. Even if Miss Morgan *did* accept the job, one eight-hour day of cleaning hotel rooms would surely change her mind.

After Jillian hung up, Alex stared unseeingly at the colorful painting hanging on the wall of his office. It was an oil painting of the hotel done by a local artist, and it perfectly captured the brilliant red of the tiled roof as the sun went down, the gold of the painted stucco walls, and the riotous colors of the blooming flowers scattered around the hotel. He often thought of the Royal Palmetto as *his* hotel, perhaps because he had been instrumental in renovating the physical structure of the property as well as restoring the hotel's reputation to its once-glamorous splendor. When he had taken over as general manager four years ago, the swimming pool was cracked and empty, the flowers dead from lack of care and watering, the formerly white stucco interior gray and faded. But Alex had seen the underlying promise and had labored painstakingly to turn the Royal Palmetto into what she was now: a charming hotel catering to upscale travelers who appreciated the hotel's quiet courtyards, well-tended gardens, and first-rate service.

Of course, it took quite a bit of work to live up to the exacting standards of these guests, and Alex guessed that Miss Morgan wouldn't last one day at it.

•   •   •

"What do you mean, it's been rejected? Try it again."
Katya pushed the plastic card back across the cold marble countertop of the hotel's front desk. This was the last thing she needed right now. Her magnetic card key hadn't worked when she'd tried to get back into her room this afternoon, and now her credit card wasn't working, either.

"I'm s-sorry, Miss Morgan. I've already tried it twice. The machine says your credit card has been c-c-canceled," the dark-haired woman manning the front desk stammered.

Katya drummed her perfectly polished nails on the counter in time with the pulse growing stronger in her neck. She could actually feel the blood slamming against her veins. How dare they refuse to accept her credit card? Yanking open the gold snap on her new Coach handbag, she pulled out a matching leather wallet.

"Here, try this one." She tossed a gold American Express card across the counter, then a platinum Visa. "How about this one? Or this." Her voice raised a notch with each card that went sailing across the cool marble.

The woman swallowed, and Katya could see in her eyes that she'd prefer it if Katya would simply leave quietly. Instead, she slid the cards one by one through the card reader.

Katya waited, impatiently inspecting the polish on her left index finger as the machine dialed. In less than twenty-four hours, she'd be on a plane back to Saint Martin, where sparkling blue water and a helpful staff awaited her return. She'd send Antoine away for a few days. He would only badger her with questions she didn't want to answer. Once she had some time alone to think, she could—

"I'm sorry, Miss Morgan. N-none of these cards worked."

Katya gathered the rectangular pile of plastic the woman had neatly arranged on the earthy-red marble counter and slowly placed each one in its slot in her wallet. Her fingernails made a satisfying clicking noise against the cards as she carefully filed each one away, her mind racing desperately. How could they have canceled her cards so quickly?

And what was she going to do now?

She looked up at the young woman on the other side of the counter. "I need to go to my room and call my accountant to find out what the problem is. I simply need another room key," Katya explained calmly, her fists clenched at her sides.

"I understand, Miss Morgan. But in order to give you a key, I need a credit card to g-guarantee the charges. You're welcome to use the lobby phone over there to make your call." The woman gestured with a nod of her head to a telephone on a table near a trio of overstuffed chairs.

Katya felt the remaining slim threads of her patience starting to snap. It had been a long, trying day. All she wanted was to go back to her room and sit in silence to absorb all that had happened. She wanted to slide into a nice hot bath and figure out a plan of action to fight her stepmother. However, she couldn't do any of this until this woman gave her a room key.

She glanced at the woman's name tag. Inez. No last name. She tried pasting a friendly look on her face, but it wasn't easy. This woman was the only thing standing in the way of Katya getting what she so desperately needed right now.

"Inez, you're just going to have to take my word that I'm good for it. I've had some trouble with my credit cards today, I have less than a hundred dollars in cash, and I need to go back to my room to make some calls to get this whole mess straightened out. Now, why don't you just give me back my key and I'll be on my way?"

Inez looked down at her shoes, refusing to meet Katya's direct gaze. "I can't do that, Miss Morgan. The r-r-rules—"

Katya's tenuous hold on her patience snapped. "I don't care about the rules. Just give me the damn key."

Several guests sitting in the lobby looked over at the scene near the reception area. Inez's face turned a bright red, but she stood her ground. "I c-can't."

Drawing herself up to her full five feet, nine inches, Katya towered over the smaller hotel clerk. "Yes, you can. All you have to do is enter something in that computer of yours." Katya waved a hand dismissively over the marble counter.

The younger woman's bottom lip trembled and Katya pushed aside a feeling of guilt. She hadn't intended to make the other woman cry, but she wasn't feeling all too happy herself. All Inez had to do was give her a key. Then she'd leave, and they could both go lick their wounds in private.

"What's going on here?"

Katya spun around and locked eyes with a tall dark-haired man. He looked vaguely familiar, but his identity didn't immediately register in her mind. He was probably one of her father's countless business associates.

In other circumstances, she might have let her gaze linger over the man's strong features, might have let herself wonder what he looked like under the concealing dark suit he wore. But, as it was, there were already too many emotions swirling around in her brain to allow herself to think of anything besides her immediate goal of finding a quiet place to stay for the night.

"Who are you?" she asked.

"I'm Alex Sheridan, the general manager of the Royal Palmetto." His golden-brown eyes regarded her levelly.

Now she remembered why he looked so familiar. She'd met him at Daddy's funeral. "Mr. Sheridan. I'm Katya Morgan, Charles Morgan's daughter. I believe we met briefly this morning."

"Yes?"

She resisted the urge to cross her arms over her chest as Alex Sheridan's eyes traveled from her polished toenails up her bare legs, stopping briefly at her breasts before meeting her eyes again. The look in his eyes told her without a doubt what he thought of her short sleeveless black dress as proper funeral attire.

Well, to hell with him. Who did he think he was, the creator of *People* magazine's Best-Dressed List? She stuck out her chest and felt a satisfying sense of triumph at the appreciative look in his eyes as the hem of her already-short skirt rode farther up her thighs.

"What's the problem, Miss Morgan?"

"The *problem,* Mr. Sheridan, is that this woman will not give me my room key. I'd like nothing more than to return peacefully to my room, but I can't do so without my key."

"Inez?" Katya noticed the man's voice softened considerably as he turned to the desk clerk.

"I'm sorry, Alex, but n-none of the credit cards Miss Morgan provided were approved."

"As I explained earlier, there's some kind of problem with my cards," Katya interjected. "I can assure you I'm good for it."

Alex shot her a sideways glance, then turned his attention back to Inez. "How much does Miss Morgan owe, not including tonight's charges?"

"Almost three thousand dollars," Inez answered, glancing at her computer screen.

Alex leaned back on his heels. "That's quite a bill."

Katya gave him a cool look. "Funny, I would think a businessman such as yourself would encourage guests to spend money at your hotel and spa."

"Oh, I do. But only if the guests have the wherewithal to pay the charges, which is why we insist on securing each room with a credit card. You might imagine the trouble we'd be in if we were to let guests run up bills of thousands of dollars which they had no intention of paying."

"I do intend to pay my bill, Mr. Sheridan," she said, pushing the words out through gritted teeth.

Alex rested a tanned hand on the marble countertop, his tone deceptively light as he continued to eye her. "That's interesting. I received a call from your stepmother a few moments ago, and she warned me you have no way of paying for your stay. So, please, tell me, exactly how do you intend to make good on the three-thousand-dollar debt you've incurred at the Royal Palmetto?"

Katya opened her mouth, but no words came out. The question spun around in her brain, ricocheting off her skull like the rubber ball in a pinball machine. How *was* she going to pay her bill at the hotel? She'd never had to deal with problems like this before. Whenever she needed money, she put a card into a machine and out popped whatever she wanted. A hundred dollars, a thousand dollars, five thousand dollars. It had never mattered before. She bought whatever she wanted and Daddy took care of the bills. It had been that way since she'd been a child.

Katya blinked back the sudden threat of tears. Why

had Daddy done this to her? Why had he died and left
her with nothing?

Clenching her teeth, she sucked in a deep breath.
She was not going to give in to self-pity. Tomorrow
she'd do whatever she had to do to fight her stepmother's
claims to Daddy's fortune. That money rightfully belonged to Katya—to Charles Morgan's only blood relative—not to some gold-digging interloper who had only
married her father for his money. She just had to get
through tonight. Tomorrow was another day.

She met Alex Sheridan's skeptical gaze and her resolve stiffened. She'd show him, and everyone else, that
Katya Morgan had what it took to survive. Without looking down, she slipped the sapphire-and-diamond bracelet
her father had given her last year for her thirtieth birthday off her wrist and held it out in front of her.

"This should be worth at least three thousand dollars. I have some more jewelry that I intend to sell tomorrow, but tonight, I need a place to sleep."

Alex looked down at the bracelet dangling from
Katya Morgan's fingers. There was no way he could
accept this as payment from her. He was about to refuse
when something stopped him.

It was her softly uttered "please" that did him in.

Nana had always said he was a sucker for a damsel
in distress.

Unfortunately, she was right. He couldn't turn away
from someone who needed his help.

With a sigh of defeat, Alex reached out a hand and
felt the cool gold slide into his palm. "I'll take this for
now, but I may be able to help you with a job if you're
interested in working it off instead."

Katya blinked, feeling as if her entire world was
tilting on its axis. Which, of course, it was. What in the
hell was Alex Sheridan talking about? What did he mean

by "working it off"? Didn't he know she had absolutely no marketable job skills, had never had any intention of doing anything other than what she'd been doing the past decade—going to parties, gambling with her friends, and enjoying her life?

Or was he talking about something else entirely?

Crooking her head, Katya looked up at him. Was he suggesting she sleep with him to even up the score? If so, it would be the easiest decision she'd ever had to make. Alex Sheridan was an attractive man, and Katya had no qualms about sleeping with him to get what she wanted.

Ignoring the audience of guests in the lobby and the hotel clerk who had been silently watching their exchange, Katya lowered her eyelids seductively and placed her hands on Alex's forearms. She'd known since she was sixteen that men found her sexy, and she'd use that sex appeal now, for whatever it was worth. Sliding close to Alex, she peered up at him through her thick black lashes. Her tongue darted out to moisten her full bottom lip. Lowering her voice to a husky whisper, she took him up on his offer. "I'd be happy to work it off, Alex. You just name the time and the place. I'm ready. Anytime."

His eyes darkened, and Katya fought back a triumphant grin. Which one of her boyfriends had said that no man could stay immune to her charms for long? Had it been Jacques in Cannes? Or was it Luc in Venice? No, it was—

Alex's voice interrupted her victory quiz. "Fine. You can start Monday morning. Report to Maria in Housekeeping at six A.M. sharp. Until then, I'll just keep this for safekeeping." He slipped the bracelet into his coat pocket before turning back to the front desk. "Inez,

you can let Miss Morgan have a room for one more
night."

The cool early-evening air swept across her skin as
Alex extricated himself easily from her grasp. Katya
watched, rooted to the spot, as he breezed out of the
lobby.

"Here's your key, Miss Morgan. I'm sorry about the
c-confusion." The dark-haired woman pushed a blue
card key across the reddish brown countertop. "Can I
get a bellman to help you with your ... uh ... your
boxes?"

Katya had forgotten all about the crates Jillian had
loaded into the taxi, the only belongings she'd been allowed to take from her childhood home. Biting the inside of her lip, Katya nodded silently at the other
woman's offer.

She was too stunned to do anything else.

"You did what?"

Alex studied the painting on the wall while ponder-
ing his sister's incredulous question. He didn't blame her
for being upset. After all, as housekeeping manager, Maria Sheridan was responsible for training new housekeepers as well as counseling experienced workers when
guests complained about the condition of their rooms.
Unfortunately, this meant that Maria would bear the
brunt of Alex's offer to help Jillian Morgan by hiring
her stepdaughter.

"I'm sorry, Maria, but you know how much money
the Morgans have brought to the hotel over the years.
When Jillian asked for this favor, I couldn't refuse."

"That's fine, but why did you have to make her *my*
problem?"

Alex listened to his sister with half an ear as he
marveled at the way the artist had painted the play of

shadows and sunlight across the cobblestone entry of the hotel. It was an elegant circular driveway with a large fountain in the middle, and Alex could almost picture well-dressed men and women stepping out of their shiny black cars for an evening of dining and dancing at the hotel. A sudden vision of Katya Morgan's golden-brown legs climbing out of a fancy car flashed in his mind and he frowned. He did not want thoughts of her intruding on his daydreams.

His sister sighed. "Alex, you're not paying attention."

He blinked guiltily. She was right. "Sorry, Maria. What were you saying?"

"I asked why you're pawning Katya Morgan off on me."

Turning away from the picture on his wall, Alex looked at his sister where she sat perched on the edge of his desk. She'd inherited her dark good looks from their mother and her height from their father. Of his four sisters, he was closest in both age and temperament to Maria. Lucy was the earth mother, content to stay at home and produce a child every few years to ensure a long line of succession; Inez was shy, and Alex hoped her job as a front desk clerk would help her learn to be more comfortable around people; Martina, the baby, was wild and headstrong, always pushing the rules to see how much she could get away with. And Maria? Maria was practical, smart, and ambitious. Maria was the only one of his sisters whom he never had to worry about. She could take care of herself.

He grinned. Maybe that's why he'd tossed her the challenge of Katya, to see if there was anything she couldn't handle.

"She's probably not even going to show up," he assured her.

"Then what are you grinning about? I know you, Alex. You're trying to punish me for something, aren't you? You aren't still mad at me for telling Nana that you prefer boxers over briefs, are you?"

Alex narrowed his eyes. He'd almost forgotten his sister's comment during their last Sunday dinner. One of the benefits of being a general manager was that he had been given a suite at the hotel. Since running a hotel was a twenty-four-hour-a-day, seven-day-a-week job, he had to be aware of what was going on at all times, and living on the premises ensured that he was. Of course, that also meant that he had no privacy, as the hotel staff routinely cleaned his rooms, did his laundry, and gossiped about him endlessly. It made it even worse that almost half of his immediate family worked at the hotel.

"Nana certainly doesn't need to know about my choice of underwear. Now that you mention it, I think having to deal with Katya Morgan is fitting punishment for you." He rubbed his chin thoughtfully. "Yes, I do think I made the perfect decision."

"Hmm," Maria snorted as she started toward the door. "Remind me to keep my mouth shut in the future."

Alex laughed. "I will. And, Maria?"

"Yes?" His sister turned.

"Go easy on Katya at first, will you? She's never had to do anything like this before."

Maria watched him, a speculative gleam in her dark brown eyes. "All right, big brother, I will. If she shows up, that is."

As the door closed behind Maria, Alex turned back to the painting on the wall and once again imagined Katya Morgan stepping out onto the gold-colored stones of the hotel's entrance. She had spent her entire life being helped out of luxury cars by valets at fancy hotels the world over, and now she was about to see just how different it was to work at one of those hotels.

He pulled the sparkling bracelet out of the jacket he'd slung over his chair and set it down on his desk. A vision of her as she'd looked that morning sprung into his mind. He remembered the look in her eyes as their gazes had locked over her father's grave, and he felt a small shiver run through his body. Having lost both of his own parents, Alex knew the sorrow could be devastating. But at least he had Nana and his sisters, not to mention the rest of his extended family, to help him over the grief.

Katya seemingly had no one. Most of the people who had attended her father's funeral that morning had been business associates and friends of Charles Morgan. There were no aunts or uncles, no cousins or grandparents. Alex had no idea what it would be like to be so alone in the world.

Slipping the bracelet into his top desk drawer, Alex couldn't help but feel a twinge of pity for Katya Morgan. He wasn't certain she knew how difficult real life could be.

"Alex, I couldn't be more pleased with how you're doing as general manager of the Royal Palmetto."

"Thank you, Barry, but it's not just me you should be thanking. There are hundreds of people who've been instrumental in restoring the hotel to its former glory," Alex said in an attempt to not take too much of the credit for himself. Barry Hampstead, the owner of the Royal Palmetto, had put a lot of faith in Alex four years ago when he'd hired him to turn the dilapidated old hotel into an upscale haven for travelers. Alex was proud of his accomplishments to date but was the first to admit he couldn't have done it alone.

"Yes, but it's been your relationships with vendors

and our employees that have allowed the hotel to become profitable so soon after renovation." Barry held up the report that Alex had handed him a few minutes ago as proof of his statement. "The profit margin at the Royal Palmetto is the highest of any of my hotels. That's no accident."

Alex felt like squirming in his chair at the unaccustomed praise. Barry was a graduate of the old school, where one was taught to lead by intimidation. Alex wasn't sure he liked this technique any better.

"It will only improve now that I'm here."

Both Alex and Barry turned to look at the third occupant of the room. Alex had almost forgotten that Barry's son, Chris, had accompanied his father to the hotel today. He and Chris were about the same age, but Chris seemed so much younger to Alex. Of course, Chris had never had the same responsibilities that had been placed on Alex's shoulders so many years ago. As the only child of a wealthy businessman, Chris had attended the best private schools in Scottsdale. He'd gone on to college and moderate success as a professional basketball player, though Alex had heard Barry deride Chris's choice of profession on several occasions. Now, at thirty-six, Chris's former glory days were almost a decade behind him and he'd spent the ensuing years doing various odd jobs for his father's numerous companies. His latest task was to try to learn everything about the hotel business from Alex. Alex had the impression that Barry was frustrated with his son and was pushing him into this in the hopes that he'd find something—anything—to excel at.

Alex ignored the other man's boast and asked instead, "How are the arrangements for the cattlemen's convention coming along?"

"Great. We're all set for their opening banquet on

Tuesday. I've been on top of every detail, and I can assure you this is one conference that will go off without a hitch."

Alex quickly hid a grimace. He'd been in this business long enough to know that it was bad karma to tempt fate by saying something like that. All he could do was hope that Chris was right—and schedule a meeting to go over all the details just to make sure. "I'm sure it will. Why don't we get together tonight after dinner to review the schedule? Say nine o'clock?"

Chris's acceptance seemed a bit reluctant, but Alex figured he'd better get used to the round-the-clock hours. Hotels and hospitals were among the few businesses that remained open twenty-four hours a day, 365 days a year. If Chris didn't like that, he should find a new profession.

CHAPTER FOUR

THE pain was almost as bad as it had been when her mother had died.

Lying on the bed in her hotel room, Katya stared blankly at the cream-colored wall and fought the urge to scream. Her father had left her, orphaned her with no money and no one to turn to for help.

Why had he done this to her? She knew he hadn't approved of her carefree lifestyle, but it wasn't just that. She hadn't lived a carefree lifestyle when she was ten years old, but he hadn't approved of her then, either. No matter what she did or how she acted, all her father saw was the constant reminder of his beloved wife. At some point in her life—even she wasn't exactly sure when—she had simply given up trying to please him. It was just no use. Her father couldn't stand to be in the same house with her because of the way she looked, so what did it matter how she acted? The end result was the same. Whether she tried to please him or not, he continued to push her away. And now he was dead. And she told herself that she shouldn't care. Aside from the money he had provided, her father hadn't been a part of her life for twenty years.

Anger and fear and aching sadness warred within her. Anger that her father hadn't been able to love her as much as he had loved her mother. Fear about where her life was going to go from here. And sadness that it wasn't really her father that she missed at all—it was the comfort that his money had provided all the years since her mother had died.

At least, that's what she tried to tell herself.

Why, then, did she feel as if her insides were being poked at with hot, sharp knives? She remembered this pain from when her mother had died, the uncontrollable urge to sob hot, fat tears until her pillow was soaked and her stomach felt empty. But she was a grown-up now and had vowed that she'd never again be ripped apart when someone left her. If she never let anyone close, she couldn't be hurt when they went away. So it wasn't as bad as when her mother had died. She wouldn't let it be.

Katya pushed her back against the pillows piled up on the bed and pulled her legs up to her chest. She shouldn't have looked in the boxes. Finding the sterling-silver-framed picture of her mother had done it. Before that, she'd been doing fine, had even managed to write out a plan of action for tomorrow, starting with a trip to the jeweler. That's what had prompted her to start looking through the boxes, to see if there was anything of value she could sell until she got this mess with her father's will straightened out.

Curled up in her hotel room, she clutched the cold metal picture frame tightly against her heart. She thought her father had gotten rid of the picture, along with everything else that had reminded him of her mother. She almost wished he had.

Her fingers tightened convulsively around the picture. The edges of the frame dug into her palms, but Katya hardly noticed.

If her mother were alive, things would be different. They'd be together in the big house nestled against Camelback Mountain, comforting each other over Charles Morgan's death.

She sniffed, refusing to give in to her tears, and the sound echoed in the empty room.

Just as her father had told her twenty years ago, crying didn't help to solve anything. It hadn't brought her mother back, and it wasn't going to fix any of her problems now.

Sitting up straighter, Katya pushed the framed photo to the bottom of the bed with her bare foot. Allowing herself to wallow in all these helpless emotions wasn't going to make anything better. What she needed was a stiff drink. And maybe some company to distract her from her problems. She didn't want to think—or feel—anymore. The hotel had a quaint little piano bar just off the lobby. She'd go have a martini or three, and then she'd feel better.

Stepping into the bathroom, Katya dabbed at the smudged makeup under her eyes, then ran a comb through her hair until it shone blue-black in the overhead light. Eyeing herself in the mirror, she decided her dress could pass without being ironed. She pulled a hand-woven black-and-silver scarf off a hanger in the closet, slid her sandals back on, and slipped out into the night.

The heat embraced her as she closed the door on her air-conditioned room. Katya stood outside for a moment, letting her eyes adjust to the soft lighting around the hotel. She remembered reading somewhere that the Royal Palmetto had been converted from the mansion of a wealthy Spanish family to its current state as an exclusive 150-room hotel. The rooms were spread out over several acres. There was a central two-story building wrapped around a courtyard with a wood-burning fireplace. Smaller one-story buildings dotted the rest of the grounds. Each room in these smaller buildings had a separate bedroom and sitting room area. Katya's favorite rooms also had their own fireplaces, where she could listen to the crackle of the mesquite burning on the rare evenings when there was a chill in the Arizona air.

She had been given one of the smaller rooms in the main building for the night, and she noticed that someone had lit a fire in the courtyard fireplace. Keeping an eye on the uneven stones of the path so she wouldn't trip, she made her way past the fire to the walkway beside the lighted swimming pool. An older couple embraced in the shadowy shallow end of the pool. Watching them, Katya felt another tug of the sadness that she had left her room to escape. Averting her eyes, she quickened her pace, still watching her feet to make sure she didn't end up in a heap on the warm stones of the footpath.

Rounding a corner, she thumped squarely into another body.

A large hand reached out to steady her. "Pardon me. I didn't see you coming. Are you all right?"

Katya stepped back instinctively from the physical contact. As a woman traveling alone, she'd learned to avoid situations where she could be seen as vulnerable. "Yes, thank you. I'm fine. Now, if you'll excuse me, my husband is waiting for me in the lobby." She waited for the man to step aside so she could pass. He was very tall. She had to crane her neck to see his face, and she wasn't exactly short.

His teeth flashed white in his face as he met her eyes. "Your husband, huh? I don't see a ring."

"I don't wear one. I'm very liberated. Now if you'll excuse me . . ." She gestured with her hand for him to move, but he ignored the hint.

"Tell you what, why don't I escort you to the lobby myself? I'd like to see if my instincts are right. I'll bet you don't have a husband at all. A jealous boyfriend I might believe, but—I've got to tell you the truth—I'm not getting the husband vibe here."

Katya sighed. She should have just stayed in her room, maybe dipped into the minibar for a couple vodka tonics. Those expensive little bags of peanuts would have sufficed for dinner, although the ambience would have left something to be desired.

"Okay, you're right. I don't have a husband. Actually, I'm a lesbian and my girlfriend, who is a champion kickboxer, is waiting for me. May I go now?"

The man laughed. "Now this I've got to see. Come on." He held out an arm for her and changed direction. Katya thought about darting past him, but it didn't appear that he had evil intent on his mind, or he'd have already hauled her off into the bushes and tried to have his way with her. Besides, hadn't she come out here for company?

Shaking her head, Katya laid a hand on his arm, appreciating his gentlemanly manners, if nothing else. That was one thing she'd noticed about men in America, especially men her own age—they didn't seem to know how to treat a woman like a lady. European men, now they knew all about taking your arm and escorting you across a room or helping you into a car. Of course, the trade-off was they didn't seem to think you were capable of intelligent conversation, but sometimes the downside was worth it. As long as they were good in bed, who really cared about conversation anyway?

They walked in silence down the path, and Katya enjoyed the stately atmosphere of the hotel. She thought about asking her escort if this was his first stay at the Royal Palmetto but found she wasn't in the mood for small talk. Instead she let the quiet lengthen until they came to a spot in the walkway where they had to turn either left for the lobby or right for the restaurant and the piano bar she'd longed for earlier.

He had started down the left path when Katya stopped him. "I'm not meeting anyone in the lobby," she confessed, looking up at him. They were standing under a muted lantern, and Katya noticed her captor had a lean face, with dark brown hair and hazel eyes that crinkled at the corners when he smiled at her.

"Then I was right on both counts. What do I win?"

Katya studied him for a moment. He seemed pleasant enough. "How about a drink? I was coming down to have a martini and listen to some music. Would you like to join me?"

"I'd love to, but only on one condition."

Here it came, the typical "I'll buy you a drink if you agree to sleep with me later" offer. Well, she should be used to it by now. "What's the condition?" she asked, prepared to turn around and head back to her room, alone.

"I pay. I'll take your company as my reward for trusting my instincts."

Katya smiled, the first real smile she'd allowed herself all day. "Agreed."

She started to relax once he'd pulled out her chair and seated her on the patio of the bar. Strains of music filtered out through the open French doors, and Katya leaned back, taking a deep breath of warm evening air.

"By the way, I never got a chance to introduce myself. I'm Chris Hampstead."

Something about his name sounded familiar, but Katya didn't want to bother to think what it might be. "Katya Morgan," she responded, holding out a hand for the obligatory shake.

He gave her fingers a too-firm once-over, and Katya had to force herself not to wince before he released her.

"Katya. That's a lovely name," he said after settling back in his own chair.

"And very unusual. I know." Katya studied her new acquaintance. She couldn't decide if the color of his eyes was greenish brown or brownish green. "My mother was Russian, and she insisted that I have a traditional Russian name, so I've gone through life explaining that my name isn't Katy or Kathy."

"What would your father's choice have been?"

The pang of sadness hit her again and she pushed it back. "I don't know." And now it was too late to ask. Knowing her father . . . well, that was the problem, wasn't it? She didn't know her father, had no idea what he would have named his only child if Anastasia Morgan had allowed him a vote in the decision.

She shrugged. "Probably something simple like Mary or Sue. I'm not sure." The waiter arrived with their drinks and Katya leaned back against the cool metal chair while a warm breeze teased the ends of her hair. She changed the subject. "I noticed your ring. It's quite distinctive," she said, spearing the olive in her martini with a sharp yellow toothpick. The salty sourness of the vermouth-soaked treat exploded in her mouth. She almost liked the condiments that came with the traditional martini more than the drink itself. Almost.

Chris turned his hand and candlelight flickered off the heavy gold ring he wore on his right hand. "It's an NBA basketball championship ring. I got it when my team won the play-offs. I didn't get to play in that game, but at least I got the ring."

Katya noticed the somewhat petulant tone of Chris's voice but ignored it. "So what do you do now?"

"Ah, what do I do? If you asked my father, the answer would be 'as little as possible,' " he answered good-naturedly. "We own real estate, and up until last year I spent my time going from property to property making sure things were running smoothly. Now I'm here, training with the general manager to learn how to run a hotel. My father wants me to take over after I'm through."

Katya looked down at the table. So that was why the name sounded familiar. In all likelihood, Chris had known her father, but he had obviously not made the connection between Katya and Charles Morgan. That was fine with her. She really didn't want to talk about her father right now. She said something appropriate, encouraging Chris Hampstead to talk about himself. He launched into an amusing story about the property manager of a high-rise his family owned in Miami, and before she knew it, Katya was sipping her second drink.

The world around her started to soften. The air was heavy with the sweet scent of orange trees and jasmine. The music floating out into the night was quieter, more beautiful than before. It was as if each note was sliding directly into her ear, caressing her with its soft kiss before making way for the next. She closed her eyes, letting the sound wash over her.

"Uh . . . Katya?"

"Mmm?"

"Have you had dinner?"

There was a hint of amusement in his voice, but Katya didn't know why. "No, thank you. I'm not hungry," she answered, taking another sip of her drink.

She liked this world, this hazy never-never land where each strike of the pianist's fingers resonated within her soul. It was a good world with no worries, no thoughts of the future, no loneliness. She sighed.

"Come on, then. We need to get you off to bed." Chris's words shattered her dreamworld. Her eyes popped open.

"I'm not going to bed with you," she said coldly.

"No, of course not. I meant off to your bed. Alone."

"Oh. Yes, of course. I'm sorry." Katya laid a hand on Chris's bare forearm. Her brightly painted nails made perfect ovals against the dark brown hair spattering his skin. "It's been a long day."

He pulled her chair out for her and Katya stood, feeling like an idiot for assuming he intended to sleep with her. After all, he had been very gentlemanly and not forward in the least. She stumbled a bit on a loose stone and he took her arm. Katya felt even more like a heel for her accusation, but the damage had been done.

They walked back to her room in silence. At the door, Katya turned. "I'm sorry, Chris. You've been a perfect gentleman, and I had no right—"

He smiled, laying a large hand against the solid wood door, effectively trapping her between his body and the wrought-iron railing. "There's no need to apologize, Katya. The truth is, if I thought you were interested I'd be inviting myself in right now. As it is, I can see you're tired, so I'll save my proposition for another time. Can I call you sometime?"

His teeth gleamed in the moonlight, making Katya think of the Cheshire Cat from *Alice's Adventures in Wonderland.* She'd always thought there was something creepy about that cat, the giant white teeth appearing and disappearing without warning. She shook her head slightly to rid herself of the absurd image. Chris seemed like a nice man, and a wealthy one at that. What more could a woman ask for?

"Yes, please do. My cell number is five-five-five five-nine-eight-five. Thank you for the drinks, and the company."

"Here, let me get your door for you." Chris reached out for the card key she held in her hand and Katya fought the odd instinct to press herself back against the door.

"Chris? Is that you? It's nine-thirty. Where have you been?"

Katya grimaced at the familiar voice. What was Alex Sheridan doing prowling around her door? Chris dropped his arm, lowering the barricade, and Katya peeked around his tall lanky body. The first thing she noticed was that Alex had changed into a pair of casual black slacks and a wildly patterned black-and-silver shirt. Looking down at her own attire, Katya realized if they stood side by side they'd look like a pair of ice-skaters in the Olympics.

The second thing she noticed was that Chris's smile seemed a bit forced as he turned to the other man. "Alex, old man. I was just coming to meet you when I got detained."

"So I see." Alex's disapproval radiated through the air, raising the tiny hairs on the back of Katya's neck.

Suddenly she was hit by a wave of exhaustion, her earlier alcohol-induced euphoria seeping through her pores to be scattered in the breeze. She mumbled a good night to Chris, ignoring Alex as she pulled the magnetic card key out of the lock and opened the door to her room. The door slid silently closed behind her as she stepped into the room. Without bothering to take off her makeup, she tossed her sandals into a corner, flung her-self down on the bed, and buried her face in the pillows. Her bare feet touched something cold and Katya at first didn't know what it was.

Reaching down, she grabbed her mother's picture and put it on the pillow beside her head. Her mother's laughing eyes looked up at her as Katya drifted off to sleep.

· · ·

"How much is it worth?" Katya asked, tapping her nails impatiently on the glass countertop.

The jeweler continued turning the diamond necklace under her loupe. "I would say nine thousand, at least. The stones are excellent quality." The woman handed the necklace back to Katya.

"How long would something like this take to sell?"

"I couldn't say. Sometimes we have items that sell within a week, and others we've had for years."

Katya raised her eyebrows. That was not a particularly helpful answer.

The other woman shrugged. "We don't get many clients who can just come in and write a check for that kind of cash. If I had to say, I would guess we're talking at least six or eight months before you'd get a buyer for something like this. Then, of course, we'd need to take our consignment fee of thirty-five percent—"

"Thirty-five percent," Katya protested. "That's robbery."

"Hardly, my dear. We have to pay the overhead—the rent here is quite expensive, as you might imagine—not to mention salaries, benefits, insurance, and a million other things."

Katya let out a frustrated breath and slipped her necklace back into its black velvet pouch. "Thank you anyway," she muttered.

"You might want to try a pawnshop," the jeweler suggested. "You won't get as high a price as we'd give you, but you'll have the money immediately."

Katya grimaced, hating the thought that she might actually have to stoop to pawning her belongings to survive until this mess was sorted out. Somehow, that seemed even worse than selling them on consignment. But on the other hand, she couldn't wait six to eight months for the money. She needed cash now to hire an attorney to fight her father's will.

She left the store and sat down on one of the wooden benches scattered around the upscale Fashion Square Mall in Scottsdale.

After a final search of the boxes Jillian had packed, Katya had found, much to her dismay, that she owned very few things of value that she could sell to tide her over until the fiasco over the will was sorted out. If she'd known Jillian was going to turn her out of her own house, she would have packed everything she had left at her father's house before leaving for Saint Martin. Although after calling the villa this morning and being told that Jillian had asked the staff to box up all of the things she had left behind on the island and ship them to the house in Scottsdale, Katya was fairly certain it wouldn't have made any difference if she had.

What had Jillian done with all her things? The closetful of expensive clothes? Her shoes? Her jewelry?

Katya gritted her teeth. They were *her* things, after all. What did it matter that Daddy's money had paid for it all?

If only she could get back into the house to get the rest of her belongings.

Absently she ran her fingers over the gold clasp of her purse. She couldn't just go knock on the front door and ask to be let in. If she did, Jillian would call Daddy's security men to stop her.

She'd have to find a way to get Jillian out of the house long enough so that she could get in to get the rest of her things. She had bought herself some beautiful jewelry over the years that would sell quite nicely, she was sure. Even if she only got fifty cents on the dollar, it was better than nothing.

But how could she get Jillian out of the house?

A smile curved her lips as a plot formed in her mind.

Pulling her cell phone out of her purse, she pushed the power button and waited for the signal to register. She dialed the number to the house and pushed SEND.

Nothing happened.

Katya looked at the display. NO SERVICE? What did it mean, NO SERVICE?

Her teeth clenched as realization dawned. They had even disconnected her cellular service.

The urge to fling the phone through the marble courtyard of the mall was almost overwhelming. Instead, Katya stuffed the slender black phone into her purse before she could give in to the impulse, then hurried off in search of a pay phone.

"Hello, Jillian. I'd like to stab you in the back like you've done to me," she muttered, walking along the mostly deserted thoroughfare. "No, that won't do. Much too honest. How about this? Stepmother, dear. I've decided to let bygones be bygones. Let's do lunch, shall we?" she mimicked in a sickly sweet voice.

"No, she'd see through that one in a minute. Hmm."

Stopping in front of a bank of phones, Katya dropped some coins into the slot, mentally rehearsing her speech.

"Good afternoon, Morgan residence," one of the staff answered. Katya didn't know the servant's name. Her father's help never stayed long. It seemed to her that as soon as she learned someone's name, he or she was gone. After her mother had died and her father had packed her off to boarding school, she'd stopped even trying to learn their names. Inevitably she'd come home for the holidays to find an entirely new set of staff members and her efforts would have been in vain.

"Good afternoon. May I have a word with Jillian, please? This is Katya Morgan."

There was a slight pause before Katya was asked to hold.

"Yes, Katya? This is Jillian."

Katya could feel her upper lip starting to curl and forced it to stop. She had to get her stepmother to believe that she was sincere or Jillian would never agree to meet her. "Hello, Jillian. I . . ." She paused for effect. "I need to speak with you. About Daddy." She added what she hoped was a convincing hitch to her voice.

"Is this about the will? I can't do anything about that, Katya. Your father's wishes were very specific."

"No. No, I've had some time to think about it, and I've realized that Daddy must have wanted it this way. I just wanted to talk to you about . . . well, about his last days. Was he in a lot of pain? Did he mention my mother at all? That sort of thing."

Katya sensed Jillian's hesitation and kept silent.

"All right, Katya. Why don't you come over to the house?"

"I don't know, Jillian. I don't think I can handle the memories." She sniffed loudly. "Maybe we could meet somewhere more neutral."

"Like where?"

"Oh, I don't know. What about Fashion Square Mall? There's a new Asian restaurant that's supposed to be very good. We could meet for a late lunch in, say, an hour?"

"Yes, I can do that. I'll see you then. I'm . . . I'm glad you called, Katya," her stepmother said before hanging up.

"I'm sure you are," Katya mumbled, telling herself she was only doing what she had to do to survive.

CHAPTER FIVE

GETTING a cab to her old home was easy.

The cabdriver didn't even bat an eye when Katya asked him to pull off the road a hundred yards from the house. Pulling a twenty-dollar bill from her rapidly dwindling roll of cash, she handed it to him and told him there'd be another twenty in it for him if he would wait for her.

There was a slight breeze in the early summer air as she gently closed the taxi door and slipped back down the road toward the elegant white mansion she had formerly called home. She wished she'd thought to wear practical shoes instead of the bright blue sandals she'd worn to match the wraparound skirt and lightweight silk tank she had on. Of course, she hadn't known when she set out this morning that she'd end up playing cat burglar by the end of the day.

Slipping into the shadows of a thick pillar near the wrought-iron gates at the end of the drive, Katya waited for her stepmother's car to appear. A fly droned lazily around her head and Katya swatted at it, but it didn't go away. She stilled as a tan Mercedes sedan came into view down the long driveway. The fly landed on her arm, but she didn't want to move and risk detection.

As soon as the car had slipped through the gates, Katya flapped her wrist to rid herself of her flying visitor. The car turned a corner and she hurried out from behind the post, sliding through the opening in the gates before they could close.

She trotted up the cobblestone drive and around to the back, figuring she'd be more likely to find an unlocked door at the rear of the house. The wide stone stairs leading up to the patio were hot beneath the thin soles of her sandals. The rear of the house took the brunt of the morning sun, but by late afternoon the heat would overtake the front. It had been a long time since she'd spent a summer in the brutal heat of the Arizona climate, but she remembered how hot the stones of the patio could get when the sun was at its worst. Winters in Arizona, however, were heaven, especially for warm-weather seekers like her. It could get chilly at night, and the top of Camelback Mountain even saw a light dusting of snow at times, but the days were usually pleasantly warm, with soft breezes constantly blowing across the desert.

Testing the handles of the French doors of her father's study, Katya was surprised to find they opened at her first try.

Finally, something was going right.

The room was dark and Katya felt the sudden urge to sit in her father's favorite chair again, to curl up in the soft leather and close her eyes. She could dream that her father had just come back from one of his frequent business trips. He'd sit in his chair, drink his usual glass of whiskey, and tell her stories of faraway places, like he had before he'd sent her off to boarding school. Before Katya's mother had died, her father had liked to talk to her about the strange-sounding cities and countries he'd been to: Shanghai, Bangladesh, Rio de Janeiro, Zimbabwe, Cairo. Whenever he'd leave on a business trip, she'd ask him where he was going so she could find him on the map, wherever he was. Sometimes she'd go months without seeing him, especially after she'd left for boarding school the autumn of her fourth-grade year.

Even then, he'd send her postcards from around the world so she could look at her atlas and know he was out there, somewhere in the world defined by Rand McNally.

Katya shook her head. This was no time for woolgathering, as one of her teachers used to scold. There was no telling how long Jillian would wait at the restaurant before realizing that Katya wasn't coming. She had to be quick about getting what she'd come here to find.

Peering around the door of her father's study, Katya checked to make sure no one was in the foyer before she dashed to the staircase. Unlike yesterday, when she'd tried the same move, Daddy's security man wasn't there to stop her. She hit the top of the stairs at a full run and turned right, heading toward her old bedroom. The carpeted hallway seemed to be a mile long as she ran across it in full view of the floor below.

She slid into her bedroom, quietly closing the door behind herself. Pressing her back to the door, she let her eyes adjust to the lighting and allowed her pounding heartbeat to slow to normal. As her eyes adjusted to the darkness, Katya stared into the room with growing horror.

It was empty.

Katya blinked, as if the act of closing her eyes and reopening them would make her old life reappear.

The room was still empty. Not a stitch remained to prove that Katya Morgan had once lived here.

Her ruffled pink canopy bed. Gone.

The chest of drawers she'd painted one summer to remind her of the ornate furnishings she'd seen on her first trip to France. Gone.

Her art books. Gone. Her old atlases. Gone.

She crossed the room and threw open the door to the large walk-in closet, tossing her purse to the floor in shock. All her clothes, thousands of dollars' worth of designer outfits and expensive leather shoes. All gone.

Visions of Bruno Magli pumps, Versace evening gowns, and pink ruffles floated round and round in her brain with the remnants of last night's overdose of gin. Katya swallowed as the first hint of bile rose in her throat. She held out a hand, steadying herself against the cool white wall of the closet. Her face felt hot; then her skin went clammy and then cold with the unmistakable knowledge that she was going to throw up.

Racing out of the closet, she pushed open the door to the connecting bathroom, barely making it to the toilet before she lost the remains of her coffee-and-croissant breakfast.

Her stomach continued to heave long after it was empty.

Katya hung her head over the porcelain bowl as tears moistened her cheeks. What had she done to deserve this? Sure, she hadn't spent much time at home these last few years, but who could blame her? After her mother died, Charles Morgan made it clear he wanted little, if anything, to do with his daughter. And once he'd married Jillian, their relationship became even more strained as Katya realized her father wasn't incapable of loving anyone—he was simply incapable of loving *her*.

She didn't know how long she sat on the cool tile floor, her head resting on her arm as her stomach calmed. It was only when she heard voices in the hall that she was spurred to get to her feet. Quietly she pressed the bathroom door closed, then pulled open a drawer in search of some toothpaste to rinse the awful taste of sickness out of her mouth. Just as she finished rinsing out her mouth, she heard the bedroom door open.

The bathroom could be entered from either the bedroom or the closet. Katya figured she'd be safer in the closet until whoever it was finished up their task, so she stepped into the shadows of the now-empty dressing room. She tripped over something near the door and leaned down.

Damn. She'd knocked over the purse she'd dropped here earlier. Blindly feeling around with her fingers, she did her best to gather the contents that had tumbled onto the carpet and stuffed them back into her pocketbook before slinging the strap over her shoulder.

The voices continued and it didn't take long for boredom and curiosity to overcome her. She moved to the entrance of the closet and pressed her ear to the door to try to make sense of the muffled conversation.

". . . my mother worked here when she was just a little girl. She wasn't so bad back then," a woman said.

"Well, that was a long time ago. Ever since I've worked for Mr. Morgan, she's been nothing but a spoiled brat," a man answered.

Katya's mouth dropped open. How dare he speak of her like that?

"Tut now. She had a hard life, with her mother dying so young and all," the woman protested. Katya had the urge to step out of the closet and hug her champion but stopped when she heard the woman's next words. "Of course, that doesn't excuse her for acting like a tramp. Why, those pictures of her running around half-naked with all those men almost made my hair curl. I thought poor Mr. Morgan was going to have a bird when that last magazine came out. Here now, help me get these drapes down."

The flash of red behind Katya's eyes erased all reason. What right did these people have to talk about her like this? Sure, she'd had a few lovers over the years, but she certainly wasn't a tramp. Not that it was anybody's business but her own how many men she chose to sleep with.

Before she had a chance to think about what she was doing, Katya pushed open the closet door and leaped into the room.

"You two have a hell of a nerve discussing me like this. You don't know anything about me. Nothing! You have no right to judge who I am or what I do, and if— no, make that *when* I get this inheritance mess straightened out, you two will be out on the street faster than you can say 'unemployment line.' "

She turned on her heel and slammed out of the bedroom, leaving the two servants staring at her with openmouthed shock as she made her way back down the hall. The front door opened just as she started down the stairs, and Katya was not surprised to see Jillian step into the foyer, followed by her husband's head of security.

"When you didn't show up at the restaurant, I thought I'd find you here."

Katya ignored the tired tone in Jillian's voice. It was probably just an act anyway, something she did to make the employees feel sorry for her and dislike Katya even more. It was obviously working, based on the sympathetic look the security man slid Jillian's way. Shaking her head with disgust, Katya continued down the stairs. "What have you done with my things, Jillian?"

"They're gone. I had everything packed up and taken away." Jillian regarded her calmly, with a touch of compassion that Katya chose to ignore.

"You had no right to get rid of my things. They belong to me, not to you, and I want them back."

"I'm sorry, Katya. It's too late. Everything's gone."

Having reached the bottom stair, Katya closed the gap between herself and Jillian. She stopped a foot from her stepmother and pasted a sneer on her face. "Well then, you can pay me what it was all worth. I had at least a couple hundred thousand dollars' worth of clothes in my room, and I expect to be reimbursed for what you stole from me."

Jillian shook her head, then lowered her gaze to the marble floor of the foyer. "You don't understand, Katya. You didn't own any of those things. Your father paid for it all, so, by rights, it was all his, and now mine, to do with as we pleased. You have to accept this and move on with your life. I can't change it."

"Can't? You mean you *won't* change it. And why should you? You've got what you wanted—my father's fortune, my inheritance. It's all yours, just as you planned when you married Daddy, right, Jillian?" Katya felt the blood pounding in her temples. The pressure in her head pulsed, like the second hand on a ticking bomb that was about to explode.

"Believe it or not, I did not intend for it to turn out this way. I never wanted your father to die. He was very nice to me, and I expected us to have many years together before he was gone. You know, as well as I do, that he didn't discover the cancer until after we were married. There's no way I could have planned for this to happen."

Katya's upper lip curled. "Yes, well, it's all worked out very well for you. You've just won the gold digger's lottery."

Her stepmother's sharp intake of breath should have made Katya feel good. After all, her barb had hit its intended target. Instead, she felt just like the spoiled brat she had been accused of being a short time ago. Not liking the way that felt, Katya did what she always had when faced with feelings she didn't like: she pushed them away and raised her chin a notch.

"Excuse me. Am I interrupting something?"

Katya glanced behind her stepmother's shoulder and glared at the intruder. What in the hell was Alex Sheridan doing here?

"Yes," Katya answered.

"No, of course not," Jillian interrupted graciously, stepping out of the doorway. "Please, come in, Alex. I wasn't expecting you."

"I was just in the area and thought I'd stop by and see if you needed anything. The gates were open, so I drove on through."

The entryway echoed with the sound of Katya tapping one sandal-shod foot on the stone floor. Impatient to leave now that she knew she was not going to get what she'd come for, Katya folded her arms across her chest. The strap of the handbag she'd slung over her shoulder rubbed against her collarbone. Ignoring Alex, she turned her attention back to Jillian. "You can bet you'll be hearing from my attorney about this. I expect payment in full for the things you've taken from me."

Jillian shook her head, the ends of her shoulder-length blond hair sweeping her cheek. "I wouldn't waste whatever money you do have fighting your father's will, Katya. You'll just lose in the end."

"Yes, well, thanks again for your advice. You'll excuse me if I choose to ignore it." Her nose tilted up in the air as she turned to the door. Alex's body blocking the doorway marred her grand exit. He refused to budge, just stood there looking at her calmly as she gestured for him to step aside.

His light brown eyes, like his hair, held hints of gold, Katya noticed as they stood staring at each other in the sunlight streaming in through the windows high above the door. Though why she should notice something like that she couldn't imagine. What difference did it make anyway? His eyes could have gold or purple or chartreuse or even vermilion in them for all she cared. It made no difference to her whatsoever. Once this mess about the will was fixed, she intended to leave Scottsdale behind as fast as she could. She'd go back to Antoine and Saint Martin or maybe one of a thousand other places she'd like to visit. Maybe she'd bring Antoine along with her after she left Saint Martin. He'd proven to be a pleasant-enough companion this last month, although he wasn't much of a conversationalist. Of course, there was something to be said for a man who simply looked wonderful and didn't try to pry into her life. Katya tried to produce a picture of Antoine in her mind but couldn't get the image of the man standing in front of her to step aside, even in her head.

Alex Sheridan's gold-flecked eyes continued to study her and Katya narrowed her own eyes irritably. "Would you please get out of my way?" she asked, finally.

"Let me give you a ride back to the hotel. There are some things I need to discuss with you."

"No, thank you," Katya answered, as if he had actually asked her if she wanted a ride instead of ordering her about like one of his employees. "I have a cab waiting."

"Actually, you don't. I saw him drive away just as I was pulling in."

The temptation to scream was almost too much to resist, but Katya did her best to contain it. "Then I'll call for another one," she hissed through gritted teeth.

"Oh, no. It's no bother," Alex insisted before turning to Jillian. "I'll catch up with you later. Why don't you call my office and we can schedule lunch sometime next week?"

"Yes, I'd like that," Jillian answered.

"Good. Come on, Katya. Let's go." The strong hand

on her arm left her without much choice but to follow. Katya tried to pull away from him anyway, but his grip only tightened as she resisted.

"Ouch, you're hurting me," she protested, even though he wasn't hurting her at all.

"Then stop struggling."

The glare she shot him did no good, either, so she gave up and went along peacefully. After all, she did need a ride, and at least this one was free. She let Alex lead her out the door and was surprised when he opened the passenger door of his Mustang convertible and handed her inside before letting himself into the driver's seat.

The engine purred to life and Alex gave a friendly wave to her stepmother before pulling around the circular drive. Katya found herself in need of a cigarette and opened the clasp on her purse as warm dry wind tossed her hair.

"Would you like me to put the top up?"

Once again, his politeness surprised her. "No, it's fine. Actually, I like it. Do you mind if I smoke?"

"Not as long as the top's down."

The road leading up Camelback Mountain was quiet in the late Sunday afternoon. Touching her lighter to the end of the slim cigarette, Katya inhaled the soothing smoke and leaned back into the soft tan leather of the seat.

"Nasty habit, smoking," Alex said after a while.

Oddly, she didn't find the comment annoying. *Must be the nicotine,* she reasoned. "Yes, it is. I don't smoke much, only when I have a real craving."

"Gives you something to do with your hands, right?"

Katya rolled her eyes heavenward. "Yes. It keeps me from slapping people who ask stupid questions."

His grin was quick; just a flash of even white teeth

and it was gone. "Seems like I interrupted a pretty nasty fight between you and your stepmother."

Her back stiffened against the seat. It was obvious where his sympathies lay, and besides, it didn't concern him. Her fight with Jillian certainly didn't have anything to do with Alex Sheridan. She shrugged, refusing to answer as she took another draw on her cigarette, then tapped the ash into the ashtray.

He let the matter drop, and silence settled between them. It was just as well, Katya thought. It was a mistake to start thinking of Alex as anything more than an adversary. A few minutes of polite conversation wasn't going to change that. "So what did you want to talk to me about?"

Alex looked across the car at his passenger and grinned. "Nothing. I could just tell that you were upsetting Jillian and I thought I'd rescue her from you."

Watching as Katya's eyes narrowed, Alex congratulated himself on his ploy. It had worked quite well, he thought, giving himself a mental pat on the back.

"Stop this car right now," she ordered furiously.

"We're five miles from the hotel, Katya. Just sit back and enjoy the rest of the ride."

"I mean it, Alex. Stop the car. Now."

Glancing over at her again, Alex saw that she had grabbed the door handle and was prepared to fling the door open at thirty miles an hour. He shook his head. Growing up in a houseful of women, he had endured his share of female theatrics. One thing he'd learned was that there were times you couldn't do anything right, no matter what you did.

He guessed this was one of those times.

Well, fine, he wasn't going to insist she ride back to the hotel with him. If she wanted to walk, he'd be happy to let her.

The tires skidded a bit on the gravel on the side of the road as he hit the brakes. Katya pushed open the door before the car had come to a complete stop and was out of her seat almost immediately. Without a word, she slammed the door behind her and started walking down the dusty road toward the hotel.

Alex watched the sway of her hips, the bright pattern of her short skirt moving from side to side as she walked. Easing his foot off the brake, he let the car creep forward a few feet.

"Come on, Katya. Get back in the car. You don't want to walk all the way back to the hotel," he cajoled.

She stopped and turned to face him, her smoky green eyes blazing with fury. "Don't you dare tell me what I do or do not want to do. My stepmother does not need protection from me. She's taken everything away from me. She has the house, the cars, the money. And I have nothing. Do you understand? *Nothing*."

Before Alex could respond, Katya turned and started running down the street. He pulled on the emergency brake and threw open the door, then cursed as his arm got tangled in the seat belt. Finally freeing himself, he looked up, only to find that she was nowhere to be seen.

Where had she gone?

"Katya, I'm sorry. Come back!" he shouted.

The hot Arizona sun blazed down on the top of Alex's head as he started down the road after her, feeling the guilt burning him with every step. She was right. He was making light of a situation that must seem very dire to her right now. Although he didn't believe that Jillian Morgan had plotted to relieve her stepdaughter of her entire inheritance, that was exactly what had happened. Katya had been left with nothing, while Jillian was now a very rich woman. Even setting the money itself aside, Alex could only imagine how much it must have hurt

Katya for her father to disinherit his only child. He felt like even more of a heel for being so quick to make jokes about Katya's situation.

After a few more minutes of shouting for her to come back, it became obvious that Katya was determined to stay in her hiding place. Alex got back in the car and put it in gear, slowly searching the side of the road for any sight of her dark hair or bright blue clothes.

"Stubborn wretch," he muttered after his third pass down the same stretch of road.

"All right, I'm leaving. This is your last chance!" Alex yelled, giving Katya one last opportunity to save herself an unpleasant walk. As bad as he felt about what he'd said, he couldn't spend the entire afternoon out here pleading with her.

There was no response from either side of the road.

Alex frowned, then put the car in gear, leaving Camelback Mountain behind in a cloud of dust.

CHAPTER SIX

"THANK you for letting me tag along," Katya said, turning to look at her former neighbor and classmate, Mindy Thornton-Lambert, as they stood in line outside the ballroom of Scottsdale's Phoenician Resort. After she'd insisted that Alex let her out of the car, Katya had hit upon an idea. If Jillian wouldn't help her, perhaps some of her old friends would. She was the first to admit that she hadn't been the best at keeping in touch, but it had been difficult when she traveled so much. Besides, Mindy had gone down a very different path from Katya herself. After graduation, Mindy had gone straight to work in her family's thriving pharmaceutical business while Katya had left to travel the world. After a while, the two had virtually nothing in common except for a shared past. Katya had hoped that would be enough.

"Not at all. It's nice to be able to catch up with you. So, besides your travels, what have you been up to?"

The line to the ballroom inched ahead. Turnout for the "Boardroom to Beach" charity auction was stellar, and the guards at the gates were carefully checking to ensure that no one gained entry without an invitation. The auction was an annual event, with all proceeds to benefit a local children's hospital. In keeping with the theme this year, the city's wealthy and successful were dressed in everything from business suits to beachwear.

"Oh, you know. This and that. What about you?" Katya deflected the question. The truth was, other than her travels, she had been up to absolutely nothing. Not

that she minded. She enjoyed her lifestyle immensely.
She was free to do whatever she wanted to do every day.
No one told her when to get up, or what to do with
herself once she did. No one pried into her affairs. No
one told her when to leave a party or when to stop gambling. In fact, no one seemed to care about her at all.

Katya turned her attention back to her former school
chum, who was just finishing up the highlights of her
résumé: created a new direct marketing campaign that
increased revenue 6.5 percent last year; supervised a department of over forty employees; responsible for an annual marketing budget in excess of half a billion dollars.

It sounded so . . . grown-up. And so boring.

"Have a nice evening," the volunteer checking in-
vitations said, waving Katya and Mindy through the
open set of double doors behind her.

Katya smiled and stepped into the ballroom teeming
with people. This was her milieu. Well-dressed, well-fed
partygoers wandered among tables laden with prizes to
be auctioned off, glasses of wine or cocktails in their
hands. As the liquor flowed, they'd become more and
more willing to bid up the prices, ensuring that this
would be a successful event for the charity.

In the adjoining room, she could see people dancing
to the music of a steel-drum band. Tables had been set
up beyond the dance floor, ready for the dinner that
would be served in an hour. One corner of the room was
taken up with a giant pile of sand, complete with beach
towels and a laptop to tie in the "Boardroom" part of
the event. If she had been in charge of the event, Katya
would have suggested a desk instead of just a laptop.
She thought the incongruity would have been more strik-
ing.

"Would you like a glass of wine?" she asked Mindy,

spying one of several grass huts that had been set up around the room to serve drinks.

"Not right now, thanks. I see the head of the ad firm we use over there, and I have some business to discuss. Would you mind if I went to chat with him?"

"Of course not." Katya dismissed Mindy with a wave. It amazed her that all some people ever thought about was their work, but she figured it was none of her concern. Instead, she stepped up to the bar and ordered herself a glass of Kendall-Jackson Chardonnay. The bartender handed her a glass filled with golden liquid and Katya paid for her drink before stuffing a dollar bill into the tip jar.

With a smile, she headed out to look over the items being auctioned off. A full day of pampering at the Golden Door Spa at The Boulders. A weekend winery tour in the Napa Valley. A week at a villa in Tuscany, complete with Italian cook. A barge tour down the Canal du Midi in Provence. Glassblowing facility tours, painting classes, music lessons, wine tastings.

She had done them all.

Caribbean cruises, gourmet dinners, photos with celebrities.

She backed away from the table, stopping when her feet touched the sand of the fake beach in the corner of the room. At thirty-one, she had done it all, seen it all, experienced it all. She should have been delighted at the thought but, instead, she felt—

"Are you all right?"

Katya whirled around. Chris Hampstead stood a few feet away, looking at her strangely. It was then she realized that her glass had slipped from her fingers and was sitting in the pile of sand at her feet.

Taking a deep breath to calm the strange sensation

that had settled in the pit of her stomach, Katya reached down and picked up her sand-filled glass.

"I'm fine, thank you. I think I'm just a bit light-headed from the wine."

Chris took her arm and led her away from the phony beach. "I guess it's a good thing they've just announced dinner, then. Shall we go in?"

"Sure." Katya set her dirty glass on a passing tray. "Are you enjoying the auction?"

Chris shrugged. "I suppose so. There's nothing being offered here that I couldn't buy whenever I wanted it, but my father would give me his 'we have to give back to the community' lecture if I didn't come. So here I am."

Katya didn't know how to respond to that, so she just said, "Hmm."

"Now that you're here, though, maybe things will get better. What table are you sitting at?"

"Number nineteen. Over there by the palm trees."

"We're at table twenty-four. Why don't you join us?"

"I really shouldn't. I came with a friend."

"All right. But if you get bored, you know where to find me." Chris smiled and let go of her arm before heading to his table.

Katya made her way to the faux palms and sat down beside Mindy, who seemed deeply engrossed in a conversation. The words "gross margin" and "strategic planning" were being bandied about, and Katya had to fight back the urge to yawn. Maybe she *would* take Chris up on his offer, after all.

As the salad course was served, Mindy quit talking about business long enough to introduce Katya to her tablemates, all highly placed employees at the Thornton-Lambert Pharmaceutical Company. By the time the main course was over, Katya wasn't sure if she should scream or fall asleep. Didn't these people realize they were at a party, not a work function?

Before one more person could politely ask her what she did for a living, Katya excused herself on the pretense of going to the ladies' room. After completing the ladies' room ritual of bladder emptying, hand washing, hair fluffing, and lipstick freshening, Katya still didn't feel prepared to face another round of the "return on investment" game being played at her table. With one hand on the bathroom door, she hesitated, then leaped back out of the way when the door was pushed open from the other side.

It was an entire gaggle of women. A veritable herd. All laughing and talking at the same time.

"Wouldn't that barge trip be f-fun, Nana?"

"We'd gain fifty pounds from eating those rich sauces for a week."

"Not me. I'd bike the path next to the canal to keep my girlish figure." This from an attractive woman who couldn't have been a day less than seventy-five.

"You can have the food; I'll take the French men," a beautiful young woman said with a toss of her waist-length brown hair.

"Martina!" a younger version of the elderly woman admonished with a shake of her head.

Katya silently agreed with the younger woman. French men were wonderful. Just listening to them talk made Katya's knees weak.

"Miss M-Morgan," one of the women said, obviously surprised to see someone she recognized in the ladies' room of the Phoenician.

It was the front desk clerk from the hotel. Katya didn't remember her name right away. "Hello. Are you

enjoying the party?" Katya asked, trying to recall the
woman's name.

"Yes, I am. We come every year. I wouldn't m-miss
it." The woman smiled, and Katya realized how pretty
she was. Her eyes reminded Katya of those of a deer
sipping water at a stream. Huge, brown, soft . . . and
wary.

Katya couldn't blame the other woman for being a
bit cautious, not after the way Katya had bullied her
yesterday. Hoping to prove that she had nothing to worry
about, Katya smiled. "I can tell you that you would love
the barge trip in Provence. There's something for everyone: great food, fabulous wine, beautiful countryside.
Not to mention the hunky Frenchmen."

"See, Nana, I told you." The youngest of the women
nudged her grandmother, a wicked grin on her face.

"Nice to see you again." Katya called as the group
moved as one toward the stalls. Once outside, she shook
her head. Talk about a little too much togetherness. She
couldn't imagine what it would be like to be part of such
a close-knit family, if indeed they were all related. She
much preferred her own situation, with no relatives to
feel obligated to visit on holidays or special occasions.
Yes, it was much better being alone than—

"I'm glad to see you made your way off of Camelback Mountain."

Katya looked up to see Alex Sheridan leaning
against the wall, his hands stuck into the pockets of a
pair of neatly pressed navy slacks. The collar of his
short-sleeved brightly patterned silk shirt was open, revealing just a sliver of golden-brown skin. "Yes, no
thanks to you," she muttered.

Alex pushed himself away from the wall and came
toward her.

Suddenly cold, Katya shivered.

"That's not fair and you know it. I would never have let you out of the car if you hadn't insisted."

She felt her face flush. He was right. She had acted just like what her father's servants had accused her of being: a spoiled brat. Damn him for calling her on it. "Okay, you win. I apologize for throwing a temper tantrum. I guess I've just had enough of people making snap judgments about me. Just because I want to have fun, I'm labeled as a bad person. So I like to party? I don't hurt anyone."

It was as if the woman in front of him had shrunk down and become a ten-year-old girl. Alex had to fight the urge to take her in his arms, push her head down on his shoulder, and murmur "there, there" in her ear as he'd done a thousand times with his sisters. Unfortunately, his feelings for Katya Morgan were decidedly not brotherly, so he resisted the impulse by stuffing his fists back into his pockets.

"Don't you ever get tired of doing nothing besides enjoying yourself? I mean, I'm all for having a good time, but don't you think there's got to be more to life than drinking and lounging by the pool?"

Katya tried to think of something glib to say, but nothing came to her. The truth was that she sometimes did feel as if her life was missing something, but that didn't mean she wanted to become like Mindy and her co-workers, either. As always, this line of thinking just led her in circles, like a dog endlessly chasing its tail.

"Tell you what. Now that we've called a truce, why don't we relax and enjoy the rest of the evening? We can leave the soul-searching for another night."

The grin he shot her melted the polish on Katya's toenails. It had a similar effect on some of her more personal body parts, too, an effect that was spoiled when the throng of women that Katya had just seen in the ladies' room descended upon them. She could barely hear Alex above the din, but she was able to make out his invitation to her to join them at their table for dessert. Given a chance to escape another hour of mind-numbingly boring conversation, Katya decided to take it. She was quickly enveloped into the group as introductions were made.

In less than five minutes, she felt like one of the family.

"Ladies and gentlemen, the auction will end in thirty minutes. Please make sure you have your final bids in by nine o'clock sharp."

As soon as the announcement was made, Martina Rivera, Alex's youngest sister, jumped up from the table. "Ooh, let's go see if our bid for the barge trip is still ahead. I would so love to go to France next summer."

Maria and Inez quickly joined their little sister.

"How about you, Nana? Do you want to go back and check on your bids?" Alex asked.

"No, thank you. I'm not willing to pay more for anything than I've already committed. Did you bid on anything, Katya?"

"No, I'm a little short on cash lately," Katya answered dryly.

Alex laughed at that. "Well, let's go check on the barge trip with the others. Lucy, are you coming?"

"No, I'll stay here and keep Nana company," Alex's oldest sister responded.

"You have a nice family," Katya remarked as he led her away from the table.

"Yes, I do. I'm glad they haven't overwhelmed you."

"I'm used to large, noisy groups."

"So, what would you have bid on if you'd had the

money?" Alex asked, changing the subject as they stepped into the ballroom.

"I don't know. I didn't really see anything . . ." Katya's words trailed off and she stood stock-still in the doorway of the room.

"What's wrong?" Alex's grip on Katya's arm tightened. She had turned a sickly white color under her tan. Had she eaten something that wasn't agreeing with her? Or maybe spotted an old lover in the crowd?

"Katya, what's wrong?" he repeated.

She started moving then. Slowly, like a mummy in one of the old horror shows he had watched as a kid. Alex followed, wondering what the hell was going on. She stopped in front of a neat row of shoes lined up on one of the auction tables. Behind the shoes, a dozen or so dresses hung from a portable wardrobe.

As Katya stood staring at the merchandise, Alex read the auction card:

Gently used designer apparel from St. John's Bay, Versace, Vera Wang, BCBG, and more. Shoes from Prada, Bruno Magli, Franco Sarto, and Cole Haan. Approximate value: $70,000. Donated by the Morgan Family Trust.

So Jillian had cleaned out her closet and donated last year's fashions to charity? Alex couldn't see why that would bother Katya.

Unless . . .

Realization dawned a split second too late.

Unless these weren't Jillian's things.

By the time Alex reacted, the damage had already been done.

CHAPTER SEVEN

SHE was enveloped in a sense of deadly calm.

These were her things, and she wasn't going to leave here without them.

With one swift movement, she reached across the table and yanked a handful of dresses off their hangers. Then she started grabbing shoes and stuffing them into her pockets. She could only fit one pair of Cole Haan sandals in her left pocket and a single Bruno Magli slingback into her right one.

She handed Alex the other slingback, then went back for more.

"Katya, stop."

She barely heard Alex's plea as she pulled another handful of dresses from their hangers. Shoving one shoe after another on top of the pile in her arms, she suddenly wished she had brought a larger purse. Her new Coach bag was small and the height of fashion this year. Too bad those giant slouch bags had gone out of style.

"Here, take these," she ordered, pushing her favorite Franco Sarto black suede knee-length boots toward him.

A hush moved about the crowd like ripples on a lake, but Katya paid it no attention.

One lone dress remained hanging. It wasn't even one of her favorites, but she was not going to leave it here to be sold to the highest bidder.

They were trying to take everything from her, and she refused to let them.

She had already lost her mother.

Then her father.

And then her money.

She wasn't going to lose anything else. Balancing her load of silk and leather, she pulled the remaining dress off the rack and added it to the pile.

Katya turned to see the formerly carefree partygoers staring at her with openmouthed shock. If her father were alive, he'd be horrified that she was making a scene, but Katya didn't care. It wasn't the first time, nor would it be the last. She lived her life as she wanted, not according to someone else's rules. She had learned early that following the rules didn't get you anywhere except shipped off to boarding school.

She started toward the door.

A neatly dressed woman scurried out of the crowd and tried to block her progress. "Excuse me. The bidding isn't over yet. You can't take those things until we're sure you've got the winning bid."

"These are mine, and I'm taking them. Kindly step aside."

The woman shook her head in bafflement. "What do you mean, they're yours? They were donated to be auctioned off for charity."

"I think I can explain. Can we go somewhere a little more private?" Alex suggested from beside her.

"Good thinking," Katya muttered, silently thanking him for the diversionary tactic. He'd get the woman's attention, and she could escape with her clothes. He might have to sacrifice the Franco Sarto boots, but at least she'd get away with the rest of her things.

"Follow me," the woman said, and turned.

Katya saw her chance and took it.

She could barely see over the pile of clothing in her arms, but she refused to let that hinder her. She was totally focused on getting outside with her loot and so didn't hear the pounding footsteps behind her.

It was only as she was tackled that she realized her plan was doomed to fail.

Instinctively her arms went out to break her fall, and shoes and dresses went flying out the wide double doors and onto the steps below. A pair of high-heeled fuchsia sandals clattered down the steps as if trying to win some sort of race.

Katya landed hard on the rough fibers of the carpet, her fall broken by the wedge heel of a red slide poking her in the stomach.

She felt as if all emotion had been pushed out of her body along with the air.

Somewhere above her, a flashbulb went off.

So this is what the bottom looks like, Katya thought, staring at the floor. She'd heard of people hitting it but had never imagined it would look like industrial-grade carpet smashed in your face, your clothes spread out all around you waiting to be auctioned off, and a two-hundred-pound man lying on your back.

"I'm sorry, Katya. I couldn't let you get away. They would have had you arrested for theft," Alex said softly in her ear. "You can have things like this again, only you're going to have to get them like everyone else does—by working for them. My job offer still stands. You could start tomorrow morning."

The emotion came back in an instant, and it was pure red-hot fury. Katya pushed herself up off the carpet—a feat made possible when Alex rolled off of her.

"No," she said, the word echoing loudly in the too-quiet room. People were watching her, horrified expressions on their faces. Even her old school friend Mindy looked appalled. "I'm going to get my life back, just like it was before. I don't want your job, or your pity." With that, she turned and raced down the steps, past the things that once had belonged to her.

Alex watched from the doorway as she pulled the last shoe from her pocket and flung it to the ground. His eyes narrowed when Chris Hampstead pushed past him, but he didn't follow. Katya was too angry and upset to think reasonably right now, and he knew from experience that the best way to handle an angry woman was to leave her alone to sort through things herself.

Apparently, that was one thing Chris hadn't learned yet.

Monday dawned crisp and bright, like almost every day in sunny Scottsdale. As he left for his morning run, Alex contemplated his good mood. The sun helped, of course. And the fact that today was his day off didn't hurt, either. Even better, he'd been able to convince the reporter from the newspaper who had snapped Katya's picture after she had fallen last night to forget about using Katya's tragedy as a lead-in to his story about the auction.

To top it all off, he had four tickets to tonight's game—the Diamondbacks versus the Dodgers. He'd invited his brother-in-law, Tomas, and his eight-year-old niece, Merrilee, who was, without a doubt, baseball's biggest fan. To round out the foursome, he'd asked a former co-worker who now worked in the corporate office of one of the largest hotel chains in the country.

Alex loved baseball. Had loved it since he'd seen his first big-league game in the seventh grade. Back then, Phoenix didn't have its own major-league team. The Diamondbacks were a relatively new team, playing their first regular-season game on March 31, 1998. Alex had been one of the 50,179 fans to see it. As exciting at that game was (even though the D-Backs lost to Colorado

9–2), it couldn't rival the first live game Alex had ever seen.

He had turned twelve that summer; the summer his mother shipped him off to his Uncle Danny's house in Seattle. He hadn't gone willingly, but his mother was insistent. From the first time Alex had set eyes on his new stepfather, he had hated him. Anthony Rivera treated Alex's mother and sisters like servants, and Alex didn't like it. He knew it caused problems when he fought with his stepfather, but he couldn't seem to stop himself. With summer approaching, the tension in the household kept mounting, and his mother finally decided something had to be done.

"Anthony is a good man," she had said to Alex, hugging him fiercely just before he was to board the airplane. "He married me, even with three children who will never be his. I know you don't like him, and I know you think you have to protect us, but you're just making things worse."

She had released him then. "I want you to enjoy your summer, and when you come back, I want you to treat Anthony with some respect. You don't have to like him, just treat him with respect."

Alex had remained silent. He wasn't sure if that was possible. But what if he couldn't? Would his mother send him away for good? Surely she wouldn't do that, he remembered thinking.

The sound of his running shoes slapping warm pavement followed Alex as he turned off Camelback and onto Northeast Twenty-fourth Street. The air was still, his movement creating the only breeze that morning. As soon as he saw the trees surrounding the opulent Arizona Biltmore hotel, he turned around and started back to the Royal Palmetto, his mind still on the past.

Rationally, he knew his mother would never choose

her new husband over one of her own children, but at the time he hadn't been so sure. He had returned to Scottsdale a bit more restrained in his behavior, but he never warmed to the man who fathered his two younger sisters. The only good things that came out of that summer, as far as Alex was concerned, were an appreciation for a different part of the country and his newfound love of baseball.

That first game with his Uncle Danny at the now-demolished Kingdome in Seattle's industrial area was one of the highlights of Alex's life. Uncle Danny had sprung for 100-level seats to the Mariners' game against the New York Yankees. Back then, good tickets were easy to come by, even when they were bought on game day.

They ate peanuts by the bucket, leaving the shells on the concrete floor in front of them. Alex knew his mother would never have let him do that, but Uncle Danny said that's what you were supposed to do. So Alex popped the unshelled peanuts into his mouth just like Uncle Danny did, sucking the salt off the shell before crunching down to break it. Then he spit the cracked shell onto the ground, chomping on the nuts left behind and feeling like a grown-up as his messy pile grew.

He supposed it had been what his sisters would call a male bonding moment.

And it only got better from there.

He got to yell as loud as he wanted. He and Uncle Danny high-fived at least a dozen times. Alex stomped and clapped along with the silly music the announcer played. During the seventh-inning stretch, he sang "Take Me Out to the Ball Game" along with everyone else. And then, in the ninth inning, he caught a foul ball that Mariner Leon Roberts popped up into the stands.

It was one of the best moments of Alex's entire life.

"I just managed to increase our occupancy to one hundred percent."

Alex shook his head, suddenly realizing that he had passed through the terra-cotta-colored wall in front of the Royal Palmetto. He was so accustomed to his morning routine that he'd made it back to the hotel on autopilot. Chris must have been waiting for him.

Alex slowed his pace, slipping into the present and his post-run cool-down mode. "How did you manage that?"

"There was a big fire over at the Camelback Inn this morning. The GM called and asked if we could handle a conference they had booked for this coming week. I told him we'd be delighted to take the business," Chris said smugly, as if he had landed the account himself rather than having it plopped down neatly in his lap.

"Are you sure we have enough staff to handle it? We were going to be running at seventy percent occupancy with just the cattlemen's convention."

"Of course we can. I talked to the heads of banquets and rooms before confirming."

"Very good," Alex said, ignoring the other man's resentful tone. It was Alex's job as general manager of the hotel to make sure things ran smoothly, whether or not the staff appreciated being questioned about their decisions. "Do we have a list of the conference events and dining requirements?"

"Yes, I got everything from the conference chairman. It's a small group, and they don't have particularly complex needs. Just a few meeting rooms with AV equipment and a closing lunch banquet on Friday."

Alex stopped walking and began his final stretching routine. "Did you have Jenny fax over a menu so they could make their selections?"

Chris sighed loudly, his frustration evident. "Yes, of

course I did. This isn't the first event I've ever handled, you know."

"I know you find this annoying, Chris, but if you were in my position, you'd ask the same questions. Taking over an event like this at the last minute can lead to a lot of mistakes. Typically, we would have been going over the details with the conference coordinator months in advance. I'm just making sure we've covered all the bases." Alex placed his palms on the side of the wall flanking the entrance to the hotel and leaned forward, stretching his calves. This was his favorite part of running—when it was all over.

"Well, you can relax. I went over the conference schedule in detail with the coordinator this morning. She's looking forward to staying at the Royal Palmetto, especially since the Camelback Inn will be paying the difference in the rates between our hotel and theirs. The only detail outstanding was the menu for the lunch on Friday, and the coordinator said she'd fax her selections back to me in half an hour." Chris glanced at his watch. "As a matter of fact, it should be here by now. Why don't you come with me while I walk it to Banquets? That way, you can be sure that I've taken care of every detail."

"All right. I will," Alex agreed. He needed to talk to Jenny about the cattlemen's convention anyway. *So much for the general manager's day off*, he thought with a wry smile as he waited for Chris to return from the lobby with the fax. Still, he had the baseball game tonight. That was something to look forward to, at least.

Chris emerged from the building that housed the reception area holding a sheaf of papers, and Alex decided it was time he gave the man a break. The owner's son had been working hard this past month, trying to please his father more than anything, Alex guessed. The trouble was that Chris was too arrogant to take advice or instruction from people who knew more about the hotel business than him. Which was just about every employee on the property. Still, maybe he was learning. It seemed as if he'd covered every detail of this event properly.

Yes, Alex decided, it was time he cut Chris some slack.

He held the back door to the kitchen open and motioned for Chris to precede him. They found Jenny Tillman, the head of the banquets department, in her office, just past the huge stainless-steel walk-in refrigerator. To Alex, the kitchen always seemed to be in chaos. Pots banging, water spraying, knives chopping, oil sizzling. Since they offered twenty-four-hour room service, the kitchen never closed. Alex could get a grilled cheese sandwich or a medium-rare filet mignon anytime, day or night. He didn't know how Jenny could stand the constant activity, but she seemed to thrive in the constantly buzzing environment.

"Hey, Cuz, I've got the menu for that lunch on Friday," Chris announced, adding the fax to the mountain of paperwork on Jenny's desk.

"Thanks, Chris. How's Aunt Susan's garden club competition going?"

Alex held back a wry smile. Nepotism was alive and well at the Royal Palmetto. Besides his own two sisters, who worked full-time at the hotel, Barry Hampstead's son and one of his nieces held jobs there, too. Jenny Tillman had been one of the original employees hired during the renovation, and Alex had been pleased with both her organizational and her culinary talents throughout the years. Conference organizers planned their events at the Royal Palmetto year after year because attendees raved about the quality of the food they were served. Without a doubt, this was one of the greatest challenges in the organizers' lives, proven by the fact that almost 90 percent of the feedback they received after a conference was related to the food. The other 10 percent complained that the meeting rooms were either too hot or too cold—with 5 percent in each camp.

Chris and Jenny chit-chatted about various family members for a few moments, and then Alex brought the conversation back to business.

"Are you sure your staff can take on the additional work?" he asked, leaning back against the door frame.

Jenny looked up, her eyes framed by small metal glasses. "We should be fine. I've called a handful of our contingent staff to see if they could work this week, and all but one was available. There's only one banquet, so that means the attendees will either want to eat at the restaurant or call room service for their meals. I'll make sure we have enough runners to handle any additional room service orders. I'm not worried."

Alex was convinced. He'd worked with Jenny long enough to trust her judgment.

Then, just as he started to relax, Jenny tossed a wrench into the works by saying, "Hmm. That's odd."

"What?" Alex and Chris asked in unison.

"They want an all-vegan menu. I didn't know this was a vegetarian group."

Alex looked at Chris, who seemed perplexed.

"They're not, at least as far as I know."

"What's the name of the group?" Alex asked.

Chris riffled through the papers in his hands, searching for a piece of letterhead. "I don't know," he muttered. "It's some animal rights group."

Alex felt as if his jaw had just come unhinged. "An animal rights group?"

A handful of papers fell out of the file in Chris's hand. "Yeah. Just a second and I'll find the name."

Pounding. The pulse in his temples was pounding to get out. To get out and strangle Chris Hampstead.

"Chris, do you realize that we have over one hundred members of the Cattlemen's Association descending upon us tomorrow?"

"Of course I do."

Alex reached out and clamped a hand over the papers Chris was still fumbling with. "Chris, the Cattlemen's Association is a group that promotes the consumption of beef. They raise cattle with the express purpose of slaughtering it and feeding it to the American people. Animal rights groups might tend to have a problem with this. Are you beginning to sense a conflict here?"

Chris was silent for a minute. One minute dragged into two. The pounding behind Alex's eyes continued.

"Oh my God," Chris said as realization dawned.

"My sentiments exactly," Alex said, attempting to rub away the pain beginning to throb at his temples.

CHAPTER EIGHT

"IN good conscience, I can't recommend anyone who'll take your case."

Katya struggled to control her mounting panic at Nathan Rosenberg's words. He just had to give her the name of someone who could assist her in fighting her father's will.

"Please, Nathan," she pleaded. "It's obvious Jillian made Daddy sign that will under duress. If he were in his right mind, he would never have left me with nothing."

"I can assure you the will was completely your father's idea. Both your stepmother and I tried to convince him that he was being unfair to you, but you know how he was when he had his mind made up about something. There was no reasoning with him."

Agitated, Katya stood up and walked over to the bank of windows. Past the sprawling city of Phoenix, the brown desert stretched endlessly in all directions, broken up only by mountains of the same color. At sunset, they would come alive with color for the briefest of moments when the sun hit them, but for now, everywhere she looked was the same drab brown. She missed Saint Martin, wanted to get back to the stunning white villa set against the bright blue waters of the Caribbean and the brilliant reds and pinks of the flowers blooming in riotous profusion. Crossing her arms against her chest to ward off the chill from the air conditioner, she turned her attention back to the lawyer.

"Why, Nathan? I know he didn't love me, but how could he have done this to me?"

He looked uncomfortable at her question and addressed his answer more to the staid darkly paneled walls than to her. "His reasons didn't concern me. I was your father's attorney in this matter, nothing more. He told me how he wanted to distribute his estate, and I made certain that his wishes would be carried through. I can assure you that everything in his will is perfectly legal, and will hold up even under the closest scrutiny. Now, if you'll excuse me, I'm already late for an appointment."

"No, wait. There has to be something I can do!" Katya wailed, following the lawyer out into the hall.

Shaking his head, Nathan stopped, then turned to face her. His sad brown eyes looked at hers with pity. "There is something you can do, Katya. You can accept that you're not going to receive any money as a result of your father's death and get on with your life. You need to get a job, find a place to live, and do all the other things that regular people without trust funds do every day."

Katya straightened her shoulders. "I'm not going to give up on this, Nathan. No matter what you say, I'm going to fight this with everything I have."

Nathan shrugged. "It makes no difference to me, Katya. Good day."

He left her standing in the hall, staring at his retreating back and fighting back anger and hurt and pure terror. What was she going to do without money? How would she live?

Once out on the hot pavement outside the building, Katya shook her head, trying to relieve the pressure of the blood pounding in her ears. What was she going to do now? She had to find someone who could help her get this mess straightened out.

After Chris had driven her back to the Royal Palmetto last night, she had lain in bed, wondering what to do. At 3:00 A.M., unable to sleep, she found herself talking to her mother's picture, knowing it was silly but doing it anyway. The only idea she could come up with was the same one that had been hounding her for days: fight the will.

Unfortunately, that wasn't something she could do on her own. She had to find someone who would take her case.

But who?

A bus roared past, lifting the hem of the emerald green shorts she'd put on that morning before setting off into the city. Katya looked up at the sound, smoothing her shorts back into place. Her eyes lit on the advertisement pasted on the back of the bus as it sped by.

"Injured through no fault of your own? Creditors at your door?" it asked in bright blue letters. "Personal Injury, Bankruptcy, our specialties. Call Paula Northcraft for a free consultation."

Katya hurriedly fished a pen out of her purse and jotted down the phone number listed at the bottom of the ad as the bus disappeared into the heavy morning traffic. She shoved the scrap of paper back into her pocketbook and looked up the street in search of a pay phone. Maybe she didn't need Nathan's help after all. She'd win this case and prove to him, prove to them all, that she could take care of herself.

"So, you'll take my case?" Katya didn't even try to hide the excitement in her voice as she looked over at the slightly overweight woman sitting across from her. Despite her somewhat shabby appearance, Paula Northcraft looked like a *Vogue* cover model to Katya right now. She had to physically restrain herself from leaping up out of the vinyl-covered chair and throwing her arms around the other woman. However, she suspected she'd leave at least the top layer of her skin stuck to the cheap chair should she attempt such a rash maneuver. Slowly, she lifted each thigh in turn, placing her hands under her legs to protect her skin from sticking like glue to the vinyl again.

"I'll be happy to take your case, Miss Morgan. Now, all we have left to discuss is the slight matter of my fee. I would expect a case like this to consume a considerable amount of my time. Your father chose a very reputable attorney, and it's going to take a lot of resources to combat someone of Mr. Rosenberg's caliber."

Katya felt her palms begin to sweat and held back a grimace of distaste as she realized the back of her knees were beginning to perspire. Whoever had invented vinyl should be shot. What were they thinking, that this disgusting plastic could in any way be thought of as a substitute for real leather?

"Yes, of course," she responded absently to her savior's previous comments. "How much will you need to get started?"

"Let's see. I'll need to set aside some funds for phone calls and copying, of course. Then there will need to be at least three or four face-to-face meetings with your father's lawyers. Yes, probably lunches, too. You know how expensive those can be."

"Um-hmm." Katya scooted to the edge of the seat so that none of her bare skin would actually be touching the slippery material.

"And I'll have to clear my schedule, which means I won't be able to accept any new clients until we get this matter resolved. Keeping all of this in mind, I'll need to set my retainer at . . ." She paused and Katya looked up, meeting soft gray eyes. "Five thousand. Yes, that ought to do it, for starters."

"Five thousand dollars?" Katya heard the squeak in her own voice and swallowed. "Five thousand. Are you sure?"

Paula Northcraft steepled her fingers on top of her desk. "Yes, I'm afraid so. This case is going to need my own personal attention, and I'll have to be adequately compensated for forgoing all my other potential clients."

Katya sighed. Five thousand dollars. Pawning her necklace would give her enough to pay the attorney, but it wouldn't leave her much to live on in the meantime. Unfortunately, she didn't have any choice. She'd called a dozen lawyers this morning before trying to get a referral from Nathan Rosenberg. Paula was her only remaining hope. She'd just have to make do.

Standing up, she slipped her purse over her shoulder and stuck out her hand.

"It's a deal, Ms. Northcraft. I'll get the money to you as soon as possible."

Where was it?

Katya tipped her purse upside down and shook it frantically. A stray slip of paper fell out onto the glass countertop and settled on top of the rest of the items she'd strewn about. Carefully she sorted through the pile again.

It had to be here.

The ascetically thin man on the other side of the counter wrinkled his nose as he watched her. His Harley-Davidson T-shirt and black leather pants attempted to project a tough-guy image, which didn't quite succeed. He looked scrawny enough that Katya figured she could push him over with one hand.

Katya looked into the man's pale eyes as if she might find her answer there but saw only indifference in his blank expression.

"It was here yesterday. I put the necklace back into the black velvet bag and put it in my purse. I know I did." She tried to keep the desperation she was feeling out of her voice.

Skinny-boy just shrugged, as if to say he really couldn't care less. Which, of course, he couldn't, Katya thought, looking at the array of second- or tenth-hand jewelry displayed in the locked glass case. Before this evening, she'd never once set foot in a pawnbroker's shop, had never realized how the walls of such a place reeked with the desperation of those who'd come before her. It fairly oozed out of the paint, threatening to suffocate her with every shallow breath she took.

She couldn't take anymore.

Her head pounded. The items in the pawnshop started spinning around in her mind. Rings, guns, knives, guitars, all moving faster and faster as she attempted to cram her things back into her purse with shaking hands. A baby's crib, a grandmother's heirloom cameo brooch, a child's stuffed animal. All of it for sale for pennies on the dollar. All of it given up for that last ounce of hope, that last dollar that would buy enough food for a day or a week or a pair of shoes that weren't already falling apart or drugs for the hopeless addict who vowed this time would be the last time.

Clutching her pocketbook under her arm, Katya raced out onto the sidewalk. Without caring where she was going, she started running, her sandals slapping the pavement as she urged herself furiously forward.

People went by in a blur of colors: men in their business suits and brightly colored ties, women in gaily

patterned dresses, everyone on their way home from a
hectic day at the office.

But she had no home to go to.

No home. No necklace. No money. No parents. No
friends. Nowhere to turn.

She ran faster, ignoring the curious looks from those
she passed, and the ache ripping into her side. She hadn't
been to church in years, but she found herself starting
to pray, *Please, God, tell me what I'm supposed to do
now. Help me.*

She stopped, suddenly realizing that her flight had
taken her right back where she had started this morning:
the Royal Palmetto. The one place she had felt safe these
past few days. She'd never been one to get particularly
attached to physical locations—she'd moved from one
boarding school dorm room to another too many times
in her early years for that—but right now she felt like
clinging to the warm stucco with gratitude. The Royal
Palmetto might not be home, but it was the closest thing
she had right now.

Calmer now, she turned into the circular drive and
walked across the sun-warmed cobblestones. The valet
on duty greeted her by name, and Katya was amazed at
the attentiveness of the staff. She nodded in greeting,
then continued on into the compound.

As she stepped onto the grounds, she felt an inex-
plicable sense of peace. It was so quiet here, the traffic
noises seemingly halted by the thick walls surrounding
the hotel. Katya walked past soothing fountains and secret alcoves just waiting for pairs of star-crossed lovers
to come for a tryst. The sweet smell of lime and orange
trees mingled with jasmine. The flowers seemed brighter
today, almost too painful to look at.

Katya took a deep breath, fumbling around in her
purse for the magnetic card key to her room. Somehow,

she knew she would find the answer to her questions once she was inside her own private sanctuary.

She put the key into the reader, waiting for the light to turn green.

Red.

She tried the door handle anyway. It didn't budge.

She tried the key again.

Still red, blinking at her.

Katya closed her eyes and laid her forehead against the warm wooden door. So, this was God's answer to her prayers?

She didn't know why she had even bothered asking for help. God knew—and so did she—that it had never worked for her before. After her mother died, she had prayed all the time, first going through the ritual of saying the Lord's Prayer, then asking God if she could talk to her mother. Thinking about it now, Katya snorted a cynical laugh against the tightly closed door of her hotel room. It was as if she had imagined God was on a phone call with her: *Okay, God, I'm done with you. Could you hand the receiver to my mom now?*

It was the only thing that had gotten her through that first lonely year of boarding school. She had missed her mother so much. Even now, just thinking about all the events she was going to have to go through without her mother made her want to curl up in a heap on the concrete and cry until she was spent.

There would be no mother to cry at her wedding. No one to tell her what to expect when she got pregnant for the first time. No one to give her advice if her baby got sick or didn't take to breast-feeding. There would be no mother to lend a sympathetic ear when she and her husband had their first major fight. As with so many events in her life, she would have to face all this alone.

Only now, she'd have to face it without money, as well as without a mother.

Alex's Mustang ate up the miles between the ballpark and the hotel with ease. He could have afforded a more expensive car, but there was just something he liked about this model. It certainly wasn't high-maintenance, like some cars out there. The minute he thought the term *high-maintenance,* a vision of Katya Morgan flashed into his head and he grimaced. He had tried to find her all afternoon to let her know he'd had to vacate her room to accommodate the last-minute conference that Chris had booked.

What a disaster this whole conference mess-up could have turned out to be. He hoped the measures he had taken would alleviate any tension between the two groups. He'd spent all morning working with his staff to rearrange meeting and guest rooms to minimize the interaction between groups. With any luck the cattlemen would never need to know they were sharing the grounds with the animal rights activists, and vice versa.

He'd left a message at the front desk for Katya, letting her know that he had her things in safekeeping. He could afford to be generous and let her have the room for a night or two if there were no paying guests he needed to house, but his generosity could only go so far. Of course, he also left her his cell phone number in case she needed help finding a place to stay for the night.

Nana was right. He *was* a sucker for a damsel in distress.

Not that he thought he had all the right answers or anything. It just seemed to be part of his nature to feel responsible for taking care of everything and everyone around him. That was probably part of what made him a good general manager.

Alex smiled to himself, feeling the cool night air rush in through the open convertible top. He loved his job, and, even more, he loved the Royal Palmetto as if it were his own.

His smile faded as he turned into the driveway of the hotel and heard the shouting.

Damn.

It looked as if his carefully laid plans had not worked out as well as he might have hoped.

"It's a good thing you're back, Mr. Sheridan," the valet said as soon as Alex pulled to a stop next to him.

"What's going on? Why didn't anyone call me?"

"Mr. Hampstead said he could take care of it," the valet answered.

"Take care of what?"

"Calf killer!" Alex heard someone shout before the valet could answer.

"Liberal freak!" another voice yelled.

Alex pushed himself out of the car and headed to the reception area at a run, his enjoyment of the pleasant evening already a distant memory.

CHAPTER NINE

AFTER her room key hadn't worked, Katya knew the last of her luck at the Royal Palmetto had run out. She hadn't even bothered to ask for another reprieve, as she had nothing more to give Alex Sheridan to make him relent. Instead, she'd had the valet hail her a cab. Her stepmother was the last person that Katya would go to for help, but Katya figured that was exactly the position she was in right now. She couldn't go to her old friends. She was certain they had all heard about what had happened at last night's auction by now. She was equally certain they would be inclined to judge her harshly. Desperation was not a quality they looked for in their friends.

No, Jillian was her last—and only—hope.

The cab dropped Katya near the top of Camelback Mountain and she forked over the last of her small pile of cash to pay the fare. Even that hadn't been enough to cover the full cost of the ride, much less a tip. After five minutes of haranguing her in whatever language was native to him, the cabbie finally realized she had nothing more to give him and sped off, leaving Katya choking on a cloud of dust.

She shrugged off the man's insults, glad she hadn't attempted to learn Farsi along with the French, German, Spanish, and smattering of Japanese she'd mastered in finishing school. She'd never been what could be considered a great scholar—her teachers continually told her she was too lazy for that—but for some reason she had adored languages. Perhaps because she had always dreamed that one day her father would call her up and invite her along on one of his many business trips.

"Katy-girl," he'd say, using the pet name she'd dreamed he made up for her, "why don't you join me in Paris? I've got a couple of meetings I can't get out of, but we can spend some time together afterward. What do you say?"

Of course she'd say yes, and they'd travel all over the city, and her father would be so impressed at how well she knew the language. Why, she'd probably be mistaken for a native, and everyone would pat her head and laugh when they found out she was an *American*. But of course, her father never asked and, instead, she'd traveled the world on her own, meeting her set in whatever city was the hot spot for the season. She'd thought her peers at least would be duly impressed with her language skills. And she thought they were, until the time she'd overheard Bitsy Smythe-Jantzen and Jason Overstreet making fun of her because all her language skills got her was the ability to talk to the servants of wherever they happened to be.

After that, she'd stuck with English, refusing to let on that she understood anything besides her native tongue, until her friends seemed to forget that she could speak anything else.

Katya sighed now as the crickets started singing their nightly song. No matter what language she said it in, she was in deep trouble.

She slumped against the warm whitewashed stucco wall that covered the perimeter of the Morgan property. The wall itself was only about three feet high. Unfortunately, it was topped off by another six feet of closely spaced spiked iron bars that Katya was not quite desperate enough to try tackling just yet.

Her foot started to cramp and she moved her left leg, wincing as the scab on the knee she had scraped on the carpet last night cracked open again. She couldn't come up with the name of even one person she could call a true friend, no one she felt she could burden with her troubles and, more important, no one who would hand her a $5,000 check to pay her attorney without a moment's hesitation.

A pale moon peeked out of the rising darkness, casting a watery light over the rocks at her feet. Katya looked up and blinked. How had this happened? How was it that she had not one person in the whole world she could depend on? Was her life really this empty?

The answer came to her immediately.

Yes. Her life was really this empty.

Katya's palms ached where they'd been abraded by the carpet. Rubbing a hand over her eyes, she wondered if any of the makeup she'd put on that morning remained on her face, then realized that it didn't matter. Her appearance was the least of her worries. She had no idea how she was going to resolve her financial problems. She had to get the money to pay Paula Northcraft to start working on her case or her life would remain the way it had been the past two days.

Stark.

Empty.

Alone.

She shuddered, crossing her arms across her chest. Jillian had to let her in. She was Katya's last hope.

Katya pushed the intercom buzzer for what must have been the hundredth time in the last hour.

"Damn you, Jillian. Please let me in," she pleaded.

There was only silence from the house.

Katya tried again. "You have to let me stay here tonight. I'm sorry for breaking in yesterday. I know I shouldn't have, and I promise I won't try to take anything if you'll just let me in."

Laying her head against the warm iron bars of the gates, Katya prayed that her stepmother would unlock them. Instead, Jillian's calm voice came over the intercom, echoing out into the desert night: "Katya, you can't stay here. Stop pressing the bell."

Katya felt her spine start to crumple and tightened her hold on the gates. What was she going to do? Where was she going to stay? Was she going to end up sleeping on the sidewalks and begging for spare change like the countless homeless people she'd passed in her life without giving them a dollar or a second thought?

Katya shuddered.

No. She'd never survive that sort of life. Jillian had to help her. She pressed the buzzer once more, fighting to hold back tears and the terror that was clawing at her insides like a pack of hungry rats.

"Please, Jillian, I don't have anywhere else to go."

Her plea was met with silence.

The sounds of the desert night enfolded her, seeming to get louder with each breath. And before the terror could destroy her, Katya turned it into raw anger. Ferociously she gripped the bars of the gates that kept her from her childhood home and yanked, trying to pull them open with the strength of her fury.

With a wild animal screech, she felt the anger wash through her.

"Damn you to hell for this, Father!" she yelled, directing her rage at the person who had caused her this anguish. She pushed at the gates, but they wouldn't budge. "You spineless coward. You didn't even have the guts to face me with this. You had to die first so you wouldn't have to deal with me. Well, to hell with you!"

she screamed once, then screamed it again because it felt so good.

She let go of the gates and turned around, pressing her back to the warm metal as she raised a fist in the air.

"You aren't going to beat me with this little game of yours. You'll see. I'm stronger than you think, and I'm not going to give up. I am not going to let you win."

Katya took a deep breath, feeling the cool air cleansing her body of toxic fury. To hell with her father and her stepmother and all of her so-called friends who hadn't even taken the time out of their empty schedules to send flowers to her father's funeral to let her know they cared.

She would emerge from this challenge as she always had: victorious and alone.

She had survived her mother's death and her own subsequent banishment, and now she would survive this, too.

But where are we going to sleep tonight? a small, childlike voice asked.

"I'll sleep right here on the ground if I have to," Katya answered the unspoken question, trying to squash the fear that was returning now that the anger was gone.

What about the animals? What if a spider crawls on us? Or a snake? her inner voice whispered.

"Be quiet," she chastised herself. That line of thinking would only destroy her. She shoved the fear away and was distressed as a more immediate, more physical, need took its place.

She looked up and down the quiet road, contemplating her dilemma. It was at least five miles to the nearest public building that would have a bathroom she could use to relieve herself. Five miles in the ever-increasing darkness, along a fairly deserted road, in flimsy sandals that were already rubbing a raw spot on her right heel. And then what? Where was she going to sleep? She certainly wasn't going to shack up on some bench somewhere and, much as the thought distressed her, she figured she'd be safer nodding off for a while behind the bushes near the gates of her old home than anywhere else. Which meant she'd have to walk all the way back here in the dark.

It was getting late. She was tired. There was no way she was going to make that trek down the hill and back up it just to go pee. She moved behind a cactus growing near the fence and unzipped her emerald green shorts. This was worse than humiliating.

Katya wrinkled her nose distastefully. A week ago, she'd been bathing in an Italian marble bath, surrounded by sweet-swelling soaps and thick, luxurious towels.

And now she was squatting with the scorpions.

CHAPTER TEN

"HOLD it right there."

If the words spoken loudly into the quiet night hadn't made her freeze, the bright spotlight glaring into her eyes would have.

Katya's hands stilled on her lowered zipper.

"Put your hands in the air and move away from the fence," the stern voice ordered.

"But—" Katya started to protest.

"Do it. Now."

She went over her options in a split second of indecision. The way she saw it, her choice boiled down to perhaps exposing her rather skimpy silk panties to whoever was bossing her around or risking death by gunshot if she made the sudden move to zip up.

She chose exposure.

After all, they were brand-new panties, purchased at her favorite lingerie shop just before she'd flown to Saint Martin. So what did she care who saw them?

Squinting against the light shining in her eyes, Katya waddled out from behind the cactus, attempting to keep her shorts in place around her waist.

"Could you get that thing out of my eyes, please?" she asked.

Apparently satisfied that she wasn't coming out from the bushes brandishing an Uzi, whoever was holding the light moved it to the side just a bit. Katya blinked, trying to regain her sight in the encroaching darkness.

A tall dark-skinned man in a tan uniform stood near a white car with a wide blue stripe marked with the emblem of the City of Scottsdale Police Department. She looked out of the corner of her eye and saw another policeman standing to her left, his gun pointed at her chest.

"Can I, uh . . ." She slowly looked down at her front, hoping they'd get the message.

The man to her left, an older man with a ruddy complexion, turned a bright pink color but didn't lower his weapon. "No sudden moves," he warned.

"Of course not," Katya muttered under her breath. "I can see the headline now: 'Policemen Killed in Deadly Zipper Incident.' "

A cough from the policeman near the car told her he'd heard her rashly uttered comment. If the other man had heard it, he either chose to ignore her or didn't have quite the same appreciation for her sense of humor as the other fellow.

"Step over to the car and put your hands behind your head."

Katya sighed. It was as if she'd been trapped in a bad version of *Dragnet,* complete with the humorless Joe Friday. Her own temporary good humor fled, however, as the tall policeman slapped a pair of cold metal handcuffs around her wrists.

"Wait a minute," she protested as he began reading her rights. "What are you arresting me for?"

"Trespassing."

"I'm not trespassing. I'm just standing here at the side of the road."

"Watch your head," the tall man said politely, putting a large hand on top of her head as he pushed her into the backseat.

"Do you have a place of residence?" the older man

asked from the front as his partner slid into the driver's seat.

Katya squirmed. "Not at the moment. But I can explain—"

"Uh-huh," the ruddy faced man said disinterestedly. "You can tell your story down at the station."

Sitting in the backseat of a police car, watching through a scratched screen of bullet-proof plastic as they passed row after row of familiar houses, being ignored by two civil servants who obviously couldn't care less what happened to her, Katya fought the urge to lay her head in her hands and weep.

Even if she decided to give in to the urge, she couldn't, since her hands were now locked behind her back, held there by the relentless grip of the handcuffs.

She thought she had hit bottom last night, but she was wrong.

Katya didn't even raise her head as one of her cellmates vomited loudly into the stainless-steel toilet openly visible from her perch on the top bunk bed. She pinched her nose closed to avoid the stench that made her own stomach heave in response.

She didn't even care that the black ink left over from being fingerprinted was probably smeared all over her face by now.

Shivering in the starkly painted yellow concrete cell, Katya stared fixedly at the door.

This had to be what the bottom looked like.

A stained and smelly mattress; an itchy blanket so small it would cover her legs or her arms but not both; the urge to pee so bad her bladder ached; a homeless alcoholic puking two feet away from her; two aging prostitutes sleeping soundly through it all. And, above it all, knowing that there was not one person in the world who cared where Katya Morgan was sleeping tonight.

It was 2:00 A.M. and she was all alone in the world.

Her cellmate threw up again. Loud, rasping retching that made Katya want to cover her ears as well as her nose.

Katya closed her eyes and felt hot tears sliding out of the corners of her eyes. It didn't matter that crying wouldn't fix anything; she couldn't stop herself.

For the second time since her father had sent her away to boarding school, she allowed the tears to flow.

Because if this wasn't the bottom—if there were worse things in store for her than this—she was not going to survive.

Alex got the message at three o'clock in the morning when he returned, exhausted, to his suite at the hotel.

He'd spent two hours soothing the ruffled feathers— or should that be leaves?—of the animal rights activists, assuring them that they could coexist peacefully with the "soulless carnivores" for four days. None of this would have happened if Chris had followed orders, but Alex was too tired to waste any energy on the other man tonight. Alex had told him to separate the two groups from the minute they stepped onto the property. He had suggested that Chris station at least two people in the lobby to direct one group to one registration desk and the other to another. Apparently, Chris's directions hadn't been very clear, so one employee was sending the cattlemen to the animal rights desk, like lambs to the slaughter.

To make sure that tonight's fiasco would not be repeated, Alex went back to his office and reviewed every detail of both conferences, ensuring that the two groups would not cross paths again.

He saw the message light on his phone blinking the minute he opened the door, but he didn't pick it up right

away. As he tossed his wallet on top of the coffee table,
he was tempted to ignore its summons altogether. He
went in to brush his teeth, but the message light continued to wink at him when he emerged from the bathroom.

With a sigh, he sat down on the couch and eyed the
baseball bat he always left perched in the corner of the
living room for when Merrilee came over and wanted to
bat a few balls around behind his casita. The message
light continued to blink.

Resigned to doing the responsible thing, Alex
picked up the receiver and punched the button to retrieve
his messages. Laying his head back against the sold pine
frame of the couch, he closed his eyes.

"Alex, this is Katya Morgan. I know I have no right
to ask you for anything, but I'm in trouble."

Alex opened his eyes abruptly and sat up straight.
She sounded small and frightened, two words he had
never thought to associate with the self-assured woman
he knew.

She continued, her voice trembling, "Jillian won't
help me, my friends think I'm a laughingstock, and I . . .
I have nowhere else to turn."

There was a long pause, and Alex scrambled to find
a pen and something to write on.

"I've been arrested for trespassing and I'm in jail."
Her voice hitched here, and Alex could only imagine
how scared she must be. Hell, he'd be scared, too. Most
people never saw the inside of a jail cell in their entire
lives. "They haven't told me anything. I don't know
what to do, or how to get out of here. I just—" She
stopped, then started again. "I'll do anything if you help
me. I'll take the job you offered me. I'll pay you back.
Anything. I'll do anything. Please." Her last word was
almost a whisper.

Alex was out the door almost before the recording

ended. He grabbed his wallet from the coffee table and raced out, only to stop a few feet from his suite when he realized that she hadn't left him the address of the police station she was at. Letting himself back into the suite, he quickly flipped through the phone book to find phone numbers for the three stations in Scottsdale. He tried the main office number, not sure whether they would even tell him if Katya had been booked there. After all, it wasn't as if he were family.

"Scottsdale Police Department," a polite voice answered on the second ring.

"Yes, this is Alex Sheridan. I'm the general manager at the Royal Palmetto. I received a call from one of my employees saying she'd been arrested for trespassing. Can you tell me if she's there?"

"What's her name?" the officer on duty asked.

"Katya Morgan."

There was some clacking on a keyboard before the officer answered, "Yes, Ms. Morgan is here."

Alex let his breath out with a *whoosh* of relief. "Can you tell me how I can get her out of there?"

"Certainly. She's only being charged with a misdemeanor. She'll see the judge tomorrow morning and a court date will be set. After that, she'll need to post bond to be released until her hearing."

"Is there any way I could get her out sooner?" Alex didn't even know if there were such things as all-night bondsmen, but he was willing to find out.

"I'm afraid not. Bail won't be set until after she sees the judge tomorrow morning."

Alex rubbed a weary hand across his forehead. "What time will that happen?"

"I don't know, sir. They'll handle the cases in the order they were received. Typically, court gets cleared out around noon, unless it's been a busy night. She should be released before lunch, though."

"Thank you," Alex muttered before hanging up the phone.

It was going to be a long night.

CHAPTER ELEVEN

THE woman Alex saw in court the next morning was not the same one he thought he knew. Her clothes were rumpled, her face splotchy. Her hair, although neatly combed, looked limp and lifeless. She didn't even look up as she was led into the room along with three other women. Alex tried to catch her eye, but her gaze remained downcast throughout the proceedings.

By the time Katya's name was called, Alex was beginning to shift uncomfortably on the hard wooden bench seat. It took less than fifteen minutes for her to plead guilty and have the judge set bail at $500.

Alex wrote a check to guarantee Katya's future appearance in court, and then he walked out into the lobby and waited for her to walk through the heavy dark door the officer behind the desk had indicated. It only took a few minutes for her to emerge. She walked toward Alex slowly, face down, then stopped a few feet away.

When she finally looked at him, Alex was dismayed to see that the inner fire he had seen lurking in her eyes had been snuffed. This was not good. Yes, she needed to learn how the other 97.5 percent lived, but not this way.

"Thank you for coming to get me. And for taking care of paying my bail. I promise I'll pay you back."

"It was no problem," Alex said, leading her out into the sunshine and away from the horror she had just experienced. He really should be back at the hotel, making sure the two factions encamped on the property hadn't decided to stage the next world war there. The kitchen would be busy getting ready for the Cattlemen's Association's beef-laden banquet, which would be held this evening, while the animal rights activists were cloistered in their meeting room discussing the merits of using red paint rather than actual blood on fur wearers. "I'm sorry I couldn't have sprung you from the joint last night. I guess I never realized the justice system was a nine-to-five gig."

Katya only nodded at his lame attempt at a joke as he opened the passenger side door of his Mustang. He closed the door behind her and she sat as still as a statue, staring fixedly out the windshield.

He had to do something to prod her out of this catatonic state, he thought, putting the car in gear. But what? He might be accustomed to feminine theatrics, but this sort of emotional emptiness was way out of his league.

The idea came to him in a flash, and Alex had to resist the urge to clap himself in the forehead. Of course. This was a job for Nana.

He turned the car around at the next traffic light and headed toward downtown Phoenix. Katya didn't seem to notice, or care, where he was taking her, so Alex turned the radio on to a soothing station and pushed the accelerator down as far as he dared. He decided it would be best if they were not stopped for speeding just now. Katya had probably had her fill of law enforcement for a while.

"Do you think you can help?" Alex asked quietly, poking his head outside his grandmother's kitchen to keep an eye on the woman sitting in the comfortable living room of his grandmother's downtown condominium. The condo suited Nana well. She didn't have to worry about tending a yard, and she'd become friendly with many of the other building tenants. Besides, it was close to the theater and art museum, not to mention the many boutiques and restaurants nearby.

He heard clattering behind him and turned back to face the woman who had taken over the job of raising his two youngest sisters when his mother had died of breast cancer twelve years ago. Anthony Rivera had been long dead of a heart attack by then, and there was no one left to raise his daughters except his wife's first mother-in-law. But Nana had been up to the task and had always treated Anthony's children with the same love she had shown her own son's children.

Nana snorted inelegantly. "Of course I can help. *Ay, Dios mio!*" she swore in Spanish. "Do you think I don't deal with this sort of thing every day with your sisters? If it's not Lucy with that headstrong husband of hers, it's Maria with some crisis from the hotel or Martina complaining about some boy. And Inez? Don't even get me started on her. If it weren't for me, that girl wouldn't have the courage to leave her apartment. And you," she snorted again. "Don't think I haven't heard things about you that no grandmother should know."

Alex grinned down at his grandmother. "Don't you listen to a word of it, Nana. You know Maria just likes to stir up trouble for me."

"It's not Maria you should worry about," Nana said mysteriously. "Now take that tray out to the living room. I'm sure Miss Katya is hungry after being in jail all night."

When Alex went back out into the living room, Katya was in the exact same position as when he'd left. She was perched on the edge of his grandmother's couch, ready to bolt at the slightest provocation. "Here are some of Nana's world-famous *empanadas*. She's fixing you some lemonade to go with them. I always take mine with extra sugar. She makes it pretty tart, just in case you were wondering." He paused, waiting for any kind of response from her, but none was forthcoming. "Anyway," he continued, "I need to get back to the hotel, but I'll be back for dinner tonight. Nana's made up the guest room for you."

Katya raised her eyes to meet his then, and he was struck again by their unusual color. Not gray and not green, but an incredible mix of the two. Only now they were filled with tears. She blinked, and two drops rolled down her face. She didn't even try to swipe them away. "Thank you, Alex. I just . . . I don't know what I would have done if you hadn't come to my rescue this morning."

Shit. He hated feminine tears. All they had to do was start the waterworks and something primitive inside him reared its head. He must have received a double dose of the urge to protect, because he had never been able to withstand a crying woman. Whatever she wanted, all she had to do was start bawling and he'd give in. It was a secret his sisters knew only too well, and they never hesitated to use it against him.

He had no choice.

Hundreds of thousands of years of evolution hadn't managed to stamp out the instinct, so he stopped fighting it.

"Come here," he said softly, pulling Katya to her feet. He pushed her head against his shoulder and stroked her back while she proceeded to soak his white starched shirt. "Everything is going to be okay. I promise."

He continued rocking her gently, letting the pain flow out of her and—apparently—onto his shirt. It wasn't much of a sacrifice, he figured. Dress shirts were fairly easy to come by.

It only lasted a minute, much shorter than he was accustomed to. She drew one last shuddering breath before pulling away from him. Alex loosened his hold but didn't let her go.

"I'm sorry," she said.

"For what?"

"For crying. I know it's silly, and it doesn't solve anything."

Alex raised his eyebrows at that. "What do you mean? Don't you feel better?"

She blinked. Once, then again. Then he saw something he hadn't expected. A smile. "Actually, yes. I do feel better. All this time, I thought . . ."

"You thought what?"

She shook her head, still with that secret smile playing about her lips. "Nothing. It doesn't matter."

Alex looked heavenward. Women. Even after growing up in an entire houseful of them, he still didn't get them.

Then she hugged him—a move so unexpected, Alex felt his jaw drop, hitting the top of her head. And in an instant, his thoughts took a decidedly unbrotherly turn. Her full breasts were pressed against him, her hips touching his. His loins were definitely stirring.

"Thank you," she said, and it took Alex's blood-drained brain a moment to realize that she was probably not thanking him for the erection he was sure she could feel pressing against her stomach.

"I'll be right there with the lemonade," Nana announced loudly, taking a moment to emerge from the kitchen.

Alex mumbled a hasty, "You're welcome," to whatever it had been that Katya was thanking him for, then bent to retrieve his suit jacket from a wingback chair. He held it casually, yet strategically, in front of him as his grandmother, who obviously had a clue of what was going on in her living room, set a tray of ice-filled glasses down on the coffee table.

"Well, I've got to get back to the hotel. You two, um . . . enjoy yourselves," Alex said, making a hasty retreat.

"Oh, don't worry. We will," Nana's laughing voice followed him out the door and into the hallway. "See you tonight for dinner."

"I'm going to give you the secret to my tamales, but you can't tell anyone. Do you promise?"

Katya looked up from the heaping scoopful of lard that she had just put into a cast-iron skillet and smiled at the conspiratorial tone of Alex's grandmother's voice. "Cross my heart," she said, marking an *X* over her chest as she had done as a child.

"I mean it. No matter how often Lucy begs you or Maria harangues you, you can't tell a soul."

Secretly touched that the elderly woman would tell her something that none of her granddaughters knew, Katya nodded.

Nana opened a cupboard and pulled out two cans of S&W fire-roasted whole tomatoes and proceeded to open them, pouring the contents into a blender. "These canned tomatoes taste much better than anything I've ever come up with. But the girls would be so disappointed if they knew I was cheating, so I've never told them. Here, we have to dispose of the evidence."

Katya took the plain brown paper sack filled with the empty cans and ran out into the hall to toss them down the garbage chute. Chuckling, she came back into the kitchen, where Nana was whirring the contents of the blender with gusto.

Who knew that cooking could be so much fun? She'd always assumed it was something distasteful. Otherwise, why pay someone else to do it for you? She'd never lived anywhere without a cook. At home, Daddy had had a chef to make their meals. At boarding school, they were served group meals from the kitchen. At college, it was the cafeteria or local pizza joint. In hotels, it was restaurants and room service. And at the villas she rented, staff was always included.

She was thirty-one years old and had never cooked a real, honest-to-goodness, made-from-scratch meal for herself.

"Careful now, don't let the grease get too hot. It'll burn the onions."

Katya turned down the flame as Nana had shown her. "Should I add them now?"

Nana peeked into the skillet. "Yes, that's perfect. You can help me shred the pork while those cook."

After watching the older woman pull pieces of cooked meat apart with a fork for a few seconds, Katya figured she could handle the task herself. It was so easy.

"Be careful not to let the onions burn. You'll need to give them a stir every now and then."

"How will I know when they're done?" Katya asked, giving the pot a stir.

"They'll start to turn a nice golden-brown color. Then we can add the tomatoes and chilies. The pork gets added last. That can simmer while we prepare the corn husks."

Katya breathed in the smell of cumin and sautéing onion. The kitchen was warm and humid from their efforts, and she felt a strand of hair fall from behind her ear. She tried to push it back with her shoulder, but of course that didn't work.

It had been a wonderful afternoon. She had poured her heart out over a plate of fried empanadas and lemonade and then had taken a long hot bath, followed by a long cool nap. Now, dressed in a pair of denim shorts and a white T-shirt depicting a skeleton propped against a saguaro and emblazoned with the words, YES, BUT IT'S A DRY HEAT, she felt like a completely different person from the wreck that had been delivered on Nana's doorstep earlier in the day.

From his vantage point across the room, Alex would have had to agree. He had quietly let himself into Nana's condo a few minutes before, not sure what he'd see when he opened the door. He certainly hadn't expected to see the former spoiled heiress wearing his sisters' castoffs and filling tamales with his grandmother. Katya's feet were bare, her toes painted a cheery shade of red. Her legs were long and tan, and her face was flushed from the heat of the steam rising off the stove.

She looked up then and caught him staring. For a moment, neither of them spoke.

Alex told himself he could never fall for someone who had never worked a day in her life. He backed that argument up by reminding himself that she was too accustomed to the glamorous life to even think about settling down in one place. Hell, she probably didn't even want children, and that was a "must have" for him.

The problem was, even knowing all that, he felt his heart lurch at the sight of her, standing barefoot in the kitchen with his grandmother.

She pushed a lock of hair out of her face and smiled.

"I hope you brought your appetite, Alex. Your grandmother's been teaching me all her culinary secrets, and I can't wait to try them out on someone."

Alex cleared his throat past the lump that had lodged there as he walked into the kitchen. "Good, because I'm starving." He dropped a kiss on Nana's cheek, then did the same to Katya, ignoring her surprise at the gesture. *Let her chew on that for a while,* he thought. "What can I do to help?"

"Why don't you pour us some wine? Your sisters should be here any—" Nana's words were cut off by a loud cacophony from the hallway. The front door was flung open and the room invaded by the remainder of Alex's family.

It was as if they carried a party with them wherever they went. Alex's oldest sister, Lucy, came first, balancing her two-year-old daughter on her hip. Her husband, Tomas, carrying a diaper bag and their youngest—a son—herded eight-year-old Merrilee through the door. Then came Maria, talking animatedly with Inez, who held the hand of her five-year-old niece. After four children, Lucy and Tomas said they were done. They could afford to have more children on his doctor's salary, but as Lucy put it, she'd done her share to populate the world with good people. It was somebody else's turn now.

Katya stood back from the group, feeling more than a little overwhelmed. She had lost her usual self-confidence somewhere; perhaps she'd left it behind in the stark jail cell last night. In any event, this raucous, happy group intimidated her a bit. Besides, Alex's sisters had witnessed her humiliation at the auction two nights ago, and she wasn't quite sure she was ready to face them again. She turned back toward the kitchen, thinking she'd hide out there for just a minute. Just until she got her bearings back. But Alex didn't give her a chance to escape. Throwing a casual arm across her shoulders, he drew her into the fray.

"Lucy, Inez, Maria. You remember Katya Morgan from the other night?" His voice was light but held a hint of warning. Obviously, the auction was not a topic he wanted discussed, either. "Martina went back to Tempe yesterday. She's a senior at Arizona State this year," he added, just in case Katya had noticed that one of his sisters was missing tonight.

Katya read speculation in three pairs of dark brown eyes, but it wasn't unkind. Just curious and a bit wary.

Alex continued the introductions, ending with the third-grader wearing a bright purple baseball cap with a turquoise A centered on the front. She had a baseball glove affixed to her left hand and continually tossed a large white ball from her right hand into the mitt and back again.

"And this is Merrilee. Merri, this is Miss Katya."

"Nice to meet you," the girl said politely around a wad of gum.

"Likewise," Katya said. "So, I'm guessing you're a baseball fan?"

"I love baseball." Katya watched the little girl's eyes light up, and it was obvious she was hooked on the game.

"Merrilee and I watch a lot of games together. She knows the players' stats better than I do."

Katya had no idea what he was talking about, but she assumed that knowing a player's stats was supposed to be a good thing, so she murmured approval.

"Have you ever been to a game?" Merrilee asked, tossing the ball up in the air and catching it expertly in her glove.

"No, but I've been to lots of other places."

"Like where?"

"Like Paris and London. Spain, Portugal, Greece. You name it, I've been there."

"Have you been to Wrigley Field?"

"Where?"

"Wrigley Field. In Chicago," Merrilee explained patiently as she sat down on the couch and scooted back so her legs stuck out in front of her.

"Oh. No, but I've been to the Colosseum in Rome," Katya offered, taking a seat next to the girl on the couch.

"Mmm. How about Yankee Stadium? Or Candlestick Park?"

Katya laughed. "Nope and nope. How about the pyramids in Egypt? I even got to ride a camel."

"Well, that's pretty cool, I guess," Merrilee conceded.

Seeing that Katya was safely settled in with his eldest niece, Alex wandered back into the kitchen and obviously interrupted the whispered discussion that was going on there. Ignoring the glare from Maria that told him to go away so she, Nana, and Inez could continue discussing Nana's houseguest, Alex asked, "So, what can I help with?"

"I have a couple bagfuls of b-books down in my car for Nana. You could h-help me bring them up."

He knew Inez was just doing her part to get him out of the room but followed her anyway. "So, what were you three cooking up in there besides dinner?" he asked, once they were out in the hall.

Inez shot him her usual serene look. "We were only helping with the tamales, that's all." She paused, then blurted, "Are you sure you know what you're d-doing with Miss Morgan, Alex?"

Alex blinked at the sudden turn the conversation had taken. Inez was usually not this direct; that was Maria's role. "I'm not doing anything with her." He stabbed the DOWN button for the elevator.

When Inez didn't say anything, Alex glanced over

at her. She was watching him with a concerned light in her eyes that struck him as ironic. Usually it was he who was concerned for his younger sister, not the other way around. Alex was struck, as always, at how fragile Inez seemed. Inez had been just shy of fourteen when their mother died of breast cancer. Alex could hardly believe she'd been gone for twelve years now. He shook his head. Back then, he had big plans of traveling the world, working in one glamorous hotel after another, before coming back home to settle down. But when Mama died, he knew he had to come back and help Nana raise the two younger girls.

Alex remembered how beautiful his mother had been, with her long brown hair, golden skin, and light brown eyes. It had been five years after his own father's death that his mother met and married local businessman Anthony Rivera, whom Alex had taken an instant dislike to. Alex had been old enough to remember the awful fights between his stepfather and his mother; the accusations of Anthony's extramarital affairs, and his excuse that the affairs were Alex's mother's fault because she had not been able to give him the son that he so desperately wanted. Anthony tolerated Lucy, Maria, and Alex, but it was obvious he would have preferred that they didn't exist. It was no tragedy to any of them when Anthony died of a heart attack shortly after Martina was born. As a matter of fact, his death brought a measure of peace to the family.

Now, as Alex looked into Anthony's elder daughter's eyes, he felt a measure of compassion for a girl who had spent her early years avoiding the animosity between her parents. It was no wonder Inez was more fragile than the rest of her siblings. Alex laid a soothing hand on his sister's arm.

"You don't need to worry about me, Inez. I can take

care of myself where Katya Morgan is concerned."

The elevator doors slid open, and Alex ushered his sister inside. He was about to ask Inez why she was so worried when the cell phone he had slipped into his front pocket rang. He fished it out and read the number off the lighted display. It was Jenny Tillman, the banquets manager at the hotel.

"Hi, Jenny. What's up?" he asked, after pressing the TALK button.

"I'm sorry to bother you, Alex, but we have an emergency."

"What's wrong?"

"Something happened at the cattlemen's banquet this evening. I'll fill you in when you get here."

What could have gone wrong? He had been there until just before the banquet began, and everything seemed to be going ahead as planned. Alex pressed a thumb and forefinger to his right temple and closed his eyes. "I'll be there as soon as I can," he said.

"Is something wr-wrong?" Inez asked, stepping off the elevator into the cool parking garage under the condominium complex.

"It seems so. Could you tell everyone I was needed back at the hotel?"

"Sure."

"Oh, and get Tomas to help you with those books, okay?" Without waiting for an answer, Alex pushed the button on his key chain to unlock the Mustang, then got in the car and headed out of the garage.

Inez walked over to her own car, a tidy green Mazda sedan. She pulled two paper bags filled with heavy books out of the backseat. "That's all right. I didn't n-need any help in the first place," she muttered to the now-deserted parking lot.

CHAPTER TWELVE

ONE hundred puking cowboys.

Sounded like the perfect name for some new rock group.

Alex laid his head atop the arms he'd folded on his desk. He'd been able to get a local clinic to send over a couple of their on-call doctors—for a hefty charge, of course—and the last patient had been given a clean bill of health fifteen minutes ago, so the worst should be over.

He didn't even want to think of the messes the housekeeping staff would face tomorrow in the guest rooms.

"Alex, what the hell is going on around here?"

At the sound of Barry Hampstead's voice, Alex raised his head. The hotel owner's face was flushed with anger, and Alex wondered how Barry had found out so quickly that there had been a mass case of food poisoning at the hotel tonight. When Chris Hampstead followed his father into Alex's office, he figured he had his answer.

"There was a problem with the food served at the Cattlemen's Association banquet this evening. Almost all of the conference attendees became ill shortly after eating. The doctors we brought in assume it was some sort of food poisoning," Alex answered, rubbing his aching temples. "I think we have it under control now, though. The last doctor just left, and Jenny and her staff are going over the kitchen with a fine-tooth comb to make sure we get rid of whatever it was that made everyone sick."

"Are we going to get sued over this?" Barry asked, sitting down heavily in the chair across from Alex. Chris remained standing, leaning against the wall next to Alex's painting of the Royal Palmetto.

Alex shrugged. "I don't know. We've done what we could to mitigate the problem, but you know as well as I do that some people will sue no matter what steps you take to fix things. I know you don't like to hear this, but that's why we have insurance."

"Yeah, with a goddamned fifty-thousand-dollar deductible."

"There's a good chance it won't come to that. We provided on-site medical attention as soon as we discovered the problem, and I've already offered a discount to the conference attendees. With any luck, the rest of the cattlemen's conference will go smoothly and we'll only be out a few thousand dollars."

"I hope you're right," Barry said, sounding calmer than he'd been a few minutes ago.

"Why don't you go on home and get some rest? There's nothing you can do here. I've got it all under control."

"All right." Barry was nodding as he stood up. "This shouldn't have happened in the first place, but you handled it very well, Alex. Chris, I hope you're paying attention. You could learn a lot from what transpired here today."

Chris's eyes narrowed for the briefest instant, so brief that Alex thought he had imagined it when the other man said smoothly, "You're right, Dad. I think I have learned something from this situation. See you tomorrow, Alex."

Alex mumbled a tired "good night" and sat back down at his desk.

Something was still puzzling him, something that wouldn't let him relax, despite the assurances he had just given Barry Hampstead.

The food from the Cattlemen's Association banquet had been delivered and prepared with the same food that was being served from the hotel's restaurant and room service menus. The steaks came from the same butcher, the lettuce from the same farmer, the potatoes from the same grocer.

So why was it that only the cattlemen had gotten sick?

As Alex hastily tied his running shoes in preparation for his usual morning run, his mind kept returning to the same thought that hadn't let him sleep last night.

Someone had sabotaged the Cattlemen's Association banquet. There was no other answer that made sense. But who? Were the animal rights people so rabid that they couldn't coexist peacefully with others who held differing viewpoints? That didn't seem right. As much as they might want to educate others about their positions, it would be counterproductive for them to cause actual bodily harm to other people.

Alex turned right onto Camelback Road, heading toward the Phoenician instead of the Biltmore today. Cars whizzed by on the already-busy road, commuters heading to the many businesses lining Camelback Road or farther into downtown Phoenix itself.

The air was warm and still; the only wind stirring was from the movement of the cars passing him from beyond the sidewalk.

With a vow to warn Jenny to closely monitor all activity in the kitchen during the next few days, Alex

decided to let the matter drop. He hadn't been lying to
Barry last night when he'd said they had done all they
could to ensure it wouldn't happen again. That was all
he could do, so he let his mind wander to other, more
pleasant things. Things like the birds singing their usual
sunrise concert as the sun peeked up across the desert.
Things like the way the mountains changed instantly
from drab brown to rich, lush red as the sunbeams
reached out to lick them.

Things like his sister honking at him as she drove
past in her well-used Mazda, a dark-haired passenger
snoozing away beside her.

Alex immediately reversed direction. When Katya
had called from jail, sounding desperate and broken, she
had said she was going to take him up on his offer of a
job, but Alex hadn't believed she was really going to go
through with it.

It looked as if he may have underestimated her.

He breezed past the valets at the entrance of the
Royal Palmetto and saw Inez's car disappearing into the
employee parking lot. He jogged behind his sister as she
drove to a spot just left of the reception area and parked
her car.

"Good morning, Alex," she greeted, stepping out of
the car.

"It looks like somebody's not quite ready to start
her first day of work," he commented, jogging in place.

"I offered to pick her up on my way to work this
m-morning and she said she'd be ready when I got there.
I'll admit that I d-didn't really expect her to be waiting
on the curb when I got there, but she was. She fell asleep
right after I pulled away, though. I didn't even t-try to
wake her."

"Why don't you go on in? I'll take care of Miss
Morgan."

Inez nodded, then grabbed her shapeless black purse before leaving him alone with the sleeping woman.

Alex quietly swung open the passenger-side door of his sister's car, leaned against the door, and propped his left foot up against the frame. Then he picked up one of the hands Katya had curled into a fist on her lap.

"Time to wake up, Sleeping Beauty," he said, uncurling her fingers.

"Hmm." Katya made a slight purring sound as she shifted slightly toward him in her seat.

He picked up her other hand and toyed with her long, strong-looking fingers. They were smooth, uncallused, though that would change after a few days in Housekeeping. Alex almost felt sorry for her then but pushed the thought away. Hard work wouldn't kill her, and it might do her some good to see how the majority of the population lived.

Alex leaned down and said quietly into Katya's ear, "Come on; you're going to be late for work."

Her eyes flew open, just inches from his. Alex knew the exact moment she stopped being disoriented. Her delightfully exotic grayish-green eyes lost their dreamy look and became sharply focused on his. "Right. Work," she repeated. "So I can make money."

Alex stifled a grin as he stepped away from the door. "Yeah, that's how it works in my world."

Katya pushed herself out of the passenger seat and slammed the car door. She stretched, and the bright yellow T-shirt adorned with a row of colorful cacti tightened across her breasts. Alex admired the view. Along with the slightly small T-shirt she wore a pair of faded blue jeans with a small tear at the knee and white Keds with no socks.

Alex opened the car door Katya had just closed, pressed the button to lock it, and closed it again before catching up with her. He slid a hand under her elbow and steered her to the right. "The employee entrance is this way," he explained with a wave.

Katya merely nodded and changed directions.

"Have you ever had a job before?" Alex couldn't help but ask. The thought was so foreign to him, having been raised in a family where it was expected that everyone would pull their own weight. He couldn't imagine what it would be like to never have to work for a living. He wondered if it would make a person feel pretty useless.

"I've never needed money before this. I wouldn't need it now if my scheming stepmother hadn't turned my father against me," she said with more than a trace of bitterness.

"Do you really think Jillian had that much power over your father?"

Katya stopped and turned to glare at him. "Of course she did. He would never have disinherited me before he met her."

Alex just shrugged before urging Katya to keep walking. He didn't say what he was thinking, which was that Charles Morgan hadn't seemed the type of man to be swayed by his wife, not even one as young and pretty as Jillian. "You say you never needed money before this, but that's not exactly true."

"I suppose you're right. I always needed it. I just never had to do anything to earn it before now."

They reached the employee entrance and Alex held the door open for her. She hung back for just a second, and Alex stifled a grin. Working in the housekeeping department would be hard, but it wasn't *that* bad. Katya acted as if she were walking to the gallows.

He gave her a little push into the darkened hallway.

"Housekeeping is the third door on the left. Enjoy your first day as a working woman."

She took a first hesitating step; then Alex watched as she squared her shoulders and tilted her chin upward in a way he found amusing. He smiled as she continued to walk away from him, her determined footsteps echoing in the quiet hall.

"I always clean the bathroom first since it t-takes the longest."

Katya stopped as Inez Rivera parked the oversize housekeeping cart just outside the door to room #115. Inez knocked on the door and called out, "Housekeeping," then waited for a few seconds before sliding her card key into the slot and tentatively opening the door.

"Housekeeping," she called again.

When no one answered, Inez pushed the door open all the way and pulled the cart into the doorway. Before they'd headed to the guest rooms, Inez had shown Katya how to stock the housekeeping cart so she wouldn't have to run back and forth during the day to restock it. Since this was their first room, the cart was loaded down and heavy with new supplies.

Katya looked around at the room, wrinkling her nose with distaste. The bed was rumpled, the comforter tossed to the floor beside the bed. The occupant must have ordered room service, because half-empty plates of uneaten food sat on the writing desk next to the phone. The odor of stale food hung heavy in the room, along with the faint musty smell of an early-morning shower.

"Why did you knock first?" Katya asked as she followed Inez to the bathroom. Earlier Inez had shown her the unoccupied-room list they worked from, showing that the occupants of room #115 had checked out early this morning.

Inez shrugged her slender shoulders, and the dark hair she'd gathered into a ponytail bobbed with the movement. "Sometimes the records are wrong, or one of the g-guests takes care of checking out while the other one is still in the shower. It only takes a few times of walking in on people to make you remember to knock f-first."

"I can imagine that would be a bit awkward." Katya paused, then asked, "Why are you training me? I thought you worked at the front desk."

"I usually do, but Maria was short-handed. Three of her regular housekeepers are out this month, so I volunteered to help. My first job ever was in Housekeeping."

Katya sat down on the rim of the bathtub and watched as Inez started to tidy up, tossing soap wrappers into the trash can under the tile counter and piling used towels and washcloths on the bathroom floor. The navy blue uniform pants that had been issued to her were already making her legs sweat. She had asked if they had anything other than polyester, only to be given a lecture that this fabric was durable, didn't wrinkle, and didn't require dry cleaning. Katya didn't understand why dry cleaning was such a big deal. The housekeeping staff had jobs, which meant they earned money and should be able to pay for dry cleaning, right? Wasn't that why people had jobs in the first place?

"What should I do?" she asked, feeling guilty that she was just sitting here watching Inez work.

Inez handed her a spray bottle filled with some sort of cleaning solution and a washrag. "You can start with the b-bathtub."

Katya looked at the items in her hands for a moment before turning around and tentatively squirting the tub with cleanser. Soapy streaks dripped down the sides of the porcelain as Katya sprayed more solution onto the green tile surrounding the enclosure.

"Thank you for showing me the ropes," she said to Inez without turning around.

Inez mumbled an unintelligible response.

Taking a deep breath, Katya turned to the other woman. "No, I mean it. I appreciate you helping me out, especially after I was so rude to you the first day we met. I can only say that I'm sorry; I was having a really bad day."

Inez looked embarrassed as she wiped out the sink. "That's okay. You didn't know I was Alex's sister."

Katya shook her head. "That's not what I meant at all. It doesn't matter that you're Alex's sister. I was rude and I'm sorry."

Inez cocked her head and gazed levelly at her, as if assessing the truth behind her words. Katya shifted uncomfortably from one foot to the other but didn't look away. Finally, Inez nodded. "Apology accepted. Now, we'd better get back to work, or these rooms will never get cleaned."

Feeling as if she had just passed some kind of test, Katya let out a sigh of relief and turned her attention back to the bathtub, grimacing when she saw a clump of long red hair clogging the drain. She supposed it wouldn't do to just leave it there, so she hesitantly reached out one gloved hand and picked it up. Clamping down on the urge to retch, she tossed the hairball into the toilet and flushed with a convulsive shudder.

It was going to be a long day.

Alex told himself that he'd take the time to check on any of the new employees at his hotel. Which was true; he would. He probably would have waited until after they'd finished their first shift, though. He certainly would have waited until after they'd had their first lunch break.

Man, he had it bad.

Still, his steps were light as he followed the trail of rooms Katya had been assigned, looking for the telltale housekeeping cart in front of the door to tell him which one she was working on. It had been a long time since a woman had intrigued him enough to drag his attention away from his two passions: work and baseball. He supposed a large part of the attraction was that he and Katya were so different. He had worked incredibly hard to get where he was. Being the general manager of a hotel was an intense and demanding job. Even when he had time off, he was still responsible for things running smoothly. Just as with last night, he was always on call. And it always seemed that emergencies only arose when he dared to set foot off the property.

In contrast, Katya had never known what it was like to be responsible for anyone but herself. Perhaps *that* was what he found so intriguing. Alex felt responsible for everyone around him, all the time. It was a role he took on willingly; it was as much a part of his nature as the stubbornness that made him keep working to get what he wanted, even when the easy thing would be to give up. But it would be nice to only think of himself and his needs for a change.

Which was probably why he was standing at the doorway of room #118, watching the very attractive hind end of Miss Morgan as she pulled the sheets off a guest bed.

He was definitely thinking of his own needs at that moment.

Nonchalantly he leaned against the door frame.

"So, this work thing isn't so bad, is it?"

Katya gave an involuntary scream and whirled

around, the dirty sheets clutched to her bosom.

"*Ay, Dios mio!* You scared me half to death."

Alex chuckled at the phrase she had so quickly picked up from his grandmother. "I'm sorry. I didn't mean to startle you."

She let out a breath and tossed the sheets at him. "Well, if you've just come to loiter, you can forget it. Put those in the hamper and come help me put clean sheets on this bed. It's a bitch trying to get all the wrinkles out by yourself."

He picked the sheets up from the floor and put them in the proper place on her cart, then followed her next order as well. "I didn't come to loiter. I just came to see if you'd driven my little sister crazy yet."

She handed him one end of a flat sheet. Inez had explained that fitted sheets wouldn't go through the enormous folding machines she'd shown Katya earlier in the hotel's laundry, so the hotel used only flat sheets, making sure to tuck the ends of the bottom one under tightly so the bedding wouldn't fall off during the night. It all made logical sense, but it was still damn near impossible to get all four corners tucked in tightly enough to avoid giant wrinkles in the middle of the bed, which, as Inez pointed out when Katya gently complained about the difficulty of the feat, would certainly make for Unhappy Guests.

And Unhappy Guests meant no return customers. No return customers meant no need for housekeeping staff. No need for housekeeping staff meant no job, no money, and no hope of ever being able to hire Paula Northcraft to take her case. So, Katya pulled the sheet as tight as she could and folded it under the bed just like Inez had shown her.

It made her wonder, though, if Inez would follow her argument all the way through to Unhappy Guests somehow leading to world hunger or the next economic recession, but in the end it was enough to know that she herself might be adversely affected by the phenomenon.

"No, I haven't driven Inez crazy. She cut me loose two rooms ago. I think I was slowing her down. She has a real knack for this housekeeping thing."

"Well, she's been doing if for a few years. She used to help out at the hotel I worked at when she was in high school. She probably knows more about the hotel business than I do," Alex said, expertly securing his second corner while Katya was still working on her first.

"So, what made you go into hotels?"

"The glamour, I suppose," he answered, a wry twist to his mouth.

Katya laughed at that. "Oh, yeah. Hotel work sure is glamorous. Especially the part about cleaning up after food-poisoned guests. That was the clincher for me, all right."

"Okay, so it didn't turn out to be quite like I had imagined. Still, it's a great industry, especially if you want a job where you can travel."

Alex grinned across the bed at her, and Katya felt her pulse quicken. She barely heard his response over the pounding of blood in her ears. Was it getting hot in here or was it just her? Whew, he was sexy when he smiled.

She moved to the last corner of the bed and swallowed. "So, did you get to do much traveling then?"

"No. My mother died just after I finished college. I came back to Phoenix to help Nana with Inez and Martina."

Katya's hands stilled on the sheet. "You did what?"

"I came back to be with my family. It was a very difficult time for us all, as I'm sure you can imagine.

Are you going to finish that corner so we can put the bedspread on?"

"Huh? Oh, yes." Katya tucked the last corner under, quickly added a top sheet, then reached out to take the corner of the cream-and-rose-patterned blanket Alex offered. He had sacrificed a life he wanted to help raise his sisters? At twenty-something years old? But why? Why would anyone do that?

Perplexed, her eyebrows drew together in a frown.

That sort of sacrifice just didn't make sense to her. His sisters probably would have turned out just fine without his help. So why give up what he wanted for them?

She pondered it for a moment while they tossed pillows onto the bed, but the concept was so foreign to her that she simply couldn't wrap her mind around it. In her world, people did not go out of their way for one another. Sure, if you were driving to the casino and someone was staying at another villa along the way, you'd see if they wanted to ride into town with you. But you didn't go halfway around the island to pick them up if you weren't already going in that direction. And that was nothing compared to what Alex had done for his family.

"So, how many more rooms do you have to clean before lunch?" Alex asked, breaking the silence.

"Just one. Do you usually eat in the employee cafeteria?"

"No. I guess rank has its privileges. I get to order from room service."

There he went with that grin again. Somebody should warn him of its knee-wobbling effect. This couldn't be good for his female—and some of his male, too, she supposed—staff.

"Of course, if all the employees were as pretty as you, I just might have to change my eating habits." He

left her with another flash of bright white teeth and a
wave and Katya stood staring after him for a good five
minutes, wondering when she had become so susceptible
to meaningless compliments.

CHAPTER THIRTEEN

HOLDING the bristly toilet brush gingerly between her thumb and forefinger, Katya poked at the rim of the toilet seat in an attempt to raise it without having to touch it. Even though she was wearing a pair of thick plastic gloves, the idea of touching a toilet seat where someone else had sat was just too disgusting to even think about.

"Ew," she grumbled, staring at the spot of . . . something gross on the rim. Reaching over to the counter, she grabbed the Lysol, then sprayed the spot a dozen times until it dissolved. She swished the brush around the water a couple of times and flushed the toilet.

Shuddering, she briefly closed her eyes before flicking the seat and lid down over the swirling water in the bowl with a heartfelt, "Thank God that's done."

She tried to remember what to do next. Oh, yes. The shower.

Katya walked over to the bathtub and pulled open the lightweight fabric curtain. Water dripped into a puddle on the green tile floor. She pushed an already-damp bath towel over the puddle with her toe, then sprayed down the sides of the shower. The cake of soap was a gooey mess that slid off the ledge and into the tub when Katya tried to pick it up. Leaning over, she scooped up the slimy bar and tossed it into the wastebasket.

Figuring she'd give the cleanser some time to do its job, Katya wandered back into the bedroom. This guest room was in one of the casitas with a separate sitting room, just like the ones Katya was accustomed to staying in. She'd always liked the more spacious nature of the casitas, but now all she could think of was that there was just more space that had to be cleaned.

She stripped off the rubber gloves, then covered her mouth with one hand as she yawned. She wasn't used to getting up so early and probably wouldn't have managed to do so today if Nana's alarm clock hadn't been so persistent. Now, even after five hours of work, it still seemed ungodly early. The bed, with its soft-looking comforter and plethora of fluffy pillows, beckoned. Eyeing it longingly, Katya decided it was time for a break. She tested the mattress with one hand.

"Heaven," she sighed before sitting down on the edge of the bed. She'd hidden a handful of gold-tipped cigarettes in the pocket of her uniform after being told to leave her purse behind in an employee locker this morning. Pulling one out now, she sniffed the sweet-smelling tobacco as she scooted farther up on the bed. She rested her back against the headboard, propping herself up on one of the unused pillows as she lit the cigarette and closed her eyes against fatigue.

She dragged in a deep lungful of smoke, knowing it was bad for her. She was smoking too much, much more than she usually did, but given the stress she was under, she decided to let it go. After all, there were only so many matters she could attend to at one time, and her increased dependence on nicotine was pretty much the least of her worries right now. The thing that had her more worried was the thought of how long it would take her to earn enough money to fight her father's will.

She had no idea how people could live on the pittance they were being paid here at the hotel. She hadn't even thought to ask what the salary was when she'd accepted Alex's offer of a job. She'd assumed it would take her less than a month to earn the five thousand dollars she needed for Paula Northcraft's retainer.

What a stupid assumption that had turned out to be. Unlike most hotels, the Royal Palmetto added an additional twenty dollars a day to each guest's bill to cover tips for the valets, bellmen, and housekeeping staff. Some guests still left tips for housekeeping on top of that, but even so, the base pay was less than ten dollars an hour.

That equated to less than four hundred dollars a week. Two-fifty once you took out taxes, the human resources person who'd helped her fill out her paperwork had corrected her cheerfully.

In one month, she'd earn less than what she was used to dropping for one meal for herself and a select handful of friends.

Her last night on Saint Martin with . . . oh, what was his name? Armand? Alfredo? Well, it didn't matter. Her last night on Saint Martin, with whatever-his-name-was latched onto her arm, she had spent nearly six thousand dollars. They'd dined alfresco at The Restaurant at the exclusive La Samanna hotel on a lovely stone patio overlooking the Caribbean. Her companion couldn't decide whether to order the grilled *ahi* or the osso buco, so he'd ordered both, complete with a bottle of Chenin Blanc for the fish and an expensive Cab-Merlot mix for the meat. After dinner, they'd driven into Philipsburg and gambled, then gone dancing till the early hours of the morning. At one point, Antoine—yes, that was his name, she recalled now, closing her eyes—had asked her for a thousand dollars cash. She'd pulled a wad of bills out of her pocketbook without even hesitating or asking what the money was for.

It was going to take her an entire month to earn what she had so blithely handed to a virtual stranger that night. A month of scrubbing toilets and making beds to come up with the same amount of cash she had laid down for one too many bottles of expensive wine and plates of food.

Her head ached.

Katya took another drag on her cigarette. Life had become too complicated in the last week. All she wanted was for things to be like they were before her father had died.

Shaking off thoughts of her troubles, Katya forced herself to relax. Wallowing in worry wouldn't do anything except add lines to her face. She'd figure out a way to solve her problems and, until then, this room-cleaning gig wasn't that bad. Except for the toilets. That part was a bit much.

But at least it kept her out of jail.

She shuddered at that thought. She'd do anything—truly anything—to never have to see the inside of a jail cell again. Just thinking of that night made her feel sick. If cleaning up after other people would keep her out of jail, then that's exactly what she'd do.

Opening her eyes, Katya stubbed out her cigarette in the ashtray beside the bed and got up. Break time was over. It was time to get back to work.

As she picked up the moist towels that the room's occupant had left behind on the carpeted floor, it occurred to her that *work* was a four-letter word.

"Alex said he'd g-give you a ride home this afternoon."

For the second time that day, Katya's heart dropped out of her chest and landed at her feet. Didn't Alex's family ever knock first?

Turning to face Inez, she mentally yanked her heart back where it belonged. "Oh, thank you. I didn't even think about how I'd get back to your grandmother's home."

Inez had a secretive smile playing about her lips but didn't say anything but, "See you tomorrow."

"Early, but definitely not bright," Katya said with a grimace, tossing several candy bar wrappers into the trash can she'd placed beside the coffee table. She looked up when Inez didn't respond to find the other woman contemplating her, a serious expression on her face. "What?" she asked, looking down at the front of her navy blue uniform to see if she'd inadvertently spilled something on herself.

"You did a good job today."

Katya's eyes opened wide with surprise. She was less amazed by Inez's quietly uttered praise than by how it made her feel inside when the other woman said it. Her cheeks turned pink, though why someone telling her she'd done a good job cleaning toilets and making beds made her blush with pride was beyond her.

She really shouldn't care. She should turn to Inez and say, "Well, of course I did. It's just simple housework, isn't it?"

But she didn't.

Instead, she barely managed to stammer out a "thank you" before spritzing the glass coffee table with Windex and wiping it off, hoping Inez would be gone when she was done.

"So, no warring between our two factions today?"

Alex looked up from his conversation with Jenny Tillman to find Chris leaning against the door frame. "No. Things seem to have settled down."

"Thank God." Chris moved away from the door and sat down across from Alex. He greeted his cousin casually and then asked, "So, what's our next big challenge?"

"Well, after the conferences end this week, the next

event we need to gear up for is the chamber of commerce's Salute Scottsdale party the Friday after next."

"What's that for again?"

"The mayor likes to use the event as a way to thank local businesses for helping to keep the city's economy as healthy as it's been. She's made it a tradition during her five years as mayor, and people always seem to have a good time. Your father's been asked to speak at the event about his own rise to success. Hasn't he asked you to attend?" Jenny asked.

Chris shifted a bit in his chair. "No."

"I'm sure that's just an oversight on his part. It wouldn't be a problem to rustle up an extra ticket if you'd like to come," Alex offered.

"Were you invited?" Chris asked.

Alex cleared his throat. "Um . . . yes. But as I said, I'm sure your father just forgot to mention it to you. I'll talk to him about it the next time I see him."

"Don't bother. It's no big deal," Chris said. "As I'm sure you're aware, my dad and I don't always get along as well as we could. I've ceased to let it bother me."

"Am I interrupting?" Katya asked, poking her head through the doorway.

Grateful for the intrusion, Alex stood up and motioned for her to come in. "Not at all. Chris, Jenny, I'm going to have to excuse myself. I promised I'd drive Miss Morgan home and I've got to stop by a friend's office before he leaves at four. I'd be happy to go over the details of the Salute Scottsdale event with you later tonight if you'd like."

Chris stood up and walked to the door. "No, that's all right. I already have plans for the evening."

"I'll see you tomorrow then. Jenny, did you have anything more?"

"No, we covered everything," Jenny answered, standing up.

Alex quickly introduced the two women, then asked Katya if she was ready to go.

"Yes. I can't wait to see what your grandmother has for me to make for dinner tonight. I never knew it could be so much fun to chop stuff up and cook it."

"We're not going to Nana's home," Alex said, turning to lock his office door once they were outside.

"We're not?" Katya asked, disappointed. "But I thought you were taking me home?"

"I am," Alex answered, not elaborating on his cryptic reply as he led her through the hallway and out into the blinding Arizona sunshine.

The elevator doors slid open about as quickly as the elevator itself had hauled them up to the fourth floor. Which was to say, about as quickly as an icicle would melt in the middle of a Minnesota winter.

Katya stepped out onto the linoleum floor in the hall of the apartment building. A strange mixture of smells assaulted her nostrils: the not-unpleasant ammonia-based smell of some kind of cleanser, the damp odor of an institutional air-conditioning system, and an odd mix of spices from a half-dozen cuisines, all seeping out from under the closed doors that opened onto the hallway.

Alex took her elbow and turned left down the hallway. They passed three brightly painted doors before he stopped. "Number Four A. Welcome home." He handed her the key with a flourish, as if welcoming her into a palace.

Rolling her eyes heavenward at his theatrics, Katya turned the key in the lock and opened the door. Alex gestured for her to precede him, then stepped back and ushered her over the threshold.

Katya walked past him, trying not to grimace. The apartment was tiny, minuscule, hardly bigger than her walk-in closet at Daddy's house. The front door opened right up into the living room, which also doubled as a bedroom. It was sparsely furnished in early Ugly American, the sofa bed some sort of cheap wood frame with an uncomfortable-looking padding, the coffee and end tables just one step up from the orange crates her classmates in finishing school used to joke about using as the deliverymen unloaded their families' precious antiques into their dorm rooms.

She didn't even have to move to see into the kitchen, which was nothing more than a glorified hallway with a refrigerator and stove on one side and a sink and countertop on the other. The sink side overlooked the living room, and the raised splashboard had its own counter that apparently served as the dining room, since two rattan barstools had been pushed up to it on the living room side.

"It's a studio," Alex announced after a long silence.

Katya looked around her with dismay. This was not a studio. A studio was what you called a charming artist's loft. This was not charming. It was claustrophobic.

"I know it's small, but it's within your price range," Alex said, pushing her into the room.

Setting her purse down on the countertop she was sure the owner would term a "breakfast nook," Katya continued looking around the tiny space.

"Oh, you mean it's free?" she asked, then almost took a step backward from the force of Alex's grin. Amusement brought out the gold flecks in his light brown eyes, eyes that crinkled charmingly at the corners as he laughed. His bright white teeth flashed against his darker skin, and for a brief ridiculous moment Katya wondered what brand of toothpaste he used. Whatever it was, it certainly was effective.

"Oh, come on. It's not that bad. Our standard hotel rooms aren't any bigger than this." Alex threw an arm around her shoulders and gave her a friendly squeeze.

It suddenly seemed a bit too hot in the small airless room. Feeling uncomfortable under Alex's embrace, Katya shrugged nonchalantly and moved out from under his arm. "At least tell me I don't have to share a bathroom," she said, cursing herself for the slight wobble in her voice.

Alex continued watching her, a smile still playing about his lips. "You get your own bathroom, although I'm sure it's not nearly as luxurious as what you're used to."

Poking her head around the corner and into the strictly utilitarian bathroom, Katya muttered, "No, it's not." She turned back around to find Alex settling himself down on the couch. "So, how much am I paying for this room with no view?"

"The owner is a friend of mine and he owes me a favor. I guess the last tenants left in a hurry and didn't take any of their belongings, so he agreed to throw in all the furnishings for free. I was able to get him to agree to two-fifty on the apartment."

Katya gasped, her eyes opening wide with surprise. "Two hundred and fifty thousand for this?" she asked, putting her arms out to her sides as if to prove that she could almost touch all four walls with her outstretched hands.

Alex couldn't help himself. He laughed so hard that tears sprang up in his eyes.

"What's so funny?" Katya asked irritably, flopping down on the couch next to him.

He wiped the moisture from his eyes.

"Stop laughing at me." She poked him in the ribs.

"Ouch." He grabbed Katya's hand to stop her from poking him again and sat back on the couch, still chuckling. "I'm sorry. You're just so funny sometimes. This apartment is two hundred and fifty dollars a month, not two hundred and fifty thousand dollars. It's not for sale, but even if it was, it sure wouldn't go for two hundred and fifty grand."

"Oh." Katya pulled her hand out of his grasp and stared at the opposite wall. She turned to the kitchen, then looked back at him. "I don't even have two hundred and fifty dollars."

"How much do you have?"

She stood up, took the two steps necessary to get her to the kitchen, and opened a few of the cupboard doors in succession. She pulled out a short scratched glass and filled it with water from the sink.

"Would you like a glass of water?" she asked, as an afterthought.

"No, thank you. How much money do you have, Katya?" He knew avoidance when he saw it. Alex unbuttoned the top button of his shirt and loosened his tie.

Katya set her water glass on the coffee table. She turned her exotically shaped grayish-green eyes to his. "I don't have any money. Not even a dollar."

Alex bit back a smile at the serious tone in her voice. He'd already suspected as much. Reaching into the breast pocket of the suit jacket he'd slung over the back of the couch, he pulled out a brown leather wallet. "Here's a hundred dollars to tide you over until payday. We're already well into the month, so I'll work it out with my friend that you can pay the remainder of June with July's rent. Okay?"

Nodding her head, Katya leaned forward to pick up the glass of water. Her shining black hair swung like a curtain between them, and Alex resisted the urge to reach out and sweep it back behind her ear. Instead, he stood up. She needed some time to figure out who she was on her own before he suggested beginning a relationship.

Today had been a big step for her, and even Inez, who was more cautious by far than he, had told him she was pleasantly surprised at how hard Katya had worked today.

Even so, there were many more challenges ahead: things like going to the grocery store, tackling that second day of work, figuring out how to get to that second day of work when nobody offered to chauffeur you there. No, for now Katya had enough to deal with.

He'd just make sure he was around after she had conquered the next round of challenges.

CHAPTER FOURTEEN

SHE was standing in the middle of the freeway, cars and oversize freight trucks whizzing by and honking, when a loud shriek in her ear woke Katya up. Pushing her hair out of her eyes, she realized it had just been a dream, one brought on, no doubt, by the traffic noises coming from just outside her living room–slash–bedroom window.

A quick glare at the squat black alarm clock by her head told her it was 4:45.

A.M.

As in morning. Or, rather, not even morning, at least not by her standards.

Katya sat up on the uncomfortable wooden-framed couch. It had taken hours to get to sleep after Alex had left, hours filled with the realization that she had nothing to do to occupy her time. The ancient television on the faux-wood bookshelves got three channels, two if she ruled out the one where she could barely make out the figures because of the static on the picture. She'd never been much of a reader, except for her regular subscriptions to *Town & Country*, *Vogue*, and *Travel & Leisure*. She was accustomed to spending her evenings getting ready for the party-of-the-night, from which she wouldn't return home until two or three in the morning. Her days would be filled with shopping or sitting in the sun, resting up before the next round of partying began.

She looked around at the sparsely furnished room, then slapped the alarm clock when it started howling again. This was not how she planned to spend the rest of her life. If she had to work at a housekeeping job and live in this tiny apartment for a while, that was fine, but she was going to do everything in her power to get her rightful inheritance back and return to her old life.

Her vow made, Katya leaped up off the couch and padded into the tiny bathroom for a shower, cursing when the tepid water did nothing more than drip out of the showerhead and onto her back. After toweling off, she didn't bother with much more than moisturizer, eyeliner, and mascara. She was too tired to do anything more than that.

She pulled on another pair of the ill-fitting navy blue pants that had been given to her yesterday morning as part of her uniform. At some point, she'd need to go shopping for some new work shoes, preferably ones that fit, Katya thought, grimacing at the tight fit of the ones Inez had loaned her for her first day of work. The inexpensive pair of panty hose Inez had given her were too short, not surprising, since Inez was at least five inches shorter than she was. Try as she might, Katya couldn't get the crotch any higher than about three-quarters of the way up her thighs. Her shirt, a white man's-style oxford, was the only thing that even remotely fit. Katya buttoned the last button, then frowned, looking down at herself. She looked like a sexless drone, utterly unstylish and frumpy.

She unbuttoned the top three buttons of her shirt, smiling a bit as the tops of her breasts became visible.

"If you've got it, flaunt it, I always say," she muttered before grabbing her purse off the coffee table and heading out the door.

The smell of fried eggs and bacon grease assaulted her as she stepped out into the hall, and Katya's stomach grumbled an empty protest. Wishing she had time to stop at a café for an espresso and a croissant, Katya instead hurried toward the stairs. The ancient elevator was too slow, and she didn't feel like standing out in the hall with a growling stomach waiting for it.

As she stepped out of the building, she noticed a large bus pulling up to the curb half a block away. She'd overheard a group of employees at lunch yesterday talking about taking the bus to work. She'd never ridden a bus in her life, but by now she knew the cab ride would cost her at least ten dollars each way. That would quickly eat up the hundred dollars Alex had loaned her, and she wasn't about to ask for any more.

"You can do this," she told herself, squaring her shoulders before making a dash for the bus. It started to pull away from the curb as she neared, and she started waving frantically.

"Hey, wait a minute!" she shouted, her purse bumping against her hip as she tried to get the driver's attention.

She slapped the door with her bare hand, and the bus stopped abruptly. The front door whooshed open and the skinny blond driver glared at her with watery blue eyes.

"Thank you," Katya muttered. She mounted the steps and started back toward an empty seat.

"Hey, lady, aren't you forgetting something?" the driver's high-pitched voice followed her.

Katya stopped and turned around, genuinely confused. "What?"

The driver, who looked barely old enough to drive a car, much less an unwieldy bus carrying fifty people, waved toward a tall metal contraption on his right. "Nobody rides for free."

"Oh, yes, of course." Katya flashed him her most charming smile. She knew it was her most charming.

Andre—or was it Jean-Pierre?—had told her so. The driver remained unmoved, however, and continued glaring at her.

Ignoring the weary sighs of the other passengers, Katya balanced her purse on her hip as she dug for some change. She had no idea how much this ride would cost. Perhaps five dollars? Half of what she'd pay for a cab? That seemed reasonable. She pulled out a twenty and flashed it at the driver.

"Here you are," she said.

"What do I look like, a cashier at Seven-Eleven?"

"I beg your pardon?" She continued waving the bill in front of the driver's nose.

"Exact change only, lady." The driver opened the door again, gesturing for her to get off the bus.

"Well, no . . . but," she sputtered. She couldn't get off the bus. She couldn't be late for her second day on the job.

"Here, I have change. One zone or two?"

Katya turned to her friendly-voiced savior. Apparently, the woman read Katya's blank expression to mean—correctly—that she had no idea what the woman was talking about.

"How far are you going?" the woman asked kindly.

"Oh. To Scottsdale. The Royal Palmetto."

"That's two zones," the woman explained, depositing some change in the machine next to the driver. He gave Katya one last glare before closing the front door and turning his attention back to the traffic.

Katya followed the Good Samaritan and sat down beside her just as the bus lurched into another lane. She settled her purse on her lap, then grabbed the bar in front of her as the bus made an abrupt turn.

"He's not the best driver we've had on this route," the woman beside her said ruefully.

Katya braced her feet on the floor to keep her balance against the drunken lumbering of the vehicle. "I think he's trying to kill us," she muttered, turning to her seatmate. "Thank you for helping me with the fare. As soon as it's safe to let go, I'll pay you back."

"Don't worry about it. You can repay the favor someday when I'm running short of change."

"I'll do that." Katya turned to look at the woman with pretty reddish brown hair. "Do you work in Scottsdale, too?"

"Yes, I'm the receptionist for an insurance broker on Camelback Road. My shift doesn't start till eight, but I get in early so I can have some quiet time to study. I go to school at night and, what with the tuition costs and all, I can't afford a car right now. So, it's the bus for me." She gave a small smile and shrugged with a healthy measure of resignation.

"What are you studying?" Katya asked to pass the time while the bus ambled toward Camelback Mountain.

"Accounting. I want to be a CPA."

"You're kidding, right? Nobody *wants* to be an accountant."

"I do. It's a good, solid field where you almost never have to worry about being laid off."

Katya looked over at the earnest face of her seatmate. "Why in the world would you have to worry about that? Unemployment is at its lowest point in decades."

"Sure it is. For everyone who has an education." The other woman laughed without humor. "I've been laid off from my last three jobs. The stock market takes a plunge and it's not the executives who lose their jobs; it's us peons. Plus, with the new voice-mail systems, receptionists are becoming extinct. I want to get an education so I won't have to save every penny I can just so I can survive when I get laid off."

Katya didn't know what to say to her seatmate's impassioned outburst, so she kept quiet. The silence lasted a minute or two; then the other woman laughed sheepishly. "I'm sorry," she said. "My mother always tells me I tend to get carried away with this college stuff. What about you? Do you have a degree?"

It was Katya's turn to laugh. "The only degree offered by my school was an MRS."

"A what?"

"An MRS. As in 'missus.' That's what most of my classmates were after, anyway. I was never particularly interested in getting married."

"Why not?"

Katya shrugged. "My father gave me everything I needed. What did I need to get married for?"

"Oh, but that's not why you get married. You get married because you love someone so much you can't stand being apart. Money doesn't have anything to do with it."

Ah, the illusions of the innocent, Katya thought, looking at the glowing face of her new acquaintance. She knew better. Most of her classmates at the all-girl school she'd attended married with the express purpose of finding someone to support them. They were happy enough to hold up their end of the deal—to provide heirs to inherit the family coffers. But no one she knew married for the quaint ideal of love.

What seemed even stranger to her was that this woman, more so than her old classmates, should be looking for someone to provide for her. After all, wasn't the ultimate goal of getting her education to ensure a secure future for herself? So, why then would she think Katya's idea of going to college expressly to find a husband was so outlandish?

Something in the back of her brain, some small niggling thought, tickled her consciousness. Maybe it wasn't enough to have everything done for you. Maybe it was better, more fulfilling, to actually do for yourself. After all, Katya herself had had financial security all her life, and where had that gotten her?

She looked around the bus, at the hardened clumps of gum stuck to the floor, the worn seats with the occasional dirty word inked permanently in the fabric, the tired-looking people doing their best not to fall asleep and miss their stops.

It had gotten her not having to live like this, that's what.

Katya threw back her shoulders and unconsciously lifted her chin. And she'd do whatever she could to get it back, too. She just had to find a way to get that money to Paula Northcraft. She couldn't do this forever, getting up at the crack of dawn to scrub toilets.

Silently thanking her new acquaintance for renewing her vow to get out of this awful situation, Katya mumbled her thanks again for the fare and stood up as the bus lurched to a halt in front of the Royal Palmetto.

CHAPTER FIFTEEN

"YOU have to r-remember to close the bathtub drain after you're done cleaning it," Inez said, her voice echoing off the tiles in the bathroom.

Katya flopped down in the tan leather chair and stared blankly at the wall of the guest room she'd just finished cleaning. Inez had cleaned three rooms for every one that Katya had done, and even then, Inez had to come in and fix several things that Katya had forgotten. It was only her second day on the job, and already she was burned out.

"I'm not cut out for manual labor," Katya muttered, flexing her aching calf muscles. She'd been on her feet for five hours solid, bending, twisting, turning. This was worse than that spa–slash–prison camp she'd gone to last winter to try to lose ten pounds.

"Is it lunchtime yet?" she called out.

Inez stepped from the bathroom, pushing a lock of her thick raven black hair behind one ear. Katya cocked her head, studying the other woman. She considered her own hair color to be black, but it was not the same blue-black as Inez's. Hers had more of a mahogany brown tint to it, especially under direct sunlight. But Inez's hair was a true black and her eyes were so dark as to almost be black themselves. Her smile was shy but mysterious, as if she knew some joke that others did not. Katya suddenly wished she had her paints—the ones that Jillian must have donated to charity along with all her other

things. She had always enjoyed painting and liked painting portraits most of all.

"Let's take our break. We're almost d-done with our
block of rooms, and I'm hungry, too," Inez said.

Katya gratefully followed the other woman out of
the room, pushing the heavy housekeeping cart in front
of her.

She parked her cart in its stall in the employee building before following Inez into the lunchroom. She'd
skipped lunch yesterday, not telling Inez it was because
she didn't have any money to buy anything. Sending a
silent *thank you* to Alex, she patted the twenty-dollar
bill in her pocket. She had no idea how she could make
the hundred dollars he'd loaned her last until payday—
she'd never had to budget before—but it was better than
the fifty cents she'd had yesterday. She'd also been able
to add ten dollars to her nest egg with the tips she'd
collected from cleaning guest rooms this morning. But
she was still a far cry from the five thousand dollars she
needed to pay Paula Northcraft's retainer.

Chewing the inside of her cheek, Katya stepped into
the lunchroom and was immediately overwhelmed by
the noise. At least thirty people in uniforms similar to
hers milled about, eating and chatting. A television in
one corner had been turned up, and the sound of a theme
song played over the din in the room.

"You can order something from the restaurant if you
didn't bring your l-lunch," Inez explained. "Employees
get a fifty percent discount, but it can get expensive eating here every day. Nana usually packs me a lunch."
She held up a bright red sack of some sort to prove it.

"Your grandmother makes lunch for you every
day?" Katya asked incredulously.

Inez smiled one of her mysterious smiles. "Yes. I
think she likes having someone to take care of."

"Don't you find that . . . strange?"

Katya stopped at the row of vending machines lining the back of the lunchroom and pulled a handful of change out of her pants pocket. She'd have to remember to save some money for bus fare for the ride home rather than repeat the scene from this morning. Fortunately, people tipped with small bills, although she wouldn't mind finding a hundred on the next guest room pillow.

She decided on a bagel and a yogurt, not because either sounded particularly enticing, but because they were cheap and filling. Scooping up the items after they dropped into the tray, Katya turned and plopped down at a small, round table with Inez.

"I lived with her up until about a year ago, and I guess she j-just got used to making a little extra for me to take to work the next day," Inez said, pulling a foil-wrapped object from her lunch bag.

"You lived at home until last year?" Katya asked, incredulous.

"Sure. The r-rent was great." Inez smiled.

Katya unfolded two paper napkins and set them in front of her. She placed the raspberry yogurt on one corner and liberated a plastic knife from its wrapper. Next, she unwrapped Saran Wrap from around the bagel, separated the two halves, and opened the small container of cream cheese that had come with it. "It's just that I don't know anyone who lives at home at our age. Hell, I didn't live at home when I was ten, much less thirty."

Inez looked at her curiously. "What do you mean?"

"I mean I went to boarding school for the first time when I was ten. I never went back home after that, except for the occasional visit. After I graduated from finishing school, I used my room at home to store my things—my clothes and whatever I didn't feel like bringing with me. But I never actually *lived* there again."

The hand Inez laid on her arm surprised her even more than the sympathetic light in the other woman's eyes. "That's awful. I can't believe your mother let you go away like that."

Katya gave a hollow laugh and pulled her arm away, ostensibly to pick up half of her bagel. "My mother died when I was ten, so she didn't have much to say about it. Even if she had lived, it probably would have been the same. Most of the girls I went to school with had mothers, and they were right there with me."

Shaking her head, Inez popped open the top of a Diet Pepsi. "I don't believe your mother would have left you all alone like that."

Katya took a bite of her bagel, noting with a small measure of disgust that it tasted exactly like what she imagined the plastic it had been wrapped in would, had she sampled it. Reminding herself that you get what you pay for, she took another bite and forced herself to swallow the doughy bread.

She looked up and met Inez's dark gaze. "I don't mind being alone. I've been alone my entire life."

Katya's eyes widened with shock when the glint of tears appeared in Inez's dark brown eyes.

"I can't imagine how lonely you must have been. I don't know what I would do without my family, especially after my mother died. I'm so sorry, Katya."

Blinking with surprise at Inez's impassioned speech, Katya felt a blush creeping up her neck. She couldn't remember anyone *ever* feeling sorry for her. From what she'd seen in her circle of friends, having a family was highly overrated. If they weren't criticizing your every move, they were trying to control your life. And those were the good ones. Most people she knew grew up just like she had—shipped off to boarding school at a young age. They'd seen their families during vacations to the

Caribbean or Mediterranean at Christmas, and some kids went home for the summer, but others, like her, did not. Some of the kids had siblings in the same school, and some of them even got along. Katya had always been a tiny bit jealous of those kids, but she'd never mentioned it to anyone. She had her own friends, many who came and went over the years, and that was enough. She'd decided at a young age that getting attached to people would only cause you pain when they left, as they ultimately would.

She was spared trying to come up with a response to Inez when a petite blonde stopped at their table and laid a manicured hand on Inez's shoulder. "Inez, dear, how are you?" she asked, flashing a 10,000-watt smile.

"I'm f-fine, Amanda. Have you met Katya Morgan yet?"

The blonde turned her attention to Katya, who was struggling to pry the foil lid from her yogurt. "No, I haven't. Katya, did you say? My, what a lovely name. I'm Amanda Harrington."

Katya looked at the other woman steadily, wondering if she had any idea how phony she sounded. Well, it was none of her concern. Setting down the accursed yogurt, Katya held out a hand, grimacing when she noticed that her own manicure looked terrible. The bright red polish had chipped, and two of the nails on her right hand had broken in ragged lines. "It's nice to meet you, Amanda. Do you work in Housekeeping, too?"

The small woman smiled wickedly. "Yes, for the time being," she said, then turned her attention back to Inez, clearly dismissing Katya. Katya rolled her eyes heavenward. *God save us from haughty housekeepers,* she thought, picking up her recalcitrant yogurt again.

"Tell Alex I said hello," Amanda said, patting Inez's shoulder.

Inez mumbled something incoherent as the blonde turned and walked away.

"I didn't quite catch that," Katya said after Amanda was out of earshot, setting down the open carton of yogurt triumphantly.

Inez's charcoal black lashes fluttered over her dark eyes before she responded, "I said, 'Yes, I'll tell him . . . when hell freezes over, that is.' "

Katya grinned, glad that Inez had seen through Amanda's veneer. "So, what did she mean that she works in Housekeeping for the time being?"

"She's worked at the hotel for almost a year now, and she's made it clear that she's happy to exchange, uh . . ."

"Sex?" Katya offered.

Blushing, Inez nodded. "Yes. She's offered *that* in exchange for a better position, more money, or . . . whatever."

"Whatever?"

"Right now she's, um, friendly with the head chef," Inez explained, then leaned toward Katya. Katya raised her eyebrows at the intrigue but followed Inez's lead and tilted her upper body toward the other woman. "I heard he makes meals for her every day. She shows up at the back door of the kitchen, and he gives her whatever she wants. For free," Inez added, for emphasis of the heinous nature of Amanda's crime.

Katya couldn't help it. She grinned.

"You don't think that's horrible?" Inez asked, obviously shocked at Katya's attitude.

Shaking her head, Katya scraped one last bite of the sweetly sour yogurt from the carton. "No. I don't think that's horrible. It seems to me they both get what they want out of the deal. Maybe if I had been more willing to give in to my father, I might have gotten what I wanted. It seems to me that Amanda knows something I didn't," she said wryly.

"What do you think your father wanted?" Inez asked, balling up her trash.

"I wish I knew. It seems that no matter what I did, he was never pleased. I guess what he really wanted was for me to not be me." Katya managed a nonchalant shrug as she scraped back her chair, the sound muffled by the chatter going on around them. She had started to walk away when she heard Inez's sigh and turned back around to see the other woman starting to gather up her trash.

"Here, I'll get that." Silently Katya cursed herself. Of course they had to clean up after themselves. When was she going to learn that there wasn't a cadre of servants hovering around, waiting to pick up after her anymore? After a lifetime of leaving her messes for others to clean up, though, it wasn't an easy lesson to learn.

Tossing her garbage in a trash can, Katya followed Inez back out into the hall, where they each grabbed a housekeeping cart.

Katya stopped on the sidewalk, enjoying the warmth of the sun on her back. Although much of the magic of the Royal Palmetto had worn off for her in the last week, she still had to admit it was a beautiful hotel. Coral-colored bougainvillea climbed sun-colored stucco walls, reaching toward red-tiled roofs. The bright blue water of the swimming pool sparkled in the early-afternoon sun, glittering invitingly beyond the wrought-iron gate. Katya wished she could strip off her clothes and dive in, wished she could spend the day lying in the cool water, rather than scrubbing bathtubs and dusting lamps. A longing for her old life struck her, hard, right between her shoulder blades.

She shook her head, scattering those thoughts. Two days of real life and she was ready to throw in the towel.

Inwardly mocking herself, she started down the path behind Inez.

"Six more r-rooms and you can call it a day," Inez said, stopping in front of a casita.

Katya sighed and closed her eyes.

"Don't forget to leave extra towels in one-eighteen. Oh, and Mrs. O'Hanlin in room one-twenty complained that her b-bathroom fan wasn't working properly this morning. It might just need to be cleaned. Be s-sure to call Maintenance if that doesn't fix it."

Pulling her cart to a stop, Katya heard Inez knock on the guest room door. "Anything else?" she asked.

Inez flashed her a quick smile. "Just remember, it will get easier the more you d-do it."

"Yeah, I'll bet that's what they tell prostitutes, too."

Katya heard Inez chuckling behind her as she pushed the heavy cart farther down the concrete path.

Alex loosened his tie and unbuttoned the top button of his light blue dress shirt. The morning had been a total waste of time. Chris Hampstead was finally taking an interest in his father's business, after almost two decades of ignoring the source of his own wealth.

Alex wished he'd stayed away for another two decades.

The trouble wasn't that Chris didn't catch on quickly. He was actually a fairly fast learner. The problem was that Chris was arrogant. He was too quick to assure Alex that he "got it" when it seemed the only thing he "got" was on Alex's nerves.

All Barry wanted Alex to do was find something— anything—that Chris would be successful doing. It didn't matter what, Barry had told him when he'd first informed Alex of Chris's decision to enter the hotel business. Alex could see that Chris had designs on his job as general manager, a job that Chris was clearly not suited for.

It wasn't just professional jealousy that made Alex so sure of his position, although he was a big-enough man to admit that jealousy played some small part. After all, he'd put himself through Cornell University, one of the best hotel management schools in the country, to get this job. He'd worked long, hard hours, hoping for the promotion that would get him to the top. So yes, he'd admit, at least to himself, that it bothered him that Chris could have his job so easily, if only he were qualified.

"You look exhausted."

Alex lifted his head at the intrusion. "Thanks, Maria. So glad you noticed," he said dryly.

Maria grinned. "No problem, Bro. That's what sisters are for."

"Hmm," Alex grunted, that one word saying everything.

"You need an office with a better view," she said, leaning her arms on the windowsill and looking out over the scrub-filled vacant lot next door to the hotel.

Alex shrugged. That was the way it was in most hotels. It was the way it should be. The best space on any property should be devoted to the guest rooms, because that's where the revenue came from. Employee areas, even the general manager's office, should be functional, not luxurious.

Alex couldn't help but laugh at people's shocked looks whenever they met in his office, a relatively small square on the top floor of the three-story building that housed the laundry, employee cafeteria, and business offices for the hotel. For some reason, they expected his office to be as glamorous as the guest rooms. He supposed the misconception came from the television series *Hotel* back in the 1980s. He could only wish his office was like that, with its penthouse view of—where had that series been set? San Francisco? But it wasn't, and no other GM he'd ever met had an office like that. Mostly they were stuck somewhere in the back of the house, as the non-public areas were called, somewhere where people had easy access to them, day or night.

Which was exactly why Alex was so tired this afternoon. After he'd come back from dropping Katya at her new apartment last night, the head of catering had cornered him, wanting to discuss how to handle an upcoming event for one of their more difficult clients. That had led to an entire discussion of continuing education and career planning for the manager, which had lasted an extra hour. Then, on the way to his suite, Alex had stopped in at the restaurant to make sure there'd been no further problems with the food, and Jenny Tillman had invited him to join her for a drink so they could discuss some menu changes the chef was hoping to make. At the end of their conversation, Jenny had wanted to talk about Chris's progress and get Alex's opinion as to whether Barry had any intention of giving his only son the Royal Palmetto to run after his official training session was completed.

It was a concern that Alex had himself, although he'd never voiced it. He couldn't imagine the Royal Palmetto with Chris Hampstead at the helm. With a wry smile, Alex told Jenny that he frankly couldn't imagine the Royal Palmetto with anyone else but *him* as general manager, but that he didn't have any insights into Barry's future plans for the hotel. It was entirely possible that Barry planned to let Chris run the hotel and there was nothing that either Alex or Jenny could do about it.

That thought did not make him feel any more relaxed. With a sigh, Alex brought a hand to his forehead and rubbed his temple.

He needed a break. Maybe he'd see if he could get tickets to tonight's game against the Seattle Mariners. It would be tough. Both teams were playing well this season—

The ringing of his cell phone interrupted his train of thought.

"See you later," Maria said, leaving his office with a backward wave. Whatever she'd come to talk to him about must not have been very important, Alex thought, pushing the TALK button on his phone.

"Hello."

"Alex, it's Chris. There's a problem with one of the folding machines down in the laundry. Could you come take a look?"

Alex sighed. What did Chris think he was, the damn maintenance department? But of course he didn't say that. Instead, he said, "Sure. I'll be right down."

He might as well take the interruption as an excuse to go get lunch and see if there were any new developments in the dueling-conferences saga.

He walked out into the hall and pushed the button to call the elevator.

"Well, Alex Sheridan. How are you today?"

Alex turned when he heard the greeting. "Oh, hello, Amanda. What brings you up here?"

The small blonde waved with an impish grin toward the housekeeping cart she had pulled to a stop a few feet away on the carpeted hallway. "It's my turn to take care of cleaning the offices this week. Fortunately, you guys are much easier to clean up after than the guests."

The elevator bell rang and the doors *whoosh*ed open. With a flourish, Alex pushed the heavy cart into the elevator and gestured for Amanda to follow. She smiled up at him.

"You make it seem as if that cart's empty," she said,

and Alex resisted the urge to grin and flex his muscles like the cavemen he knew men were often accused of being.

"It's nothing."

"We could both fit in here. I'd be happy to make room for you," she said, batting her eyelashes up at him.

"That's all right. I'll just take the stairs. I need the exercise anyway," Alex said, despite the fact that he'd completed his customary five-mile run that morning. The last thing he wanted was to be crushed into an elevator with Amanda Harrington. She tended to look at him the way a starving vegetarian might eye a nice ripe peach. Not that he minded being ogled every once in a while, but he had the feeling this was one woman who'd devour him whole.

Alex pushed open the door to the stairwell but his steps halted when he heard a heart-stoppingly loud crash.

What in the hell was that?

He hesitated for just a second before flying down the steps to find out.

CHAPTER SIXTEEN

IT was only 9:30 when the knock sounded on her door, but Katya was already fast asleep.

This toilet-cleaning business was taking its toll on her.

At first, she tried to ignore it, hoping whoever it was would give up and go away. But when her neighbor started banging on their connecting wall, shouting through the paper-thin drywall for her to answer her damn door, she got up.

"Just a minute," she grumbled, tugging her pewter-colored silk bathrobe on over the matching nightgown. At least there were some things she had managed to keep, her favorite nightwear among them.

"Katya, it's me, Alex."

She took the four steps necessary to get her from the couch to the front door and yanked it open. "Alex? What are you doing here?"

"Oh, I'm sorry. Were you in bed already?" he asked, crowding her back into the room.

Katya blinked up at him. He looked as tired as she felt. His five o'clock shadow had lengthened, dragging him well into the evening. He'd changed from his usual starched dress shirt and loosened tie into a pair of thigh-hugging faded blue jeans and a burgundy polo shirt that set off his dark coloring and made his skin glow with a golden hue.

She stepped back to let him in.

"What's the matter?" she asked.

He stood near the breakfast bar, overpowering the room with his presence. He radiated energy, a force that seemed to swell until all the oxygen in the room was gone, leaving her breathless. Katya plopped down on the couch, pulling the faded orange blanket she'd found in the closet last night over her bare feet.

"Amanda Harrington was seriously injured this afternoon. The elevator she was riding in dropped almost two floors before the safety cable caught. She was nearly crushed by her housekeeping cart."

"What? How in the world could that happen?" Katya asked, recalling the petite blonde she had met at lunch today.

"I don't know." Alex was quiet for a moment, staring off into the darkness outside the window in her living room. Then he turned to her, and Katya could read the shock in his eyes. "I was supposed to be in that elevator. She just happened to finish cleaning up the offices just as I pressed the call button. If she hadn't come up behind me with that cart, it would have been me."

Katya didn't have many maternal instincts, but it was obvious that Alex was in need of some comfort. Reaching out, she put her arms around his shoulders and pulled him to her. "But it wasn't you. Everything's all right."

"No, it isn't. It's my fault that Amanda—one of *my* employees—was injured. It should have been me."

"Alex, that's ridiculous. You were just being nice. You didn't cause the accident."

Alex was shaking his head. "But she was my responsibility. And now she could die."

Katya didn't know what to do beyond what she was doing, so she just continued to hold him and pat his strong, muscled back and feel more inadequate than she had ever felt in her life. Why couldn't she be more like him? He always seemed to know what to do to make her feel better. She had no idea what to do to comfort him.

"Would you . . ." She hesitated, then began again, "Would you like to go to the hospital and see how she's doing?"

Alex raised his head, his golden-flecked eyes filled with pain. "I don't know. She has a brother, I think. I'm not sure he'd want to see me."

Katya gave him a fierce hug. "Oh, Alex, no one could possibly blame you for this except yourself. You are not responsible for everything that happens to everyone around you."

He laughed without amusement. "Well, we'll see if Amanda's brother agrees with you."

"He will."

Alex paused, then put two strong fingers under her chin and lifted her face to his. He brushed her lips lightly with his, just a fleeting touch, and then he was gone. "Would you come with me?" he asked softly.

Katya felt dazed by even that tiniest bit of contact. She had no idea what kind of spell this overprotective man had on her, but it certainly was nice. She cleared her throat. "Yes, of course. Just let me change my clothes. I won't be a minute."

Gathering up the well-worn pair of jeans and white tennis shoes, as well as the red GOT MILK? T-shirt she'd put on after work, she stood up and pulled the gray silk nightie over her head.

She heard Alex's sharply indrawn breath before he bellowed, "What are you doing?"

She stood in front of him, wearing nothing but a silky pair of white thong panties, and Alex's heart nearly leaped out of his throat. It wouldn't have been such a difficult feat, since he was certain there was no blood left in it. It had all drained down to his penis, which, despite his earlier distress over what had happened to Amanda, was quite ready to set sadness aside and get down to the business of having sex with the woman standing before him.

"I'm getting dressed," she said, sliding the red T-shirt on over her full breasts.

That didn't help in the slightest.

Alex closed his eyes to keep his eyeballs from popping out of his skull. Apparently, they wanted to join his heart, which was lying in a bloodless heap at Katya's pedicured feet.

When he opened his eyes again, she had pulled the jeans on over her hips and was struggling to button them. "Maria needs to gain some weight," she muttered, fastening the last button.

She sat down next to him on the couch to slip into her shoes, and Alex tried to come to terms with the fact that she had absolutely no idea what she had just done to him. He laid his forehead in his palm.

All she had to do was take her clothes off and he went instantly, pantingly hard.

He was a dead man.

"There it is, ahead on the right. The 'Wuthering Heights' mobile home park." Katya double-checked the slip of paper Alex had handed to her on which he had written Amanda's address. Amanda's brother hadn't been at the hospital when they'd dropped by. Amanda had some serious internal injuries, but at least she was in stable condition. Not content to leave it at that, Alex had asked Katya if she would mind coming with him to talk to her family.

Since he was taking this so hard, Katya had agreed.

Besides, what else did she have to do this evening but sleep?

"It says here they live in number thirteen."

Alex slowed down to make the turn, his headlights sweeping the faded blue-and-gray sign that marked the entrance of the trailer park. It was a nice community, as these things went. Most of the trailers were set on permanent foundations, with well-tended patches of grass surrounding them. A few residents had added artistic touches, such as a plywood cutout of a female gardener, bending down so her polka-dotted lace underwear was revealed, or giant yellow-and-brown butterflies attached to the metal siding, along with the obligatory pink flamingo or two.

"Number thirteen, you said?"

"Yes, here. It's this one." Katya pointed to a single-wide on the left.

Alex stopped the car, then backed up, since he had missed the driveway to the Harringtons' home. He pulled up alongside the front door, then put the car in park and pressed the button to release his seatbelt.

"It's going to be all right." Katya reached out and gave his hand a reassuring squeeze, for which Alex was grateful. He hadn't expected her to be any good at this and was surprised at how much her presence comforted him.

He squeezed her back, then got out of the car.

The front door of the mobile home was flung open before he reached the first step. He saw the blur of amber-brown fur before he heard the first bark, and instinctively stepped back. He hadn't been around dogs much in his life and wasn't sure if the noises being made were friendly or menacing but hoped for the former.

A young man stepped out just as a light on the porch went on, blinding Alex momentarily.

He heard a low growl to his right, which dashed his hopes that the dog was just being friendly. "Katya, don't move," he said to the woman who was plastered against his back.

"Don't worry, I won't," she squeaked.

"Hello. I'm Alex Sheridan, the general manager of the Royal Palmetto. Are you Bobby Harrington?"

"Yes, I'm Bob Harrington. Daisy, heel," the young man commanded.

The dog ceased her growling and trotted back up the stairs, stopping next to Amanda's brother and eyeing them warily.

"Daisy? The dog's name is Daisy?" Katya whispered into Alex's spine. "Killer I could see. But Daisy?"

Alex silently agreed but didn't say anything aloud. The dog looked as if she would be happy to be given the order to rip their throats out, and he didn't want to push his luck.

"Bob, I need to talk to you about your sister. Can I come in?"

"Of course."

Alex slowly inched up the stairs, watching the dog out of the corner of his eye. Bob Harrington turned around, ushering the dog inside the trailer. Alex followed, motioning for Katya to come with him.

Bob sat down automatically in a worn leather recliner, and Alex pulled Katya down next to him on a lumpy couch. Daisy curled up at Bob's feet and laid her head on her front paws but didn't take her eyes off them.

"What kind of dog is that?" Alex asked, trying to ease into the conversation.

"Boxer. Amanda got her because she looks mean, but she's really very sweet."

Alex looked at the sharp fangs protruding from the dog's lower jaw. Right. Very sweet. Alex cleared his

throat, knowing he had to tell Amanda's brother the truth
sometime. "Bob, I'm so sorry about what happened to
Amanda. I feel responsible. I let her take the elevator
before me. I should have made her wait to take the next
one."

Bob shook his head. "I don't blame you, Mr. Sheridan. It was just an accident. This is just so difficult."
He paused, drawing in a ragged breath. "We're all each
other has. We made a pact to stick together. She can't
die. She can't leave me!" The last was said on a wail,
as Bob put his head in his hands and started sobbing.

Katya looked over at Alex, who had a helpless, desperate look in his eyes. She didn't know what to do,
either, in the face of the young man's grief, so she
thought back to when her mother had died. What had
she most wanted someone to do then? The answer came
easily, immediately.

Katya got up off the couch, very slowly so as not
to alarm the dog. She walked over to Bobby and
wrapped her arms around his shaking shoulders, whispering nonsensical words of comfort in his ear.

No, everything wouldn't be all right. Bobby's world
might never be the same, as Katya well knew. But what
did it hurt to murmur soothing words that might ease the
pain in the young man's aching heart? Would it make
him weak, unable to cope with his loss? Would it have
done that to her if someone had made the effort to heal
her after her mother had died? She didn't think so. In
fact, it might have made the healing easier, to know that
someone understood what she was going through.

At last, Bobby's sobs became hiccups, and finally,
he settled. His eyes, when he raised them to her, were
tinged with sadness and a touch of embarrassment. "I'm
sorry," he sniffed.

"Don't be. You love her. You have every right to

be scared." Katya gave his shoulders another squeeze, then stood up and went back to the couch.

"Do you work with her?" Bobby asked, wiping his face with a Kleenex.

"Yes, I do," Katya answered, knowing what Bobby wanted. He wanted her to say something nice about his sister, something he could file away in his memory box to take out later, when he was worried about her. "We hadn't known each other for very long. I only started working at the Royal Palmetto a few days ago. But I knew from the minute I met her that she was smart and she wanted a better life for the two of you. I could see that she was very determined about that."

"Did she mention me at all?" Bobby asked eagerly.

"Um, yes, she did," Katya said, stalling for time. Frantically she looked about the room. She spied some textbooks stacked on the dining room table and crossed her fingers that they didn't belong to Amanda. "She told me how proud she was of your, uh, scholastic achievements."

Katya held her breath until Bobby answered, with a sad smile, "She was the one who should have gone to college, but instead she worked so I could go. She lets me live here, rent-free even, so I don't have to work more than part-time. She's the best sister a guy could ever have."

This started off a whole new round of sobbing, and by the time Bobby had calmed down again, it was well past midnight. Katya tried, unsuccessfully, to hold back a yawn, smothering it with the back of her hand instead.

She looked over at Alex, an unspoken question in her eyes. Did he think Bobby would be all right if they left? Alex nodded imperceptibly.

"Bob, try not to believe the worst is going to happen. Amanda's a strong woman, and she's got great medical care. You don't have to worry about money; the hotel's workers' compensation coverage will pay for everything. Here's my card. Please let me know if there's anything we can do to help."

Katya stood up and clasped Bobby's hand. "If there's anything we can do, anything at all, please let us know."

Bobby looked up at her with sad brown eyes. "There is one thing. . . ."

"Yes, what is it? We'll do anything we can to help."

"Well, I hate to ask, but . . ."

"Yes?"

"It's Daisy," Bobby blurted. "I don't have the time to take care of her, what with school and my job and everything. Sometimes I'm gone twelve, even fourteen hours a day, and no dog can go that long without having an accident. I just can't do it all. She hates being boarded, and I can't take her back to the pound. Amanda just got her a few weeks ago, and if I take her back, it would be like putting her to death."

Katya looked at Alex. He looked back at her.

There was no way they could tell Bobby no.

"All right. We'll take her," Katya said.

Alex's eyes widened, but he had the good grace not to contradict her. "Do you have a leash?"

"Yes. I'll get her things. This means so much to me."

Bobby hustled around the small trailer, tossing various objects into a paper sack. When he was done, he handed the sack to Alex, then clipped a heavy red leather leash onto Daisy's collar. "Here, why don't you take her out to your car and I'll get her food?"

Bobby disappeared. Katya held the end of the leash. Daisy hadn't moved from her supine position on the floor, except to fix her large brown eyes on Katya.

"What the hell are we going to do with her?" Katya whispered to Alex.

"I have no idea. I'm not even sure your apartment allows pets, much less ones as large as Killer here. And I can't take her to the hotel. Barry would fire me on the spot."

"Oh, God, Alex, what are we going to do?" Katya all but wailed.

"Well, for now, let's just get her out to the car. Maybe after things have settled down, we can find a good kennel and get her boarded."

"You're right. That's perfect." Katya started to follow Alex out of the mobile home but stopped short when the immobile object at the end of the leash remained in place. "Uh, here, Daisy. Come on, puppy," she cooed, giving the leash a tug.

Daisy stayed right where she was.

"Oh, come on, Dog. It's late. I want to get to bed." She tugged again.

"Heel, Daisy," Bobby called from outside.

"Eek!" Katya shrieked as the dog leaped up and dashed out the door. Katya clattered down the stairs in her tennis shoes in an attempt to keep up, trying not to break her neck in the process.

Bobby stood by the trunk of Alex's Mustang, an enormous bag of dog food at his feet. "Can you help me get this in the trunk?" he asked Alex.

"Um, wow, thanks for all that food. That must last you about, what, six months?" Katya asked.

Bobby laughed. "No, Daisy will go through this in about a month, won't you, girl?" He ruffled the dog's pointy ears playfully. "I'm going to miss you, but don't you worry. Mommy will be out of the hospital before you know it."

Katya opened the passenger-side door of the Mustang. Daisy jumped in immediately, looking as if she would be more than happy to ride shotgun.

"Oh, no, you don't, Dog. Get in the back." She pointed to the backseat and was amazed when the dog obeyed her command.

Maybe having a dog for a while wasn't going to be so bad after all.

CHAPTER SEVENTEEN

IT wasn't the snuffling or the grunt in her ear that woke Katya—after all, she'd slept with enough men in her life to get used to that—instead, it was the wet sneeze, right in her face, that had her bolting upright with a screech.

"Oh, that's just gross." She wiped her hand across her face, grimacing when it came away wet. She looked for somewhere to wipe it, then spied the glossy tan coat of the culprit. "Here, I believe this is yours," she said, wiping her slobber-soaked hand down the dog's fur.

"What'd you do that for?" she asked, not expecting the dog to answer. "Didn't I make you a nice bed in the kitchen? Didn't I—Where's my robe?" Katya looked around but didn't see the silk garment where she had left it last night, hanging from the edge of the ancient television set. Instead, she saw small bits of gray scattered throughout the apartment. Small bits of gray that looked suspiciously like—

"Aagh!" she roared. "You ate my favorite bathrobe, you mongrel. That's it. As soon as I'm dressed, I'm taking you to the pound. First you sneeze all over me; then you dismember my robe. You're going, and that's final. I'm not putting up with this; I don't even like Amanda in the first place."

She leaped up off the couch in righteous indignation, intending to fling herself into the bathroom for the quickest shower ever, leaving her plenty of time for a trip to the pound.

Katya stopped when she heard a soft whimper from

behind her. Daisy—or The Dog, as Katya was getting used to calling her—had slumped into a lying position, her head resting on her outstretched front paws. Katya narrowed her eyes at The Dog.

"Stop looking at me like that. I do *not* feel sorry for you. I doubt you even know your own name, much less that your previous owner is . . ."

Daisy's eyes had filled with sadness, and if Katya didn't know better, she might have thought The Dog was about to cry. But that was ridiculous. Dogs didn't cry. Especially not bathrobe-eating, slobber-sneezing ones.

No, she probably just needed to go out. Grumbling, Katya changed direction. She tugged on her borrowed jeans and pulled a black sweatshirt with PRINCETON UNIVERSITY embroidered in orange lettering on it over her head. It took a few minutes to locate The Dog's leash, and then a few more to get the animal to follow her.

"Heel," seemed to work best, and Katya couldn't understand why The Dog didn't come when she said "come." The only explanation she could muster, as she trotted down the stairs with The Dog at her heels, had a sexual connotation she didn't want to explore further. As long as she'd found some way to get T.D. to move, she'd just leave it at that.

As she stepped out the front door of her apartment building, Katya discovered another early-morning dog walker out. Not knowing exactly what the routine entailed, she followed the other woman, hoping she'd discover some dog-walking secrets. Instead, she discovered the dog park.

At least, she would think of it forever after as the dog park. There were dozens of people out, wandering around with leashes in one hand and plastic bags in the other. She followed Daisy for a few minutes, trying to give the dog her privacy and wishing she'd hurry it up so Katya could get back to the apartment and get ready for work.

After about ten minutes, she figured she'd given The Dog ample time to relieve herself and turned to leave.

"Excuse me," a tall, beautifully dark-skinned woman said, a belligerent tone to her voice.

Katya wondered what in the world she'd done. Had she invaded the woman's private territory? Had The Dog done something to this woman's small, yapping terrier?

"Yes?" Katya asked, trying to muster some attitude of her own.

"You're supposed to pick up after your dog. If you don't follow the rules, we could all be banned from this park."

"I'm so sorry," Katya apologized, then waited a moment, hoping realization would dawn. But after a minute or two, she still had no idea what in the world the other woman was talking about. "What do mean, exactly?" she asked, finally.

The woman shook her plastic bag in front of Katya's face. It was filled with something brown. "Pick up after your dog. You know. Scoop the poop."

"Oh my God. You mean, you expect me to actually . . ." Katya swallowed. "You want me to pick it up?"

"Yes, that's what the bags are for. The city provides them for dog owners. They're sanitary." The woman thrust an empty bag at her, obviously expecting her to take it.

Katya grabbed the bag, then turned to where she had tried to ignore The Dog making a particularly repulsive mess on the lawn. Unfortunately, it was either clean it up or duke it out with the rather strong-looking woman who was still eyeing her with a healthy measure of disapproval.

She chose the poop.

"This is just too disgusting," she grumbled, kneeling down next to the pile.

"No. Look, you stick your fingers in it, like a glove, then pick it up and pull your hand out," the woman instructed just as Katya was about to make an apparently fatal mistake with the bag.

"I didn't realize there was a wrong way to do this," Katya muttered. But she followed the directions, and it really wasn't so bad. Holding the bag between her thumb and forefinger, she stood back up.

"Now what do I do with it?" she asked the apparent authority on dog excrement.

"There are specially marked waste containers located throughout the park. You just put it in one of those."

"Fine." Katya located the nearest appropriate receptacle and made a beeline for it.

"We dog lovers thank you," the woman called.

Katya merely grunted, hauling The Dog behind her as she disposed of her doggy deposit and made her way back to her apartment.

"The consultants from Overland will be here later this afternoon to start investigating what caused the elevator to drop so suddenly," Alex said to Barry Hampstead as they stood looking at the yellow tape covering the elevator doors on the first floor.

"I'm sure it was just a mechanical failure," Chris said, behind them.

"Hmm. Speaking of mechanical failure, what was wrong with the folding machines yesterday afternoon?"

"The what?" Chris asked.

"The folding machines. You called me and said there was some sort of a problem."

"Oh, that." Chris shrugged dismissively. "One of the

machines just needed to be reset. I took care of it."

Alex wondered why Chris couldn't have just done that in the first place but didn't want to say anything in front of the other man's father. Chris and Barry had enough tension in their relationship. Alex didn't need to add fuel to the fire.

"All right. Keep me posted," Barry said before turning to leave.

Once the older man was out of earshot, Chris looked over at Alex. "The accident made the front page of the *Arizona Republic*. The reporter also found out about the food-poisoning incident we had earlier this week. This is going to be really bad for business."

Alex rubbed a tight spot on his neck. "Yes, it could be," he agreed. He couldn't believe the things that were happening at his hotel, the hotel he had put his heart and soul into making a success this last four years. "We'll just have to work extra hard and pray that nothing like this happens again."

"Yes, I guess we will," Chris agreed.

They both turned when they heard the raucous barking coming from a few feet away.

"Damn it, heel, you stupid dog," Katya cursed from the other end of the thick red leash. "And stop that noise."

"Miss Morgan, how are you this morning? You're looking lovely as always," Chris flattered as Katya finally managed to get the dog to stop dragging her down the hall.

Alex gritted his teeth when Katya laughed and held out a hand to be kissed. "Why, thank you, Chris," she twittered, then said sharply, "No, Daisy. Stop it. Er, heel."

Alex heard the dog growling low in her throat. Her

teeth were bared as she took a menacing step toward Chris's outstretched hand.

"I'm so sorry, Chris. I don't know what's gotten into her. Heel, Daisy," Katya repeated.

Chris muttered something unintelligible, shot Alex an amused glance, and excused himself.

"Good morning, Katya. What can I do for you?" Alex asked.

"You can take this damned dog off my hands, that's what you can do. Do you know what I had to do this morning?"

"Why don't you tell me?" Alex leaned back against the wall and watched Katya pull the resisting dog behind her as she flopped down into a chair near one of the enormous washing machines in the first-floor laundry.

"I had to ... to ... Well, never mind. It's too awful to talk about. Suffice it to say that I'm not cut out for dog ownership. You'll have to take her."

"I can't. There's no way I can have a dog here at the hotel."

"What about your grandmother? Or one of your sisters? How about Lucy? I'm sure Merrilee would love to have a dog."

"Nana lives in a condo that doesn't allow pets. Inez lives in an apartment that might even be smaller than yours, Maria is not the dog type, Martina lives in the dorm at Arizona State, and Lucy can barely keep up with her brood, much less an animal. I'm sorry, Katya, but you're going to have to keep her for now. We can't get rid of her; it would break Bobby's heart."

There was a long, drawn-out sigh from the slumped figure in the chair. "That's what I was afraid you'd say."

Alex tapped his fingers on the wall behind him. "Um, by the way, why exactly did you bring Daisy with you to the hotel?"

Another sigh greeted his question. Katya looked at him, her gray-green eyes so intensely sensual that Alex almost forgot his question by the time she answered, "I had to. I didn't get five feet from my door when she started howling and barking. Mr. Eggers, my next-door neighbor, came out and threatened me with bodily harm if I didn't keep her quiet. You should have seen the struggle I had getting her on the bus." She shook her head woefully.

Alex leaned forward, taking in the fact that Katya hadn't buttoned the top buttons of her uniform and the tops of her taut, round breasts were easily visible from where they spilled out of her white shirt. "How did you convince the driver to let her on the bus with you?" he asked, distracted.

Katya licked her lips and pushed a lock of mahogany hair behind one ear. When her eyes met his, Alex could almost have sworn he saw genuine amusement lurking there. "I told him that she's being trained as a Seeing Eye dog, and I asked if he wanted to bring the wrath of the American Association of the Visually Challenged down on the Valley Metro Transit Authority."

"The American Association of the Visually Challenged?" Alex raised an eyebrow at that.

"Yes. I told him that Ray Charles and Stevie Wonder were charter members. I think I might have mentioned Roy Orbison, too. I couldn't think of anybody younger."

"Roy Orbison? He wasn't blind."

"Oh." Katya paused. "Well then, why is he always wearing those funny-looking glasses?"

"I don't know. Besides, he's dead."

"Oh," Katya said again. "I didn't know that. I hear his songs all the time. I guess the driver must not have known, either, because he let The Dog on."

Alex had to hand it to her; that was some creative thinking.

"If you're not going to take her, then you're going to have to let her come to work with me for a while. At least until she gets used to staying at my place by herself."

"All right. But do the best you can to keep her out of sight."

"Will do, boss." She stood up to leave. "Come on, Dog, we have work to do."

Daisy stopped a few feet away and looked up at him. Her dark brown eyes were fixed on him seriously, as if she were assessing his character. Alex wished he had some doggy treats to toss her. In his experience, most reluctant creatures could be won over by a little something in their belly.

"I'm off to scrub some toilets, maybe see if I can rid a few rooms of dust bunnies. Ta-ta." Katya added a jaunty wave to her tongue-in-cheek *au revoir*.

"Wait a minute, Katya. Would you have dinner with me tonight? There's a new Southwestern place down the road that's supposed to be really good."

"Does it have outdoor seating?"

"I don't know. Would you like me to call them?" Alex asked, wondering why in the world she wanted to know that.

"Please. Since I can't leave The Dog home, we'll have to make it a threesome." She held up the red leather leash, winked at him, and was gone.

"Good morning, Inez," Katya said, wondering whom she should thank for her uncharacteristic good humor this morning. Perhaps it was the anticipation of what might happen after her dinner with Alex Sheridan this evening. There was something about that man that made her toes curl whenever he was within ten feet of her. Maybe to-night she'd have the chance to see what effect he had on her when he was even closer than ten feet away.

She looked up to see Inez watching her and refused to blush at the thought that she had just been contemplating sex with the other woman's brother. After all, she was an adult and was entitled to contemplate the occasional sexual interlude.

Katya pulled her cart out of its spot, looped The Dog's leash around the handle, and started pushing. "So, why doesn't your brother have a girlfriend?" she asked.

Inez, who had been following her, stopped on the warm gray pavement. "What?"

"You heard me. Why doesn't Alex have a girl-friend? He's awfully cute."

Katya heard Inez's footsteps behind her, the heels of her leather flats clicking in the early-morning quiet. "He's had a f-few over the years. He doesn't tell us much about them."

"Why do you think he doesn't have a more permanent relationship?"

"M-me?"

"Yes, you. What do you think is the reason your brother isn't attached by now? Is he secretly gay? Does he have a thing for sheep?"

Inez giggled at that. "N-no, I think he likes women just fine." She was quiet for a minute as Katya helped her get her housekeeping cart into the first room of the day. "I think Alex isn't the type to waste time on the wrong woman."

Katya thought about that statement as she tried to decide whether it would be best to leave The Dog tied up to her cart outside the casita for a minute while she talked to Inez or let Daisy come inside. The Dog made her own decision by lying down next to the cart on the suite's welcome mat. "Make yourself at home," Katya muttered before turning her attention back to Inez. "What do you mean by that?"

Inez gathered up a light blue bucket filled with cleansers and a scrub brush and headed to the bathroom. Katya counted out the supplies she'd need to restock the bathroom and followed her. She might as well help Inez clean up while they chatted.

"I m-mean that Alex is fairly quick to decide if the woman he's dating is not going to be *the* one. If she's not, he figures, why bother?"

"Why bother?" Katya repeated incredulously. "Well, sex, for starters."

"Yes, but having s-s-sex with someone you're not in l-love with isn't the same, is it?" Inez sprayed down the shower, then turned back to Katya with a dreamy look on her face.

Katya rolled her eyes, noticing as she did that one of the ceiling tiles around the bathroom fan was out of place. "Honey, if you think that, you must not be doing it right. Sex is great, no matter *who* you're doing it with. As least, it should be, or what's the point?"

"Well, I think you're wrong and I think Alex would agree with me. Sex with someone you don't love isn't worth it. You feel emptier after it's over than if you'd never done it in the first place."

Katya noticed Inez hadn't stuttered, even once, during her speech and decided she must be pretty serious about the matter to speak so strongly about it. She tossed the used bar of hand soap into the trash can and wiped down the soap dish, thinking about Inez's point. It wasn't true for her, of course. She thought sex could be mutually satisfying, and the quaint notion that love had to be involved be damned. But Inez must believe it. And Alex? Would a man think this way, too?

She doubted it. Probably Alex just liked playing the field and Inez used her own romantic notions to explain why her brother hadn't settled down yet. Yes, that was undoubtedly the case. Katya knew some women believed that sex and a strong emotional attachment went hand in hand, but not her. She had an active and very satisfying sex life, and she hardly considered herself emotionally attached to any of her partners. Hell, she could hardly even remember the last one's name. What had it been? Arturo? Antonio?

"Um, Katya?"

Antoine! Yes, that was it.

"Katya?"

Katya lurched out of her reverie. "Yes, Inez?"

"You've already replaced that bar of soap three times."

She smiled over at her fellow housekeeper. "I guess I have. Well, this one will have to do then. I'd better get going. The Windex awaits."

CHAPTER EIGHTEEN

"I brought the boxes you left in your hotel room last week," Alex said as Katya opened her apartment door to him.

"I'd forgotten all about them." Katya stepped back to allow him in, pressing the back on her earring to keep it in place. She missed her jewelry—the emerald-and-diamond studs she'd bought herself, the ruby teardrops, also a gift from herself, the sapphire bracelet, the diamond choker . . . also bought for herself with her father's money. Katya stopped in the process of putting on the other earring.

Hadn't anyone ever bought jewelry for her? She thought back over the years, to all the men she'd dated. Most had been in her own financial class, where gifts of precious gems were reserved for engagements and the like. Other men she'd dated—like Antoine—were handsome and charming but were the types of men one bought gifts for, not expected gifts from, especially not ones of much value.

She stabbed the gold post through the hole in her ear. What did it matter, except that if the jewelry had truly belonged to her, she could have used it to fund her attorney? As it was, she had nothing but a pair of in-expensive diamond earrings and a lousy-paying job.

Alex set down the last of the boxes and turned to her. "What's wrong?" he asked.

Katya's eyes met his, and he could see the storm

raging in their gray-green depths. She shook her head but didn't say anything.

"Don't want to talk about it? That's fine." He stepped closer then, putting a hand under her chin. "You look beautiful." He kissed her then. Lightly, but with lots of promise. "Are you ready to go?"

Katya's eyes fluttered open, and Alex was glad to see the storm in them receding. He hadn't lied; she did look beautiful. The silvery-gray dress she wore shimmered in the overhead light, stopping a relatively demure three inches above her knees.

"Let me just get The Dog," she answered, her voice low and breathy. Alex was glad to see he wasn't the only one who was affected by their nearness.

"Why don't you call her by her name?" he asked, trying to lighten the conversation.

"Tell me, does she look like a 'Daisy' to you?"

The dog stopped in front of him, holding her leash in her mouth. She looked up at him with her round, dark brown eyes and out-jutted bottom jaw. Then she cocked her head at him, and Alex smiled. "No, but she's cute in her own way."

"Right. Like children. They're cute in their own way, too. Especially when they're throwing up on you, or their diaper needs changing." Katya led the way out into the hall. Alex took the key from her outstretched hand and locked her front door, then handed the key back.

"You don't like children?" he asked as they started down the hall.

She paused, then reluctantly admitted, "Actually, I do. I just don't think I'm ready for them yet."

Alex knew his family would be scandalized, but he felt much the same way himself. He loved his sister's children but wasn't ready to become a father. After helping Nana to raise his sisters, after finally—almost—getting the last one into adulthood, all he wanted was to be free from the responsibility for a while.

"By the way, how is Amanda doing?" Katya asked, changing the subject.

Alex frowned. "I talked to Bobby this afternoon, and he says she's still in critical condition. She's conscious but can't keep any food down. The doctors aren't sure what's wrong. He's promised to keep me posted on her condition, but I know it's hard for him to talk about it."

Alex pressed the button for the lobby and watched the elevator doors inch shut. At the last moment before they closed, a brawny arm covered with dark hair slid into the opening. The doors crept open again, revealing a well-muscled man wearing torn blue jeans and a white T-shirt.

"Good evening, Mr. Eggers." Alex was surprised when Katya greeted the man, who grunted in response.

"Alex, this is my neighbor, Mr. Eggers. Mr. Eggers, my, uh, friend, Alex Sheridan." Katya performed the introduction with perfect politeness. Since Mr. Eggers didn't offer a hand for him to shake, Alex merely nodded in the man's direction.

As the doors started to slide shut again, Katya turned to Alex, only to be interrupted when the leg of a metal walker jammed the doors. He tried not to sigh. At this rate, they'd never get out of the elevator, much less make it to the restaurant on time.

"Hello, Mrs. Wagner. Here, there's plenty of room for you." As the self-appointed greeter of the elevator, Katya welcomed the newest occupant, a short gray-haired lady whose walker sported a bright pink wicker basket with a white flower on the front. An oversize orange-and-cream-striped cat sat in the basket, eyeing the other occupants of the elevator with cool distrust.

Alex was about to ask if it might be better if Daisy and the cat rode down to the lobby in separate elevators when disaster struck. The only warning was the slight growl, low in Daisy's throat, before she leaped. Katya had relaxed her grip on the dog's leash but must have tightened it at the last minute. Daisy stopped inches from Mrs. Wagner's cat, but the cat wasn't waiting around to see if there was going to be a last-minute reprieve. With a yowl, he leaped from the basket, landing on Mr. Eggers's shoulder.

Having eighteen pounds of hissing feline, including outstretched claws, land on him must have come as something of a shock to Mr. Eggers, who screeched and hurled himself out of the elevator. Daisy put all her formidable strength into following, catching Katya off guard.

Katya tried to hold on to the dog's leash but somehow got tangled up in the red leather. The heel of one four-inch silver sandal caught a tear in the worn carpet and she fell, half in and half out of the elevator. Alex would have made an attempt to catch her but had his hands full of Mrs. Wagner, whose walker had tipped over when the cat leaped out.

Katya pulled herself out of the way just as the doors started beeping, giving one final warning that they were closing, no matter what.

Alex's last glimpse of her was not particularly flattering, since her legs were splayed and her skirt had ridden up well past a modest level. But it was tantalizing, all that golden-tan skin exposed. As a matter of fact, the image burned into his brain so much so that when he looked down into the wrinkled face of Mrs. Wagner, he had to stop himself from leaping back in shock.

"Thank you, young man," Mrs. Wagner said.

Alex cleared his throat. "You're welcome. Here, let me help you with your walker."

Once the walker was righted, Alex got it situated so Mrs. Wagner could let go of his arm. She gave his bicep one last squeeze before letting go. "My, but you're a strong one. That Miss Morgan certainly is lucky," she twittered, batting her lashes up at him.

Alex smiled. "Well, thank you, Mrs. Wagner."

"Oh, you can call me Emma, dear."

"Emma, then. Do you think your cat's okay?"

"Tiger? Yes, he should be fine. He's a tad over-weight, but he gets around all right. I'll go right back up and check on him." She punched the button for the fourth floor.

Alex thought the cat was more than a *tad* overweight but didn't bother to argue with Mrs. Wagner. Instead, he stepped out of the elevator when it finally stopped on the first floor. "I'll see you back up there, then. It was nice to meet you," Alex said with a wave before turning to the stairs. He could have sworn he saw Mrs. Wagner eyeing his backside before the elevator doors slid closed, but he dismissed the thought as being ridiculous. He'd bet she wasn't a day under ninety. Surely she wouldn't be checking out his ass, Alex thought as he pounded up the stairs.

He flung open the heavy fire door on the fourth floor to find Katya standing in the hallway, holding a sheepish-looking Daisy by the collar.

"You are a bad, bad dog. Do you hear me? You frightened Mrs. Wagner's cat, and just look at poor Mr. Eggers's shoulder."

Daisy stood listening, her stump of a tail drooping and her head cowed. Katya turned to Mr. Eggers, who was pressing a wet washcloth on the scratches on his arm and eyeing Daisy with disgust. "I am so sorry, Mr. Eggers. This won't happen again."

"It had better not or I'm going to lodge a complaint against you and that damn dog. As if the barking wasn't enough," the hairy man muttered, pushing past Alex on his way downstairs.

"Bad dog," Katya repeated, wagging her finger at the boxer.

"Oh, come on," Alex said as the door to the stairwell closed. "It's not that big of a deal. Daisy couldn't help it. Dogs chase cats; that's just what they do."

"That's easy for you to say. You're not the one who has to live next door to Mr. Eggers. And you're not the one whose favorite shoes are ruined." Katya turned and limped toward her apartment.

"And I'm not the one with a sprained ankle, either. Are you all right?" Alex caught up with her and noticed her wincing.

"No. It hurts."

"Here, stop for a second." She obeyed, and Alex knelt down. He passed a hand over her ankle. It wasn't swollen, which was a good sign.

"Ow, that hurts," she complained when he touched her.

"Let's get you into your apartment and get some ice on this." In one swift movement, he picked her up and carried her to her door. She fumbled around in her purse for a second or two, then awkwardly opened the door just as Mrs. Wagner stepped off the elevator. The elderly woman's eyes widened with surprise and a hand fluttered to her open mouth.

"Oh, my dear, are you all right?"

Alex felt, rather than heard, Katya's sigh. "Yes, Mrs. Wagner. I think I may have just twisted my ankle a bit."

"Well, do let me know if there's anything I can do."

"We will, Mrs. Wagner. Thank you. I hope you find your cat." Alex stepped over the threshold with Daisy following at his heels, then closed the door as Mrs. Wagner stood staring at them. He laid Katya down on the couch, propping her up against some pillows.

"I think Mrs. Wagner likes you," Katya said, attempting to sit up. Alex helped her scoot back, trying not to notice her skirt creeping up her thighs.

"What's not to like?" Alex teased, going into the kitchen in search of some ice to put on Katya's ankle.

"Your inflated ego, for one thing."

Alex grinned at Katya over the countertop. "I think she was admiring my butt back there. Where do you keep your dish towels?"

Katya rolled her eyes with mock disgust, secretly agreeing with Mrs. Wagner on that score. Alex had shown up wearing a pair of black trousers and a patterned silk shirt, with no suit jacket covering the piece of his anatomy in question. She had to admit, at least in the privacy of her own mind, that Alex Sheridan had a very nice backside—probably one of the nicest she'd ever had the pleasure of admiring. But he didn't need to know that. It appeared he had plenty of confidence in that area already.

"I'm not sure," she answered his question about the location of her dish towels. "So far, I haven't had much need for the kitchen." She heard Alex opening and closing drawers; then the freezer *whooshed* open. He emptied a handful of ice cubes into the towel, then came back out and set it on the coffee table.

Gently he slid the sandal off her injured foot and arranged the towel over her ankle. Katya winced at the cold.

"It'll feel better in a minute," he said, then gently unclasped the broken sandal from her other foot and put the pair neatly under the table. "I'm sure you can find a shoe repair shop that will be able to fix your heel."

At the word "heel," Daisy stuck her wet nose against Katya's arm. She patted the dog's head absently.

"Thank you, Alex. I'm sorry, but it looks like our date is ruined. Perhaps we can try this some other time," Katya suggested, disappointed that Alex would be leaving. For whatever reason, she had been looking forward to this evening all day. Maybe it was just the opportunity to eat something different than the Top Ramen she'd found on sale at the grocery store the other day. But whatever the reason, she had felt that little stir of excitement all day. And now it was over, ruined because of The Dog. She shot the boxer an irritated glare, at which point Daisy went to curl up in the corner on a discarded pillow and the remains of Katya's favorite robe, which she'd found under the couch. Her big brown eyes had a liquid quality that almost made it look as if she'd been crying.

Katya had to swallow around a sudden lump in her throat. The Dog looked so forlorn, so lonely, curled up into a ball, as if to protect herself from the pain of the outside world.

As quickly as that, Katya's anger dissipated. She dropped a hand over the side of the couch. Daisy looked at it for a moment, wary, then silently unwrapped herself from the corner and took the few hesitating steps to bring herself to Katya's side.

Katya put a hand on top of the dog's head, then tentatively scratched the soft patch of fur behind her ears. Daisy gave a heartfelt slobbery sigh, then lay down on the floor beside her. All of this took mere seconds, but Katya felt as if something had shifted in her world, in her self. But before she had time to ponder what it might be, Alex's voice interrupted her thoughts.

"Why don't we order dinner in? I'd offer to cook something for you, but I need something more than ramen noodles and diet soda to work with. Unless you're not feeling up to it, of course." Alex cocked his head questioningly.

Katya felt a slow smile bubbling up from deep inside her. Alex wasn't going to cancel their date because she couldn't go out. It felt nice for a change for someone to want to spend an evening with just her, not with her society friends, hoping to see and be seen, but simply to sit and talk. The smile bubbled out, spreading across her face. "Do you know what I'd really like to do?"

Alex rocked back on his heels, stunned for a moment at the force of Katya's smile. He had no idea what had happened to make such radiance shine from her eyes, but he hoped it had been something he'd done. "No. What would you really like to do?"

"I'd like to order pizza. I haven't had pizza—real pizza, not that silly barbecued-chicken or goat-cheese-and-spinach stuff that seems to be so trendy now—in years."

Alex grinned. "What about pepperoni? And black olives?"

"And mushrooms. I love mushrooms."

"Done. I know just the place." He flipped on his cell phone and dialed the number for his favorite Italian restaurant. "They said it'd take about forty minutes," he informed her after placing the order.

"What shall we do until then?" Katya asked, sending him a look that sent his blood pressure up at least ten points.

He swallowed. "Cards. Let's play cards."

Katya laughed, obviously seeing his ploy for what it was. "All right. Cards it is. I think I saw a deck over there," she said, nodding in the direction of the book-case.

Alex searched for a minute or two before finding the well-worn blue-and-white rectangular package neatly secured with two rubber bands. He turned to find Katya staring at him in much the same manner as Mrs. Wagner had been studying him in the elevator.

And women said *men* were only interested in one thing, he thought with a grin. It certainly was a fascinating change, to be the pursued rather than the pursuer. Flattering was the only word he could think of to describe it. Usually women were much less obvious about their attraction to him.

"So, what do you want to play? Old Maid?" Alex suggested with a wicked grin.

"How about poker? I love to gamble."

I'll just bet you do, Alex thought, watching her laugh as she tossed her dark hair over one shoulder, preparing for the challenge.

"I can't believe I lost again," Katya wailed, tossing her cards down on the now-empty pizza box on the coffee table. "My luck was terrible tonight."

Alex took a drink of his beer and hid a grin. It wasn't luck that had betrayed her; it was her expressive eyes. He knew instantly what sort of a hand she had by the light in their exotic depths, but he wasn't about to tell her that. Who knew when that sort of knowledge might come in handy again?

"You know, I'm a little short on cash these days."

The purring note in her voice should have warned him, but Alex was too busy gloating over his win to notice it at first. By the time he did, it was too late. One minute she was sitting beside him on the couch; the next she was straddling his lap.

"Your ankle—" Alex started to protest.

"Is fine. Now, why don't we talk about what you might be willing to accept in exchange for cash? I'm sure I might be able to think of something I have that you might want." She teased open the top button of his shirt, which opened without protest.

Alex leaned his head back on the couch as she opened the next button, and the next. Her lips trailed down his exposed skin, achingly slow, button by button, until they were all undone.

"There, I think that's worth at least five dollars, don't you?" She lifted her head from his abdomen and looked into his half-closed eyes.

"Ten," Alex growled before burying his hands in her silky hair and pulling her lips to his. Alex let his hands wander down her back, around the curve of her buttocks to her firm thighs, the skin exposed as her soft gray skirt crept upward.

"You feel good," Alex groaned as Katya rubbed her hips against his.

"So do you," she whispered against his neck, reaching between them to caress his erection. It was then that Alex realized this was going too fast. He was not one of those wham-bam-thank-you-ma'am types. He preferred to take it slow, to get to know every inch of his partner before the act was done. Nudging Katya off his lap, he stood and held out a hand.

"Let's take a shower."

"A shower? What for?"

Alex pulled Katya to her feet and wrapped an arm around her waist. "Because I want to slow this down."

"What? Why?" Katya almost stomped her foot with frustration. She wanted it, now. She was ready. He was ready. Why should they slow anything down?

Alex smiled down at her, a slow, seductive smile. "Humor me. I promise you'll enjoy it."

Katya gritted her teeth, then let her breath out slowly. An answering smile spread across her lips. She'd never met a man she couldn't control sexually, and she'd guess Alex Sheridan wasn't going to be the first.

"Lead the way."

CHAPTER NINETEEN

HER guess was wrong.

Absolutely 100 percent incorrect.

He'd taken his time, touching her here, kissing her there, until she'd begged him to end the torture. Still, he'd waited. He'd dried her off, his hands gentle with the threadbare towel, before leading her back out into the living room.

Now, as she knelt before him on her narrow couch, every bit of her skin felt electrified, as if one touch from him would send her over the edge. In an attempt to exact some measure of revenge, she took him into her mouth, running her tongue around the tip of his erection. Alex groaned, and she knew he was as close to exploding as she was.

"Enough," he growled, pushing her back onto the pillows, sheathing himself with a condom, and entering her in one swift movement.

Katya raised her hips to meet his thrusts, nearly screaming his name as each long slide brought her closer to release.

Alex touched one swollen nipple—just touched it—and she shattered. Her vision went black and she heard herself cry out, as if hearing the sound from under water. Her limbs went numb and heavy and, as she heard Alex's answering sounds of satisfaction, her entire body relaxed.

•   •   •

It felt like hours before her bones returned to her body.

Katya stared at the dark blue fabric of the couch, trying to think of something witty and clever to say, but her mind was still floating somewhere out over Camelback Mountain. Alex rolled off of her and Katya felt a momentary sense of relief.

Good. He was leaving.

But he just grabbed the blanket she'd left folded on one of the rattan chairs and came back to the couch, nudging her to her side so he could lie next to her. He threw one thickly muscled thigh over her legs and an arm around her waist before pushing her hair off her nape with his lips.

"Comfy?" he asked quietly, his breath tickling her ear.

Katya nodded, still searching in vain for some pithy comment that would let him know it was fine with her if he wanted to leave. She wasn't a cuddler, neither needed nor wanted this after-sex intimacy, but couldn't seem to make her brain come back to life just now.

Closing her eyes, she figured it would be fine. Alex would get tired of lying on the cramped couch soon, and then he'd go.

It was the last thought she had before drifting off to sleep.

He had stayed. All night. His leg thrown over her like some caveman protecting his latest conquest.

The thoughts whirled around in her head like the repeating loop of a tape. He had stayed. And she had let him, hadn't even realized it until he woke her up with whispered words about wishing they could lie in bed all day, but they had to get to work.

Katya had gotten up and run through her morning routine, trying not to bump into Alex at every turn, which wasn't easy, considering the size of her apartment.

Now, as he parked his Mustang in the employee parking lot, he put a hand on her arm before she could leap out of the car.

"Are you feeling all right?" he asked. "You've been awfully quiet this morning."

Katya thought of a surefire way to get him to let her go. "I think I'm starting my period."

"Oh." Alex blinked. "Well, do you have anything to take for the cramps? If not, I'm sure that Maria or Inez will have something you could borrow."

She closed her eyes briefly. She should have known that Alex wouldn't be horrified at her mention of female troubles. After all, he *had* grown up with four sisters.

"I'm fine," she mumbled, flashing him a halfhearted smile. "Come on, Daisy; we don't want to be late." She tugged on the dog's leash, but Daisy didn't budge from the backseat.

"Are you sure? You seem upset to me."

"I'm sure. I'm just not much of a morning person, that's all." Katya flung open the car door, still tugging at Daisy's leash. "Come on; let's go."

Alex got out of the driver's seat and came around to her side of the car. He put his hands on either side of her face, forcing her to look up at him. "I had a great time last night, Katya. Even without the sex, which was pretty terrific."

The smile he shot her could have leveled a small town. Katya felt that boneless feeling again in her knees but forced herself to remain standing. The early-morning sun picked out the golden highlights in his hair and kissed his eyes with sherry-colored lights.

She had to get away from him. She had no idea what she said, but he released her.

"Heel, Daisy," she said the magic words, and the

boxer leaped out of the backseat. Katya turned and fled into the hotel, leaving Alex standing in the parking lot staring after her.

"What in the world was that all about?" he mused aloud. He'd never had a woman flee from him like that, especially not after a night of pretty good—no, make that fucking fantastic—sex.

Just as he was closing the car door, he noticed a splash of red on the floor. Absently he leaned down to pick it up and realized that Katya had forgotten her purse. He closed the door, smiling. Obviously she was a bit flustered this morning.

He locked up the car, taking Katya's purse with him. It gave him a good excuse to have to talk with her later. He had enjoyed her company last night and he intended to continue seeing her. As a matter of fact, there was a party tonight that he had to go to and—

"Nice purse," Chris Hampstead's wiseass comment interrupted Alex's thoughts.

Alex felt his face suffuse with color but refused to respond to Chris's remark, answering instead with only a polite "Good morning."

Fortunately, Chris didn't press the point. With a wave and a mocking smile, Chris headed one way down the sidewalk while Alex went another, heading for his suite, where he could change for work.

"Well, hello there, Miss Rivera, Miss Morgan."

Katya and Inez stopped their carts together on the already-warm pavement on their way to the guest rooms.

"Good morning, Chris," Katya said.

"Mr. H-Hampstead," Inez acknowledged.

"Lovely day, isn't it?" Chris asked, then continued without waiting for an answer, "Can I have a word with you, Miss Morgan? In private."

Katya looked at Inez and shrugged imperceptibly. She had no idea what Chris wanted. Daisy took her usual stance, glaring at Chris with her round eyes, her bottom teeth jutting out belligerently. Inez got her cart rolling again and continued on down the sidewalk.

"Your dog doesn't like me," Chris observed.

"She doesn't like most people," Katya lied. In truth, the only person Daisy had taken an instant dislike to was Chris, but she wasn't about to tell him that.

"Listen, I was wondering if you'd like to come to a party with me tonight? It's at my father's house and there should be plenty of free booze."

Katya opened her mouth to decline, then closed it again. Why shouldn't she go out with Chris? After all, she and Alex hadn't agreed to see only each other. Besides, he didn't mean anything more to her than anyone else she'd ever had sex with, so why shouldn't she accept Chris's invitation? It would probably be fun—just like the old days.

"I'd love to come. Why don't I meet you there? Say seven o'clock?" Katya told herself she didn't want to ride with Chris because she didn't know what she was going to do with Daisy. She knew he wouldn't understand that the dog refused to be left alone, and she couldn't see him allowing the big, slobbering animal to ride in the minuscule backseat of the Porsche she'd seen him hop into a few days ago. That's what she told herself, not putting words to the thought that she felt the tiniest bit uncomfortable about being alone with him. It was a feeling that had grown over the past couple of weeks, from something almost unconscious the first time they'd met to this niggling drip, drip, drip of unease that tickled the hairs on the back of her neck.

Chris took her suggestion in stride, however, not bothering to argue about giving her a ride. "Fine. I'll see you there at seven. I look forward to this evening." He kissed her hand gallantly and strode away, leaving Katya with the strange impulse to wipe the back of her hand on her pants.

Shaking her head at the absurd notion, she turned and made her way to the first room on her list. She was in the bathroom, squeegeeing down the tile, when Inez spoke from behind her. "What did he w-want?"

Katya almost fell into the tub. "You and your brother need to start wearing bells on your shoes," she admonished, turning to face the other woman.

Inez didn't give her her usual Mona Lisa smile. Katya frowned.

"What did he want?" Inez repeated.

"Who? Chris?"

Inez raised her eyebrows.

"Um, he wanted to ask me to accompany him to a party this evening."

"Oh. Well, I'm glad you won't be g-going. I don't like him."

Katya fiddled around with the makeup the room's occupant had left on the countertop. She picked up one jar. Ah, Lancôme. Her favorite. She hoped her own supply of moisturizer would last awhile. At fifty dollars a bottle, she'd have to work for . . . She did the math, then almost gasped as she realized how many bathtubs she'd have to scrub to keep herself in moisturizer.

"Who said I'm not going?" she asked absently, setting the jar on top of a clean washrag on the corner of the counter. How did normal people afford necessities like good makeup if they had to work an entire day just to be able to buy one jar of cream? And what about eye shadow and lipstick? How was she ever going to pay for all the things she'd taken for granted before?

It was a question she was left to ponder at a later

time, because at that moment she had an angry adoring sister to protect herself from. She had always figured Inez as a gentle, peace-loving soul, but Katya was forced to revise her opinion when the younger woman stalked right up to her, pinning her to the bathroom wall.

"What do you mean, you're going?" she hissed, with no trace of a stutter.

"I . . . uh . . . I told Chris I'd go with him. What's wrong with that?"

"What's wrong?" Inez repeated incredulously. "What's wrong is that you and Alex had a d-date last night. And I already heard that he didn't come back to the hotel until this morning. So, it's obvious that you two . . . you . . ." Inez's face blushed bright red as she tried to spit the words out.

Katya folded her arms across her chest and looked at Alex's sister calmly. "It's obvious that we slept together, is that what you're trying to say?"

"Yes." Inez nodded defiantly. "And you can't do that with my brother one night and then go out with C-Chris Hampstead the next."

Her first instinct was to tell Inez that this was really none of her business, but for some reason Katya didn't do that. Instead, she slowly uncrossed her arms and said, "Inez, Alex and I did have a date last night, and what happened between us is our own business. But I can assure you that I'm not betraying your brother by accepting a date with Chris. We don't have any sort of exclusive arrangement. We've only had one date, after all. It's not like Alex asked me to marry him."

Inez snorted inelegantly, then poked Katya's arm with a strong forefinger. "I'm warning you, you'd b-better not hurt my brother."

"I think your brother can take care of himself," Katya said, resolutely turning back to the tub.

She didn't hear Inez retreat, which wasn't surprising. Instead, she sensed the other woman's withdrawal after a moment's hesitation. Katya didn't bother turning around to check.

She already knew that she was alone.

By the time she was ready for her lunch break, Katya was just as irritated at Inez as the younger woman had been with her. After all, Katya thought as she stomped through the employee building on her way to her locker, she had every right to go out with anyone she wished, and it was nobody's business but her own.

She yanked open the metal locker, cursing when it banged into the next one and snapped shut again, forcing her to re-key the combination. She reached inside for her purse, then stopped when she realized the locker was empty.

Where was her purse? Had somebody stolen it?

"That's great. Just what I need." She slammed the door shut and marched out of the women's locker room, intending to report the theft to Personnel.

As she turned the corner, she ran headlong into Alex. He put his arms out to steady her, and Katya felt the skin on her arms tingle, as if he were filled with some kind of electric charge.

"Just the woman I was looking for. You left this in my car this morning." He released her, took a step back, and handed her the red Coach bag she'd grabbed this morning when they'd left her apartment.

He looked gorgeous, as usual, his plain white shirt unbuttoned at the collar, his navy-and-green tie just a bit askew. The only difference was that now she knew exactly what he looked like under all those clothes and now she was the one feeling as if too many of her own buttons were done up. He smiled down at her, still holding her purse out to her.

Katya took it, with a mumbled "thank you," then almost tripped over Daisy when she turned to leave. The dog moved out of the way with a yelp.

"Wait a minute, Katya. I'd like to see you again. I have to go to a cocktail party at Barry Hampstead's house tonight, and I'd love it if you could come with me. We could leave early, maybe make up for the dinner we missed last night. That is, if Mrs. Wagner's cat will cooperate."

He grinned at her, his teeth white and straight against his dark skin.

The longer she stared at him, the more frightened she became. He looked so good to her, so handsome and kind, but all she could think of was that she wanted him to go away. He was dangerous to her in a way that very few people in her life had ever been—in the same way her mother had been, the way that made her know he'd break her heart, her spirit, when he left.

And he would leave.

They all left eventually.

"No. No, I can't. I already have a date." She ran then, back into the women's locker room with Daisy at her heels.

Alex waited a moment, too surprised to do anything but stare after Katya in openmouthed shock. Then he went after her, banging on the door of the locker room first to make sure she was alone. Only she wasn't there at all. The back door was still swinging, but by the time he burst out into the sunshine of the parking lot, she was nowhere to be found.

CHAPTER TWENTY

KATYA'S hands shook as she attempted to fasten the clasp of the costume choker she'd bought for $4.99 at a secondhand shop on the way home. The triple row of rhinestones winked and sparkled at her in the bathroom mirror. The red gown she'd brought with her from Saint Martin gathered just under her full breasts, then swept to the floor in a smooth line. She knew the dress was flattering with the front cut low to show off what were, besides the exotic eyes she'd inherited from her Russian mother, her best assets.

"Damn it," she cursed as one of the matching earrings slid from her fingers into the sink.

She knew in all probability she'd run into Alex tonight. It shouldn't matter. She'd told Inez the truth earlier. She and Alex didn't have an agreement to see each other exclusively. So why was she so nervous about seeing him again?

Daisy snorted from behind her, a decidedly unfeminine sort of noise.

"Don't touch my dress with that wet nose of yours, dog."

The dog tilted her head to one side, and Katya couldn't help but admit that she was just the tiniest bit cute when she did that. She patted Daisy's head, then shooed her out of the bathroom.

"I don't suppose I could leave you here tonight, huh, girl? If you behaved, I'd even bring you a treat. Wouldn't you like that?" She picked up her small strapless black evening bag and stepped out into the corridor, hoping Daisy would lie down and go to sleep.

The whining started first. Katya thought perhaps it was because the dog could still smell her. She stepped farther away from the door. That's when the barking began.

Mr. Eggers popped his head out into the hall, but before he could say a word, Katya held up her apartment key. "I'll get her, Mr. Eggers. I just had to give it a try."

Chewing on the inside of her cheek, Katya stared at the boxer. What was she going to do? Daisy looked up at her expectantly, then dashed to the corner and came back with her red leather leash between her teeth.

"I know you want to come with me, but you can't. It's a party. At a house. A very elegant house," she added for emphasis.

Daisy dropped the leash and lay down at her feet.

Katya sighed. Well, she'd just have to bring Daisy along. Surely at a place the size of Barry Hampstead's there would be somewhere unobtrusive she could tie up the dog.

She clipped the leash onto Daisy's collar and was about to leave when she saw that the dog had barely touched her supper. They'd be gone for at least four hours. Could Daisy go without food and water for that long? She supposed not.

"Hold on," she said, closing the front door again.

She picked up the two plastic bowls and brought them into the kitchen. She emptied the water back into the sink and dried out the white bowl with a dish towel. Then she looked at the red food bowl. Sniffing the contents, she wrinkled her nose.

"Ugh. You eat this stuff?"

Daisy cocked her head again. The doggy equivalent of a shrug, Katya supposed.

She poured the food back into the sack it had come from and stacked the two bowls together. "I can't just walk around carrying these. What do I have to put them in?"

She walked around the apartment, looking for something, without success. Her eyes narrowed on the boxes Alex had stacked in the living room last night. Maybe there was something in there she could use. Quickly she rummaged through the first box, then the next. In the third box she hit pay dirt in the form of a monogrammed tote bag.

Katya gingerly lifted it out of the box. It had been a gift from Jillian the first Christmas after she'd married Katya's father. Katya had barely even acknowledged the gift then. Now, as she took it out of the box, she realized it was full of art supplies—sketch paper, charcoals, pot after pot of paints.

It wasn't elegant, but it was thoughtful. Much more thoughtful than anything her father had ever given her, Katya grudgingly conceded as she emptied the art supplies back into the box.

The tote itself was roomy. It was also a pretty silvery gray color that matched her eyes. Katya put it over her shoulder. It hung nicely, comfortably, at her side, making her feel even worse for being such an ungrateful brat.

Feeling guilty all of a sudden, she tried reminding herself that Jillian had convinced her father to change his will and disinherit his only child.

"But if he loved me, he never would have listened to her," she said to herself in the quiet apartment. And there it was again, that flash of pain laced with anger she felt whenever she thought about her father. Pressing a fist against her aching heart, Katya closed her eyes.

"I need a drink," she mumbled, startled when a cold, wet nose was pressed against her palm. Katya opened her eyes again and scratched Daisy's head. It wasn't quite the same as a double vodka martini, but still she felt some measure of comfort when Daisy looked up at her with pure doggy adoration.

The toot of a taxi's horn blasted from four floors below, hastening Katya's pace. She'd decided to splurge on a cab, not wanting to fight with another bus driver about allowing Daisy to ride with her. *How do people without cars manage to take their dogs to the vet?* she wondered, stuffing Daisy's bowls into the tote bag. She tossed her evening bag on top, grabbed Daisy's leash, and dashed out the door before the cabbie could rouse all the occupants of her building.

The cabdriver didn't want to let Daisy ride in his cab, either, but Katya's assurance that she was donating the boxer to charity—to the Seeing Eye Dog Foundation of Arizona, a partner with the American Association for the Visually Challenged—convinced him to let Daisy in.

"Thank you very much, sir. The people of Arizona appreciate your support." Katya shook the man's hand as she and Daisy disgorged themselves from the cab at their destination. The cabbie had been kind enough to offer to let her ride for free, seeing as how she was donating this fine and expensive animal to such a worthy cause, but Katya insisted on paying her fare. She already had enough in her life to atone for. Telling a little white lie about the dog was fine, but taking advantage of a hardworking cabdriver was too much.

She'd never been to Barry's house before. It was beautiful, a white Georgian mansion with dark green shutters and a rounded balcony on the second floor that would be perfect for giving speeches to the masses. He looked surprised to see her, and even more surprised to see the dog she had in tow.

"Mr. Hampstead, so good to see you again. And,

Mrs. Hampstead, that dress looks fabulous on you." Katya gave the couple her practiced society hug, nothing touching but the arms, of course. "Chris invited me to attend this evening," she said in answer to their unspoken question. She leaned forward conspiratorially. "I agreed to watch a friend's dog, only she didn't tell me it's afraid to be left alone." She gave them the usual Seeing Eye dog routine, then finished with, "I know it's a terrible inconvenience, but I thought you wouldn't mind if I tied her up somewhere out of the way. She won't be any trouble, I assure you."

The Hampsteads hadn't gotten where they were in society by being rude or opposing such popular animals as Seeing Eye dogs. Mrs. Hampstead assured Katya it was no trouble, of course, then led her around the back way to the terrace.

"This is perfect. Thank you so much." Katya looped Daisy's leash around the wrought-iron railing lining the patio at the back of the house.

The tall French doors were open to the elegant living room beyond, which, if Katya's first guess was correct, was furnished with expensive Louis XIV antiques. She followed Mrs. Hampstead up the stairs and into the party, looking back to make sure Daisy wasn't going to make a fuss. The dog seemed content to lie under the wisteria, listening to the music and tinkling of glasses and polite laughter wafting out the doorway of the room beyond.

Chris's mother wafted away on a cloud of blue chiffon, back to join her husband at the front of the house, Katya presumed. Katya stood near the back doors for the time being. For some reason, she didn't feel much like partying tonight. Maybe she just needed a glass of wine or two to loosen her up.

But first things first.

"May I please have a glass of water?" she asked a passing waiter, who held a full tray of drinks balanced on his shoulder. "No, make that two glasses. Large ones."

"Yes, ma'am," the man acknowledged her order with a nod, then went off to deliver his drinks.

Another waiter drifted by, this one holding a tray of hors d'oeuvres aloft.

"What do you have there?" she asked.

"Beef carpaccio, ma'am." The man held the tray of thinly pounded raw meat under her nose.

"Ooh, that's perfect. I'll take the whole tray."

"Pardon me?"

"The tray. I'll take the whole thing. Thank you." So saying, she relieved the waiter of his burden and turned to go outside. Just then, the first waiter returned with her glasses of water. "Here, follow me." She gestured to the first man, who was doing his best not to look curious. *The Hampsteads must be paying him well,* Katya thought.

She stepped out onto the terrace and handed the man the tray of meat so she could get Daisy's bowls out of her bag. Setting them side by side, Katya took the glasses off one tray, dumped the water in the water dish, then proceeded to empty the tray of hors d'oeuvres into Daisy's food dish.

Handing the now-empty tray back to the man, Katya nodded with satisfaction. Now she could go enjoy the party.

"Thank you for your assistance, my good man." She clapped the waiter on the back and preceded him back into the party.

The waiter looked back at Daisy, who was happily munching her expensive dinner, muttered something about rich folks sure being different, and followed Katya inside.

"Hello, Jillian. What a nice surprise. I didn't expect to see you here tonight."

"Alex, how nice to see you." Jillian Morgan turned slightly from the group she was chatting with and gave Alex a friendly almost-kiss on the cheek. "You know everyone here, right?"

"Yes. Good evening, Jack. Lillian. How are you, Dr. Liu?" Alex joined the group, making polite small talk about the usual things while he studied Katya's stepmother. She said the right things and laughed at the right moments, but Alex could see that her smile didn't quite reach her eyes. She looked tired, worried, and it was a small shock to Alex to realize her husband had been dead less than two weeks.

It seemed odd to him that Charles Morgan's death seemed to have affected his wife of less than two years more than his own daughter. But from what Alex had observed, Charles and Katya had not been particularly close. He wondered why. Katya's mother's death should have been the catalyst to bring the two closer together, but it seemed to have done the opposite.

"How is Katya doing?" Jillian asked.

Alex realized that the rest of the group had drifted away, leaving him alone with Jillian. And she had just provided him with the opening to satisfy his curiosity. "Surprisingly well. I expected she would have quit by now, but she's still hanging in there."

Jillian nodded, and Alex heard her small sigh of relief.

"I was just wondering about something, though. About your husband and Katya?"

"Yes?"

"Why were they so distant? I mean, Charles was Katya's only family, but they didn't see each other very often. Why was that? I would have thought they'd be very close because of the death of Katya's mother."

"I wasn't around back then, of course, but I can hazard a guess as to what went wrong. Do you mind if we sit down? I feel as if I've been on my feet all day."

"Of course." Alex put a hand under Jillian's elbow and led her to one of the fancily upholstered couches that had been placed near a bank of windows over-looking the manicured back lawn. Jillian took a seat on the couch and Alex sat down in a wingback chair next to her.

"Not long after Katya's mother, Ana, died, Charles sent Katya away to boarding school. He loved Ana dearly and I think Katya only served as a reminder of what he had lost."

"Does Katya look like her mother?"

"She's almost an exact replica. I don't think Charles consciously set out to hurt her—I doubt he even realized what he was doing at the time—but the fact remains that within a few months, Katya, in effect, lost both of her parents. I think . . ." Jillian hesitated.

"Yes?"

"Well, I believe that Katya's outrageous behavior as an adult was simply a way to get her father to notice her. Unfortunately, he did, but in entirely the wrong way. Every time he criticized her, she'd do something even worse. I don't think she's a bad person. A bit spoiled perhaps—"

Alex laughed at that and Jillian nodded to acknowl-edge her understatement. "All right. More than a bit. Charles gave her everything she could want monetarily but cut her off emotionally."

Alex was about to ask why Charles had disinherited

his only child when a commotion at the other end of the room interrupted his train of thought. He looked toward the French doors and his hands tightened on the arms of his chair.

"Aw, come on, let's dance. This party needs a bit of livening up," Chris Hampstead's slurred voice echoed off the high ceilings of the living room as the partygoers became quiet, but it wasn't the sight of Chris tottering in from the terrace that had Alex tensing. It was the statuesque brunette by his side. The grayish-green-eyed one wearing the shimmering red dress that outlined every curve of her body—all the curves he had explored last night, and into the early hours of the morning.

"Oh, Katya, no," he heard Jillian whisper from beside him, but didn't turn his head.

"Let's kick this party up a notch. What do you say?" Chris reached out to grab a rose out of a large flower arrangement set on a table in the middle of the room. He gave a hearty jerk to the stem, then bumped the table when the rose finally came free.

Alex watched in frozen shock as the vase started to wobble. Chris had turned away, sticking the rose between his teeth as he grabbed Katya and began a lurching impression of the tango.

The vase fell to the hardwood floor with a loud crash, splattering those standing nearby with water. Either Chris was too drunk to hear it or he simply didn't care about the mess he had made. Alex wasn't sure which, but he had seen enough. He leaped to his feet and went over to the couple now spinning in circles around the room.

He grabbed Chris's shoulder. "That's enough, Hampstead. You're causing a scene."

"Hey, get your own girl, Sheridan," Chris said, trying to push past him and continue his dance.

Katya looked up at him, her cheeks flushed. "Alex, I—"

Alex ignored her for the moment, turning back to Chris. "I said enough, Chris. It's time you went to bed. You're drunk."

"Damn right I am. And I'm gonna be even drunker before the night's over."

Chris whipped Katya around, but she stumbled on her high heels and crashed into Alex. Before he could reach out a hand to steady her, she slipped in the pool of water at her feet and went skidding across the floor.

"Whoo-hoo! That was some move," Chris hooted before he, too, slipped in the liquid on the hardwood floor. He was making a desperate grab for the lapels of Alex's jacket when Alex saw a flash of buff-colored fur leap into the air. He heard a low growl, then a thump as Chris and the dog hit the floor. Chris screeched as Daisy attacked, instinctively crossing his arms in front of his face to protect himself.

"Daisy, no!" Katya screamed just as the boxer was about to go for Chris's jugular. The dog looked over at her, still growling.

"No. Bad dog."

Daisy stepped back.

Katya had pushed herself into a sitting position on the floor, attempting to straighten her dress as she did, when the blinding snap of a flashbulb popped in front of her eyes.

Oh, great. This was just what she needed. First Chris had accosted her out on the patio, and now the papers would have her splashed across the society pages, sitting in a puddle of water and looking like a fool.

Well, it wasn't as if this were the first time she'd had to deal with bad press.

Pushing a lock of hair behind her ears, she gratefully

took the hand Alex extended to help her up off the floor.

"Thanks," she muttered, tugging down the hem of her dress.

Alex just grunted, then picked up Daisy's red leash from the wet floor.

"Are you ready to go?" he asked.

"Yes, just let me go get Daisy's things," Katya said, ignoring the whispering around her as she marched resolutely back outside to get the dog's bowls. Once alone, she closed her eyes and let out a ragged sigh. Despite what her father may have thought, she didn't go seeking notoriety. It simply seemed to find her wherever she went. Of course, he would have argued that she put herself in its path by the lifestyle she led, but she'd never known exactly what sort of life it was that he expected her to lead. She wasn't cut out to work at some high-powered corporate job. The finishing school she'd gone to taught her how to appreciate art and music, how to paint and speak foreign languages. Basically, they taught her how to be a good rich man's wife, something Katya had no intention of ever becoming.

She had never wanted what many of her peers did. She liked living alone and liked changing boyfriends with every new place she went.

That ensured that they never got too close.

"Katya?"

She opened her eyes at hearing Alex call her name.

"I'm coming," she said, pushing her thoughts away as she gathered up Daisy's things.

CHAPTER TWENTY-ONE

ALEX had left the top of the Mustang down, and the warm June air pushed its fingers through his hair.

Katya hadn't said a word since they'd left the party. Instead, she sat next to him in the passenger seat, her hands folded primly in her lap. Daisy sat in the middle of the backseat, blocking his view in the rearview mirror. Of the three occupants of the vehicle, she seemed the only one unaffected by this evening's events. As a matter of fact, the dog looked decidedly happy with the wind picking up her jowls and filling them with air as her long pink tongue lolled over to one side of her mouth.

Finally, just to break the uncomfortable silence, Alex said, "Things should calm down a bit at the hotel after tomorrow, with both conferences winding up."

Katya didn't look at him. "Why don't you just say it?"

Alex flipped the right turn signal and pulled onto Lincoln Drive. "Say what?"

"That I embarrassed you. That I caused a scene back there. That my picture's going to be all over the tabloids tomorrow, and I'll look like an idiot."

Tapping the brakes, Alex slowed at the next intersection and hooked a left onto Invergordon. Briefly he glanced over at Katya. "It sounds to me like you don't need anyone to tell you those things. It seems you're already beating yourself up enough without any input from me."

Katya leaned down and pulled her purse from the

oversize tote bag at her feet. She pulled out a rectangular box, opened it, then swore when she discovered it was empty. Damn. She really could use a cigarette right now.

"Besides," Alex continued, "why would I blame you for Chris getting drunk and behaving like an ass? As I recall, it was him—not you—who knocked the vase over and decided to attempt the waterfront tango."

She looked at him then, still holding the empty cigarette box in her hands. "So you're not mad at me?"

Alex shrugged. "Of course not."

Katya looked away again.

"At least not for that."

Her spine straightened and she crossed her arms across her chest. "Oh?"

"The thing is, Katya, if you and I are going to be sleeping together, I expect to be your only partner."

"I didn't have sex with Chris. I just attended a cocktail party with him."

Alex slowed the car, but not for a turn this time. Instead, he pulled into a bus turnout, leaving the motor running. Then he turned to face her. Katya kept staring straight ahead, so he reached out and took her shoulders, forcing her to make eye contact. "Look, Katya, I don't run in the same sort of circles you do. In my world, when you're committed enough to have sex with someone, you're committed enough to stop dating other people. If that's not something you can do, just tell me and we'll end it right now."

Katya opened her mouth to tell him there was no way she would agree to just seeing him exclusively. Then she closed it.

His request wasn't unreasonable. As a matter of fact, she'd always followed that same rule—although unspoken—with her other lovers, despite what he might think.

So why did it seem so much more serious when Alex voiced his request?

Alex smiled at her then and stroked his hands up her bare arms, trailing goose bumps in his wake, and she melted into a puddle of lust beside him. His fingers moved up to tangle in her hair, and he pulled her closer to him. Then he kissed her, his tongue softly caressing hers, and she shivered in the warm night air.

He lifted his lips from hers. "I promise I'll keep you plenty satisfied," he said.

And after last night, she was certain of that. So, why resist and miss out on some of the best sex she'd had in her life?

"I'm sure you will," she said, her voice sounding husky to her own ears.

As she went to pull Alex's lips back to hers, there was a loud, wet sneeze from the backseat, which served as an instantaneous desire-buster.

"Oh, Daisy," Katya wailed, wiping at the back of her neck. "That's gross."

Alex just laughed as he put the car in gear and pulled back out into traffic.

CHAPTER TWENTY-TWO

"YOU h-had a message up at the front desk."

Katya jerked with surprise, then reached out and grabbed the shower curtain rod before she lost her balance and plummeted into the bathtub. Damn Inez and her stealthiness. And damn Daisy for not barking or something to alert her to an intruder. Instead, the dog came padding into the small bathroom alongside Inez, pushing her head into the other woman's palm as she did.

Some watchdog she was.

Katya stepped off of the ledge of the bathtub, where she'd been inspecting the fan that Mrs. O'Hanlin in room #120 kept complaining about, and reached out for the pink slip of paper Inez held out to her.

"Thank you," she said, glancing down to see that it was Paula Northcraft who had called.

Inez shot her a look that could have chilled dry ice, then turned to leave.

Katya put a hand on the other woman's shoulder. "Inez, please talk to me," Katya pleaded.

Still nothing.

"Look, what happens between Alex and me is private, but I will tell you that, in retrospect, I see that I shouldn't have agreed to go out with Chris while I'm having . . . uh, while I'm dating your brother. Okay?"

More silence.

"As a matter of fact, my so-called date with Chris was a disaster from start to finish. It's actually pretty funny, now that I've had some time to think about it."

"I'm sure this is all pretty f-funny to you. Rich girl gets to play housekeeper and toy with the general m-manager for a few days. Ha ha."

"No. That's not what I meant. Believe me, I don't find anything amusing about persistent stains or mildewed grout."

Katya knew she was in trouble then. Inez didn't even crack a smile.

"Please, don't give me the silent treatment. I can explain—"

Inez sat down on the closed toilet lid and shrugged. "F-fine. Then explain to me the picture I saw in the paper this morning of you and Chris. Why don't you l-leave Alex alone and take Chris instead? He can give you the kind of life you seem to want."

As a diversionary tactic, Katya sprayed glass cleaner on the mirror and started wiping it down. Inez made a very good point. Why didn't she simply latch onto Chris Hampstead and leave Alex alone? Chris was probably in line for a trust fund, would probably inherit the Royal Palmetto itself when his father died. Certainly he had more promise of giving her back her old life than Alex Sheridan did.

So why was the idea so distasteful to her?

Even before Chris's drunken groping last night— something she'd certainly experienced often enough with other men in the past—she hadn't been attracted to him. It was Alex who turned her insides to molten lust, not Chris. And as wild as she may have been in the past, she had never dated a man simply because he was rich. In fact, it was typically her money that funded the relationships she'd had. Or, rather, her daddy's money.

But how could she explain this to the raven-haired

sister who so obviously wanted to protect her sibling from harm?

Katya put the cleanser down on the counter and sat down on the edge of the bathtub. "I don't care about how much money Alex does or doesn't have. I have an attorney who is going to help me get my inheritance back. It's just going to take some time. In the meantime, I'm going to continue dating your brother." She held up her hand when Inez started to protest. "No, hear me out. Alex and I are attracted to each other, nothing more. He's not looking for any more of a commitment from me than I am from him. If he's okay with that, why aren't you?"

Inez looked at her then, her eyes as dark and sad as Daisy's. "I think you're lying to yourself. I think Alex wants m-more."

Katya smiled at that, feeling sad inside. "Inez, look at me. Look at my life. I travel from town to town. I go to glamorous parties and dance until all hours of the night. I drink. I gamble. I lie by the pool. Do you really think Alex wants a long-term relationship with someone like me?"

Inez cocked her head at that, appearing to consider it from a different angle.

"I guess you're right," she said slowly and without stuttering. "I guess he couldn't expect anything more from you than that."

Katya felt a red-hot knife of pain in her chest. She tried taking a deep breath to put out the flame, but that didn't work.

What was that saying? she asked herself, staring up at the ceiling as she blinked back tears.

"Sometimes the truth hurts."

Yes. That's the one.

She blinked again to clear up the last bit of moisture

in her eyes. And that's when she saw it. She got back into the position she'd been in when Inez had first intruded, balancing on the bathtub ledge, her back against the cool green and white tiles.

"What are you doing?" Inez asked, looking up at her from her seat on the toilet lid.

"Trying to find a way to escape this conversation." Katya knew she was at least momentarily forgiven when Inez chuckled at that. "No, I just saw something protruding from the fan that Mrs. O'Hanlin keeps complaining about. Here, give me a hand, would you?"

Inez hopped up onto the bathtub ledge and helped hold the grate in place while Katya untwisted the screws with her fingernail. Thinking this was a game she needed to be a part of, Daisy jumped into the bathtub with them and put her front paws up onto the tile.

"I'm not certain I want to know the answer to this, but what's going on here?" Alex asked dryly from the entrance of the bathroom, startling them all.

Katya gasped and lost her precarious balance on the ledge of the tub. She fell first, barely missing Daisy, who started barking at all the fun. Inez toppled next, landing on Katya's back. Fortunately, she wasn't heavy and hadn't had far to fall.

Alex was across the room and up on to the rim of the bathtub in two quick strides, catching the fan grate just before it fell away from its loosened screws. It landed squarely in his hands, weighted down by a small black electronic box of some sort with a wire protruding from one end. It was this wire that Katya had seen poking out of the grate.

She sat up in the bathtub and Inez scrambled out. Daisy sat down and started panting, the occasional dribble of drool dripping onto the porcelain.

"What's that?" Katya asked as Alex turned the box over in his hands.

Alex was silent for a moment, then looked down and met her gaze. "I think it's a video camera," he answered.

CHAPTER TWENTY-THREE

"I'M sorry I acted like such a jerk last night."

Chris Hampstead caught up with Katya and Alex just outside the door to Alex's office. "I don't know what got into me." He paused, then gave a short laugh. "Well, yes, I guess I do. A bit too much bourbon is what got into me."

Alex just shrugged. He had more to worry about than the owner's son's poor behavior. Finding a camera in one of the guest rooms was a GM's second-to-worst nightmare; the worst being a hotel fire that could kill or injure a large number of guests. While taping guests in their rooms wouldn't lead to death or injury, it could lead to the demise of the hotel that Alex had worked so hard to restore over the past four years.

He shuddered, remembering the scandal a few years back when a hotel chain had been accused of installing their peepholes backward so anyone in the hallway could look into a room and see what the occupants were doing. It had rocked people's sense of security. For whatever reason, people seemed to believe that they were safer at a hotel than they were in their own homes. Alex didn't know why that phenomenon existed, but he had seen it firsthand too many times to ignore it now. Normally cautious people who wouldn't think of unlocking their front doors for strangers would open their hotel room to anyone announcing himself as a hotel employee. They didn't pay attention to the person lurking behind them in the hallways, never for a minute thinking that person might follow them into their hotel room to rape, rob, or murder them. They left valuables out in the open with balcony doors unlocked, unconcerned about who might be in the next room or wandering around the property, just waiting for such an opportunity.

And now, at his hotel, this unwritten promise of safety and privacy had been violated.

Alex swallowed the bile rising in his throat.

"Is there anything I can do to help?" Katya asked, and Alex realized that he had somehow managed to sit down behind his desk without even realizing it. The black box sat atop a neat pile of papers, staring back at him.

He didn't know how she could possibly help him when he had no idea how to handle this situation. The first thing he would do was order a search of all the guest rooms. With so many guests checking out today, it would be relatively easy to have the head of security and his staff perform room inspections before the next wave of guests checked in.

Alex hadn't thought any further than that. He didn't know who had placed the recording device and had no way to tell how long it might have been there. What if pictures of his guests were plastered over the Internet or being sold at adult video stores? The camera had been placed with a full view of the bath.

Thinking of the shower he and Katya had shared two nights ago in her apartment, Alex fought a wave of anger. How would he feel if it had been them who had been taped, if it had been his suite that had been rigged? He could only imagine the embarrassment his family would go through if they saw pictures like that. Not that he was ashamed of having sex with a consenting adult. It was purely a matter of violating people's privacy.

"No. I need to think about how to handle this.

Would you both excuse me?" Alex asked, clearly dismissing both Katya and Chris.

Katya tried not to feel offended as she shut the door behind her, but it wasn't easy. She was not accustomed to being dismissed.

Katya was halfway through dialing the number Paula Northcraft had left on the message Inez had handed her before they called a truce when an idea struck. Katya hung up the receiver and sat down at the desk in the guest room she was cleaning. Who would have thought her own mildly scandalous behavior might come to her rescue someday?

Hurriedly she dialed the familiar number of her old family home, hoping that Jillian would be in.

The phone was answered on the third ring. Yes, Mrs. Morgan was at home. Would she hold for a moment?

Katya cleared her throat in the ensuing silence.

"Hello, Katya," Jillian answered, a heavy dose of caution in her voice.

"Hi, Jillian. Do you remember the year before last, when I got into some trouble with that Spaniard who threatened to sell pictures of us to that tabloid unless Daddy paid him off?"

"Of course I remember. It happened during our honeymoon."

Katya grimaced. "Oh, right. I'm sorry."

There was a long painful pause during which Katya found herself almost wishing her stepmother would say something like, "It's all right. I forgive you." But she remained steadfastly silent, and Katya supposed she couldn't blame her.

"Well, anyway, Daddy refused to pay the man off, knowing the blackmail would never end, but there was virtually no scandal. Did Daddy pay someone to hush it all up?"

"Not exactly."

"What do you mean?"

Jillian sighed a long-suffering sigh. "I mean he paid a public relations firm that specializes in disaster control to be at the ready. Fortunately, your boyfriend either decided to do the honorable thing—which I doubt was the case—or really didn't have the photos he claimed to have. In the end, the whole thing just blew over."

"I told Daddy I didn't believe Enrique had us photographed," Katya said triumphantly. She may have been a bit wild at times, but she wouldn't have willingly let the man take pictures of them in flagrante delicto. As she recalled, Enrique had been *muy* delicto. Until he tried to blackmail her, of course. At that point, he became persona non grata, in whatever language you wanted to use.

"Do you happen to remember the name of the PR firm?"

"Why? Katya, please tell me this whole thing with Chris Hampstead isn't any worse than what we all saw last night."

Katya frowned at that. Why would Jillian care if her stepdaughter's name was dragged through the mud? It wasn't as if it made any difference to her now that Charles Morgan was dead. Katya hesitated, then asked the question. "Why would it matter to you if it was?"

Jillian's answer was too quick to be a lie. "Because, Katya, underneath all of your spoiled brat behavior, I always thought that you were a good person. I wanted to believe that all you were after was some much-needed attention from your father. I tried to tell him that, but he wouldn't listen. Please don't tell me I was wrong."

"You . . . You always thought I was a good person?"

Jillian laughed shortly. "Yes. Despite the drinking and the gambling and the scanty clothes."

"But why?" Katya asked, feeling as if she were ten years old again.

"I never saw you do anything cruel to anyone. And you always remembered to send your father a gift on his birthday. That meant a lot to him."

If Katya hadn't been sitting down before, she would have sat down now. Was this the only evidence Jillian had to determine the type of person her stepdaughter was? And was she really so one-dimensional? It was as if Katya Morgan only existed on the surface, as if she were one of the paper dolls she and her mother used to play with when she was a child. Put the party dress on the Katya doll and have her go out dancing. Put on the thong bikini and prop her up by the pool. Have her say hello to the butler who's paid to be nice to her. And make her remember her father's birthday because that proves the paper doll has a heart.

Katya held the receiver to her ear while twin tears dripped down her face and splashed on the veneered surface of the desk. She closed her eyes and two more tears dripped out and onto the pink message slip where her attorney's contact information was written.

She was standing at the edge of an abyss, peering into the unknown blackness. It was dark down there. And scary. This was the problem with having personal conversations like this. They hurt too much. It was far better to drink and gamble and lie by the pool with people who called you friend but knew nothing about you and wanted to keep it that way. All they really wanted to know about you was if you were up for a party.

And if that made her one-dimensional, then so what? At least that one-dimensional being didn't spend all her time crying and feeling guilty and lonely.

She opened her eyes, letting the tears dry by themselves.

"It's not me who needs the PR firm this time. It's Alex. There's been some trouble at the Royal Palmetto and I thought he could use some professional help."

"Oh," Jillian said, sounding surprised. "Let me look through my address book. I'm sure I kept the number just in case we needed it again."

Katya drummed her ragged fingernails on the desk, trying not to look at them. She needed to get to a salon to have the acrylic tips stripped off, but she didn't have the money. She had taken to the habit of putting the cost of everything into "I have to clean x number of rooms to pay for this" terms. It would cost her six rooms to get a manicure, and that was way too high a price to be paid. Especially when she needed to save all her money for the attorney who could give her back her old life and the one-dimensional status she missed so badly.

Jillian came back on the line and gave her the information, then wished her well and hung up.

Katya looked down at the pink piece of paper in her hand.

She'd call Paula Northcraft first, then give Alex the number for the PR firm.

After all, she had her priorities.

"I'm sorry, Paula, I don't have your money yet."

"I figured as much when I didn't hear from you. We'll need to get that squared away before I can start your case in earnest, but in the meantime I did some preliminary checking around in the public records."

Katya sat up straighter in the uncomfortable chair. "What did you find out?"

"Not much."

Katya slumped back to her original position.

"The will was very brief. Pretty much word for word what you told me. Your father bequeathed some minimal amounts to the current staff and stipulated that the remainder of his estate go into the Morgan Family Trust."

"What are the terms of the trust?"

"I don't know. That's not a matter of public record. A lot of wealthy people handle their estates this way. It's really the only way to ensure that the details of their bequests remain private."

"Well, why can't we just go down to the bank and ask to see the trust agreement? As Daddy's only living blood relative, I should be entitled to see it."

"Actually, you're not. The trust agreement can be made as secret as the creator of the trust wishes it to be. You say your father's attorney mentioned that your stepmother is the only one with access to the details of the agreement?"

"Yes. That's what he said on the day of the funeral."

"Hmm." Paula paused. "I'm going to have to think about this for a while. You do realize your father was not obligated to leave his money to you, don't you?" she asked, not unkindly.

Katya sighed. "I know. It just seems so unfair that he left it all to Jillian. They'd only been married for two years."

"I can see how you'd feel that way, and I'm happy to try to build a case for you. I just want you to know that, in the strict eyes of the law, your father could leave his money to anyone he wanted. Even if he'd wanted to fund research into a cure for cancer in fleas or donate it all to the Loyal Order of Labradors, he could do that."

"Then why would you even bother to take my case?"

"Because I think there's some precedent out there that might help us. But there are no guarantees how a jury will decide. You've got twelve people in that jury box, twelve people who probably have no idea what it's like to grow up rich and who may just resent the hell out of you because of the cushy life you've led. Now, I'm not saying they will, mind you. I'm just saying they could, and then you'd end up with nothing besides bills from me."

"I understand," Katya said with a sick feeling in the pit of her stomach. A week ago, she had been so certain that she was in the right and Jillian in the wrong. She had felt confident that all she had to do was hire an attorney and this issue would be resolved.

Now she wasn't so sure.

What if she didn't win?

Daisy padded over with her leash dangling from her jaws—her signal that she needed to go outside. Katya stood up and clipped the leash onto Daisy's collar.

Five thousand dollars. That's how much she'd have to pay Paula just to get started.

How many hotel rooms was that?

Katya stopped abruptly on the warm sidewalk. Daisy tugged on the leash, but Katya didn't budge.

Eight hundred and fifty.

That's how many toilets she'd have to scrub, how many minibars she'd have to restock, how many TVs she'd have to dust, in order to pay her attorney's retainer. And if she lost, she'd be even worse off than she was now.

Daisy tugged the leash again, and Katya blindly followed the dog over to an intriguing clump of flowers that begged to be sniffed.

The answer was easy, she supposed.

She just couldn't lose.

CHAPTER TWENTY-FOUR

BY seven o'clock that night, the cattlemen had all checked out, followed by the animal rights activists. The PR firm had been called and they were busy brainstorming, promising to call him first thing tomorrow. Apparently, handling scandals was a seven-day-a-week job, too, Alex thought, leaning back in his chair.

In the painting hanging on the wall across from him, the Royal Palmetto looked calm and elegant, as if nothing could disrupt its soothing ambience.

Looks could certainly be deceiving.

He had to stop thinking about it, stop worrying about it, or he'd go crazy. Just the thought of this sort of scandal tainting the Royal Palmetto—tainting *his* hotel—made him feel as if he were about to throw up.

He had to get out of here.

Grabbing his cell phone and his suit jacket, Alex left the office, carefully locking the door behind him. He was in his convertible moments later, speeding away from the hotel he loved so much and toward the woman who made him forget everything but her.

He would have called first, but she didn't have a phone. Alex made a mental note to take care of that tomorrow, then smiled for the first time since they'd discovered the camera in the guest room. He was doing it again—taking care of his damsel in distress.

The thing was, it made him feel good to do it. He liked taking care of people, so why fight the urge? Besides, he'd never met anyone who needed help worse than Katya Morgan.

Alex was still smiling when he pulled to the curb outside of Katya's apartment building.

The sun was sliding down Camelback Mountain in preparation for disappearing for the night, but they had a good thirty minutes to go before it got dark. Squinting, Alex watched the mountain change from drab brown to a rich red as the sun's rays touched it.

Just as he finished putting up the convertible's top, a woman rounded the corner and headed his way. Alex admired the acres of smooth, tanned skin exposed by a pair of denim shorts. She had on a loose red T-shirt and wore her Keds without socks, as usual. Her hair glinted red in the sun's path, much like the mountain rising up behind her had.

He never tired of looking at her.

She saw him then and smiled, waving with a hand loaded down with a grocery bag.

Alex stepped out of the car and pressed the appropriate button on his key chain to lock the doors.

"Here, let me get those for you," he offered, moving to stand in front of her on the warm sidewalk.

"Thank you." She handed the heavy bags to him without protest, and Alex grinned when he saw that she had tied two plastic grocery bags together and arranged them over Daisy's back like saddlebags.

"I see you've put the dog to work."

Katya shifted Daisy's leash from her right hand to her left so she could push a lock of mahogany-colored hair behind her ear. "I figured it was fitting punishment."

"Why?"

"She won't let me go anywhere—including the grocery store—without her. This way, at least she can be of some use. I only give her the light ones to haul, but at least my arms don't get so loaded down that I can't see around the bags. She doesn't seem to mind. When I get my inheritance back, she might come in handy at Bergdorf's annual sale."

That comment darkened Alex's mood considerably. He hadn't realized Katya was still thinking in terms of when she became rich again, had thought that she'd accepted her new life. Apparently, he'd been wrong, but it wasn't something he wanted to discuss tonight. Tonight he simply wanted to relax.

"Of course," Katya continued, obviously unaware of his mood shift, "I guess she'll be back with Amanda by then."

They stopped in front of the glass doors leading to the entry hall of the apartment building and Alex held out a hand for Katya's keys, but she was already unlocking the door and pulling it open.

As they stopped to wait for the elevator, Katya pulled the grocery bags from Daisy's back.

"You'll be back with your real owner in a few weeks, dog. It couldn't be soon enough for me," Katya said, absently scratching Daisy's head as the dog looked back at her with enormous brown eyes.

Alex watched the exchange, wondering if Katya thought she was kidding anyone with her act. She certainly wasn't fooling him.

The pampered princess and the bucktoothed boxer had bonded.

The elevator bell rang and the doors wheezed open as Alex kept his eyes peeled for Mrs. Wagner and Mr. Eggers. Not that he hadn't immensely enjoyed how his last date with Katya had turned out, but he really didn't want to risk bodily injury to get laid again.

Alex stepped into the elevator after ushering Katya inside. He pressed the button for the fourth floor and waited for the ancient machinery to begin working.

"So, what brings you here?" Katya asked, after telling Daisy to sit. "You can't tell me that you missed me already."

"What if I said that I did?"

Katya smiled at him then, and Alex was struck again at the exotic tilt of her grayish-green eyes. He'd be willing to bet she'd left a few broken hearts scattered in the wake of her travels. She dropped Daisy's leash on the floor of the elevator and stepped forward to close the gap between them. "I'd say," she began, her voice low and husky, "that's a good answer."

With that, she slid her hands around his neck, tangling her fingers in his hair. She pressed her lips to his, her tongue tangoing with his as if they'd been doing this dance for a lifetime, rather than just a few days.

Alex let the grocery bags slip to the floor and wrapped his arms around her waist. It was so hard to take things slowly with her. It seemed that all she had to do was smile up at him and he was instantly ready to throw her down onto the floor—or push her against the elevator wall—and make love to her.

She wrapped her left leg around him and rubbed against him like a cat after a bowl of cream. Alex groaned, knowing the elevator doors were going to open much too quickly for his liking.

He opened his eyes and reluctantly pulled his mouth from hers. "Katya, we have to stop."

She looked up at him, a teasing light in her eyes. "We can always stop the elevator if we need more time."

Alex groaned again when Katya pressed against him. "We couldn't do that."

"Why not?"

"We can't have sex on the elevator. They only do that in movies."

Katya reached backward and pressed a button. The elevator hissed to a stop. "Hold on, Alex. It's going to be a bumpy ride," she said, stealing a line from said movies.

Alex opened his mouth to protest, then closed it again. Was he insane? This was every man's dream, a beautiful woman offering him sex on an elevator. Of course, the dream typically didn't include a drooling dog and a week's worth of groceries, but a guy had to take what he could get.

So he did.

Alex had never considered the logistics of elevator sex before, but somehow they managed. It helped that Katya seemed to know what she was doing. First she led him into the corner, and then she stripped him of his tie. Next she teased his tongue with hers until Alex didn't care anymore that they were tying up the elevator. Then she unbuckled his belt and unzipped his pants and Alex stopped thinking about anything except her hands stroking him, her thumb sliding around this tip of his penis, making him want to come right then and there.

He pulled back for a moment, just to make sure he didn't waste this opportunity by ejaculating into her hand like an uninitiated teenager.

"Your turn," he said softly, licking the tender skin just below her ear. He grinned with male satisfaction when she let out a moan. He trailed kisses down her neck while his hands were busy with the snap of her shorts. They stuck a little as he pulled them off her hips and slid them down her legs.

He touched her then, running his fingers lightly across the sensitive skin at the juncture of her thighs. Her breath was coming faster now and she threw her head back, crushing her long straight hair against the wall of the elevator.

Alex slipped a finger inside her, feeling her close around him. She squirmed when he moved out of her, then back in, his thumb teasing her slowly. Katya pulled his head down to hers and kissed him, her tongue mimicking what his fingers were doing to her. Her breath came in little pants, and Alex knew she was about to come apart. She pulled her mouth from his and whispered into his ear, her voice sounding desperate, "Fuck me, Alex."

Instead of being shocked at her words, Alex was turned on. What a nice surprise to have a woman who was not shy about initiating sex, who didn't have to be wooed into it with flowery words and chocolates.

Slipping his fingers out of her slick wetness, Alex obliged her. Balancing her hips on the metal railing that ran along the sides and back of the elevator car, Katya wrapped her legs around his waist. Alex guided himself into her, surprised at the force of his lust. Her heels dug into his back as he thrust into her once, then again.

That was all it took for them both.

Alex felt his brain explode behind his eyeballs, his thoughts disappearing into a vortex of sensation. Katya stiffened against him, their moans of pleasure mingling in the otherwise quiet space.

They remained locked together for a moment . . . or a lifetime. Alex wasn't sure which.

"*Ay, Dios mio!* That was—" The elevator lurched, cutting off whatever prayer it was Katya had started.

Still lost in the aftermath of his orgasm, it took Alex a few seconds to realize what was happening. Fortunately, Katya seemed to have recovered a bit faster. He watched her slide her shorts back up and tug on the zipper. Then she turned to him and grinned.

"Here, let's get you back in order," she said, tucking in all the necessary parts before zipping him back up.

She had just finished buckling his belt when the elevator doors slid open.

Alex blinked rapidly, trying to recapture his brain, which seemed to have blown out of the top of his head a minute ago.

"I don't know what in the world is wrong with this elevator," Mrs. Wagner said, rolling her walker toward him. Fortunately, Tiger must have stayed in the apartment this trip.

Alex tried not to blush, since he knew very well what had held up the elevator just now.

Katya, on the other hand, looked to be totally in control of the situation. She picked up Daisy's leash and her two grocery bags and said, "I know, Mrs. Wagner. It's amazing how slow it can be sometimes. Alex, would you be a dear and get those other two sacks for me?"

Alex reached down to pick up the plastic bags, then whipped around. He was certain he'd felt someone pinch his ass. But surely Mrs. Wagner wouldn't . . .

The elderly woman looked at him and winked as Alex stepped off the elevator. In a sex-filled daze, he followed Katya to her door.

"Mrs. Wagner has a crush on you, you know," she said, entering her apartment.

Alex set the grocery bags on the counter in her tiny kitchen. "I think I just realized that."

"She caught up with me the other day in the lobby and asked when I thought you were going to come by again. She told me she thinks you're cute."

"Hmm," Alex said, opening the refrigerator to put away the butter and milk Katya had bought.

Katya came up behind him and slid her arms around his waist, pressing her hips against his. "I agree with her on that."

Alex smiled, folding his arms over hers. He felt her

breasts against his back, but rather than feeling lust, he felt tenderness instead. Turning, he pulled her to him and dropped a kiss onto her forehead. "Are you sure you're not just saying that to get me to make you dinner?"

She cocked her head up at him, looking very much like Daisy, who was sitting beside them on the linoleum floor making the same gesture. "Would that work?"

His smile turned to a grin and he noticed Katya's eyes darken but couldn't read her expression. "Yeah, I think it would."

Her voice sounded husky when she answered after clearing her throat twice, "I'll file that away for future reference. However, tonight I'll make *you* dinner."

"I thought you didn't know how to cook?"

It was Katya's turn to smile. "I don't. Fortunately, your grandmother isn't stingy with her recipes. I called her and she walked me through a handful of things that even I should be able to make. She also told me I could call her if I got stuck. It makes trying something new so easy when you have someone to help you."

That was certainly a telling statement, whether she realized it or not.

The air from the open refrigerator was cool on Alex's back, but he didn't move away.

Did she really not have anyone she could lean on in her life? Alex thought about it. There was her father, who had sent her away when she was young. Presumably she had friends in her circle, but it seemed to Alex that they wouldn't know much more about life's more practical aspects than Katya herself did. Jillian would probably have come to her stepdaughter's aid, but Alex couldn't see Katya asking her for help.

Once again, Alex was struck by the differences in their lives. He had always had someone to turn to, whether it be for advice or money or knowledge. But Katya had had to do it all on her own.

No wonder she was not inclined to change her lifestyle. She had no one to show her how to do it.

He hugged her a little bit tighter and then let her go. "I'm no slouch in the kitchen myself. If you need any help, you can come to me."

Katya looked at him strangely. "Thank you, Alex. Would you like a beer?" she asked, taking a step back and bumping into Daisy, whom she patted absently on the head.

Alex let her go. "Sure. By the way, what's for dinner?"

"Chicken enchiladas."

"Ooh, my favorite," Alex said, twisting the caps off of two bottles of beer. "Did Nana share her secret sauce recipe with you?"

Katya broke out in a sudden fit of coughing. "Yes, she did," she answered, once she had her breath back. "But you'll have to go in the other room while I make it. I promised I wouldn't share her secret."

Alex grumbled good-naturedly when Katya shooed him away from the grocery bags. He went to sit on one of the barstools overlooking the kitchen as she disappeared into a small walk-in pantry. "Oh, by the way, I meant to ask you if you'd like to come with me to the Salute Scottsdale party next week."

Katya emerged from the pantry with a secretive smile playing about her mouth. "I'd love to. Anything to give me an excuse to buy a new dress."

She filled a pot of water from the sink and swung around to put it on the stove. Then she moved to the refrigerator to pull out a plastic-wrapped Styrofoam container of chicken. During all of this, Daisy lay down in the middle of the floor, stretching her legs out so she covered almost the entire space.

It didn't escape Alex's notice that Katya didn't step on the dog.

Not even once.

CHAPTER TWENTY-FIVE

KATYA was just finishing up her last room on Monday when Alex stopped by. He looked as knee-meltingly delicious as always, and Katya wondered if it would be considered prostitution if she managed to convince him to have sex with her on the freshly made bed while she was still on the clock. Technically, she figured it wouldn't. After all, she'd be getting paid *while* having sex, not getting paid *to* have sex. She might have to talk to her attorney about the legal nuances of that one.

But it would mean she'd have to strip the bed down and make it again, and she was really much too tired for that. So, for now at least, she decided to shelve the idea.

"The PR firm you recommended handled the camera situation beautifully," Alex said as Katya mentally tried to replace the bones in her knees while straightening the bedspread.

He tossed a newspaper down on the bed, then went to sit in the oversize leather chair next to the couch. Daisy scooted closer on the rug so he could rub behind her ears.

Katya picked up the paper and read the story plastered on the back page of the *Arizona Republic*:

Local Hotel Discovers Cameras in Guest Rooms

The staff at the upscale Royal Palmetto hotel in Scottsdale was dismayed to discover a wireless

camera in one of their guest rooms. As Alex
Sheridan, the general manager of the Royal
Palmetto, said, "We realize that this is a guest's
worst nightmare. They come to our hotel,
expecting to be pampered and safe, and, instead,
they discover their privacy has been violated."
Mr. Sheridan admits that all hotels are
susceptible to similar breaches. While new
employees go through standard background
checks, if a potential employee has not been
caught in the act of installing such devices, their
behavior would not be known to previous
employers.

Hotel experts agree that opportunities for
crimes such as this are endless in the hospitality
industry. Despite this, Mr. Sheridan has
undertaken measures at the Royal Palmetto to
decrease the likelihood of such an event
occurring again. According to Peter R.
Hoffman, director of security at the hotel,
"We've searched all 150 rooms and found no
evidence of another camera. We've also trained
our housekeeping staff on what to look for to
do our best to make sure this sort of thing
doesn't happen again." Mr. Sheridan added that
the housekeepers know each room intimately
and are often the first ones to notice something
amiss. Indeed, it was a member of the
housekeeping staff who discovered the camera
in the initial guest room.

The article went on to explain to the reading public
what signs to look for themselves and ended with this
quote from Alex:

The entire staff at the Royal Palmetto is committed to providing our guests with the safest, most enjoyable experience possible. While other hotels might be tempted to cover up something like this, we felt our guests needed to know that, even in the best hotels in the world, they still need to be cognizant of their surroundings for their own safety and privacy.

Katya plopped down on the couch and set the paper on the coffee table. "I told you they do great damage control."

"You were right. I was worried that their advice to make this public knowledge right away was going to backfire. Since only a handful of us knew about the camera, I thought we might have been better served to keep quiet until something leaked."

"I agree with the PR firm," Katya said, rubbing Daisy's stomach with her foot. "If you tried to keep it a secret, someone would inevitably find out, and it would seem as if you were covering up something far worse than just one camera. And you say that only a few of us knew, but the security staff who searched the rooms knew, and you can bet they mentioned it to their families. Things like this have a way of not staying secret for long."

"That's exactly what the PR firm said, and I'm convinced now that they were right. We've received several phone calls from concerned guests, but none that were directed at the hotel. This could have been a real nightmare, Katya. Thank you for helping me make sure it wasn't."

Katya leaned forward and fiddled with the newspaper. "It was no problem. All I did was give you someone to call."

Alex laid his hand on top of hers and remained silent until she looked up. "That was enough to turn this from a potential public relations disaster to what it really was—an unfortunate event that we all hope will never happen again."

She was saved from coming up with an answer to that when Inez breezed in, coming to an abrupt halt just inside the door. Instinctively Katya tried to pull her hand out from under Alex's grasp, but he just held her tighter.

"Hi, Inez. How are you today?" Alex asked.

"F-fine. Katya, are you finished for the day?"

Katya gave up trying to wrestle her hand away, but not without giving Alex a glare for good measure. She and Inez had a fragile truce going, and she didn't want to jeopardize it. She had even asked Alex's little sister if she'd come shopping with her to find a dress to wear to the Salute Scottsdale party at the end of the week. Katya had no idea where to shop for bargain clothes, and besides, what fun was shopping by yourself anyway?

"Yes, I'm done. I just have to change my clothes and then we can go. We'll need to drop Daisy by my apartment. Mr. Eggers said he'd dog-sit for me for a few hours."

The dog's ears perked up at hearing her name, then perked back down as the conversation turned away from her.

"Mr. Eggers?" Alex asked, incredulous.

"Yes. Turns out that he loves dogs—just as long as they're not barking when he's trying to sleep. He works nights and he apologized to me the other day about being so grumpy about Daisy. I guess the former neighbors left their dog alone in the apartment all day and it barked and whimpered for hours. Poor Mr. Eggers said it almost broke his heart to hear the poor thing."

Alex started toying with her fingers then, drawing Inez's attention back to their intertwined hands.

Katya tugged on her hand again. "Alex, would you please let go of me?" she asked, exasperated.

He gave her another one of his grins that made Katya glad she was sitting down, then finally let her go. "You two have fun. I'll see you both tomorrow."

Katya had a hard time forcing herself not to stare at him as he left. Damn. And she thought having sex with him a few times would have dulled the strength of her attraction.

Unfortunately, it seemed to have done just the opposite.

"Here, let me just get Daisy's water bowl," Katya said, handing Inez the dog's leash as she ducked into the tiny kitchen of her apartment. She made sure there was plenty of kibble in Daisy's food dish, then said a loud, "Come in," when a knock sounded at her door.

"I'm ready to take that dog of yours for a walk," her neighbor said, stepping into her apartment.

Katya looked up when Mr. Eggers muttered a hasty, "Oh, excuse me."

He had obviously not expected someone to be standing in the living room, since he'd bumped into Inez when he entered the room.

Inez looked up at him and smiled that secretive smile of hers. "It's all right. Let me just g-get out of your way."

"No, no. You're not in my way at all."

Katya tried to hide a grin when Mr. Eggers started blushing. It seemed that he couldn't take his eyes off of Inez. Katya made the proper introductions, but she doubted either of them heard her.

Trying not to interrupt the moment, she slid out from

behind the counter with Daisy's food and water bowls and said, "I'll just take these over to your apartment, Mr. Eggers."

As she pushed open her neighbor's door, she immediately noticed how tidy he kept his place. Clean dishes were stacked in a plastic draining thingy near the sink. A folded washrag hung over the faucet to dry. She would have expected his apartment to be strewn with empty beer cans and pizza delivery boxes, but instead, his neatly stacked recycling bins held only cans of Coke and a week's worth of newspapers. She set the bowls down in the kitchen and wondered how long she could stall before they became suspicious.

Slowly she wandered around the apartment that was identical in layout to hers. Then, peering out onto Mr. Eggers's balcony, she gasped.

Her neighbor had built his own secret garden out there.

Katya quietly pushed open the sliding glass door and stepped outside. Brilliant orange hibiscus interlaced with tiny fragrant white flowers hung from a trellis. A fountain had been placed in the corner of the balcony, with a tiny plaster fawn drinking from a pool. A small wooden bench sat off to one side, and Katya resisted the urge to sit down and take it all in.

She would never have expected her burly neighbor to be the type to build something like this.

Hearing voices in the hall, Katya stepped back into the apartment and quickly slid the balcony door shut.

"So, Friday night at seven it is. I'll pick you up," Mr. Eggers said.

Inez was smiling as she and Daisy preceded Katya's neighbor into the room.

Well, surprise, surprise, Katya thought, busying herself in the kitchen as Inez shyly gave Mr. Eggers her address.

"Are you ready to go?" Katya asked, straightening from her make-believe task as the silence in the apartment lengthened.

Both Inez and Mr. Eggers laughed nervously, and the spell between them was broken. "Yes, let's go," Inez answered, handing Daisy's leash over to the man standing beside her.

"Bye, baby," Katya cooed, stopping for a moment to scratch the dog behind her ears before following Alex's sister out the door and down the hall.

"How is everything, Miss Morgan?" her personal shopper, ever attentive, asked.

The silk fabric of the dress slipped through Katya's fingers, pooling on the floor at her feet.

She blinked and the beautiful vision faded away. Her bare toes wrinkled against the scratchy carpet in the dressing room. Tossed-away pins and pieces of plastic littered the floor, and she did her best to avoid touching the scuffed once-white walls as she tugged on the inexpensive unlined dress.

Katya sighed. She had come a long way since those days spent at Bergdorf's.

Unfortunately, it had been a slip in entirely the wrong direction.

"Does it f-fit?" Inez asked from the other side of the dressing room door.

Katya opened the door. "Yes, but it feels terrible. Why do these synthetic fabrics have to be so uncomfortable?"

Inez shrugged. The mysteries of polyester were obviously not going to be solved here in the discount department store dressing room. "It looks great on you, but everything does."

Catching the hint of wistfulness in Inez's voice, Katya turned from craning her head to look at her own backside in the mirror. Her eyes narrowed as she contemplated her subject. Inez's problem was that she dressed as if she were twenty years older than she really was. To make matters worse, she picked the most unflattering tones of tan and beige, colors that leached the golden tones from her skin and made her dark brown eyes look drab and lifeless. She'd look fabulous in navy blue and white, or bright red. Even black. Anything but the drab brown she usually wore.

But Katya didn't know how to say all that without risking damage to their fledgling friendship.

She wished suddenly that she had a sketch pad and her paints. It had been months since she'd painted, since before her father had died. She thought of Jillian's present, of the paints and charcoals back at her apartment, and her fingers itched. She'd love to show Inez what she would look like if only she dressed a bit more daringly or did something different with her hair.

Mr. Eggers would really be wowed by her then.

It was a cliché, Katya knew, the whole thing about having a makeover and changing your life. Then she looked down at herself, at the cheap green dress she wore, and bit back a laugh. Her own forced makeover had certainly changed her life, though not in quite the same way she was hoping a makeover would change Inez's life.

"What's so funny?" Inez smiled, and Katya noticed she had the same beautiful white teeth her brother did.

"Nothing. Here, let me take this off. I think I'll just wear one of the dresses I already own to the party on Friday. I just hope no one notices that I'm wearing something they've seen before." She stepped back into the dressing room and let the dress fall to the floor without bothering to close the door. As she pulled on her denim shorts, she noticed Inez's attempt to look at the ceiling . . . at the floor . . . at the yellowed stain on the wall from God only knew what . . . at anywhere but Katya.

"Sorry," Katya said, pulling a blue T-shirt on over her head. "I was in all-girl schools most of my life. There wasn't much need for modesty, since we all had the same equipment."

"Yeah, but some people's equipment is better tuned than others."

Katya laughed, then picked the flimsy dress up off the floor. She stood for a moment, looking at her new friend. And instead of seeing a drab and colorless person, she saw a kind and beautiful soul, the type of person who would do anything to help a stranger, even one who wasn't always so nice in return.

Before she could stop herself, she flung her arms around Inez's shoulders. "Thank you," she mumbled, giving the other woman a quick squeeze.

Inez tentatively put her arms around Katya. "You're welcome." She paused. "For what?" she asked, puzzled.

Blinking rapidly, Katya backed away. She laughed uncomfortably, already embarrassed at her impulsive gesture. "For coming shopping with me. I would never have known where to get clothes at such a . . . um, such a reasonable price."

"Oh, you're welcome," Inez repeated.

"Do you want to check out their makeup section before we go?" Katya asked, hoping to find some way to start repaying Inez's kindness.

"Sure," Inez answered.

Katya followed Inez out of the dressing room area and across the store. They spent half an hour giggling like teenagers over glittery blue nail polish and black eye shadow.

As they stopped in front of a dazzling array of eye shadows, Katya decided to take a chance. "You know," she said tentatively, "you have really beautiful eyes. Have you ever thought about wearing eye shadow?"

Inez shrugged. "It wouldn't m-make a difference. People don't notice me for anything except this st-stupid stutter."

Katya's hand stilled on Garden of Gold #5. She turned to Inez, who was frowning at the threadbare carpet. "Would you like to change that?"

"I c-can't."

"Of course you can. If there's anything I've learned over the past month, it's that people can change if they put their minds to it. And I'm not talking about major personality issues here. All I'm suggesting is that you learn how to put on a little bit of eye makeup and wear a few more bright colors. That's all."

Inez tentatively reached out a hand and touched a smoky gray eye pencil. Then she looked up at Katya. "All right. Let's give it a t-try."

Katya smiled. Finally. Now here was something she knew how to do!

"Great," she said, taking charge. "Sit here."

After getting Inez settled onto a stool in front of a small round mirror, Katya left on her quest to find the perfect eye shadow. At first, she thought about trying something in the lavender family, or maybe a nice dark green. Then she found the perfect shade of golden brown and knew she'd hit the jackpot. It was neutral enough not to shock the novice makeup wearer—which would be perfect for Inez—but had enough color that Katya knew it would set off the gold tints in the other woman's eyes. Of course, that was just the outer eye color. That still left her to find the right shades for the inner crease, eyelid, and under-brow areas. Not to mention an eyeliner, mascara, and blush. Oh, and lipstick, too. Plus a lip liner pencil. Katya grabbed one labeled DIABLO DUSK and added it to the ever-growing pile of cosmetic samples in her arms.

Inez's eyes widened when Katya returned, bringing what seemed to be half of the store's entire stock of makeup with her. Katya set her loot on the counter and stared critically at Inez's face. Inez resisted the urge to squirm. Finally, Katya nodded and Inez let out the breath she'd been holding. Apparently, Inez had passed the test.

"I want you to watch what I do so you can do this yourself whenever you want to wear makeup," Katya said, handing her the small mirror that had been sitting on the counter.

Inez took it, then watched Katya slide open a tester case of brown eye shadow, pull a Q-Tip out of a jar on the counter, and swish it over the surface of the shadow.

"See, first you cover the entire eyelid with this nice light brown. That will provide you with a base of color to start with. Don't go above the brow bone, though. We'll put a lighter color on up there that will help make your eyes look even bigger than they are," Katya explained, showing Inez how to apply the first layer of shadow. "You really should buy a nice set of brushes. You wouldn't believe how much easier it is to put your makeup on properly if you have the right tools." She turned to a hovering clerk. "Do you carry a line of brushes that you could recommend?"

The clerk nodded. "Yes, I think we do. Most people just use the applicators that come with the shadows, though."

Katya snorted indelicately. "Well, that's their first mistake. It's impossible to apply makeup with the proper

nuances using those clunky things. We need something
more precise. Perhaps something in sable?"

"I'll see what I can do," the clerk said skeptically,
and Katya figured that she was probably going to be
disappointed with the clerk's selection.

Shrugging, Katya turned back to Inez. "In order to
do this next step properly, I really need a better brush,
but I'll try to make do with what we've got. All right,
next you want to put this darker shade just above the
crease of your eyelid. Many people make the mistake of
putting the darker shade in the crease itself, but if you
do that, you can only see the color when you blink and
that doesn't make any sense. If you put it just above the
crease, it will give your eyes a more wide-open look,
plus it will help bring out their exotic color." Katya expertly swished on a line of shadow.

Inez glanced at herself in the mirror, shocked to discover that Katya was telling the truth. Her eyes suddenly
did look larger and more glamorous than they had seconds before.

"We'll put this light rose color just up to your brow
line. Be sure to blend it in really well. Otherwise, it will
look funny." Katya showed her how to smudge the line
between the colors, making them run together a bit, then
brought out the last pot of eye shadow with a flourish.

"This color is my favorite. It's going to give you
that final bit of polish a look like this needs."

"Here's the only set of brushes we carry," the clerk
announced, handing a plastic-wrapped package to Katya.

Katya took out one brush and looked it over, frowning. "Hmm. They're not sable, but they'll have to do."
She pulled the smallest brush out of the set and swished
it around in the dark brown powder. Then she tapped
the brush on the edge of the shadow case to get rid of
the excess powder and expertly brushed the color on just

the very edge of Inez's eyelid. Finally, she lined both the top and the bottom of Inez's eyes, added some mascara, and lightly brushed a bit of blush over her cheeks.

"We're all done except the lips. What do you think?"

"Wow," Inez said, staring at herself in the hand-held mirror and wishing she could honestly say she didn't like the image looking back at her. But she couldn't. Her eyes looked huge and luminous, as if they held a secret in their depths. And she had cheekbones. She never realized that she had cheekbones. But there they were, high up on her face.

While she watched, Katya put the finishing touches on Inez's lips and stepped back to evaluate her handiwork. She made a few minor adjustments, then put the lid back on the lipstick she had just finished with.

"Wow," Inez said again, unable to take her eyes off herself. She blinked, her lashes feeling heavy from the unaccustomed weight of the mascara Katya had slathered on them.

"You look great," the clerk who had been watching them said.

"Yes, you do," Katya agreed.

"Wow," Inez repeated for the third time. Apparently, wearing makeup had lowered her IQ a few points, she thought with a wry smile. Then she stopped smiling. "Did I mess up my lipstick?" she asked, horrified, as she grabbed for the mirror.

Katya laughed. "Well, it didn't take long to convert you to the dark side. No, of course you didn't smudge your lipstick. Even if you had, we could fix it in no time. Once you get the hang of it, it's very easy."

"Hmm," Inez muttered skeptically.

"Why don't you just bring your makeup to work

with you in the morning and we can go over it again
and again until you feel comfortable?"

"You wouldn't mind doing that?"

"Of course not," Katya said, unconsciously stiffen-
ing when Inez flung her arms around her and gave her
a heartfelt hug. It took her a moment to relax and start
patting her friend on the back.

"Thank you." Inez let her go, then turned and started
picking through the items on the counter.

"What are you doing?" Katya asked.

"Oh, I can't afford all of this," Inez answered. "I'm
just going to get a few things right now. I can come
back for the rest when I get paid."

"Why don't you just ask Alex for a loan? Surely he
makes enough to help you out now and then."

Inez smiled her Mona Lisa smile. "Alex has helped
us all out enough in his lifetime. I don't like to ask him
for more than he's already given to me. Did you know
he paid for my first three years of college?"

"He did?"

"Yes. My grades were pretty good, but I just
couldn't seem to decide what I wanted to major in. I
changed my mind four times, and then I finally gave up.
Alex has never once complained about all of the money
I wasted." Inez sighed, toying with one of the rectangular eye shadow cases. "I wish I could repay him, but
without a degree I doubt I'll ever make much of myself."

Katya frowned. "Since when does having a degree
determine a person's worth? Look at me—I have a degree and I'm not half the friend you are. And God knows
you have ten times the work ethic that I do."

Inez grinned at her then, her doelike eyes large and
luminous and dancing with good humor. "That's true.
But at least you're trying."

Katya grinned back at her friend. "Yes, I am. I've

even surprised myself," she said before turning back to the makeup on the counter. Mentally tallying up the cost of each item she'd used on Inez, Katya deducted that amount from the tiny amount of cash she had left from Alex's loan. It wouldn't leave her much to live on until payday, but she wanted to do something to repay Inez's many kindnesses.

She turned to the salesclerk. "We'll take it all," she said, waving a hand over the counter.

"No, I—"

"Just think of how surprised Mr. Eggers will be when he comes to pick you up on Friday night," Katya interrupted, smiling. Pulling her next-to-last twenty-dollar bill out of her purse, she pushed the pile of cosmetics toward the salesclerk.

"We'll take it all," she repeated.

Katya watched Inez glance at herself in the rearview mirror for the twentieth time in fifteen minutes and felt a tingle of satisfaction in the pit of her stomach. Who knew that doing something nice for someone else would feel so good?

As they pulled up in front of the squat apartment building that Katya now called home, Inez turned to her, her eyes shining.

"Thank you again, Katya."

"You're welcome," she answered, wondering if Inez realized she hadn't stuttered at all since they'd left the store. "I'll see you tomorrow morning."

She stood on the warm sidewalk and waved as Inez pulled away from the curb. She had just turned to go into the building when a voice shouted from above.

"Thank God you're back, Katya. Daisy's sick!"

She looked up to see Mr. Eggers frantically waving at her from his fourth-floor window.

"I'll be right up," she shouted before racing inside and pulling open the heavy stairwell door.

Questions rolled through her mind as her tennis shoes slapped the concrete. What could possibly be wrong? Daisy had been fine when she'd left three hours ago. Was she simply playing hypochondriac to punish Katya for leaving her? Were dogs smart enough to do that? Katya would bet money that Daisy certainly was.

She hit the fourth-floor landing at a run. Mr. Eggers waited out in the hall, frantically waving her into his apartment.

Daisy didn't even look up when Katya knelt down on the floor next to her prostrate body. Katya laid a hand on the dog's brow. Her soft fur felt hot to the touch. "What's wrong, baby?" Katya asked, as if the dog could tell her.

"She's been lying on the rug like that since about an hour after you left and hasn't moved, except for the two times she got up to throw up on the balcony outside."

Katya looked up at her neighbor and winced, knowing how that would have affected his private sanctuary. "I'm so sorry, Mr. Eggers. She's never done this before. Did she eat something after I left? Maybe you left some chocolate out or something. I think that's bad for dogs."

Mr. Eggers was already shaking his head. "No. I don't care for the stuff myself. I've been in the living room with her the whole time since you left because I was watching the D-Backs beat the socks off the Devil Rays. So I know she hasn't gotten into anything she shouldn't have."

"All right. Let me just call a veterinarian then. I don't know what else to do."

He waved her to the phone perched on the breakfast nook of his apartment, and Katya frantically flipped through the yellow pages of the phone book looking for the *V*s. She quickly found a vet with a twenty-four-hour emergency number listed in the phone book, dialed the number, and then turned to watch Daisy, who still hadn't moved from her spot on the carpet.

A pleasant-sounding woman answered the phone and Katya hurriedly explained the problem.

Without hesitating, the woman on the other end of the line told Katya to bring in Daisy as soon as possible. Dogs didn't vomit for no reason, and if Daisy hadn't eaten anything recently that had made her sick, it could be something serious.

Feeling sick herself, Katya hung up the phone.

"Mr. Eggers, I hate to trouble you further, but do you have a car? I have to take Daisy to the vet right now."

"No, hon, I don't. I just have the Harley, and that won't do for you, me, and the dog. Would you like me to call you a cab?"

"No, I'll do it. I could use a hand getting her downstairs, though."

While Katya dialed the cab service, Mr. Eggers went to Daisy and gently picked her up in his arms. Katya watched them go, blinking back the tears that threatened to spill over her lashes. Why was it that every time she started to care about something, it got taken away from her?

She pulled in a deep breath and gave her address to the dispatcher before hanging up the phone and returning it to its cradle. She clenched her teeth and felt a shiver go through her bones.

"You don't care about that stupid dog," she whispered angrily into the empty room. "She's not even yours. She's Amanda's, and as soon as Amanda gets better, you have to give her back. Besides, it's just a stupid dog. That's all."

With that, Katya quietly pulled the door of Mr. Eggers's apartment closed behind her and stepped out into the hall.

CHAPTER TWENTY-SIX

ALEX was fast asleep when the telephone beside his bed jangled to life. He jolted awake immediately.

Damn. What could be wrong now?

With the camera crisis averted, he had hoped for one good night's rest.

He had hoped for too much, apparently.

"Yes?" he answered, trying not to sound groggy. Sleepily he wondered why people always tried to sound as if they hadn't been sleeping when others called at unreasonable hours. He immediately forgot his question when he heard Katya's voice on the other end of the line.

"Alex, I hate to trouble you, but I need a ride."

Her words sounded garbled, and Alex wondered if she was at a party and had been drinking. If so, he applauded her decision not to ride home with other partygoers, who were probably also inebriated, but was still faintly irritated about being woken from his own slumber to rescue her from the situation.

He sat up in bed, running a hand through his hair to smooth it down. "Where are you?"

She gave him an address half an hour from the Royal Palmetto and then said, "I'm sorry for calling you so late. I would have taken a cab, but I spent my last twenty dollars getting here."

Alex grimaced into the receiver. Leave it to her to spend the last of her cash to get to some party. It was a good thing she had him to make sure she had enough money to buy food and pay her bus fare until payday. He'd spare her the lecture about fiscal responsibility until the morning, but she really was going to need to learn how to live within her means.

"I'm leaving right now," he said, standing up to pull on a pair of jeans with one hand while holding the phone in the other.

She hiccupped before saying good-bye and ending the call, and Alex wondered how she was going to feel about all this when 5:00 A.M. rolled around. One thing he would say for her: she had made it to work every day, on time, since she'd started working at the hotel. He hoped that trend wasn't about to end, because he would have to be tougher on her than a regular employee. Even now, he knew he was treading a fine line from a human resource standpoint. He'd even considered asking a friend of his at the Phoenician if he had an opening in the housekeeping department there. But he hadn't, in large part because he knew that she wouldn't have the same support network at another hotel that she enjoyed here at the Royal Palmetto.

Alex pulled a T-shirt over his head, grabbed his wallet and keys from the top of the dresser, and slid his feet into a pair of Top-Siders before trotting outside into the warm night. The desert was abuzz with the yelping of coyotes hunting down a midnight snack, mixed with the ever-present chirping of crickets, and Alex drew in a deep breath and listened as he walked to his car.

He loved the desert, loved the surprises and contrasts brought about by the extreme weather, the squat and seemingly ugly hedgehog cactus that was the first to bloom in the spring, with its bright red flowers that hummingbirds loved; the little javelina pigs that traveled in herds and looked like tame farm animals but whose razor-sharp tusks could drive off even bobcats; the rock formations that stuck out of the ground like some giant child's toys left on the ground millions of years ago.

With the top down on his Mustang, Alex sped out of the parking lot of the hotel and into the night. Stifling a yawn, he tuned the radio to a station that played the music he'd grown up with. As Alex pondered the fact that he was old enough to remember music that was now considered "oldies," Michael Jackson protested that Billie Jean was not his lover, despite evidence to the contrary.

By the time Alex turned into the parking lot of the address Katya had given him, he'd been down memory lane with some of his old favorites: Def Leppard, Foreigner, Journey, Van Halen, Bon Jovi. *Funny to think that those bands used to be considered hard rock,* Alex thought with a wry smile.

Then he came back to the present, surprised to find himself not in some upscale housing development, as he'd expected, but parked in front of a veterinarian's office. Katya was sitting all alone on the concrete front steps, with her knees together and her shoulders stooped.

It looked as if his socialite hadn't been out partying after all. She looked so sad that Alex almost wished she had been.

He parked the car and killed the engine before stepping out onto the pavement.

"What's wrong?" he asked, sitting down beside Katya on the cool concrete.

She drew in a shuddering breath. "Daisy's sick. The vet wants to keep her overnight to keep an eye on her. They've run some tests but won't have the results until tomorrow afternoon."

Alex put an arm around her shoulders and pulled her close. "Is it something serious?"

"They said they didn't know, but they kept giving

each other these looks that told me they suspect something but don't want to tell me until they're certain. But it doesn't matter. She's not my dog anyway. I'm just taking care of this situation because Amanda can't. That's all."

"Uh-huh," Alex said, silently wondering what Katya was going to do when Amanda regained her health and asked for Daisy back. He hoped the two women would find a way to work out joint custody of the dog, as it was obvious that Katya had become attached to her. "Are you ready to go home?"

Katya looked up at him then, her grayish-green eyes suspiciously watery. "Could I stay at your place tonight?"

Alex gave her shoulders a squeeze. "Sure. Do we need to stop by your apartment for anything?"

"Not if you have an extra toothbrush I could use. I always carry emergency makeup in my purse, and I have a uniform in my locker back at the hotel."

Alex stood up and offered her a hand. Katya entwined her fingers with his and allowed him to pull her into a standing position. As she stood on the step above him, her face was just about level with his. Alex put a hand in her hair and pulled her closer until their noses touched. "It will be all right," he said.

Katya kept her eyes focused on his. "You can't guarantee that."

She had him there. Unfortunately, as much as he might want to make everything right for the people he cared about, there were some things he couldn't control.

Damn, he hated that.

"No, I can't. But I can guarantee that I'll be here for you if things go wrong. That's the best I can do."

Katya blinked, and twin tears slid out of her eyes and dripped down her face. "That's not good enough," she said quietly, pulling herself out of his embrace. "Can we go now?"

Alex frowned at her back as she walked away. What did she expect? A risk-free life? Now there was something that neither he nor anyone else could ever provide her. And all of the money in the world couldn't buy it for her, either. Life just didn't work that way.

Since she was already upset, he spared her the sermon and simply followed her to the car instead. The ride back to the Royal Palmetto was quiet, with each of them lost in thoughts they chose not to share. As they pulled into the parking lot of the hotel, Alex waved off the valet and continued on to the employee lot.

They walked in silence to his suite, where Alex pulled his card key out of his wallet and slid it into the card reader. The lights blinked green, but before he could turn the handle he felt Katya's hand snake around his waist from behind. She rubbed her breasts against his back and whispered into his neck, "Make love to me, Alex."

She moved her hands lower, below the waistband of his jeans, and caressed him. Alex closed his eyes, enjoying her exquisite torture as his penis pressed against the fly of his jeans, trying to get closer to her magic hands.

She was very good at this.

Alex put his hands over Katya's to stop her, then turned in her arms.

"Let's do this inside," he said, before reaching backward to open the door.

Burying his hands in her silky hair, he lowered his mouth to hers. He pulled her with him through the open door without breaking their kiss.

She curled her tongue around his, sucking gently, and Alex groaned.

Katya wrapped her arms around him and caressed his back, her hips rubbing against his.

On the drive back to the hotel, she couldn't stop thinking about Daisy. About the cute way the dog had of looking at her with her lower jaw sticking out and her head cocked. About how she'd follow Katya around in the morning, holding her own leash in her mouth until Katya was ready to take her outside. About how she'd started crawling up on the couch with Katya at night and snuggling against her feet, her head resting on Katya's calves.

Why couldn't God just leave her alone? Wasn't it bad enough that He'd taken her mother and her father, not to mention her inheritance? Did He have to take Daisy, too?

She didn't want to think anymore. All it did was make her more miserable.

In her old life, she could push the pain away by going out drinking and partying. But now she was trapped, forced to listen to the thoughts running through her brain over and over again.

So she turned to sex to keep the thoughts at bay. She wouldn't have to worry about Daisy or think about anything other than how good it felt to have Alex touching her breasts and running his lips down her throat.

She started toward the bedroom and Alex followed, as she expected he would.

He stopped her before she could enter the room, however, pushing her back against the wall.

"Wait. Slow down and enjoy it," he said, running his hands over her arms and making her shiver.

Katya wanted to scream at him, to make him hurry and get to the good stuff. Then he brushed his fingertips over her nipples, still covered by her bra and T-shirt, and she realized this *was* the good stuff. Closing her eyes, she laid her head back against the wall as Alex continued to tease her.

His strong hands caressed her bare legs, traveling ever closer to the parts she most wanted him to touch. He slid one hand under the fabric of her shorts to caress her buttocks and Katya barely had the wherewithal to recognize that he didn't even have to slide his fingers beneath her silken panties—she was ready for him now.

With a breathy moan, she pushed her hips forward to rub against his.

Why was it that he could get her so hot without doing anything more than this heavy petting?

Then he brought his hands around to the front of her shorts and rubbed his thumb over the magic C.

"Yes," she moaned, pushing her shoulders back against the wall.

Alex slid his thumb under her panties then and moistened it in her own slick wetness before returning to taunt her again.

She thought about making him stop for about a nanosecond; then she stopped thinking at all when he started caressing her breast with his free hand. He bent down to kiss the tender skin just under her ear, and Katya felt overwhelmed by the sensations washing over her. She was in serious danger of coming apart right there in his hands, but she didn't care. He smelled so good, and what he was doing to her felt so good, that she just wanted to lose herself in him.

He stroked her again, and she did just that, groaning out his name with the force of her climax.

His fingers stilled while she convulsed against him.

When she had enough energy, she opened her eyes, only to find Alex watching her with a serious look. He kissed her tenderly on the mouth, smoothing her panties back into place with one hand.

"Are you ready to go to sleep?" he asked.

"But . . . but what about you?" Katya sputtered, bewildered.

Alex grinned at her and grabbed her hand, tugging her into the bedroom. "I'm saving myself for next time. Come on; let's go to bed."

He went to the dresser beside the king-size bed and pulled out his wallet, laying it on the sturdy pine top. Then he tossed his keys next to his wallet, opened a drawer, pulled out a dark blue T-shirt, and handed it to her. "Do me a favor and wear this. I can't get any sleep when you go to bed nude."

That same grin was playing about his mouth, and Katya didn't know whether to be flattered or offended as he ushered her into the bathroom with a pat on the rear and a calmly uttered, "There's a spare toothbrush in the top right-hand drawer. Ladies first." She pulled the door closed behind her and sat down on the toilet, staring at the green-tiled wall of the shower.

She'd never known a man who'd turn down freely offered sex.

What in the hell was wrong with him?

She pondered the question but never came up with an answer. Instead, she gave up and got up off the toilet to brush her teeth and take off her makeup.

Alex was fast asleep when she returned, his body sprawled across the king-size bed. He'd pushed the sheets into a pile at the bottom of the bed and lay with his arms curled around his pillow. Katya stood still and looked at him, holding her neatly folded clothes in her arms. He wore pajama bottoms, probably a habit learned from growing up as the only male in a house of females. His skin was a delicious shade of golden brown, his arms tanned and strong. A lock of hair had fallen across his forehead and Katya was tempted to smooth it back, but she didn't. Instead, she stayed where she was for a moment more, drinking in the sight of him as he slept.

Finally, she set her clothes down on a chair beside the bed and crawled in next to him. Alex's body radiated warmth, so she didn't bother pulling a sheet up to cover herself. Instead, she tentatively scooted closer to him and laid an arm across his waist.

Sleepily he turned over to face her and muttered a whispered, "I love you," before kissing her lightly on the forehead, rolling back over, and pulling her arm tighter to him, forcing Katya to rest her head against his smooth back.

She closed her eyes, trying not to think about Daisy, who was sleeping alone in a cage at the vet's office.

She felt the tears start behind her eyelids and willed them away. Crying wouldn't comfort the dog, and it certainly wouldn't make her feel any better, either. Screwing her eyes shut more tightly, Katya closed the remaining inch between herself and Alex, letting his soothing warmth seep into her.

And, finally, she slept.

"Don't leave me," Katya begged, tears streaming down her face and splattering over her neatly pressed pleated navy skirt.

"I have to. My dad's got a new job in Switzerland, so I'll be going to a school there. I promise I'll write to you every day." Karina Gold, her best friend of almost two years, was crying just as hard as Katya as they sat on the well-tended lawn of the exclusive all-girl school they attended in Connecticut.

Unlike Katya, Karina didn't live at the school. Instead, she was picked up in the family sedan and taken home every night by her mother, a pretty blond-haired woman who never seemed to mind having her daughter's best friend come to visit. Being Jewish, they ate different foods and had different customs from those Katya had always known, but she enjoyed hearing the stories that accompanied the rituals. As Passover that year, she had even found the afikomen and was rewarded with a bag of travel games that she was hoarding for the five-hour flight back home this summer. She would only be home for a few weeks before her father would send her back to school. He'd tell her it was because he had business to attend to, but Katya knew the truth.

Since her mother had died, her father didn't want her around anymore. He might love her in his own way, but she was too much of a reminder of what he'd lost. Even at twelve, she knew that. Every time she looked in the mirror, she saw more and more of her mother there.

In some ways, it was a comfort—as if Mama wasn't really gone.

In other ways, it was a curse. Especially at Easter or Christmas, holidays her mother used to love making a big fuss over. Her father probably had the same good memories that she did, which had to be the reason he managed to be "away on business" every time these holidays had rolled around since her mother had died.

So, rather than going home during her school breaks, she went to stay with Karina and her family, who, of course, didn't celebrate either Easter or Christmas.

But at least she hadn't been left alone at school like some kids were. At least she'd had Karina's family celebrations to keep her mind off of her loneliness—even if they weren't the same ones she'd grown up with.

Only once Karina was gone, Katya would lose even that.

"Please, can't you make your dad change his mind?

I want you to stay here," Katya pleaded, desperate to stop the inevitable.

Karina pulled up a handful of sweet-smelling grass and tossed it to the wind. "I want to stay here, too. But Dad says we have to go."

Katya felt two more tears drip off her chin. She looked up at the soft blue sky filled with cotton ball clouds and wondered how her life could be falling apart on such a beautiful day. She blinked then and wiped her eyes.

Her father was right.

Crying wasn't going to stop Karina and her family from moving away. All it did was give her a headache.

She should have learned better than to let herself start to care about someone else. Every time she did, they just went away.

That day in the grass, watching her friend continue to cry, Katya decided this was going to be the last time she was going to bother caring about anyone. She would concentrate on having fun from now on. She'd be involved in every activity she could, but she wasn't going to have friends anymore. She'd have people to hang out with but nobody she would really share her feelings with. Because when the people you cared about left you, you were worse off than you were before, and it just wasn't worth it.

Katya blinked and realized that she was staring at the golden wall of Alex's back, not the bright blue sky of a Connecticut afternoon. Still half-asleep, she saw it all in her mind, though. That last day with Karina, sitting on the grass in the sunshine. How she'd turned to her friend with an outstretched hand, very politely, and said, "It's okay. You're going to have lots of fun in Europe. Don't bother writing to me. I'm sure you'll make new friends and be very happy."

And then, without waiting for a reply, she stood up, smoothed the pleats of her skirt, and walked away.

That was the day she learned that it was better not to cling to the people you cared about. Even when you did, they still deserted you. So what was the point of losing your heart—and your pride—by trying to make them stay?

Drawing in a ragged breath, Katya realized that her arm was still around Alex's waist and her legs were tangled with his. His breathing was deep and even, his hand still covering hers where it lay on his stomach. She inhaled the scent of him, knowing this would be the last time they'd be together like this.

He made her want to forget that lesson she'd learned almost twenty years ago.

He made her want to cling.

To him. To his family. To that stupid dog.

But eventually, it would all be taken away from her. Alex would stop caring about her once the attraction he felt for her waned. Then Inez would stop being her friend. Nana would die. And Daisy was sick. She could tell from the looks the vet kept giving his assistant last night that something was seriously wrong with the dog's health.

Once again, she'd be left with nothing except a broken heart.

Carefully extricating herself from Alex's grasp, Katya slid out of bed. Without a sound, she padded over to the chair where she'd left her clothes.

Not bothering to put on anything besides the T-shirt she wore, she quietly let herself out of Alex's suite. She stopped on the front stoop and looked around to make sure she was alone. Then she pulled on her shorts and tennis shoes. She could put her bra on in the employee locker room when she got ready for work.

Although she had almost an hour before she had to clock in, she decided to get started early. Housekeeping was still understaffed and Inez had told Katya she could work as much overtime as she wanted to. This morning, Katya was happy to oblige. After all, more work meant more money. And more money meant she could pay her attorney to start working on fighting her father's will.

Because, she reminded herself as she set off toward the front of the hotel, getting her inheritance back was the only thing that was really important to her.

CHAPTER TWENTY-SEVEN

"ALEX t-told me about Daisy. I'm so sorry."

Katya looked up as Inez poked her head into the bathroom that Katya was cleaning. Katya noticed that the other woman had attempted to copy the makeup application that they'd practiced yesterday afternoon in the discount store. She'd done a fairly good job of it, too.

Squelching the pleasure she felt at seeing her friend— no, make that co-worker, she thought—Katya sat back on her heels. "It's no big deal. The vet is supposed to call this afternoon, and I'll pass whatever he says on to Amanda's brother."

Inez blinked a few times. "Oh. Alex said it might be serious. I thought you'd be upset."

Katya shrugged, then wiped at a soapy spot on the tiled wall of the shower. "Why? She's not my dog."

"I . . . Is something wrong?"

"No. I'm just busy. And sick of this dumb job. I tell you, once I get my inheritance back, I'll be sure to tip the housekeeping staff ten times what I used to give them. This is a rotten way to make a living."

Inez frowned at that. "It is not. It's hard work, but there's nothing wrong with that."

"Yeah, well, it's too hard, if you ask me. I don't see why we have to clean the rooms every day. I mean, people don't clean their houses every day, right? So why can't we just clean between guests? Does Mr. Miller really care if he gets fresh sheets every night? I could just make his bed and he'd never know the difference."

"It d-doesn't matter if Mr. Miller knows the difference or not. You would know, and that should be enough. We get paid to care that the sheets are clean, and that the minibar's stocked, and that the guests have enough towels. That's our job."

Katya stood up and grabbed a bottle of Windex. "You can spare me the lecture, Inez. I didn't say I wasn't going to do it. Just that it's not a particularly fulfilling way to spend your life."

Inez drew herself up to her full five feet, four inches. "Do you realize how insulting that was?"

Katya closed her eyes briefly. *You have to do this,* she told herself. Inez was too soft-hearted to stop being friendly to Katya without good reason. So Katya had to give her that reason, no matter how difficult it might be. It would be better for them both this way.

Wiping the mirror with a soft cloth, Katya answered nonchalantly, "Sorry. I wasn't trying to be insulting. I was simply stating my opinion."

Inez didn't respond. Instead, she stood in the doorway of the bathroom, staring at Katya for one long minute.

Katya held her breath and kept wiping at the mirror until Inez finally turned around and left the guest room. She heard the front door open and close, quietly and with great control. If it had been Katya, she probably would have slammed the door. But, of course, that was the difference between the two of them. Inez was reserved and thoughtful, while Katya was impetuous and uncaring. And outrageous.

And unlovable.

And alone.

She was in the cafeteria eating lunch by herself when Alex came striding into the room. Katya saw him stop in the doorway and felt her stomach start to tingle. His silky brown hair was mussed a bit, as if he'd been running his fingers through it, and his bright red tie was askew. He looked so serious and businesslike in his black suit—that is, until he spotted her and smiled.

It was then that Katya knew that leaving Alex was going to be the most difficult thing she'd ever had to do.

Because it wasn't just her knees that melted when he was around—it was her heart.

As he strode toward her, she tried to remind herself that it would be better not to prolong the inevitable. Why let him get closer and have even more of an ability to hurt her?

No, it would be better to end it now.

Alex sat down in front of her, looking happy and relaxed. "You left before I had the chance to say good morning."

Katya looked down at her half-eaten bagel. "I couldn't sleep."

Alex's smile instantly turned to a frown. "Oh. I'm sorry. Were you cold? You should have pulled the blankets up."

Katya resisted the urge to smile. That was Alex, all right. Ever the problem-solver. "No, I wasn't cold. It's just hard to sleep with someone else, that's all. I prefer sleeping alone most of the time."

Alex's frown deepened, but before he could say anything more, Katya decided she'd had enough emotional turmoil for one day. She had already dealt with Inez; Alex could wait until tomorrow. She stood up, gathering the remains of her pitiful lunch. "Look, I have to get back to work. Was there something you needed?"

Alex leaned back in the plastic cafeteria chair, and Katya tried not to stare at him. He was just so damn handsome, with all that golden skin she knew was hiding underneath his conservative suit and those eyes that looked as if they'd been kissed by the sun.

"Actually, there are two things I wanted to discuss with you. Can you come up to my office?"

Katya shrugged. "Sure. I'm done eating."

She tossed her trash in the garbage and met Alex at the entrance of the cafeteria. Neither of them spoke until the newly repaired elevator had chugged its way to the top floor.

As they walked down the hall to his office, Alex said, "I ran across my tickets to the Salute Scottsdale party on Friday and I realized that we hadn't firmed up the logistics on this. I need to stay at the hotel to make sure the arrangements all come together as they should before the party starts. If you want to bring your clothes with you when you come to work in the morning, you're welcome to get ready in my suite after your shift. Or I could send a cab to your apartment to come get you. I'll take you home after the party, of course. You don't need to decide today, but I wanted to at least give you your ticket in case I'm not around when you arrive." He handed her a brown-and-white slip of paper and ushered her into his office.

"Thank you," Katya muttered, slipping the ticket into her purse as she sat down across from his sturdy cherry desk. With everything that had happened last night, she'd forgotten about the party on Friday. Wondering if she should tell him now that she wasn't going to go, she almost missed his next words.

"The second thing I wanted to do was to give you this back."

Alex slid the sparkling sapphire-and-diamond bracelet across the top of his desk toward her.

Katya just stared at it for a few seconds. It was the bracelet she'd asked him to take as payment for her hotel bill the day she'd learned she'd been disinherited.

"But why? I still don't have the money to pay my bill."

"I know. We'll be able to get some of the money from the credit card company. After all, they did authorize many of the transactions on your bill. As for what's left"—Alex shrugged—"well, we'll figure out some way for you to pay it back over time."

Katya reached out and picked up the bracelet. The stones were cool to her touch, the diamonds winking at her gaily in the light from overhead. If she pawned this, she'd probably have enough to pay a large portion of Paula Northcraft's retainer. She would finally be on her way to getting her inheritance back.

So why wasn't she elated?

She forced a bright smile. "Thank you. Now I'll have the money to pay my attorney."

"Pardon me?" Alex asked quietly.

Katya swallowed and resisted the urge to scoot back in her chair. He was furious. His voice was calm and controlled, but his gold-flecked eyes were shooting fire directly at her. "I can pawn this to pay my attorney," she repeated, holding the bracelet so tightly that the prongs dug into her palms.

"I thought you might want to use it to pay Daisy's vet bill. If there is something seriously wrong with her, it could be expensive to fix."

"She's not my dog. I'm sure Bob and Amanda . . ." Her voice trailed off when Alex pushed her chair back and stood up, looming over her.

"Do you really think either Bob or Amanda has that kind of money?"

"It's not my problem," Katya said resolutely. "Daisy is Amanda's dog, not mine. If she doesn't have the money to save the dog's life, that's none of my concern."

Alex narrowed his eyes and sat down on the edge of his desk, right in front of her. Katya tried to focus on the painting of the Royal Palmetto on his wall and not look at the strong, yet gentle, hands of the man sitting before her. All she wanted to do was lay her head down in Alex's lap and let him stroke her hair and tell her that everything was going to be all right.

But she knew better.

Everything was *not* going to be all right.

She would never be able to recover from losing Alex and his family and Daisy, if she let herself care any more than she already did. She had to protect herself. She had to not care.

"You can't tell me that you'd just sit by and let Daisy die. I don't know why you're putting on this act, but I'm not buying it."

Katya stood up, to get away from Alex's nearness more than anything else. "It's not an act," she said, doing her best to keep all emotion out of her voice. "You're asking me to make a choice between myself and a dog. Of course I'm going to choose myself. Besides, what if I did spend the money on Daisy and she died anyway? Then where would I be?"

Alex cocked his head at her and scowled. "That's the risk you have to take when you love someone," he said, and Katya knew then that this conversation was no longer about the dog; it was about them.

She snorted derisively. "Haven't you figured out by now that I'm not capable of loving anyone, Alex?"

"Of course you are. You just have to stop pretending that all you're concerned with is partying and having a good time. You and I both know that it's all a lie. You care about Inez. And Nana. And me. And that damn dog."

"Maybe," Katya said slowly, sliding the bracelet

into the front pocket of her navy blue uniform pants. "But I care about myself more."

She turned to leave, but Alex's voice stopped her. "If you call your attorney instead of the vet, we're through."

Katya squeezed her eyes shut, wishing she could shut out the pain in her chest as easily.

"Good-bye, Alex," she said, closing his office door behind her.

CHAPTER TWENTY-EIGHT

ON Friday evening, just as Alex was stepping out of the shower, he heard a commotion from the living room of his suite at the Royal Palmetto. Hastily donning the thick terry-cloth robe that had been hanging from a hook on the wall, he pushed open the door of the bathroom to see what was going on.

"What are you doing here?" he asked, surprised to see Nana, Inez, and Maria all watching him with varying expressions on their faces.

"I'm sorry, Alex. I tried to stop them," Maria said, flopping down on the couch.

"Stop them from what?"

"From coming here and butting into your personal life," Maria answered, sounding more amused than anything else.

Alex cocked one eyebrow at the gathering of his relatives and leaned against the doorjamb of the bathroom, crossing his arms across his chest. "That's okay. I'm used to it by now. So, go ahead. Let me have it," he said to his grandmother and Inez.

"Maria told us you'd given Katya an ultimatum," Nana began, her voice calm and soothing.

Alex knew he was in trouble when Nana used that voice on him. It was her "wounded animal, come to me" voice—the one that had small children climbing into her lap in two minutes flat and pouring out all their troubles to her. Alex's spine stiffened. He was no hurt child who needed maternal comforting; he was a grown man with a real problem.

He had fallen in love with the wrong woman.

This was not a simple matter of lifestyle differences between him and Katya. It wasn't just the issue of whether she spent her money on Daisy's vet bill rather than paying for an attorney. If it had only been the money, Alex would have written her a check four days ago and not forced her hand. But it went much deeper than that.

This was about her core values, about what was most important in her life.

And in choosing to fight her father's will over fighting for something that she loved, she had proven to Alex that a relationship between them would never work. Because, to him, you sacrificed for those you loved. They were what you really lived for, not glamorous vacations or luxury cars or a mansion so large that you needed a map to get around in it.

He was certain he and Katya could have made a go of it for a while. The sex was fantastic, and he enjoyed being in her company, even out of bed. But what would happen when the really important things in life happened? When the kids got sick or his sister got her heart broken? Or he had to face the choice between a nursing home and home care for his grandmother?

Alex looked at Nana then, knowing how easy that choice would be for him to make. He wasn't wealthy by Katya's standards, but he'd do whatever was necessary to make sure that Nana was loved and well cared for until her last breath on earth.

But what if that meant he couldn't afford to buy Katya the most expensive clothes or luxurious vacation? Alex was willing to bet that she'd begin to resent him for it, and that was no way to live.

Alex uncrossed his arms and stepped farther into the room, taking his grandmother's worn hands in his. "Yes, I gave Katya the choice between money and love, and she chose the wrong one."

Nana squeezed his hands tightly, her weathered skin wrinkled, yet soft, under his. "Are you sure that's how she saw it, Alex? Things aren't always so black-and-white to other people, you know. And you must remember that the poor girl's father abandoned her a long time ago, withholding everything from her except his money."

"D-do you think," Inez began, then stopped, as if searching for the right words. "Do you think that Katya equates love with money? I mean, as a child, you believe that if nobody else in the world loves you, your parents do, right? No matter what."

Maria frowned and scooted to the edge of the couch, propping her chin in her hands. "So, what happens when one of your parents dies and the other sends you away?"

"Exactly," Inez said, warming to the topic. "You have to believe that parent loves you, because if you don't . . ."

"If you don't, you simply couldn't survive," Nana finished quietly.

"So you start grasping at things, trying to find evidence that this love exists. Like, if your parents hit you, you tell yourself they're only doing it because they love you. Or if they mock you and make you feel small, you say it's only because they want you to do better for yourself."

"And if they withhold emotional affection, or send you away and never want to see you—" Alex began.

"You look at the money they provide and tell yourself that *this* is the proof you need that you are worthy

of being l-loved," Inez finished, not bothering to wipe
the tears from her eyes.

"So, you're trying to tell me that in Katya's mind,
money equals love?" Alex asked skeptically.

Nana released the grip she had on his hands. "We're
not trying to tell you anything, Alex. There are some
things you just have to figure out for yourself."

And with that, she gathered his sisters around her
and left, leaving the small room feeling empty and too
still in the oppressive heat of the desert summer.

With one hour to go before she had to leave for the
Salute Scottsdale party, Katya sat on the couch in her
apartment, Daisy's head resting in her lap.

"What am I supposed to do?" she asked, looking
from the check she held in one hand to the cash gripped
in the other.

Daisy cocked one ear and stretched out her hind legs
but didn't provide any insights.

"Do you realize that Amanda doesn't want you
back, dog?" Katya frowned. She had called Amanda's
number that morning after finally getting conclusive results back on Daisy. The news hadn't been good, and
Katya had hoped the problem would no longer rest on
her shoulders once she talked to Amanda.

"I can't deal with this," Amanda had responded
when Katya had told her what the vet had said. "I just
came home from the hospital yesterday and I'm so weak
I can barely lift my head. Besides . . ." She hesitated,
clearing her throat. "Besides, I didn't really like having
a dog anyway. I thought I would, but it's just too much
trouble. I had to get up even earlier than usual. And
everything she needs is so expensive. Not to mention the
slobber." Katya could almost hear Amanda's shudder
over the phone line. "To tell the truth, I was going to

take her back to the pound the night of the accident. I didn't say anything to Bobby because I didn't want him to be disappointed in me."

"But what if they put her to sleep?" Katya had asked.

"The way I see it, that's not my problem. I mean, I tried. I really did. Can I help it if I just didn't like her?"

Katya set the wad of cash on the table, then reached down and scratched the soft fur behind Daisy's ears. "She could have at least given you a chance. If she really wanted to love you, she would have given you a chance."

Daisy licked Katya's thigh with her bright pink tongue, as if to say that she agreed.

"But that's not my problem. I was only doing Alex a favor by taking you in for a while. You understand why I have to take you back to the pound, don't you?" Katya asked, trying to control the wobble in her voice. "I can't afford your vet bills, not on my pittance of a salary. Just look at the size of this check." She waved the piece of paper she was still clinging to with one hand in front of the dog's nose. "And who knows if I'll ever get my inheritance back? Even if I do, I travel all the time. That's no way for you to live, flying from one overcrowded city to another whenever the urge strikes me. No, you'll be better off with someone more stable. Someone with a nice, big backyard for you to run around in."

The dog closed her eyes and sighed, the flaps of her jaws billowing out. Katya drew in a shaky breath. It was the right choice. She knew it was.

So why, then, did it feel so wrong?

CHAPTER TWENTY-NINE

"YOU handled that camera situation beautifully, Alex," Barry Hampstead said, clapping Alex heartily on the back.

"Thanks, Barry." Alex tried to let some measure of pride at the hotel owner's compliment come through the gloom he was feeling, without much success. It had been four days since the scene in his office with Katya. Four miserable days when even the Diamondbacks' victory over the Colorado Rockies hadn't managed to improve his mood. Nor had his discussion with Nana and his sisters done his spirits any favors.

All of the psychobabble in the world couldn't change the fact that when the chips were down, Katya Morgan was only going to do what was in her own best interests—and the rest of the world be damned.

How could he have been so wrong about her?

He would have been willing to bet the Royal Palmetto itself that Katya had changed, that she cared more about Daisy than she did about continuing down the futile path of trying to fight her father's will.

It was a good thing nobody had taken that bet. He'd have lost his beloved hotel.

"Still, it shouldn't have happened in the first place," Chris Hampstead said, bringing Alex back to the moment.

They were in the main ballroom of the Royal Palmetto, a bustling hive of activity half an hour before the Salute Scottsdale party was to begin. The florist for the event was busy setting centerpieces on the round tables spaced around the ballroom floor. He had already placed an enormous spray of fragrant lilies and delicate roses on the rectangular table at the front of the room where the guests of honor would be seated. Jenny Tillman's staff bustled about, making sure the place settings were all in order before the first guests arrived.

Alex turned to look at the hotel owner's son. He assumed Barry had invited Chris to attend the party this evening after all, since Chris had changed from his usual business attire into an expensive-looking black tuxedo. Alex had just come back from changing clothes himself, having been tied up with overseeing the final arrangements for the party all day. No matter how competent the staff or the event organizers, there were always last-minute glitches that had to be addressed before they turned into full-blown disasters. At this event, it had been the unexpected illness of one of the scheduled speakers—the star forward of the Phoenix Suns. The event organizer had called in a panic, so Alex volunteered to call the starting pitcher for the D-Backs, a man Alex had become acquainted with when he'd first moved to Arizona and had stayed at the Royal Palmetto while searching for a home in the area.

With that crisis averted, Alex had come to do one final check of the ballroom when Barry and Chris had arrived.

"Tell me, Chris, what would you have done to prevent someone from planting a camera in a guest room?" Alex asked, trying to keep the irritation he felt out of his voice.

"You should have realized this sort of thing could happen and educated the maids earlier."

"I don't agree. You and I both know that there's a potential for all sorts of bad things to happen at a hotel.

A guest could tap the phones, or plant another camera, or hide listening devices in the couch. Or do a million other things I couldn't even conceive of right now. The only way to ensure that didn't happen would be to hire a security service to sweep every room between guests, and that's just not practical. We have a great track record here at the Royal Palmetto and we're doing everything within reason to make sure our guests enjoy a relaxing—and safe—stay at the hotel. That's all we can do."

"I agree with Alex," Barry said, his voice loud in the relative quiet of the ballroom.

"Of course you do," Chris muttered under his breath as his father turned to leave.

Alex frowned but didn't say anything.

"I'm going to go get a drink. You coming?" Barry asked, not bothering to turn around.

"Yeah. I'm right behind you," Chris answered.

Still frowning, Alex watched the two men leave. He probably shouldn't have put Chris on the spot, especially not in front of the other man's father. But Chris was always so cocky, so sure that he, and only he, had all the right answers. He refused to accept that people who had more experience than he did might know a thing or two about this business.

Shaking his head, Alex decided it was time he sat Chris down and had a serious talk with him. Chris would never succeed if he didn't stop alienating the people he worked with.

Tomorrow he'd solve this problem with Chris Hampstead for good.

Tonight, however, he had other things to deal with. Spotting Jenny Tillman as she strode into the room with a clipboard in her hand, Alex forgot Chris for now and waved her down.

"Jenny, how are you holding up?" he asked, meeting her halfway across the ballroom.

"Fine, so far. Two of the extra staff I had scheduled for the evening called in sick, but I think we'll be able to manage."

"Jenny, my girl. How's your old man doing?" Barry boomed from behind her, clapping the banquets manager on the back.

Alex noticed Jenny's grimace before she turned to greet her uncle. "He's fine, Uncle Barry."

"Is he still driving that bus part-time? Can't imagine why a man his age would want to do something like that."

"I don't think it's a matter of 'want,' Uncle Barry. You know my dad's pension isn't enough to cover Mom's nursing care bills, even with their Social Security." Jenny's supposedly good-natured smile was more than a little bit forced, but Barry didn't seem to notice.

Barry just laughed, which made Alex wince. He knew Jenny's mother, Barry's sister, had Alzheimer's and that Jenny's father had cared for her for as long as he was able before finally giving in and putting her in a nursing home. What Alex didn't know was why Barry refused to help out his own sister and brother-in-law with some much-needed cash, but he didn't think that was exactly a question he was in a position to ask.

Hoping to defuse the situation, Alex asked, "Will you excuse us, Barry? Jenny and I have some last-minute details to attend to."

When they were out of earshot, Jenny mumbled, "Thanks, Alex. Uncle Barry can be such a pompous asshole sometimes."

Alex just grunted, figuring it would be best if he didn't add fuel to that fire.

· · · ·

"Invitation, please."

Katya pulled the brown-and-white ticket out of the beaded silver bag at her side and handed it to the volunteer guarding the entrance of the Salute Scottsdale party. He tore the ticket in half and handed one piece back to her.

Looping Daisy's red leather leash around her hand, she put the torn scrap of paper back into her purse and started into the ballroom.

"Just a moment, ma'am. You can't take that dog in there," the volunteer said, putting a firm hand on her arm.

Katya turned and smiled brightly at the man. "Oh, I'm sorry. I guess I should have mentioned that Daisy is here as a representative of the Scottsdale Tracking Society. She's their top search-and-rescue dog, and holds the record for finding the most lost hikers in Grand Canyon National Park two years running." She added an eyelash bat or two for good measure. Daisy did her part by sitting next to her calmly, her head cocked as she watched the exchange.

"Oh. Well, then, I guess it would be all right to let her in. I apologize for the confusion. No one mentioned to me that we were expecting a dog."

Katya patted the man's shoulder comfortingly. "It's perfectly all right. All's well that ends well, I always say."

Turning, she gathered up the slack in Daisy's leash and said, "Heel," and the dog obediently trotted behind her and into the party.

In keeping with her renewed resolve to get back to her old way of life, Katya had decided that she was coming to the party tonight, whether Alex liked it or not. He had given her a ticket and she wasn't going to pass up the opportunity to take advantage of free food and booze. She had to bring Daisy because Mr. Eggers was on his date with Inez and couldn't dog-sit for her, but secretly Katya was just as happy to have the dog with her.

She had picked Daisy up from the vet's office on Monday night after her fight with Alex. Daisy's temperature had been dangerously high when Katya had brought her in, but they'd managed to bring it back to normal with cool water baths. The blood tests they'd taken had shown elevated potassium levels, which the vet said indicated that Daisy might have a serious illness called Addison's disease that was caused by an insufficient production of hormones by the adrenal gland. They had run one more test to see if this was the problem, and the results had come in this morning. Daisy did have Addison's, which meant she would have to have daily doses of costly steroids, and a stressful event could throw her into a crisis situation, when she'd have to be rushed to the vet and treated with intravenous fluids.

Katya kept telling herself she was glad that this would all be the humane society's problem soon, but then she worried about whether they would even bother to pay for Daisy's treatment with so many other pets to care for.

Reaching down, she patted the soft skin of Daisy's head. "Not that it matters to me, you know. You are not going to be my problem much longer."

Daisy closed her eyes in doggy ecstasy and wagged her stump of a tail.

Katya resisted the urge to bend down and bury her face in the dog's neck. *You don't want to risk getting your dress dirty,* she told herself, looking down at the red-sequin creation she had decided to wear this evening. The sequins covered a silky material that clung to her curves as she moved. The thin straps that looped over her shoulders made wearing a bra impossible, but the dress's tight fabric did a fine job of pushing her breasts together and up to give her a nice mound of cleavage to show off. She'd picked the dress initially because it matched Daisy's red leather leash. But it was also one of her favorites, and even if people did notice she'd worn it last season, at least she knew she looked sensational in it.

"Katya, my dear. You look lovely this evening."

Even before Daisy started to growl, Katya recognized Chris Hampstead's voice. "Easy, girl," she whispered, plastering a smile on her face before turning to greet Chris.

"Hi there. You're looking very dapper tonight yourself."

"Well, you know how it goes. If you want to be a successful hotel owner someday, you've got to dress the part."

Katya frowned at that. It was odd to think of Chris owning the Royal Palmetto, but of course, he would probably inherit the hotel when his father eventually died. For some reason, that just seemed so wrong. Alex Sheridan was so much more a part of the personality of the hotel than the current owner's son. She couldn't imagine anyone but Alex owning and managing the Royal Palmetto.

But, of course, that was not the way it would be.

Chris would inherit the hotel, and from the way the two men interacted now, Katya could clearly see that Alex would be the first employee to leave.

"Can I get you something to drink?" Chris asked.

"Yes, please. Some champagne would be nice."

Chris trotted off to the bar, and Katya stepped away from the crush of bodies mingling around the ballroom. Normally, she'd be right in the middle of the action,

small-talking with the best of them. But tonight she felt
restless and edgy, more content to stand on the outskirts
of the festivities than to be a part of them.

Looping Daisy's leash once, then twice, around her
hand, she watched the partygoers, making up conversations in her head.

The mayor's husband pumped away at another
man's hand. "Hey, Earl," she imagined him saying.
"Haven't seen you at the club lately. Everything all
right?"

And Earl would answer, "Just been busy at work,
you old dog. You know, not all of us have got wives
who make a nice living running an entire city. My missus is doing her part, though. She's keeping the economy
of Scottsdale going by spending all our money on new
clothes at Nordy's." This would be accompanied by a
hearty laugh, of course.

In another corner, two serious-looking women were
wrapped up in their own conversation.

Probably talking about the lack of funding for the
city's orchestra, Katya thought, absently scratching behind Daisy's ears.

Or the trials of menopause.

Or the state supreme court's latest unpopular ruling.

Then she spotted her stepmother, looking as calm
and cool as ever in an ice blue dress that shimmered
whenever she moved. Katya tilted her head, trying to
look objectively at the woman who had come to person-
ify Katya's ambivalence toward her father. Jillian took
a sip of wine and smiled up at her companion, but her
smile seemed strained and her movements controlled, as
if she had to force herself to go through the motions of
having a good time. And, for the first time since her
father's funeral, Katya felt a twinge of pity for the other
woman.

Jillian had been right. When she'd married Charles Morgan two years ago, there was no way she could have known that she'd be widowed so soon. She may have ended up with all the money, but if she had truly loved Katya's father, what sort of comfort was that?

Katya blinked.

Had she really just thought that? How could she feel any sympathy for the woman who had charmed her father into disinheriting his only child? In a flash, Nathan Rosenberg's words came back to her with full force: *"I can assure you the will was completely your father's idea. Both your stepmother and I tried to convince him that he was being unfair to you, but you know how he was when he had his mind made up about something. There was no reasoning with him."*

It was time that she stopped blaming Jillian for the mess she was in and put the responsibility back where it belonged—firmly on her father's shoulders. She was even willing to share in the blame, fifty-fifty. But none of what was happening to her now was her stepmother's fault, and Katya vowed right then to stop treating Jillian as some spoiled teenager would.

As for her father, Katya wasn't quite ready to stop being angry at him. She wasn't certain she ever would.

Looking away from her stepmother, she saw Chris threading through the crowd with two champagne flutes at the same time she caught a glimpse of Alex out of the corner of her eye. Instinctively she turned toward him, and felt her toes start to curl in her expensive silver sandals.

He looked gorgeous, all dressed up in a black tuxedo over a crisp white shirt with white buttons and a black bow tie. It was just a traditional tux, but on him it looked special. Katya was reminded of the line from a ZZ Top song: "Every girl's crazy 'bout a sharp-dressed man."

She didn't know about every girl, but she knew he looked sharp . . . and she knew she was crazy about him.

He glanced her way then and their eyes met. And held.

"Miss Morgan. I didn't expect to see you here."

Katya pulled her eyes away from Alex to see Paula Northcraft approaching with Chris at her heels.

"Here you are, Katya. To the most beautiful woman at the party," Chris toasted, thrusting the champagne glass into her hand and clinking the rim of his drink with hers. "And who might this be?" he asked, turning to Paula.

Katya performed the introductions, then looked back to where Alex had been standing.

He was gone.

It was probably just as well. She had some business to conduct with Paula anyway—business that Alex didn't approve of.

Unconsciously Katya patted the small beaded bag at her waist. She had pawned her bracelet yesterday and had received more money than she had expected for it. Four thousand dollars. Almost the entire amount of Paula's retainer. She was afraid to leave that much cash lying around her apartment, so she had brought it with her.

And now she had the chance to hand it over to the attorney, to get her to start working on fighting her father's will.

So why was she hesitating? This was what she wanted, right?

Daisy pushed her cold, moist nose into Katya's palm and snuffled. Two weeks ago, Katya would have been disgusted, would have raced to the nearest ladies' room to wash her hands.

Now she just shrugged. It would dry in a minute.

Besides, a little dog slobber never killed anyone.

She looked down at the dog, who looked back at her with huge dark brown eyes. Katya scratched under Daisy's chin and the dog's stubby tail immediately started wagging. It was so easy to make Daisy happy. All Katya had to do was touch her and the dog looked at her with an adoration that made Katya feel as if Daisy thought she was the best person in the whole world.

It was a very satisfying feeling, all in all.

But if Katya gave Paula Northcraft all her money, she wouldn't have anything set aside if Daisy got sick again.

If she didn't keep the money, Daisy might die.

The dog shifted position, rolling onto her left hip and propping herself against Katya's leg. Katya felt off balance and adjusted her stance. Daisy snorted her "happy dog" sigh and closed her eyes.

And suddenly it didn't matter that Daisy wasn't her dog. At that moment, standing in a crowded ballroom surrounded by strangers, Katya realized that she couldn't just tell herself not to care about Daisy and make it happen.

She loved Daisy, and there was nothing she could do to change that.

Just as she loved Alex and could no more stop loving him than she could stop the Earth from revolving around the sun. It didn't matter that Daisy might die or that Alex might leave her. She couldn't make herself feel differently than she did, and she'd just have to live with the risk that they'd desert her one day.

As the wave of emotion rose up, threatening to drown her, Katya murmured a hasty, "Excuse me," and fled to the bathroom with Daisy trotting behind her.

Not caring who might walk in and see her, Katya collapsed on the overstuffed plum-colored couch in the ladies' lounge and let the tears flow unchecked down her face.

How arrogant she had been to believe that she could decide how to feel or not feel about people. All these years, she had played at being shallow to keep people at bay. If she never really knew anyone, she couldn't begin to care. And if she did start to get close to someone, all she had to do was pack up and leave before it deepened to anything beyond minor affection. But now, being trapped at the Royal Palmetto and forced to really interact with Alex and Inez and Nana and Daisy and Mr. Eggers and even Mrs. Wagner down the hall, she had no choice but to become a part of their lives, just as they were now a part of hers.

Katya wrapped her arms around Daisy's neck and sobbed into her soft fur as the dog clambered up into her lap. Sixty-five pounds of pure adoration can cure a lot of ills, and Katya immediately felt better when the dog licked her face.

She hiccupped and wiped her wet face on Daisy's shoulder. "I promise I won't ever let anything happen to you," she said, feeling the tears start to drip down her face again.

Daisy laid her head down in Katya's lap and sighed contentedly.

CHAPTER THIRTY

IT took Katya half an hour to get her tears to stop. By the time she emerged from the ladies' room, though, she felt as if the old Katya Morgan had been left behind, wrapped up in the Kleenex she'd used to dry her eyes and tossed into the trash where the old Katya belonged.

The new Katya felt a bit shaky, her feet wobbling a bit on too-high silver sandals. She missed her comfy Keds, although she *did* still love this dress.

Some things would never change.

She stopped at the entrance of the ballroom and Daisy sat down next to her. Barry Hampstead was speaking, and she didn't want to cause a scene by walking to one of the tables in the middle of his speech. Instead, she stayed where she was, leaning up against the door frame for support.

"I can't tell you all how much this award means to me," Barry said, holding up a glass oval with a gold base. "Scottsdale has been my home for over a decade now, and I was so pleased to have the opportunity four years ago to be able to invest in the local economy by buying the Royal Palmetto. This hotel will always mean a lot to me, because it's part of what I've come to consider as my hometown.

"And, while I'd like to take all the credit for the success the Royal Palmetto has become, I can't do that. This hotel would not be what it is today if not for the efforts of a man who put his heart and soul into the renovation of this property and continues to put that same love into running it every day.

"So, to Alex Sheridan, the general manager of the Royal Palmetto and a man who is just like a son to me—this award belongs to you as much as to me."

There was much clapping and cheering, and Katya searched the crowd for Alex, who she knew would be immensely pleased at Barry's praise. She spotted him at a table in the front, looking sheepishly at Barry as his tablemates clapped him on the back.

Barry walked over to Alex and enfolded him in a bearlike hug, then made him pose with the award between them as several photographers snapped off pictures.

Katya smiled and started forward to take an empty seat now that she could do so without interrupting the program. That was when she noticed Chris, whose face was about the same color as a pickled beet, getting up from a table in the back and racing out of the ballroom.

Poor Chris. He'd be so much better off if he'd get out from under his father's thumb and find a job that made him happy, rather than trying to take jobs that would please his parents.

Shaking her head, Katya sat down in an empty seat. Daisy crawled under the table and lay down with her head on Katya's feet. Katya wiggled her toes into the dog's fur as the next speaker took her spot at the podium.

Katya surreptitiously fed Daisy pieces of her filet mignon after the entrée was served, explaining to her seatmate that the dog had been nominated for Scottsdale's Most Valuable Citizen Award, but lost to a doctor at Children's Hospital who had raised over $5 million to fund research for leukemia.

"You just can't compete against that," the man said. "That's what I told Daisy, but she was still very disappointed," Katya agreed. Having a neurotic dog wasn't such a bad thing after all, she thought, passing another piece of meat under the table. At least it provided her with an interesting topic of conversation at parties.

By the time the meal was over, the speeches were, too. A band was set up in one corner of the ballroom, and the banquets staff carted dishes out of the room as people finished their dessert and coffee to make way for the dancing that was to start in half an hour.

Katya thanked her seatmate for being such a pleasant dinner companion, then stood up to search for Alex. She wanted to tell him she wasn't going to pursue fighting her father's will anymore. More important, she wanted to tell him that she had realized that she loved him.

She spied him at the front of the room, surrounded by well-wishers. Figuring she'd have to fight her way into the throng, she tugged Daisy's leash and said, "Come on, girl."

Before she got far, she was stopped by Paula Northcraft.

"Miss Morgan, I'd really like to talk to you."

"I'd like to talk to you, too, but I have something important to do now. Can I call you on Monday?"

"Of course, but I think this is something you'd want to hear about now."

Katya watched as Alex turned away and started to leave the room. She had to talk to him, and now. The new her just couldn't wait to tell him how she felt.

"I'm sorry, but I've got to go. I'll call you on Monday," she said distractedly before hurrying after Alex's retreating back.

"Alex, wait," she called as she drew nearer.

His shoulders stiffened, but he didn't stop walking.

Katya almost ran to catch up with him.

"Wait," she said, reaching out to grab his arm.

He stopped, then slowly turned to face her. "We don't have anything to say to each other, Katya."

Katya smiled. "Yes, we—"

"Mr. Sheridan," a husky voice interrupted, "I'm Beth Ginger from the the *Arizona Republic*. I'd like to talk to you about the renovation of the Royal Palmetto and how you think the hotel fits into the mayor's plans for the future of Scottsdale." She paused. "Unless I'm interrupting, of course."

Katya's smile dimmed somewhat. The old Katya would have told the reporter to go away, that they were having a personal conversation here. But she wasn't that person anymore. Good publicity for the hotel was important to Alex, and he didn't need to pass up the opportunity to talk about his vision for the Royal Palmetto to hear about Katya's emotional breakthrough.

Besides, she had all the time in the world to tell him that she loved him.

"No, of course not," Katya answered smoothly. "Alex, I really do need to talk to you. Would you meet me back at your suite when you're finished with Ms. Ginger?"

Alex frowned but obviously couldn't think of a polite way to refuse her request in front of the reporter, so he agreed before turning his attention to the other woman.

Katya turned back to the party and sighed. She didn't want to spend the next half hour drinking and chatting with strangers. She looked for Paula Northcraft, figuring she had time now to see what the attorney wanted to discuss with her, but the lawyer was nowhere in sight.

"Well, Daisy, how would you like to take a walk?"

The dog grabbed her leash in her mouth and Katya grinned. Reaching down, she ruffled the dog's fur. "You are such a goof. Come on."

The cool evening wind tickled Katya's skin as she walked the grounds. Although it was summer, it was relatively cool this late in the evening. It was also very quiet. Even the birds seemed to be asleep. She wondered briefly why the crickets weren't chirping but decided that maybe it was still too early. A lime fell off a nearby tree as she passed, startling her with the sudden *plop* it made when it hit the ground.

She meandered through the main courtyard, taking a deep breath of the mesquite wood that was stacked by the outdoor fireplace. There would be no need for a fire tonight.

Just as she had that thought, she noticed a strange orange flickering in the distance.

"*Ay, Dios mio,* Daisy. What is that?" she said, fearing she already knew the answer as she started running toward the light.

CHAPTER THIRTY-ONE

"So, Ms. Northcraft, I understand that Katya Morgan is a client of yours," Alex said, taking a sip of his Chardonnay.

"Actually, no. She and I have discussed some matters pertaining to her father's will, but she's never put me on retainer."

"I'm sure it won't be long now," Alex said evenly, wondering why Katya hadn't turned over the money from her bracelet yet. He figured that she'd pawned it first thing on Monday night, even before going to pick Daisy up at the vet's office.

"Actually, I have some news that will make it unnecessary for her to hire me. I tried telling her tonight, but she seemed preoccupied."

"What do you mean?"

Paula smiled in a friendly manner. "I'm sorry, I can't discuss the details with anyone but her. I'm sure you understand."

Alex took another sip of wine. "Yes, of course. I didn't mean to pry. I just know how important the money is to her."

"Well, it is a considerable amount that she lost. How would you feel if your father left you with nothing and no explanation for why he was punishing you?"

After three hours of listening to his family's not-so-subtle lecture loop over and over in his head, Alex was ready to concede the point. Maybe they were right. Maybe he was oversimplifying the issue, pretending it was black-and-white rather than an entire rainbow of shades in between.

He tried to picture himself in Katya's shoes, but couldn't quite do it. Then he imagined his eight-year-old niece, Merrilee, motherless, sent away to one impersonal boarding school after another while her father refused to send for her because she reminded him too much of her mother. And, right then, he felt it—the loneliness of a little girl willing to believe her father loved, her because at least he paid her bills.

In a flash, he finally understood what Nana, Maria, and Inez had been saying earlier that evening. In the absence of real love, people will grasp at anything they can to feel that they're not worthless and unwanted. And if they find that one thing that makes them feel loved, and you try to take that away, you threaten to destroy the very thing that helps them to survive in an often uncaring world.

All this time, he had thought the choice was so easy.

Pick one: money or love.

He had been so foolish, so arrogant, to think he had all the answers. For someone like Katya, who had grown up with nothing but money, losing that, too, must have seemed like the last straw.

And he had been ready to give up on her.

What sort of person did that make him? He claimed to love her, but he hadn't really. Not until this instant, when he saw inside her heart and her mind and understood that, for her, choosing money *was* choosing love. Fighting for her inheritance was not about the cash or material possessions it would bring. It was about trying to win back her father's love from beyond the grave. Why hadn't he been able to see that before?

In truth, she had adapted extremely well to the financial hardships since her father had died. Yes, she'd grumbled about the size of her apartment and having to get up early to go to work, but, really, for someone accustomed to the luxuries that she had lived with her entire life, she had taken the physical setbacks incredibly well.

It was the emotional setback that was crippling her.

In that moment, Alex knew that he honestly loved Katya Morgan, warts and all. He also knew that he had to go to her, to tell her that he understood and that he would stand behind her, whatever she decided to do about her father's will.

Because when you loved someone, you didn't turn your back on her—even when her behavior disappointed you. At some point, she'd have to admit that she cared as much about Nana, Inez, Daisy, and him as they cared for her. Maybe then she'd realize that loving someone wasn't really such a risk.

"Are you all right?" Paula Northcraft asked, looking at him strangely, making Alex realize he had been staring blankly at the woman while having his epiphany.

Alex blinked and cleared his throat. "Yes, sorry, I'm fine. Katya and I are supposed to meet back at my room this evening. Would you like to tell her your news tonight?" he asked, knowing Katya would want to hear any news the attorney might have about her inheritance.

"I'd love to. She said she'd call me on Monday, but I can guarantee you that this is something she'd want to know right away."

Alex set his half-full glass down on a tray and started to lead Paula outside. Just before he got to the doors, someone tapped him on the shoulder. He turned to see Jillian Morgan standing there, looking as cool and untouchable as always.

"I'm sorry to interrupt, Alex, but do you happen to

know where Katya went? I . . . I have something I urgently need to discuss with her."

Alex sighed. It looked as if he were going to have to take a number to talk to the woman he loved. "Yes, we're going to meet her right now. Would you like to join us?"

Jillian nodded and preceded him and Paula out into the still night air.

Alex looked up at the inky night sky dotted with twinkling silver stars, obscured here and there by thick, heavy rain clouds. The desert sky seemed so huge and open, as if the sky were larger here than anywhere else. He took a deep breath and rolled his shoulders back.

Today had been—

His thoughts were interrupted by Paula Northcraft's gasp. "Oh my God. It's a fire."

Alex opened his eyes, following Paula's pointed finger. Off in the distance, an eerie orange light burned bright against the dark sky. "Go call nine-one-one," he ordered, taking off at a run toward the flames.

Katya got close enough to realize that the orange light she saw was, indeed, a fire. It was already burning too fast for her to try to put it out by herself. She had to go get help.

Turning, she prepared to sprint back to the party, then drew up short when Jenny Tillman appeared in front of her.

Jenny held a baseball bat in one hand and was thwacking it against the palm of her other hand menacingly.

"Miss Tillman, what are you doing?" Katya asked, grabbing Daisy's leash to keep her out of harm's way. She could feel the vibrations from the dog's throat thrumming through the leash as Daisy growled.

"I'm burning this fucking place down, that's what I'm doing." She smacked the bat hard against her palm again. "And when Alex comes running to stop me, I'm going to kill him with his own baseball bat. I'd say that would be a fitting end to this story, wouldn't you?"

Katya swallowed past the lump in her throat. "No. I would say that's crazy. Alex hasn't done anything to you."

"You don't know anything about this. I was supposed to get the job as general manager at the Royal Palmetto, and I would have, too, if Alex hadn't sucked up to my Uncle Barry four years ago. And now he's training my shit-for-brains cousin to take over, instead of me. I'm sick of always being passed over for a job I've worked almost my entire life preparing for. It's not fair, and I'm not going to put up with it anymore. If I can't run this hotel, no one can."

"That doesn't make any sense. Burning down the hotel and hurting people isn't going to get you what you want. Maybe you just need to go back to school for some more training or something," Katya said, trying to remain calm and not blurt out that perhaps what Jenny really needed was a nice dose of Prozac and a long stay at the funny farm.

"Shut up," Jenny said quietly, continuing to thwack the bat against her palm threateningly. "Or maybe I'll kill you, too."

Katya grabbed Daisy's leash with both hands as the dog started dragging her toward Jenny. She would have let the dog go, but she was afraid the other woman might be able to get a damaging blow in before Daisy could knock her over. As it was, the chunky heels of Katya's own impractical sandals sank into the soft earth as she tried to hold Daisy back.

"Alex Sheridan has done everything he could think

of to turn my uncle and my cousin against me. I've tried to show them that Alex doesn't know what he's doing here, but they just won't see it."

"How have you tried to show Barry that Alex isn't competent?" Katya asked, using her most reasonable voice. Maybe if she could stall Jenny long enough, help would come. Surely the fire alarms would be going off by now. Of course, they were in one of the most remote areas of the property behind Alex's suite, which was away from the guest rooms, affording its occupant at least some small measure of privacy. But she could still hope.

"I set fire to the Camelback Hotel and suggested to the GM that the Royal Palmetto could accommodate their conference, knowing the animal rights activists were booked to stay there at the same time the Cattlemen's Association was supposed to be here. I thought having the two groups here together would cause problems, but Alex managed to come out smelling like a rose, like always. Then I put Ipecac into the mashed potatoes at the cattlemen's banquet to make them sick, but not even one of them has sued. I even planted a camera in one of the guest rooms, but it took forever for someone to find it."

Katya tried to marshal her expression into something other than disbelief.

This woman was freaking nuts.

"I couldn't wait any longer to see what would happen after the camera was discovered, and I figured I'd had enough of Alex Sheridan. That elevator accident was meant for him, not that poor little maid. Alex was the one who was supposed to die.

"But he didn't. Oh, no. Nothing sticks to Alex. But this time I've got him. I've poured gasoline all over the place and it's going to go up like a tumbleweed. Alex will see the hotel he cares so much about going up in flames and there won't be a thing he can do about it. Then he's going to come back here and see what's happened to you." Jenny giggled, and Katya tried to take a step back from the force of her insanity.

"I almost hate to ask this, but what's going to happen to me?" she asked, struggling to stay calm.

"I've decided that I am going to kill you, after all. I might toss your body into the flames, but that might make you unrecognizable. But it would be great for effect, don't you think?"

Katya didn't know quite how to answer that, so she let Jenny ponder it herself. In the meantime, she assessed her captor, wondering if she could overpower the other woman. Unfortunately, Jenny was wearing a short-sleeved T-shirt and it appeared that she worked out. Regularly. Unlike Katya, whose only form of exercise was bending over to make beds or reaching up to clean soiled grout in the showers.

"We need to get the fire started back here," Jenny said, obviously deciding that the question of whether to barbecue Katya or not could wait for later. Gesturing with the bat, she pointed to a can of gasoline. "Pick that up and start pouring it on the building. And don't let go of that fucking dog or I'll kill you both right now."

Katya eased her hold on Daisy's leash a bit so she could pick up the gas can. Tugging at the tight leather to get the dog away from Jenny, she awkwardly juggled the heavy metal container as her heels sank into the grass, hindering her progress.

"Hurry up!" Jenny shouted.

"I'm trying. I'm not exactly dressed for arson."

It took Katya a few tries to raise the gas can above her waist while still holding Daisy's leash, but she finally managed to pour fuel on the bougainvillea surrounding

Alex's suite of rooms. She tried to spill as much as she could on the grass, where it wouldn't do much more than fry a couple of worms, but she wasn't entirely successful.

When the can was empty, she set it on the ground and turned back around to face Jenny. "Now what?" she asked.

"Pull your lighter out of your purse. I've seen you smoking with the other housekeepers, so don't try to tell me that you don't have one."

Katya looked steadily back at Jenny, trying to think of a way out of this mess. "I don't have a lighter with me. I had to quit smoking this week. I couldn't afford the brand I like, and bargain cigarettes taste terrible. They're so . . . harsh."

Jenny sighed. "Fine. I'll give you mine." She lowered the bat for just a moment as she dug one hand into the front pocket of her navy slacks.

Katya saw her chance.

She released Daisy's leash and the dog lunged. But rather than going for Jenny's throat, Daisy clamped her strong jaws down on the bat she had been brandishing at them.

"Good dog. Stay!" Katya yelled, bending down to pick up the end of Daisy's bright red leash.

As Jenny struggled to get the bat out of Daisy's hold, Katya ran around her in ever-tightening circles. She pulled on the leash, and Jenny was trapped, unable to move.

With one mighty shove, Katya pushed the other woman to the ground, where she struggled futilely against the sturdy leather that bound her.

"Daisy, down," Katya ordered, and the dog released her hold on the bat, which was now tied up tightly against Jenny's leg. Daisy stepped back, which only served to constrict the bindings holding Chris's cousin.

Katya looked down at the struggling woman on the lawn. Well, she'd managed to subdue her attacker, but now what? If she let go of her end of the leash, Jenny would get away. And she couldn't send Daisy for help. She might be a smart dog, but real life wasn't Disney.

Fortunately, she was saved from having to figure out what to do next when Alex arrived on the scene, panting.

"Katya, are you all right?"

"I'm fine. And your timing is impeccable."

Alex stopped at the corner of the building, trying to take it all in. Katya and Daisy stood at opposite ends of Jenny Tillman's body, each one holding an end of a red leash as if they were playing some strange game of tug-of-war. He'd come running to save the day, only it looked as if his services were no longer needed.

His damsel in distress had apparently saved herself with a handful of leather and a loaded boxer.

Alex grinned at her, and Katya got a strange look in her eyes and dropped Daisy's leash.

A crack of thunder erupted overhead, startling them both.

Jenny took the opportunity to unravel herself enough to get a hand free and wrap it around Katya's ankle. She let go with a yell when Daisy grabbed hold of Jenny's ankle with her teeth.

Almost immediately, the sky opened up in one of the torrential downpours that were so common in Scottsdale in the summer.

Alex was at Katya's side in two strides, uncaring about the rain drenching them all. With Daisy doing a stellar job as jailer, he wrapped Katya in his arms and buried his face in her silky hair.

"I was so scared when I realized you were out here," he said, stroking her back.

"I was a little scared myself. I never realized that Jenny was nuts. Did you?"

"What do you mean?"

"She's the one who started the fire. And caused a lot more trouble at the Royal Palmetto besides."

Alex crushed her even closer to him, her wet hair dripping onto his tuxedo jacket. "I don't want to talk about Jenny now. The fire department is on their way, and we can hand her over to them as our arsonist."

Katya smiled up at him, and Alex moved his hands up to frame her face.

"I love you, Katya Morgan."

"I love you, too, Alex Sheridan."

Alex dropped his hands in surprise. "What?"

"I said, 'I love you, too.' Why are you so surprised?"

They both heard Jenny's yelp of pain behind them but ignored it. Being chewed on but Daisy was the least that she deserved.

"I didn't think you were ready to admit it to yourself yet. I thought, after you decided to choose the attorney over Daisy, that you were still entrenched in your old 'I don't care about anyone but myself' attitude."

"But I didn't."

"Didn't what?" Alex asked, confused.

"I didn't choose the attorney over Daisy. I was going to call Paula on Monday and tell her that I didn't want to retain her services. I have to save my money for Daisy's medical care. I just can't take the risk that she'll need something I can't afford to provide for her. I care too much about her, even though she's neurotic. And she snores. And slobbers."

Alex rested his forehead on hers and smiled down at her. "I know," he said. "Ain't love grand?"

"Would you two please stop making googly eyes at

each other and get this dog off me?" Jenny hollered.

"No," they responded in unison, right before they heard the sirens at the front of the hotel.

Ignoring the noise of the fire trucks and Jenny's wailing, Alex lowered his mouth to Katya's and kissed her tenderly.

This was one damsel in distress he wouldn't mind rescuing for the rest of his life.

CHAPTER THIRTY-TWO

ALEX let Katya go when he heard the sound of someone coughing behind them. He kept his arm around her shoulders as he turned around. After dumping on them for less than a minute the rain had stopped, but that had been enough to put out the fire that Jenny had started.

Barry Hampstead stood beside Jillian, Paula North-craft, and a blond fireman. *Or would that be firewoman? Fireperson?* Alex wondered, given the sex of said rescue worker.

"Jenny? Alex? What's going on here?"

Katya answered before Alex could, "Mr. Hampstead, I'm so sorry to tell you this, but your niece is the one who started the fire at the Royal Palmetto tonight. She also tried to burn down the Camelback Inn a few weeks ago. And she poisoned the cattlemen. And planted that camera in the guest room. And sabotaged the elevator that Amanda was injured on."

"Is this true?" Barry asked, looking down at his niece with a horrified expression on his face.

"Yes, it's true, you stupid bastard. You let Alex have my job, and then you were going to give the hotel to Chris. But I'm the one who deserved it. Me!" Jenny screeched, wriggling ineffectually against the damp leash that bound her.

"What are you talking about? Alex doesn't have your job."

"I was supposed to be the GM. You were supposed to hire me." Jenny was sobbing now. "But you didn't.

You've always resented me because my father took my mother away from you when she got pregnant with me. That's how you saw it, isn't it, you jealous fool?"

Barry's face had turned the same shade as the fire trucks in the parking lot of the Royal Palmetto. "That's ridiculous. If your mother was foolish enough to run off with your father—who I always told her would amount to nothing—I can assure you I never held it against you. And I was certainly not jealous. I simply felt that your mother had made her own bad choices, against my advice, and she should have to live with the consequences."

"You pompous—" The rest of Jenny's diatribe was muffled by the mouthful of lawn she inhaled as her writhing positioned her face-down in the grass.

"I'll take it from here," the fireperson said. "You can call off your dog now."

Katya moved to Daisy and unclipped the leash from her collar. Daisy continued to growl at Jenny but stepped back as they unraveled her leash from Jenny's body.

"Good dog," Katya said, patting Daisy on the head as Jenny was led away.

"I don't know what that fool girl was caterwauling about," Barry complained. "She was never in line for the job of general manager at the Royal Palmetto, and neither is that fool son of mine. I wouldn't make the mistake of putting him in charge of such an expensive property. Now, I do own a nice Motel Six down in Alabama that I thought he might be able to handle." Barry wandered away, continuing to mutter to himself.

"What a crazy family," Alex said, turning to Katya with the intent of continuing to avow his love for her.

"I'm sorry to keep intruding, Miss Morgan," Paula Northcraft interrupted just as Alex opened his mouth to speak. "But I really do have some good news that I think you'd like to hear."

Katya grabbed Alex's strong hand and laced her fingers with his. Her other hand stayed on Daisy's head, and Katya felt that she couldn't be happier than she was right now, standing between the man and the dog that she loved. But, obviously, the lawyer had something to say and Katya wasn't going to stop her.

Squeezing Alex's fingers, Katya smiled at the other woman. "Shoot," she said.

"All right. Well, first I have to tell you how I came about this information. You see, a few years back, I got a call from my sister, who drives ambulances for a living. Now, before you let loose with any 'ambulance chaser' wisecracks, let me just say that this is *not* my usual way of drumming up business. But in this one instance, my sister responded to a call involving a car accident. The driver of the car was injured pretty badly through no fault of her own, and the guy who hit her was a contractor who filed for bankruptcy and refused to pay her medical bills. She didn't have the money to fight him, but she remembered that my sister had given her one of my cards and told her to call me if she needed help.

"Anyway, I ended up taking her case and we won. During the process, she got really interested in the law and decided to start working toward a law degree. In the meantime, she's been working as a paralegal at Rosenberg, Powell, and Kingman," Paula said, naming the firm Katya's father had used.

Katya scratched behind Daisy's ears, only half-listening to the attorney's drawn-out tale.

"I guess that's a long way of telling you that I have a friend at RPK who felt that she owed me a favor. She and I had drinks together the other day and I mentioned that I might be doing some work on your case. I didn't ask her to do any snooping for me, mind you. I am not unethical, and I wouldn't even share this with you if you weren't going to learn about it next year anyway."

"What are you saying?" Alex asked, impatient to get this over with and get Katya alone so he could demonstrate properly how pleased he was at how this evening had ended.

"I'm saying," Paula Northcraft said, pulling a set of folded papers from her purse, "that Miss Morgan will be getting her inheritance in just over ten months."

"What?" Katya squealed, feeling as if her eyes were about to drop out of her head and fall to the lawn.

"Yes, that was part of the agreement that your father made me sign," Jillian said, seeming to glide over the lawn toward them.

Paula seemed as stunned as Katya and Alex by the interruption.

Jillian stopped ten feet from them, her gown glowing as if she were a moon unto herself. "When your father realized he hadn't much time to . . ." She paused, a creamy white hand fluttering to her throat. "When he realized that he was going to die soon, he had his attorney draw up some papers for me to sign. You see, he knew that if he left his money to you outright, Katya, you'd continue on the unhappy and unproductive path you'd been on for so long. He knew he had been a neglectful father, and that he was much to blame for your outrageous behavior, so he decided that he would try to put a stop to it in the only way he knew how."

Jillian's speech was interrupted by the deafening roar of a motorcycle engine. They turned as a group as the Harley turned off the sidewalk and onto the lawn, turning sideways at the last minute like in some Hollywood movie.

"What now?" Alex groaned, tightening his hold on Katya's hand. All he wanted was to drag her back to his casita and tell her how much he loved her, and have her tell him the same thing in return. Okay, and maybe get laid in the shower. And on the couch. And in bed. And—

He totally lost that train of thought when his sister— his timid younger sister who had never done anything out of the ordinary in her entire life—pulled the helmet off her head and threw one leg off the Harley in a perfect dismount.

"Inez? Mr. Eggers?" Katya sputtered from beside him. "What are you doing here?"

Inez grinned, her hair falling loose and wild around her shoulders and her eyes sparkling like some beautiful brown gemstone that had yet to be discovered. "Derrick—that is, Mr. Eggers—is a detective in the Scottsdale Police Department. We were back in his apartment, um, playing chess when he heard the call go out about a fire at the Royal Palmetto. We got here as soon as we could. Is everything all right?"

Katya couldn't seem to clamp her jaw shut. "Playing chess, my eye," she wanted to say, but the words wouldn't come out. Inez looked like a totally different woman tonight, and it had nothing to do with the makeup.

"Everything's fine," Alex answered, still looking more than a little baffled at this turn of events. "Maybe we should go inside?"

Everyone thought that was a grand idea, and they commenced traipsing across the lawn to Alex's suite. Katya handed out towels to everyone, making sure to save one to dry off Daisy, who seemed to think this was all some sort of grand game. Alex was in the middle of ordering drinks from room service when a perfunctory knock on the door sounded before it opened, letting in another forty people.

At least, that's what it seemed like to Alex, who wanted nothing more than to be alone with Katya right now.

Instead, he was being invaded by his entire family.

Damn. Inez must have called them before racing over on her boyfriend's hog to save the day.

He ordered more drinks, then went over to the couch and laid claim to the spot next to Katya, squeezing out one of his sisters. Daisy was curled up at Katya's feet, happily watching the crowd of people as they darted about in the small room.

Beside him, Katya smiled contentedly and laid her hand over his.

"Look at all these people," she said.

"I know. I can't get rid of them," Alex answered, lightly tracing the lines on her palm with one finger. "Believe me, I've tried."

"No," she said, raising her gaze to meet his, "that's not what I meant at all. I feel so . . ." She swallowed visibly and her eyes filled with tears, and Alex put his arm across her shoulders, having no clue as to what was the matter. She buried her head in his chest, her shoulders shaking as she cried.

"Aw, dammit. Don't cry," Alex pleaded, feeling his heart constrict. As always, he felt helpless in the face of tears. Give him a problem to solve and he knew what to do. But this sobbing just left him feeling totally inadequate.

Katya lifted her head and sniffed. "I'm sorry. I'm just . . . I'm just so used to being alone."

Alex put a hand under her chin and brought her lips to his, kissing her tenderly. "Marry me and I will guarantee that you'll never be alone again," he whispered.

"You're going to need to wait on that for a year."

Katya and Alex gasped in unison and turned at the dryly uttered comment.

Alex was the first to regain his composure. "Why do you say that?"

Jillian sat down in the newly vacated chair beside them, and, seeing them, Paula Northcraft wandered over to join the conversation.

"Is this about the will?" she asked, and Jillian nodded.

"Yes, this is about the will. It seems that Paula has already discovered your father's secret, but perhaps it might help if I explained it."

"Go ahead. I'd love to know the 'why' of it," Paula conceded, settling herself on the floor.

"As I was saying earlier, your father knew he was dying and felt it was important for him to try to do in death what he hadn't had the courage to do when he was alive. He wanted you to learn how to live a normal life," Jillian said, speaking directly to Katya.

Katya dropped Alex's hand and leaned forward, listening intently to Jillian's words. "But why? I was happy with my life as it was."

"Were you really?" Jillian asked, then continued without waiting for a reply, "He didn't think so, and neither did I. We both thought that your behavior was going to become more and more outrageous in a desperate bid for attention, until you did something that couldn't be fixed with money. My suggestion was to put you on a strict budget, but your father . . . well, honestly, I don't think your father had the courage to stand up to you. Whenever he saw you, he saw your mother, and his resolve crumbled."

Katya dropped her gaze then, looking at Daisy with tear-filled eyes. "Why couldn't he ever see past that? I loved my mother and I needed him when she died, but he just pushed me away."

Jillian hesitantly reached out, offering Katya her hand. Katya gripped her stepmother's hand ferociously, as if trying to regain some connection with her father.

"I don't know, Katya. I wish I did, but I don't. All I can say is that he tried to do what was right at the end."

Katya squeezed her stepmother's hand compassionately. It had to be difficult for her to talk about those last days. Katya had never thought about it before, about how frightening it must have been for Jillian to be with her husband, both of them knowing he had so few days left to live.

After a long pause, Jillian continued, her voice calm and controlled, as if she just wanted to get through this next part so she could leave, "Before your father died, he convinced me to sign an agreement to take away your inheritance. If I didn't sign it, he was going to donate it all to a variety of charities, and, while I'm all for supporting a good cause, I could not, in good conscience, just step aside and watch your birthright disappear. So, I agreed to his wishes."

"And you knew about the conditions?" Paula Northcraft asked from her seat on the floor.

"Yes," Jillian replied, smiling faintly.

"What conditions?" Alex asked.

"First, Miss Morgan had to get a job and remain gainfully employed for at least ten of the next twelve months," Paula interjected.

"Ah," Alex said.

"What do you mean, 'ah'?" Katya asked, suspicious.

"Jillian asked me if I'd give you a job at the hotel. I wondered at the time why she seemed so anxious to see you working. Now I know why."

"You did that?" Katya felt a growing sense of shame, especially when she remembered how she had tricked Jillian into leaving the house so she could ransack it.

"Yes, she did," Alex answered when Jillian would have remained silent.

"Thank you," Katya said, feeling a wave of gratitude for her stepmother.

"There were other conditions, too," Paula continued. "Your picture couldn't appear in the tabloids more than three times during the year."

Katya smiled. "Well, I guess that means I have two more shots," she said, remembering the picture of her and Chris Hampstead on the floor of his parents' living room on the night he'd gotten drunk and made asses out of both of them. "Anything else?"

"Yes, there were two more conditions," Jillian answered. "The first was that I was not to help you in any way. I had to get rid of anything you might be able to pawn for cash. I couldn't let you come stay at the house, or give you any money, or let you know that you could regain your inheritance by satisfying these conditions. If I did, we would both lose everything."

"We would?" Katya asked, horrified. It seemed that her stepmother had just sacrificed her own inheritance, as well as Katya's, to come clean.

Jillian looked from Paula to Alex to Katya. "Yes. I have ten million dollars at stake here. The other conditions are measurable; they're things that Nathan Rosenberg can see and tally up. But not this one."

"So, why are you telling us this now? It seems to me that you've just sacrificed a hell of a lot of money yourself," Alex said, pulling Katya closer to him on the couch. He couldn't seem to get enough of touching her. The smooth skin of her bare arms against him was driving him wild. He had to get rid of all these people, and soon, or he'd go crazy.

Jillian answered his question, looking directly at Katya, "Because I'm not as strong as your father believed me to be. I can't stand seeing you suffer any more than he could. And I think he was unfair to you. He threw you out into the world and expected you to meet his expectations without telling you what those expectations were." She paused, rubbing her hands up and down her own bare arms. "I don't think he even knew what he wanted from you. I refuse to be a party to this anymore. I got rid of everything that wasn't a gift, just as I was supposed to. But that's it. I'm done. And the four of us . . . well, we all have our own reasons to keep this quiet until the year is out, don't we?" She looked pointedly at Paula, who shifted her gaze to the carpet, which Alex took to mean that the attorney would be well compensated for her silence.

"Why did the conditions of the will need to remain a secret in the first place?" Katya asked. "The end result would have been the same, so why the subterfuge?"

"Your father thought that if you knew this was only going to be temporary, you'd just go through the motions. You'd get a job and stay out of trouble for twelve months just to get the money, but then you'd go right back to your old life."

"Oh," Katya said, feeling more than a little bewildered. One part of her was furious that her father had felt the need to manipulate her into doing what he wanted, but another part wanted to believe that he must have loved her just a little to care so much about what became of her after his death.

She sighed. Why did her feelings for her father have to be so damn complicated? Why couldn't he have made things easy for her by not throwing this at her? If he had disinherited her for good, she could continue feeling righteous anger toward him for the rest of her life. Now she had to wrestle with more emotions than she knew how to deal with: resentment, guilt, hate, love.

At that moment, Alex touched her shoulder with his hand. It was a fleeting touch, nothing more than a butterfly's caress, but Katya leaned into it. And suddenly she didn't feel quite so overwhelmed anymore. Somehow, just knowing that there was someone in the world who really, truly loved her made all the difference. So what if her father hadn't been able to see past her resemblance to her mother? That didn't make her a bad person. It made *him* weak and confused and bitter and unlovable, but it was not a reflection on her. It had been him all along.

Jillian slid forward on the chair next to her, interrupting Katya's thoughts. "I need to leave now, but maybe one day we can—" She broke off, her voice hitching.

Without hesitating, Katya moved off the couch to embrace her stepmother, bending down awkwardly to hug her. "We will, Jillian. Thank you for trying to believe in me. I know I didn't give you much to go on."

Jillian hugged her back. "I hope you've decided that you want to change. For your own sake, more than anything else. Your father's gone, and whatever he wanted for you or from you"—she paused with a shrug, then continued—"it really doesn't matter anymore. This is your life, and the choices you make from now on should be the ones that are right for what you want out of life, not things you do just to spite people or try to get attention."

Stepping back, Katya reached for Alex's hand and smiled. "I think I finally understand what you mean."

"Good." With that, Jillian pushed herself out of the

chair and glided through the crowd of Alex's family and out into the night.

Alex thought it was high time his family cleared out for the evening so he could give Katya a proper proposal, although she'd have to make do with only the promise of an engagement ring. Standing up, he cleared his throat loudly and announced, "All right, everyone, listen up. Katya and I appreciate your concern for us, but as you can see, we're both fine. It's getting late and we both have to work tomorrow, so, if you don't mind, we'd like to call it a day."

There was much mumbling and grumbling and it took a while to get people moving toward the door (after all, it wasn't every day that such drama entered their lives), but at long last Alex and Katya were finally alone.

Alex closed the door behind his grandmother after dropping a kiss on her soft cheek and promising to come to dinner tomorrow night. With a heartfelt sigh, he turned to the living room and pulled Katya into his arms. Daisy got up off the floor and pushed her nose between them. Katya reached down to scratch the dog's ears, enjoying the feel of Alex's strong hands caressing her back through the filmy fabric of her dress.

"Katya Morgan, will you marry me?" he asked, looking down at her solemnly.

"Alex, I—"

Her response was interrupted by the insistent clang of the doorbell.

Alex groaned. Pulling Katya behind him, he stalked to the door and flung it open. "What now?" he asked irritably, without waiting to see who it was.

Paula Northcraft blinked and took a step backward at Alex's abrupt tone. "Sorry, I just realized that I'd forgotten to tell you about the final condition of your father's will."

"Yes?" both Katya and Alex said at once.

Paula shuffled through the handful of papers she was holding. She reached the one she wanted and handed it to Katya, pointing with a neatly manicured finger at a paragraph near the bottom. "Here it is. You can't marry anyone with a net worth of over a million dollars during the year. It seems that your father wasn't going to reward you for taking the easy way out."

Katya looked questioningly at Alex. Surely he wasn't—

Alex shook his head with a rueful smile. "Sorry, honey. I invested well during the nineties and got out before the market cratered. It looks like we're going to have to wait a year."

She grinned up at him, her eyes sparkling as she hastily thanked Paula for the information and closed the door on the bemused attorney. "That's just fine," she said. "Because I'm going to need that much time to pull off the perfect wedding gift."

EPILOGUE

One Year Later

"ALEX, please let me in!" Katya shouted, pounding on the door of his suite at the Royal Palmetto.

"No," came his muffled reply through the heavy oak door. "It's bad luck for me to see you in your wedding dress."

"You've already seen me in my dress. Don't you have the portrait I did of Daisy, Inez, and me hanging in your office?" she asked, knowing full well that the painting she had labored over for months hung right next to his painting of the Royal Palmetto.

"That's not the same thing at all. It's just an image of you in your dress."

"Who would have ever thought he'd be so traditional?" Katya asked, looking down at Daisy, who had sat down beside her on Alex's front stoop and leaned her weight against the heavy fabric of Katya's white wedding dress.

She had protested the color, of course. She was hardly a virgin, after all. Especially not after she and Alex had . . . um, experimented with some new and interesting ideas, she thought, feeling her face flush at certain memories of the past year.

"Miss Katya, you look beautiful."

Katya whirled around at the comment, instantly mortified that her nine-year-old soon-to-be niece had caught her reminiscing about things nine-year-old little girls shouldn't know about. She fanned herself with the end of Daisy's leash—a brand new white leather one in honor of the occasion.

"Thank you, Merrilee. You look mighty fine today, too."

Merrilee self-consciously straightened her dove gray dress, patterned in the same fashion as Katya's slim white sheath. "Hmm," she answered, obviously not certain she believed the compliment.

Before Katya could ask how the D-Backs were doing against the Mariners in that day's game, Inez came flying around the corner of Alex's casita. "Katya," she said, sounding horrified, "you know it's bad luck for Alex to see you before the ceremony. What are you doing here?"

Laying a hand on Daisy's head, Katya sighed. She couldn't seem to do anything anymore without someone knowing about it.

She grinned.

Wasn't it wonderful?

Daisy pressed her ears against Katya's fingers, and Katya smiled down at the dog she loved so fiercely. Her heart started to ache as she thought about how lonely she had been before her father had given her the greatest gift he could have given her: a life. One that included a job as the first-ever multi-lingual event planner at the Royal Palmetto, a family, a husband, a dog, and so much love that she felt at times her body couldn't contain it all.

Katya looked up into Inez's smiling face. Her almost-sister-in-law looked as happy as Katya felt inside. And no wonder. In less than half an hour, they were both going to wed the men they loved.

"Oh, no," Inez wailed, watching Katya's face start to crumple. She started banging on the door of Alex's suite. "Alex, come out here quick. She's going to start crying again and ruin the makeup I spent an hour on this morning."

Immediately Alex flung the door open. "Aw, honey, please don't cry," he pleaded, folding Katya into his arms.

Only that just made it worse, Katya thought, running her fingers up and down his back and watching his golden eyes darken as he held her. Their love gave them all such power over her, but not in the way she'd expected.

Sometimes she'd look over at Alex or Daisy or Inez or Nana and fear would squeeze her lungs until she was breathless. What would she do without them? How would she ever survive if she lost them?

That was the power love had, the power to scare her until she felt like the weight of it would crush her.

At times like that, she'd see her lover and her dog and the entire family she had inherited, and she knew that's how she'd survive. Because she wasn't alone anymore. And she would never be alone again.

Alex wiped the tears from his bride's eyes but didn't ask what was wrong. He knew what was wrong. She was remembering her old life. She'd told him before that the tears she cried were tears of gratitude for all that he had given her.

Sometimes he'd joke with her that it was an even trade—his family for the Royal Palmetto, her surprise wedding gift to him.

More often than not, though, he just let her cry.

After all, Alex thought, pulling her close, she had finally learned that money couldn't buy the one thing her old life lacked.

And that was love.